THE DRAGON'S MATE

THE SHIFTERS SERIES
BOOK SEVEN

ELIZABETH KELLY

EK PUBLISHING INC.

Edited by:
L. Nunn Editing

Cover art by
The Final Wrap

THE DRAGON'S MATE

A spark of attraction ignites flames of obsession.

As a dragon shifter, Kaida knows the clan rules – the clan always comes first, and a dragon never reveals their true nature to other shifters or humans.

But by saving a yearling human and an injured fox shifter, she's breaking all the rules.

Now she's in Bren Matthews' crosshairs. A by-the-books detective and the sexiest human she's ever laid eyes on.

Kaida knows she needs to stay away from Bren, but her dragon's interest in the human is obsessive.

To Bren, Kaida is exquisitely fascinating. Everything about Kaida, from her compassion to her bravery to her abnormal strength and speed, is intoxicating. Unfortunately, knowing her secret could be fatal.

Yet the danger isn't enough to keep him away.

But prejudice is a killer. Now, Bren and Kaida must fight for their love and their lives.

CHARACTER NAME
PRONUNCIATION

Dear Reader,

Are you like me and easily distracted by proper name pronunciation when reading? Nothing takes me out of a story faster than constantly wondering if I'm reading a character's name correctly. To that end, here is a list of a few characters in "The Dragon's Mate" and the proper pronunciation of their names.

Happy Reading!

Elizabeth

Kaida – Ky-da
Sika – See-ka
Javee – Jay-vee
Kova – Koh-va
Avena – Ah-vee-na
Makeda – Ma-kee-da

CHAPTER 1

"I knew it. You're fucking faggots."

Tyler's stomach dropped, and he pulled his mouth away from Corey. He looked behind him, and fear slipped into his gut. Jeff Howell and three of his football teammates were standing just behind them.

Corey's cold, shaking hand slipped into his, and Tyler squeezed it tightly.

"Get lost, Jeff," he said with a bravery he didn't feel. He glanced at Corey. The smaller boy's face was pale and pinched with worry, and Tyler's fear heightened.

"It'll be okay, honey," he said.

"It'll be okay, honey," Jeff mimicked in a high-pitched voice. He shook his head with disgust. "Jesus, you two are gross."

Tyler didn't reply. He had been schoolmates with Jeff since kindergarten, and he knew from experience the best way to handle him was to ignore his taunts. Although Tyler had never publicly announced he was gay and had done his best to quietly blend in, he'd been targeted by Jeff and his oafish friends for most of his life.

"Tyler, let's go." Corey tugged on Tyler's hand, and Jeff glanced at his friends. They spread out in a loose circle around them, and Corey moaned quietly with fear.

They were too far for anyone to help them. They'd ridden their bikes to the edge of the woods, and he and Corey had walked for nearly an hour into the trees to the long, wide river that wound its way through them. Tyler had grown up on the city's outskirts and spent many happy hours playing in the woods. Now, he lived with his father in an apartment in the city's downtown core.

Adrenaline was lighting sparks through his veins. Corey had moved to the city two years ago, and although Tyler was aware of him and admired how his lean, lithe body moved when he played soccer, he and Corey didn't start dating until this final year of high school. Corey, the captain of the school's soccer team, was failing Spanish, and Tyler was assigned to tutor him. It hadn't taken long for them to fall in love.

Tyler squeezed Corey's hand again. They had kept it quiet. In fact, many of the girls in their grade regularly swooned over Corey, and he had no idea how Jeff had figured it out.

"Why the fuck you'd want to stick your dick up his ass instead of some girl's pussy, I'll never fucking know." Jeff shook his head again. "Or are you the bottom? You strike me as the kind of guy who likes to take it up the ass, Wagner."

"You seem to know a lot about the lifestyle, Jeff," Tyler said. "Are you and your friends a little closer than you want people to know?"

Corey moaned again as Jeff's face turned bright red. "You'll pay for that, you fucking faggot."

"Original. Of course, I can't expect someone with your IQ to come up with better insults, can I?"

"Tyler shut up," Corey whispered.

Tyler shook his head. The fear on Corey's face, the way his body trembled, had buried his fear under a sudden, hot, throbbing pulse of anger, and he embraced the unfamiliar feeling.

"You and your idiot friends should leave, Jeff," Tyler said.

"Oh, we're not leaving until we teach you what happens to queers like you. What you're doing is sick." Jeff and his friends closed in on them. "We'll see how you feel about your little boyfriend when you're in the hospital with a broken -"

He took a step back when Tyler suddenly threw himself at him. He rammed his shoulder into Jeff's stomach, knocking the bigger boy backward as he shouted, "Corey! Run!"

He dropped on Jeff and swung his fist. His hand screamed in agony when it connected with Jeff's broad jaw, but he ignored it grimly and raised his hand again, smashing his fist into Jeff's nose.

Jeff howled with anger and threw Tyler to the ground beside him. He pounced on him, wrapping his large arm around his neck and hauling him into a sitting position as his nose gushed blood down Tyler's shoulder and arm.

He squeezed tightly as Tyler choked and clawed frantically at his arm. He released it enough for Tyler to drag in a whooping gasp of cold air.

"You and your boyfriend are going to burn in hell," Jeff whispered.

Eyes bulging, Tyler watched as Jeff's friends knocked Corey to the ground and began to kick him in the ribs and back.

"Corey!" Tyler tried to scream as one of the boys delivered a brutal kick to Corey's face, and his eyes rolled up in his head.

"What the fuck?" Jeff's hot breath puffed in his ear, and his arm relaxed around his neck.

"Corey?" Tyler whispered. Corey's limp body was rippling and changing, the clothes tearing away, and the boys watched in fascination as he shifted to a small, orange fox. Blood trickled steadily from the fox's nostrils as one of the boys reached down and prodded at it with the toe of his sneaker.

"Holy fuck." He turned to Jeff. "He's a paranormal."

Jeff grunted with surprise when Tyler nearly wiggled out of his grip.

"Let me go! He's hurt!" Tyler shouted.

Jeff tightened his grip until Tyler gagged. "It's not bad enough that you're fucking a dude, but he's a paranormal too? What is wrong with you?"

His face going purple from lack of oxygen, Tyler reached for Corey. He had to get to him. He had to help him. He clawed again at Jeff's muscular arm as black roses bloomed in his vision.

"Let him go."

The voice was soft, but its tone was hard steel. Jeff dropped his arm from Tyler's neck and stood up. Tyler lay on the ground, gagging and gasping in air as Jeff scowled at the woman standing a few feet away.

"Get out of here, bitch. This isn't any of your business." Jeff wiped the blood from his nose with the heel of his hand.

"You're trespassing on my land. That makes it my business," the woman replied. She wore a long dark blue cloak with a hood, and she pushed the hood back to reveal her face as she glanced at the fox lying on the ground.

Tyler stared at the woman. She was tall, he guessed close to six feet, and she had long dark hair with streaks of blue woven throughout it. Her skin was pale, and her eyes seemed to glow in the growing dusk.

"Fuck off!" Jeff clenched his ham-like hands into fists. "I'm not into hurting women, but I'm willing to make an exception for you."

"Lucky me," the woman replied. She eyed the others before shifting her gaze back to Jeff. "Go on. You and your little friends scurry off like the ugly rodents that you are. I grow tired of you."

"Bitch! You'll pay for that," Jeff huffed again. He glanced at the three other boys, and Tyler gave a hoarse shout of warning as Jeff suddenly rushed forward, and his friends followed.

The woman sighed loudly, and Tyler watched in stunned silence as she beat the shit out of his classmates.

———

The woman, who wasn't even breathing hard, bent and picked up the unconscious fox. Scattered around her, Jeff and his friends were lying on the ground, moaning softly, but she completely ignored them.

Tyler staggered to his feet and lurched after the woman as she walked into the woods.

"Wait!" He grabbed her arm and coughed hoarsely into the crook of his elbow. "He needs to go to the hospital."

"We can't take him like this. The hospital won't treat him until he shifts to his human form, and he's not going to shift while he's unconscious," the woman replied.

"Wh-where are you taking him?" Tyler squeezed her arm.

"To get him help." The woman frowned as she stared at his hand. The knuckles were bruised and swollen. "Is your hand broken?"

"I don't know."

He glanced behind them at Jeff and the others. "What about them?"

"Leave them," she said dismissively. "They'll crawl home and lick their wounds."

She started walking again, and Tyler followed her, not knowing what else to do.

"Who are you?" he panted. The woman was setting a brisk pace, and he could barely keep up with her long strides.

"My name is Kaida."

"I'm Tyler. That's Corey."

The woman nodded, and Tyler lapsed into silence as he followed her into the trees. He could barely wrap his head around what had just happened. Corey was a shifter, and the woman carrying him in her arms had just beaten up four teenage football players like it was nothing.

"Where did you learn to fight like that?" he asked.

"My grandmother."

"Your grandmother?" He stumbled to a stop in his surprise.

She kept going, and after a moment, he hurried after her. "Well, thank you for helping us. I appreciate it."

"You're welcome." She glanced at Corey, and her pace quickened further. Tyler was nearly jogging to keep up with her.

"Where are we going?"

"To my home. Hold these." She handed him Corey's clothes. Balancing the fox carefully in one arm, she reached into the pocket of her cloak and pulled out a cell phone. Tyler breathed a sigh of relief. The woman looked like she had stepped out of a time capsule with her long cloak and odd accent, and to see her holding a cell phone comforted him a little.

The woman held the phone to her ear. "Hey, it's me. Can you meet me at my house? I have an injured fox shifter that needs your help."

She listened silently for a moment before smiling a little. "I know. Thanks. I'll see you in ten."

She hung up the phone and made it disappear in the pocket of her cloak before glancing at Tyler. "What were you two doing out here, anyway?"

Tyler cleared his throat. "We were just, uh, hanging out."

"Why did those boys attack you?"

"I – no reason. They're assholes."

She eyed him carefully. "Is that so? It has nothing to do with the fact that they caught you two kissing?"

He blushed and stared at the ground. "They're assholes and homophobes."

She grinned a little, her straight white teeth flashing in the gloom. "That they are. Why do you hide that you're gay?"

"My family doesn't know," he said.

"Why not?"

"Well, my brother knows, but my mom and dad don't. I'm not close to my mom. My parents divorced when I was a kid, and she left us with our dad. I haven't even spoken to her in two years. My dad, well, it's complicated."

"It usually is," she replied.

"Corey and I have been dating for nearly six months, and I had no idea he was a paranormal," he said.

She raised her eyebrows at him. "That's strange."

"Yeah." He touched his knuckles lightly and winced. He knew damn well why Corey hadn't told him he was a paranormal, and he felt a combination of guilt and anger. He was nothing like his father, Corey knew that, and the fact that he hadn't trusted him enough to share that he was a paranormal was like a knife in Tyler's heart.

The trees were starting to thin, and he realized with a start that he knew where they were. For as long as he could remember, a small community of shifters lived in the woods. They kept to themselves, and most city people had forgotten about them. The rumour was that they were bear shifters who had grown tired of the underlying tension between the humans and the paranormals and had retreated into the woods to escape it.

The trees opened up into a man-made clearing. Cabins were scattered throughout. Tyler counted nearly twenty nestled among the trees, and he could see a dirt road winding past the cabins and into the woods.

"Where does that road go?" he asked.

"Back to the highway." She strode past three cabins before stopping at one of the smaller ones. Flowers were planted in large pots on the tiny front porch, their blossoms starting to fade, and she climbed the steps and opened the front door.

Tyler hesitated at the bottom of the stairs, and she gave him a slightly impatient look. "Hurry up."

He took one last glance at the other cabins before hurrying after her.

THE CABIN MAY HAVE BEEN RUSTIC ON THE OUTSIDE, BUT THE inside boasted a sleek and modern décor. The contemporary furnishings and stainless-steel appliances should have looked odd against the log walls but strangely didn't. The living room and the kitchen were combined into one big room. The kitchen was on the smaller side with a fridge and stove, one mid-sized length counter with cupboards above and below it, and a small round table with four chairs crowded around it. A narrow marble-topped island helped divide the kitchen from the living room. There was a small couch and an armchair in the living room with a metal and glass coffee table and a television mounted to the wall.

He stared at the old woman bent over a pot on the stove. She was bigger than Kaida, standing well over six feet with wide hips and shoulders, and dressed in faded green pants and a bright pink t-shirt with 'sugar mama' written across it in large yellow font. Her hair was pure white and hung in a neatly made braid to her waist. Like Kaida, there were streaks of colour in it, although her colour was a rich, emerald green rather than the blue that Kaida sported.

"Hello, sugarpie." The old woman straightened and gave Kaida a generous smile. Her eyes were the same golden colour as Kaida's, and she dropped a small wink at him. "Who's this handsome young fellow?"

"Hi, Gram. This is Tyler," Kaida jerked her chin in his direction, "and this is Corey."

"Put the fox on the couch, and I'll take a look at him," Gram said cheerfully.

Tyler followed Kaida to the couch and stood anxiously at the end of it as Kaida laid Corey down. Gram joined them and poked and prodded at the fox's body before lifting his eyelid. His eyes were still rolled up in his head, and Tyler made a soft groan of dismay.

"It's all right, dearie," Gram said. "He'll be fine."

She felt his skull and his face carefully before wiping away some of the blood that had dried under his nose. She sniffed it carefully, and Tyler made a low sound of disgust when she licked it from her finger.

"What happened to the poor thing?" she asked.

"A bunch of human boys were beating him," Kaida said. "Three against one, and they were all twice his size."

Gram shook her head. "Human or paranormal – teenage

9

boys are the worst." She grinned at Tyler. "No offense, dearie."

She stepped back and straightened. "Well, I can't do anything for the poor boy until he wakes up."

"What if he doesn't wake up?" Tyler said. "What if he -"

"Oh, he'll wake up, don't you worry. Fox shifters got heads like rocks," Gram said. "Now, let me look at your knuckles while we wait for your boyfriend to come to."

He blinked at her, and she chuckled. "I might be old, but I still know a thing or two about love." She took his hand and surprised him by leaning in and inhaling deeply. "Plus, you got his scent all over you."

They must be bear shifters, Tyler decided. She had to be a paranormal if she could smell Corey's scent on him. He flinched when Gram probed at his bruised knuckles, and she made a sound of sympathy.

"Ayuh, I imagine that hurts. Well, don't you fret – old Gram has a poultice to ease the pain and help with the swelling." She pinched his cheek and returned to the stove.

Using his left hand, Tyler fumbled his cell phone out of his pocket and groaned. He had two missed calls and three texts from his brother.

"I need to call my brother and tell him I'm okay," he said to Kaida. "I was supposed to meet him over an hour ago, and he's freaking out. I'll, um, ask him to come by and get me, all right?"

He stared anxiously at the dark-haired woman. Truthfully, he wasn't going anywhere until Corey woke up, but the thought of being alone with a bunch of bear shifters as darkness fell made him nervous.

Kaida glanced at Gram, and a silent communication seemed to pass between them. Gram stirred the liquid in the pot. "That's fine, dearie. Call your brother. Tell him the road is off highway fifteen. If he gets lost, he can -"

"He won't get lost," Tyler said. "We grew up around this area."

CHAPTER 2

He drove up to the front of her cabin with a recklessness that raised her eyebrows. She was standing on the porch, and he slid out of the SUV, slamming the door and bounding up the stairs with an effortless grace. The man in front of her was tall with wide shoulders and a narrow waist. His dark hair was a little long, and dark stubble covered his lower jaw. She inhaled deeply. God, he smelled delicious for a human. She studied his light blue eyes filled with anxiety.

"Tyler! Where is he?" His tone was worried and impatient.

She opened the front door, and he pushed past her. As he hurried to the table, she watched the large muscles in his back before dropping her gaze downward. He wore faded jeans that clung to his ass, and she could feel the warmth starting in her stomach almost immediately. She snorted to herself and forced her gaze away. She needed a human, like she needed another hole in her head.

"Tyler? Are you all right?" The man knelt next to Tyler, who was sitting at the table. He touched his head.

"I'm fine. I hurt my hand when I punched Jeff in the face," Tyler replied.

"Is it broken?" He examined the wet cloth draped over Tyler's knuckles. "What is that?"

"It's a poultice," Tyler said.

"It smells like a dead dog." The man grimaced, and Kaida hid her smile. The poultice really did smell like death and it would take forever for the smell to dissipate. She'd have to sleep with every window open tonight.

While she and everyone else in their clan had no need for Gram's poultices, it hadn't stopped the old woman from learning the art of healing. Call it a side hobby.

"Yeah, but it's making my hand feel better," Tyler said.

The man glanced at Gram, who was sitting next to Tyler.

"Hi, I'm Gram. What's your name?"

"Bren Matthews." He held out his hand, and she shook it, a smile creeping onto her face.

"Bren?" Gram glanced at Kaida. "German descent, is that right?"

Bren nodded, and Gram's smile widened. "Meaning flame?"

"I guess. I don't really know," he said absently.

"Pretty sure that's what it means," Gram replied cheerily. "You're a good-lookin' devil then, aren't you?"

Bren blinked at her. "Uh, thanks."

"You're welcome."

"Tyler, are you sure you're okay?" Bren looked his brother over anxiously.

"Yeah, I told you on the phone I was okay."

Bren touched the top of Tyler's hand, frowning when the teenager hissed out a breath and pulled his hand away. "This might be broken."

"His hand isn't broken, just bruised," Gram said.

"Are you a doctor?" Bren asked.

"Nope. But I've seen my fair share of injuries over the years." Gram smiled at him again.

"You're going to the hospital for an X-ray," Bren said to Tyler.

"I don't need one," Tyler protested. "It's already feeling better. I swear, Bren."

"Tell me exactly what happened," Bren said.

"Corey and I rode our bikes to the edge of the woods after school. We were going to go hang out by the river for a while. I guess Jeff and the others followed us. They caught us kissing and -"

Tyler's voice clogged in his throat, and his face turned pale. Kaida watched as Bren squeezed his shoulder gently. "It's okay, Tyler."

"Jeff called us faggots and said that we were going to find out what happened to faggots like us," Tyler whispered. "I punched Jeff in the face and yelled at Corey to run, but the other boys started hurting him. They were kicking and punching him and -"

He stopped, blinking back tears as Bren squeezed his shoulder again. "They wouldn't stop hitting him, and Jeff had me in a chokehold, and I – I couldn't get free. I tried to stop them. I swear."

"I know," Bren said reassuringly. "It wasn't a fair fight, Tyler. Where's Corey?"

"On the couch."

Bren stood and glanced over the top of the couch. His mouth dropped open, and he turned to stare at Tyler again.

"I didn't know he was a shifter," Tyler whispered. "He never told me. One of them kicked him in the face, and he shifted before he lost consciousness."

"How did you get away?" Bren asked.

"She saved us." Tyler looked over Bren's shoulder at her. Bren followed his gaze, and a shiver went down her back as he studied her eyes. Her dragon made an odd sound – something between a growl and a mating call - and she twitched in surprise.

"Thank you," Bren said.

She focused on a spot on the wall just over his left shoulder. Staring directly at the human was making her dragon weird. "You're welcome."

"It was amazing, Bren," Tyler said. "Kaida kicked the shit out of all four of them. They didn't stand a chance."

Bren took another look at her, his gaze lingering on her eyes. This time, her dragon made what was definitely a mating call, and she briefly considered running from the cabin and hiding in the woods for a few hours. What the hell was going on with her dragon?

"Corey needs to go to the hospital." Bren was still looking at her, and her dragon practically rolled over and showed her goddamn belly to the human.

Stop it, you idiot!

Her dragon hissed grumpily at her, and she tasted smoke in the back of her throat. Jesus, the last thing she needed to do was start spewing smoke out of her mouth and nose in front of two humans. She inhaled the smoke that lingered in her mouth and throat.

She moved to the couch – she needed to do something to distract her dragon - and knelt next to the fox shifter. "Not when he's in his shifter form." She stroked the fox's fur. "Until he wakes up and shifts to his human form, there's no point in taking him to the hospital."

"He could have a concussion or internal injuries," Bren argued. "We can't -"

The fox made a soft whining noise and twitched under

Kaida's hand. Tyler dropped the poultice on the table and hurried over to join them.

"Corey?" he said anxiously. "Can you hear me?"

The fox twitched again before his eyes opened. He stared unblinkingly at Tyler before abruptly shifting. Kaida grabbed the blanket draped over the back of the couch and covered Corey's naked body.

"Corey!" Tyler sat beside him and touched the boy's forehead. "How do you feel?"

"My head hurts," Corey rasped as Gram pushed past Tyler and laid her worn hand on his shoulder.

"Stay still, boy. Let me have a look at you, all right?"

She patted Tyler's shoulder. "Why don't you wait outside with your brother and Kaida?"

"I want to stay here with him," Tyler said.

"I know, dearie, but it'll only be a few minutes. Go on now. Be a sweet boy and listen to Gram." Her grandmother's voice was firm.

Tyler hesitated and then squeezed Corey's hand. "I'll be outside, Corey."

Bren took Tyler's arm and guided him outside. Kaida shut the door behind them and sat on one of the wicker chairs as Bren paced back and forth.

"I'm going to the school on Monday and talking to the principal first thing." He raked his hand through his hair. "This is going beyond bullying. You and Corey could have been killed."

"No, Bren. Don't do that," Tyler pleaded. "It'll make it worse."

Bren stared at him in disbelief. "Tyler, do you understand what I said? You could have died. This asshole kid needs to be expelled, and his parents need to know what he's done."

17

"If he's expelled, he'll go after Corey and me again," Tyler argued. "You know that, Bren."

"I can't sweep this under the rug, Tyler. Hell, I should arrest this kid for assault."

"Bren, no!" Tyler nearly shouted. His entire body was trembling lightly, and Kaida could smell the tangy scent of his fear. "That will make it worse. Don't you get it? He knows I'm gay now. The best thing we can do is lay low, hope that he doesn't -"

"Doesn't what? That homophobic asshole won't leave you alone. What would you have me do? You need to be protected, and I can't follow you around. I have to work and -"

"You could teach him to fight." She mentally berated herself for interrupting. This wasn't any of her business.

"Stay out of this," Bren said.

Anger rippled through her even though the human was right. Still, just because it wasn't her business didn't mean she wasn't making a good point. "If he knew how to fight, he could protect himself."

"Listen, I appreciate what you did to save my brother, but -"

"She's right, Bren," Tyler said. "If I could fight like Kaida, this wouldn't have happened."

Bren blew his breath out. "Tyler, fighting isn't going to solve the problem."

"Nothing will solve the problem," Tyler said, his voice tinged with anger. "Don't you get that, Bren? You think that going to the principal, that meeting with Jeff's parents will solve the problem, but it won't! He might back off for a few weeks or even a few months, but sooner or later, he'll come after us again. You have no idea what it's like to go to school every day and pray that you aren't noticed. To hope that Jeff and his stupid football buddies don't pay any attention to you. I can't go on like this! I can't! And now that they know about Corey and me and that Corey is a shifter, it'll get worse. I need to learn to fight! I'm not a child!"

The tears that Kaida sensed had been threatening for hours finally erupted. Tyler sat down with a heavy thud on the top step, burying his face in his arm.

Bren crouched beside him and rubbed his back. "I'm sorry, Ty."

"Don't." Tyler shifted away from him.

Bren scooted closer and rubbed his back again. "Ty, look at me."

"Leave me alone!" Tyler shouted and shoved him hard. Not expecting it, Bren fell back onto his ass with a hard thump.

Tyler flinched and cradled his hand against his chest. "Please leave me alone."

The genuine fear and sorrow in his voice made Kaida's chest ache. She stood and joined Tyler on the front step, sitting beside him and putting her arm around his thin body. To her surprise, Tyler threw one arm around her waist and buried his face in her neck. She rocked him back and forth as she rubbed his back.

"There, there, mostoirín," she murmured. "It'll be all right."

She continued to rock him back and forth and pressed a kiss against the top of his head. Tyler's shuddering slowed, and he sat up, wiping at his nose and knuckling away the tears still on his cheeks. He stared at the step between his feet, his cheeks a dull red, before muttering, "Sorry."

"You have nothing to be sorry about, mostoirín," she said.

"What does that mean?" Tyler asked.

"Mostoirín is an Irish word," she replied. A hint of red was climbing into her cheeks.

"What does it mean?" Tyler repeated.

"My little darling." Her cheeks were very red now, and she gave Tyler an embarrassed look. "Sorry, I picked that up from Gram."

"I don't mind." Tyler smiled faintly, and she squeezed the back of his neck.

Bren sat down beside them, and Tyler said, "Sorry. I shouldn't have shoved you."

"I get it, kid. You've had a rough day," Bren said.

"Yeah," Tyler said. "I need to learn to fight, Bren."

"I know." Bren stared moodily at his vehicle. "I'll teach you some self-defence moves, and we'll get you into some classes at the -"

"Kaida could teach me to fight," Tyler said.

Bren shook his head. "No, buddy. That's not a good idea."

"It is," Tyler insisted. He stared pleadingly at Kaida. "You can teach both Corey and me. If we can do what you can, we'll be able to protect ourselves the next time Jeff tries something. Please, Kaida."

Spending time with the humans was the absolute worst idea in the world. She opened her mouth to say no and almost choked in surprise when her dragon pushed forward and said, "Yes."

Bren stiffened, the slightest hint of unease flickering across his face. She got it. Unlike other shifters, dragons could speak the human language, but the sound wasn't exactly music to the ears. Her dragon's voice sounded much deeper and thicker than her normal speaking voice – like she was gargling with sand.

Tyler hadn't appeared to notice her not quite human

sounding response. Happiness washed over him in waves, and his body vibrated excitedly. "Yeah?"

Afraid her dragon would make another push for control if she disagreed with it, she nodded. "Yes. I'll teach you to fight."

"Thank you, Kaida," Tyler said.

The door opened, and Gram stuck her head out. "You can come back in, Tyler."

He stood and followed Gram eagerly into the cabin as Bren sat on the step beside Kaida. He wasn't sitting that close, but she immediately shifted away. Unbelievably, her dragon purred to the human, and her eyes widened. Shit. Had she purred out loud?

The human wasn't staring at her like he'd heard the purr, but unease crowded into her chest. What the fuck was wrong with her dragon?

KAIDA WAS UNDENIABLY GORGEOUS, BREN DECIDED. HER PALE skin and long dark hair were a striking combination, and he stared at the streaks of blue in her hair for a moment before he shifted his gaze downward. The odd cloak she was wearing hid the curves of her body, but a woman as tall as Kaida would have full breasts and hips.

He felt an unexpected bite of lust and didn't look away when she turned to face him. Her eyes were stunning – an odd golden colour that fascinated him. There were tiny flecks of blue in the gold, and he leaned closer. Contacts, he decided, she must be wearing contacts. No one – shifter or human – had eyes that colour.

"You're staring."

He twitched when he felt her hand on his broad chest.

She pushed him back, not that lightly, and frowned. "It's rude to stare at a person like that."

"Sorry." He stared at the other cabins scattered throughout the trees before raking his hand through his hair. Anger was bubbling up inside of him again, and he wanted to jump in his car, drive to that asshole teenager's house, and arrest the little shithead for battery.

"Thank you for helping him," he said.

"You're welcome." She studied her hands for a moment. "I'll teach him and the fox to fight, but it won't do them much good if the other boys go after them again immediately."

He sighed. "I know. I'll have to talk to the school, at least let them know the bullying is out of control and ask them to keep a close eye on the boys."

"Do you think that will work?"

"Honestly? No. But I don't know what else to do. I could talk to Dad about pulling him from school, maybe transfer him somewhere else to finish the year, but then he'll want to know why and Tyler... he won't want him knowing any details."

He swallowed down his bitter laugh. If his father knew Tyler was gay, he'd lose his shit. The man didn't just have a problem with shifters. He was also a homophobe, a misogynist, a racist, and a shitty father. If asked, Bren would be hard-pressed to say one good thing about the man who shared his DNA. Excellent at bullshitting the general public, maybe.

He stared at his hands. He needed to be figuring out how to keep Tyler safe, not worrying about his asshole of a father. "It's before and after school that I'm really worried about. Even if he comes straight home after classes, there's still the opportunity for them to go after him when he's biking home."

He paused. "I could try to be there to drive him and Corey home every day, but my job isn't exactly a nine to five. I work weird hours, and if I'm on a case, I might not be able to get away to drive him home."

"A case?" Kaida said.

"I'm a detective with the fifty-third precinct," Bren replied.

"Tyler doesn't strike me as the type who likes to be babysat anyway," Kaida said.

He snorted. "Yeah, he isn't. He's scared, but he'll also be pissed about being watched like a child. I don't blame him. Those pricks are the ones who deserve to be punished, yet he'll be the one punished. He deserves to live a normal life and not have to worry about being beaten up because of who he loves."

His hands were rolled into tight fists, and he slammed them on his thighs in frustration. "He's a good kid, always sees the good in people, and I hate that he's learning the truth about them."

"Humans suck." There was no malice in her voice, only a weary resignation.

"Yeah, we really do."

"I might know someone who can help you," she said.

"Oh yeah?"

"Yes." The sun was low on the horizon, and he watched the dying light flash in her eyes. "I have a friend who owns a private security company. They mostly provide personal security for paranormals, but I know they also provide their services to humans. I'll give Bishop a call tomorrow and -"

He started to laugh, and she frowned at him. "What's so funny?"

"You're talking about Bishop King, aren't you?"

She jerked all over. "Yes. Do you know him?"

"Yeah."

He said nothing else, and she raised one perfect eyebrow at him. "How do you know him, human?"

"His girlfriend had some trouble with a guy a while back. The guy murdered Ava's friend and was stalking her, and I was assigned to the case. We never did find him, and the case has gone cold, but I've had some interactions with Bishop and Ava on and off since then."

"What kind of interactions?" she asked.

"Social stuff, mostly."

If a person referred to saving the giant grizzly shifter from another grizzly about to rip his head off and helping him and his friends rescue a phoenix shifter from a mad scientist as 'social stuff,' then, yeah, it was totally social.

"Human?"

He glanced at Kaida. "Sorry, what?"

"I said if you know Bishop, then you know he can help. You should call him."

"Yeah, maybe I will."

The grizzly shifter wouldn't be happy to hear from him because he still believed Bren had a thing for Ava, but Bren would do whatever he had to to keep Tyler safe.

"It's a good idea," he said. "Thanks."

"You're welcome."

They watched in silence as the sun slowly sank below the horizon.

CHAPTER 3

"**Y**ou should have told me, Corey." Tyler squeezed Corey's hand as he sat beside him on the couch.

The shifter started to sit up, and Gram appeared. "Oh no, you don't, fox shifter. You need to stay still. Nothing's broken, but your ribs are bruised badly, and you're lucky you don't have a concussion."

Corey touched the side of his face gingerly. Dark bruising had risen on his tanned skin and his cheek and jaw had swelled to twice their size.

Gram draped warm, steaming cloths across his ribs before pressing another against his jaw. Corey's nose wrinkled, and Gram laughed. "Ayuh, I know. It stinks, but it'll help. Trust me."

Tyler frowned when Gram reached to touch Corey's forehead, and the boy sniffed at her hand. A weird look crossed his face, and his eyes widened as he looked at Gram.

"There, there," Gram said, "old Gram ain't going to hurt you. Don't you worry now, boy."

Corey stared nervously at her as she rested her hand on

his forehead momentarily. She winked at him and went back to the stove.

"Why – why did you bring me to them?" Corey whispered.

"I didn't *bring* you to them. The woman, Kaida, showed up and saved us. She beat the hell out of Jeff and the others. You were unconscious and in your fox form, and she said she knew someone who could help you. I didn't know what else to do," Tyler said.

He glanced at Gram before squeezing Corey's hand again. "Why are you frightened of her?"

"I'm not." Corey licked his lips.

"You are. Do bear shifters and fox shifters not, uh, get along normally?" Tyler asked.

"Bear shifters?" Corey hesitated and then gave Tyler a weak smile. "Fox shifters are cautious around other shifters, that's all. We're not as big as some of them, you know?"

"You should have told me you were a paranormal," Tyler said.

"I don't tell anyone, Ty," Corey replied. "Not even my foster parents know."

"Why do you keep it a secret? Most humans don't care. They're not -"

Corey shook his head. "You, more than anyone, know that isn't true."

"I'm not like my dad," Tyler said. "Why would you ever think that I was?"

"I know you're not," Corey said. "But you're naïve about paranormals and humans. There are humans who aren't frightened of us, who think we deserve to be treated as equals, but there are plenty of people like your dad who think we should be locked away."

"He doesn't think you should be locked away," Tyler protested. "He just…."

He couldn't get the words out. He knew exactly what his father wanted.

Corey sighed. "He hates the paranormals. What would he say if he knew his son was dating one?"

"I'm nothing like my father," Tyler repeated miserably.

"I know." Corey smiled at him. "But I thought it would be better if you didn't know. You already have to keep secrets from him. I didn't want to add another to the list."

"I love you, Corey," Tyler said.

"I love you too," Corey said. The door to the cabin opened, and Bren and Kaida walked in.

"Hi, Corey. How are you feeling?" Bren asked.

"Hey, Bren. I'm okay." Corey's gaze slid to Kaida.

"This is Kaida," Tyler said. "She saved you."

Bren was studying Corey and Kaida with a thoughtful and considering look. Tyler could sense the tension radiating from both Corey and Kaida. Corey was squeezing his hand so hard that his fingers were going numb.

"She saved you," he repeated.

"Thank you." Corey looked away.

Kaida turned to Gram. "Can we move him? We should probably get him home before his family starts to worry."

"Nope." Gram shook her head. "He really shouldn't go anywhere for a few days."

"He can't stay here, Gram," Kaida said.

"We don't have much choice, mostoirín," Gram said.

"His family won't allow him to stay with strangers," Kaida replied.

"They don't care," Tyler said. "They're his foster folks, and they don't give a shit about him."

"I can't stay here," Corey said with growing alarm. "I'll be fine. Help me up." He started to sit up and groaned in pain before grabbing at his side and falling back to the couch.

Gram frowned at him in disapproval. "I told you not to move, fox shifter."

Tyler stroked his arm. "It's only for a day or two, Corey and then you can come stay at my house."

Corey laughed weakly. "Yeah, that wouldn't make your dad suspicious at all."

"I'll come by tomorrow morning, okay?" Tyler smiled at him. "Bren, you have the weekend off, right?"

His brother nodded, and Tyler said, "Will you bring me out here?"

"Sure, if it's okay with Kaida and her grandmother."

"Tyler, don't leave me here alone," Corey said.

"They won't hurt you. In fact, Kaida has offered to teach us how to fight so next time Jeff and his asshole buddies attack us, we can defend ourselves," Tyler said.

Corey stared at him in disbelief, and Tyler said, "What? What's wrong?"

"All right, time for the fox shifter to get some rest," Gram said before Corey could reply. She patted Tyler's arm. "Don't worry. Your boyfriend will be fine with us. You can come by tomorrow morning and spend the day with us."

"Gram…" Kaida sighed.

Gram ignored her and patted Tyler's arm again. "I'll see you tomorrow, boy. All right?"

"Okay." Tyler leaned forward and kissed Corey's mouth. "I love you. I'll see you in the morning."

Corey stared at Kaida with fear, and Tyler looked uncertainly at Bren. "Maybe I should stay with him just -"

"No," Kaida said impatiently. "The fox shifter will be fine. You can come by in the morning."

"But I -"

"Enough, Tyler," Bren said. "We've imposed on Kaida and her family enough. It's time to go."

"Right." Tyler kissed Corey again before resting his forehead against the smaller boy's. "It'll be okay, Corey. I'll see you tomorrow."

———

KAIDA STIRRED THE SOUP ON THE STOVE BEFORE TASTING IT. She stirred it again, then looked at the fox shifter lying on the couch. Gram had left half an hour ago, and the boy hadn't said a word since she'd left.

"The soup will be ready in a few more minutes."

He didn't reply.

"Are you hungry?" Kaida asked.

"Not really," he said.

"You should try to eat." She frowned at him and could immediately smell his fear rolling off of him in waves. "You do not need to be afraid, little fox. I promise I will not harm you."

She'd hoped that Corey wouldn't figure out what they were, but she should have known better. Foxes were well known for their sense of smell and how he looked at her, and Gram suggested he had an idea, at least.

It was confirmed when he said, "Your kind is supposed to be extinct."

"And how do you know what my kind is?" she asked.

"You smell like smoke and… flame," he said. "One of the foster homes I was staying in, they had a children's book about you. You smell like smoke, it said."

She didn't reply, and he said timidly, "You're a dragon. Aren't you?"

"Yes, little fox. We are dragons."

"Holy shit," he said. "Holy shit."

There was excitement under his fear now. She needed to impress upon him how important it was to keep this to himself. She believed that Cadmus would let the fox shifter live – if she hadn't, she would never have brought him here – but if the kid didn't realize how important it was to keep their clan's existence a secret and Cadmus picked up on that...

"How many are in your clan?" he asked.

"Twenty-five, but there will be a hatchling born soon."

She spooned some soup into a bowl and helped Corey sit up before handing him the bowl. He sniffed it gingerly, and she heard his stomach rumble.

Kaida smiled briefly. "Eat, little fox. The sooner you regain your strength, the sooner you'll be able to leave."

"Right." He ate some of the soup as Kaida sat down in the armchair. "Did you tell Tyler you were a bear shifter?"

She shook her head. "I did not."

"He thinks you are."

"That's better for him. In fact," she leaned forward and stared directly at the teenager, "if you tell Tyler what we are, it will not end well."

"What do you mean?" Corey whispered.

"We will burn you to a crisp, little fox. You, your boyfriend, and his brother."

"I...what?" Corey's face had turned white, and she hated that she was scaring him, but she had no choice.

"No one can know of our existence. I brought you here because I feared you had a serious head injury, and my grandmother is a healer. But, by doing so, I have revealed a secret you were never meant to know. In the morning, you will go before the council of elders. They will decide your fate."

"My fate?" Corey held the bowl of soup in a tight grip.

"If you can convince the council that you will not reveal our existence, they will allow you to live. If they believe, even a little, that you won't keep our secret…"

She inhaled and then allowed a small plume of smoke to escape when she exhaled. Corey's eyes widened and, in a quivering voice, said, "They'll kill me."

"Yes, little fox, they will."

He'd lost so much colour now, he was practically transparent. He stared at the bowl of soup in his hand before setting it on the coffee table. "I won't say anything," he said. "Not to Tyler, not to anyone. I promise."

"I know," Kaida said. "Be very clear on that point when you meet with the council in the morning."

"I-I will." His voice was quivering again, and she leaned forward and rested one hand on his shoulder. He flinched, but she only squeezed lightly.

"Get some more rest, little fox. Do not worry about tomorrow. If you truly mean what you say about keeping our secret, the elders will see that."

She drew the blanket over him when he curled up on the couch before taking his bowl to the counter. She rubbed at her forehead, feeling nauseous and a little like a monster. What kind of shifter told a child he would die?

It's for his own good.

Yes, it was. She took a deep breath. Cadmus would let him live. He would never harm a child. The other elders in the council might argue, but Cadmus was the high elder. They would bend to his will.

She stood in the kitchen and ate a bowl of soup before

washing the dishes and putting the leftovers in the fridge. By the time she was finished, Corey was sleeping again on the couch.

There was a knock on the door, and she hurried to open it before Corey woke. She groaned inwardly at the shifter standing on her front porch. He was over six feet tall with broad shoulders. His shoulder length dark red hair had streaks of green throughout it, and his golden eyes had flecks of emerald.

"Good evening, Drago."

He peered around her at the fox shifter sleeping on the couch before snorting in disgust. "The council wants to see you."

"Yes, I imagine they do." She threw her cloak over her shoulders and followed the red-headed dragon into the darkness.

BREN STEPPED INTO THE FOYER OF HIS APARTMENT BUILDING. He usually took the stairs, but bone tired and ready for a hot shower and cold beer, he took the elevator to his apartment. He'd just slid the key into the lock when the door across the hallway swung open.

"Bren!"

He groaned inwardly. It wasn't that he didn't like his neighbour. He was just really fucking tired and in no mood for small talk. Pasting a smile on his face, he turned around. "Hey, Helen."

Helen eyed him up and down, her light blue eyes studying his before a frown crossed her wrinkled face. "You look like shit."

"Thanks."

The old woman hobbled forward. One hand carried a foil-covered plate, and the other held her elaborately carved cane. The cane banged rhythmically against the floor. "Bad night at work?"

"No, I was off today. There was a bit of trouble with Tyler."

Her eyebrows rose in alarm. "Ty? Is he okay?"

"Yes, he's having problems with a few kids at school."

Helen thumped a little closer. "You tell Ty to come see me if he needs a little spell to put those assholes in their place."

How bad was it that Bren was actually considering whether the old woman's offer could be a viable solution?

He smiled at her. "That's kind of you to offer, but there are some pretty firm no shifting, spell using, or blood sucking rules at Tyler's school."

"Humans and their rules." Helen snorted and glanced behind her at her apartment. "Why don't you come in for a visit? Elora is finishing her shower, but you can have a few beers and… visit."

"Thanks, but I'll take a rain check. It's been a long day."

A scowl flitted across her face before she shoved the foil-covered plate at him. "All right then. Take these muffins. They're banana – you're favourite. I baked them especially for you."

He took the muffins. "Thank you, Helen."

"Make sure you eat one tonight," she said, "you're looking a bit thin."

"I will. Thanks again. Good night."

"Night."

He stepped into his apartment, closing the door behind him. He rubbed his forehead and walked into the kitchen, flicking on the light. He peeled off the foil from the plate and stared at the two banana muffins on the plate before opening the garbage can and dumping them in.

He set the plate on the counter and grabbed a beer from the fridge, twisting off the top and pitching the cap into the garbage before taking a long drink. He leaned against the counter and closed his eyes. Immediately, Kaida's face popped into his mind - her pale skin, the full curve of her bottom lip and those oddly appealing golden-coloured eyes with their blue flecks. Where did someone get contacts like that? Online, maybe?

He wondered what the natural colour of her eyes was. Not that it mattered. She'd be sexy as hell no matter what colour her eyes were. Just the sound of her voice had made it difficult for him to concentrate. Low and raspy with a slight accent that he couldn't place. How would she sound when he had his face buried between her legs?

What the fuck, man? Since when did you start imagining going down on a woman you just met?

Since now, apparently. But could you blame him? Kaida pushed all of his buttons, and he definitely looked forward to seeing her again tomorrow. His dick twitched, and he reached down and adjusted himself roughly.

His brother was in trouble, was now really the time for getting his rocks off over a weirdly hot bear shifter who lived in the middle of the damn woods? He needed to be figuring out how to keep Tyler and Corey safe, not wondering what Kaida's body looked like under that cloak or how her pussy would taste.

He took another swig of beer as someone pounded on his front door. "Bren!"

"It's open," he shouted.

The door flew open. He heard it slam shut and then the hurried thud of footsteps down the hallway. Elora ran into

34

the kitchen, her brown hair soaking wet, her face free of makeup, and her t-shirt on inside out. A large crow, its midnight black feathers dripping wet, was clinging to her shoulder.

"Don't eat the muffins!" she shouted.

Bren grinned at her and took another drink of beer. "I didn't. They're already in the garbage."

"Oh, thank God." Elora grimaced before opening the fridge and grabbing a beer. She twisted off the cap, tossed it into the garbage to join the muffins, and drank some beer before collapsing in one of the kitchen chairs. The crow flapped its wings, spraying a fine mist into Bren's face before settling on Elora's shoulder again.

"What's in them this time?" Bren asked.

Elora made a face. "Another love potion."

Bren sighed. A year ago, Helen and Elora had moved into the apartment across from his. Bren had helped Helen carry some groceries into her apartment about a week after they moved in, and from that moment on, she'd been trying to make a romance happen between him and Elora.

"She really wants us to fall in love," Bren said.

"Tell me about it. I keep telling her it isn't going to happen, but my grandmother is persistent. She can't accept that I'm not into you at all." Elora made a face that suggested she'd rather eat dirt than date him.

"Hey, I'm not that bad," Bren said.

"You're a total babe and smart and employed, and I have absolutely zero sexual attraction to you."

"Ouch."

"Oh please, is there any part of this," Elora pointed to her face and then her body, "that makes you go, 'Oh baby, break me off a piece of that'?"

There should have been. Elora was an attractive woman,

and there was no reason why he shouldn't find her hot. Only he didn't. Was she funny as hell and unbelievably smart? Yes. Did he want to bang her? No.

"Exactly." Elora could read his face disgustingly well for having only known him for a year. "Other than that one night, you have never once been attracted to me."

Bren groaned. "We agreed never to talk about that, remember?"

"Hey," Elora took another sip of beer before reaching up and stroking the crow's sleek chest, "it's not your fault you ate a love-potion laced brownie from Helen and thought I was your soul mate."

Bren finished his beer and grabbed another from the fridge. "Thank God you handcuffed me to the bed before I could declare my undying love for you to the entire apartment complex."

Elora burst into laughter, making the crow caw in a decidedly disgruntled manner. "I figured it was bad enough that you changed your Facebook status to in a relationship with me and wrote that terrible poem on your wall. How did it start again?"

"Don't," Bren warned.

Elora straightened in the chair and held her hand over her heart. "Her love is a quilt that covers me from head to toe. Her beauty is -"

"We had an agreement, Elora," Bren said. "We never speak of that night. Keep bringing it up, and I'll arrest you for the dozen unpaid parking tickets I saw in your glovebox."

Elora giggled before slumping against the chair. "I still can't believe you didn't arrest my grandmother for drugging you like that."

"She meant well. She wants you to be happy," Bren said.

"Yeah, well, if she keeps drugging unsuspecting humans,

the WWC is gonna label her a dark witch and have her imprisoned." Elora's tone turned somber.

Bren sat down and reached across the table to squeeze her hand. "Do you want me to talk to her?"

"It won't make a difference. Helen does what she wants and always has. She was a little better when Sarina was around, but now…"

Bren squeezed her hand again. Sarina was Elora's half-sister. He'd never met the shapeshifter, but he'd heard many stories about her from Helen and Elora. "Have you heard anything from her lately?"

Elora shook her head. "No. She hasn't responded to any of my texts in over a week. Normally, she responds right away. Helen says not to worry about it, that Sarina can take care of herself, but… I do worry. You know?"

"Yeah, I get it."

He watched as the crow hopped from Elora's shoulder to the table. It pecked at the wood, and Bren poked at the shiny, damp feathers on its back, pulling his finger back when the crow whipped around and pecked viciously at him. "If she shits on my table, I'm tossing her out the window."

"It was one time," Elora said. She reached out and stroked the crow's head. The crow rubbed her beak along Elora's fingers before turning her black-eyed gaze to Bren.

A shiver went down his back. "You know a group of crows is called a murder, right?"

Elora laughed. "You think Lilianna is going to find some crow friends, break into your apartment, and murder you while you sleep?"

"I am now," he said.

She laughed again, and they both watched Lilianna groom her wet chest feathers.

"I can't believe you shower with her," Bren said.

"How else will she get clean?" Elora said. "She doesn't like to be dirty."

"Yeah, but she's a human trapped in a crow's body."

"So?" Elora said.

"So, you don't feel weird showering with her?"

"No." Elora reached out and stroked Lilianna's head. "I thought I found the spell to break Lilianna's curse."

"Really?" He leaned forward and stared at the crow. "What went wrong?"

"I don't know. It just… didn't work. It *should* have worked. I don't know if it failed because I'm not a powerful enough witch or if I was wrong about the spell," Elora said.

"Did you show the spell to Helen?"

Elora sighed. "You know how she is about Lilianna. She refused to even look at the spell. She keeps saying that there must have been a reason that Lilianna was trapped in the crow's body, and releasing her could be a terrible mistake."

"To be fair, she could be right," Bren said.

"Maybe," Elora replied. "But if she isn't and Lilianna is an innocent witch trapped… I can't live with myself if I don't try to help."

"Elora, are you even sure that -"

"Don't, Bren," Elora said. "Lilianna is a witch, okay? She's not an ordinary crow. I know you think it's stupid of me to believe the word of a stranger, but it isn't just that. Lilianna is special. I knew it from the moment I saw her."

"All right," Bren said. "But I think it's a bit suspicious that you stumble onto a witch trapped as a crow in a cage in a potions store of all places. I mean, why did the store owner even have her?"

"I don't know, but I couldn't leave her locked in the cage once the store owner told me what she was," Elora said. "Even if, and this is a big if, you're right, and she's only a crow, Lilianna was dying in that cage. I couldn't walk away from her."

The crow cawed softly before flying back to Elora's shoulder. She stroked Elora's cheek with her beak before running her beak over a lock of Elora's wet hair.

They drank in silence for a few moments, the only sound in the room the light rasp of Lilianna's beak as she groomed Elora's hair repeatedly.

"I thought Tyler was spending the weekend with you," Elora said. "He texted me on Wednesday to see if I would join you guys for your *Alien* movie marathon."

"He's coming by tomorrow. He had plans with Corey tonight."

"Had?" Elora said.

"He and Corey ran into some trouble with some shit-heads from school this afternoon."

"What happened?" she said in alarm.

"How much time do you have?" he asked.

She stood and grabbed a second beer from the fridge. "Plenty. Tell me what's going on."

"I COULD DO A PROTECTION SPELL FOR TY AND COREY." ELORA picked at the label on her beer bottle.

Bren shook his head. "The use of magic at Ty's school is strictly forbidden. If they find out he has a protection spell cast on him, they'll expel him, and Dad will lose his shit. But thank you for offering."

Elora pulled thoughtfully at a few strands of her hair, and Lilianna immediately began smoothing them down again. "You said the female bear shifter – Karen -"

"Kaida," Bren said. "Her name is Kaida."

"Right, Kaida. You said she offered to teach them how to fight. That seems weird."

"Tyler can be persuasive when he wants to be."

"Don't I know it," Elora sighed. "He's why I have a four-leaf clover tattooed on my calf."

Bren laughed. "At least you don't have a skull tattoo on your shoulder. Talk about a cliché. Why we keep letting a seventeen-year-old boy pick out tattoos for us is beyond me."

Elora grinned at him. "You'd think a detective and a witch would know better. Anyway, this Kaida will teach them how to fight, and you'll hire Bishop to keep an eye on them."

"Yeah."

"Think he'll do it? He still believes you have a thing for his girlfriend, right?"

Bren rubbed at the scruff on his jaw. About six months ago, he'd gone for drinks with Elora, had too much whiskey and told her about his short-lived crush on Ava and about Bishop and the rest of the shifters at the BKF Securities company. "Yeah, but I don't. That ship has sailed. They have a kid, and they live together. Hell, I knew I didn't have a chance the day I asked Ava out at the coffee shop and she turned me down. She wasn't technically dating Bishop yet and still had no interest in me."

"Man, it's so weird to even hear about a grizzly mating and having babies with anyone, let alone a human," Elora said. "They're usually loners."

"Bishop's different, I guess. I'll talk to Mal or Kat about it if he says no. Bishop isn't the sole owner of the company."

"It'll be expensive, yeah? I don't know much about personal security, but it can't be cheap."

"I don't have much choice. The kid who attacked him, Jeff, is a football player and twice the size of Ty. He could seriously hurt him, and if the beating Kaida gave Jeff was as bad as Tyler said it was, I'm sure he'll be looking for revenge against Tyler and Corey," Bren said.

"Will you speak to Jeff's parents?"

"Tyler doesn't want me to."

"Yeah, but Tyler is seventeen, Bren," Elora said gently.

"I know, but I think he might be right in that it'll make things worse. Kids like Jeff – they don't give a shit about authority." Bren set his bottle down on the table. "Fuck, I hate that Tyler is going through this. He shouldn't be bullied for who he loves."

"Life isn't fair," Elora said. "Honestly, I'm more worried that this Jeff kid will tell your father that Tyler is gay and dating a shifter."

Bren ran his hand through his hair. "I didn't say anything to Tyler, but I'm concerned about it too. Tyler's worried enough about Corey. I didn't want to freak him out even more by mentioning Dad."

"What did he say when you took Tyler home?"

"He wasn't home. He was at some charity event."

"If he does find out about Tyler…"

"Dad will kick him out," Bren said bluntly. "And then Tyler will have no choice but to live with me."

"It bothers you that he won't live with you now, doesn't it?" Elora said.

"Yeah. I understand why he isn't. Tyler wants to believe that Dad is a good guy, but I worry about him living there. Dad doesn't give a shit about him. It's all about public image for our father and having a gay son who's dating a shifter? Dad will disown Tyler."

"I'm sorry," Elora said.

"Me too," Bren replied.

They sat in comfortable silence for a minute or two before Elora stood, Lilianna clinging tightly to her shoulder.

"I should go. It's getting late." She leaned down and pressed a kiss against Bren's forehead. "I'm sorry you've had such a bitch of a day, buddy."

"Thanks, Elora. And thanks for listening."

"Anytime. If you or Tyler need me, text me. And remember," she ruffled his hair affectionately, "don't eat anything my grandmother gives you."

CHAPTER 4

They hadn't walked five feet toward the community cabin before Drago turned to her. "What the hell were you thinking, Kaida?"

"They were being beaten. I couldn't leave them to their fate."

"You could have and should have done so." Smoke was starting to drift from his nostrils.

"Calm yourself, Drago," she said.

"Do not tell me what to do. You brought a fox shifter and two humans into our clan. Have you gone mad? You'll be lucky if the council does not banish you for what you have done."

"If they choose banishment, I will accept the punishment." Her voice was calm, but she felt far from relaxed. Her pulse was racing, and panic was singing through her veins. She might often feel smothered by the clan rules, but banishment meant madness and death.

Drago grabbed her arm and pulled her to a stop. "If you would only stop your foolishness and accept my mating proposal, you would not have to worry about being banished. They won't dare banish you if you're my mate."

"Why? Because you believe you are next in line to be an elder?" She arched her eyebrows at him. "Believing you should be an elder doesn't make it true."

He snorted. "I am the best candidate for the position, Kaida. You know as well as I do that Cadmus will appoint me to the council. It would be wise not to anger me."

"Are you threatening me?" She pulled her arm free of his tight grip. "That's not a good idea."

"For God's sake, I'm not threatening you. But you need to see that your foolish ways will lead you into trouble. It's like you want to be banished, Kaida."

"Just because I don't believe the old ways are still appropriate for us doesn't mean I want to be banished."

Drago threw his hands up in annoyance. "The old ways have protected us for years. If the humans were to find out about our existence, what do you think they would do? We'd be hunted and left with no choice but to destroy them. Is that what you want? For humanity to fall beneath our flame?"

"Of course not," she said. "But who are you to say what the humans will think or do if they learn of us?"

"They have proven time and time again that they do not trust the paranormals. Are you really that foolish, Kaida?"

Sick of his questions, she stomped toward the community cabin.

"If you were my mate," he was hurrying after her, "the first thing I would do is curb you of your ridiculous ideas about humans and dragons living in harmony."

"Thinking you can tell her what to do is exactly why she'll never bang you, dude," a voice drawled from the darkened porch of the community cabin.

The dragon shifter stepped out into the moonlight as Drago made a low hiss. "Mind your own business, asshole."

"Hello, Kaida." The shifter ignored Drago.

"Hi, Bones." She studied the giant shifter in the dim light. At almost seven feet tall and with a body thick with muscle, he was one of the larger shifters in their clan and the head of security for the clan. Somewhat ironic, considering he'd earned the nickname Bones for being abnormally skinny as a yearling and even into adulthood. But now, his large size, shaved head, and numerous tattoos intimidated many in their clan and other clan dragons.

What Kaida had always found fascinating was that Cadmus had appointed Bones to be the security head before he'd started to fill out. The other elders objected strenuously, but Cadmus would not be swayed. She shouldn't have been surprised by it, Kaida supposed. Cadmus often made decisions that seemed strange but ultimately were perfect.

She joined him on the porch. "Why are you here?"

Bones tugged at his chest-length goatee. The thick black hair was threaded with silver. Before he could reply, Drago said, "Why do you think? There's been a security breach, one that you caused when you brought a human into our midst. You're lucky he did not slaughter the humans immediately."

Kaida glanced at Bones, who rolled his eyes and said, "Do me a favour and tone down the fucking dramatics, would you, Drago? The human was just a kid."

"One of them was just a kid," Drago sneered. "The other was a cop."

Kaida twitched in surprise. "How do you know that? Were you hiding in the damn bushes next to my cabin while I spoke with the human?"

"Of course not," Drago said.

"Javee took his license plate number and did some," Bones hesitated, "research on him."

Kaida sighed. Why she thought for even a moment that she could keep the humans a secret from the rest of her clan was beyond her. They would have smelled Tyler and Corey as soon as she brought them close, and the council would have immediately begun assessing the risk and investigating the humans.

"You're lucky that we didn't call for his death the moment we discovered he was a cop," Drago said.

"We?" Bones turned toward him. "Your desire to be on the council is well-known, Drago, but until Cadmus appoints you to the council, don't act as though you have any say in their decisions.

Drago's upper chest glowed, and more smoke drifted from his nostrils and mouth. "You'll want to watch that smart mouth of yours, Bones. When I am on the council, you may find yourself working in the kitchen rather than security."

"Perhaps," Bones replied. "But until that happens, you'll watch your tone with me. Having your say on the council will be difficult if you're missing your tongue."

Drago snarled at him before yanking open the door to the cabin. "Are your threats supposed to frighten me? Kaida, come."

Her dragon snarled in fury, and Kaida crossed her arms over her chest. "Tell the elders I will be in shortly."

Drago snorted, flames shooting out from his nostrils. "I am not your messenger boy. Tell them yourself."

He disappeared into the large cabin, slamming the door behind him. Kaida rubbed at her forehead as Bones said, "Jesus, what a douche that guy is."

She smiled a little despite the nausea running rampant in her guts. "What's Cadmus's mood like?"

Bones shrugged. "You could probably tell better than I can, but he seems calm. Ever since Valen died, nothing seems to rile him up. The council asks him daily to appoint another member – Ryul hounds him about it, to be honest – but he seems in no hurry to do it."

"Do you think he'll appoint Drago?" Kaida asked.

"Fuck, I hope not." Bones rubbed at his shaved head. "Drago will have us fucking living in caves in the middle of Siberia if he gets appointed to the council. I know Ryul, Collette, and Oben are hoping he is appointed. They're old school like Drago, and having him on the council will give them the majority when it comes to voting."

He stared glumly at her. "We really will be living in caves in Siberia."

She squeezed his tattooed arm reassuringly. "Cadmus is still high elder. He has the power to overrule the council's vote."

"That's true, but Cadmus has been high elder since we were yearlings. How many times have you seen him use that particular high elder perk?"

"Only once," she said.

"Exactly. He didn't overrule their decision when you approached the council for permission to help Bishop protect his human mate from that rogue dragon, and he likes Bishop."

"I remember," Kaida said, "but you know as well as I do that Cadmus likes living near the humans. He always has. If he had his way, dragons would reveal themselves to the world like the other paranormals."

"Jesus, what a fucking shitshow that would be," Bones said. "You don't think Cadmus would do it, do you? I mean, it's one thing to wish we didn't have to be in hiding, but if he tried to show humans that dragons existed – high elder or not, he would be banished."

"No, I don't think he would," she said, but there was doubt in her voice. Ever since Cadmus's mate Valen died, the old dragon seemed almost indifferent to the council and the clan. He'd always been calm and slow to anger, but now he was nearly catatonic in his mannerisms. With Valen gone, she had a feeling that Cadmus believed he had nothing to live for anyway, and that could lead to dangerous consequences for the dragon.

"You'd better get in there," Bones said.

Kaida followed Bones into the cabin. It was the largest cabin, and it served as their community hall. The clan ate their meals here, social events were held in the cabin, and the council's monthly meetings occurred here. Any clan member was welcome to sit in on a council meeting but rarely did. Tonight, though, was an exception.

"Shit," Kaida said.

Bones stared at her before studying the dragons that filled the chairs lined up in neat horizontal rows in the large room. "Yeah, news spreads fast, right? They all want to know if the humans will be barbequed."

She took a deep breath as Bones sat in the last row next to Javee. The dragoness, short and curvy with long brown hair streaked with a rich dark red, smiled affectionately at him. Bones draped his arm across the back of her chair, and she leaned into him before giving Kaida an encouraging look.

Kaida walked down the center aisle toward the long and narrow table at the front of the room. The six council members sat behind the table. Kaida stared at the empty chair next to Cadmus where Valan used to sit, a sharp pang of loss eating at her insides.

She stopped in front of the council table and bowed to the elders. "Good evening, elders."

"Good evening, Kaida," Walter, the oldest of the elders, replied. His long hair was completely white, and its purple streaks had long since faded to a pale lilac. "Do you know why the council has summoned you?"

"I do," she said.

"Explain yourself," Ryul said sharply. "You brought humans into our clan. What were you thinking?"

"The fox shifter was injured badly by humans. I worried his head injury would be fatal, so I brought him to Gram for healing. The human is dating the fox shifter."

"You should have left the fox to die," Ryul said. "The problems of other shifters are not our concern."

"Perhaps they should be." The soft-spoken reply came from the blonde dragoness sitting next to Cadmus. The streaks in her hair were a dark red, and the flecks of red in her golden pupils almost looked like blood. "Avoiding other paranormals is a mistake we need to rectify."

"Not tonight, Leia," the dragon next to her sighed. "It is already late, and this is not the time for another discussion on why we should join forces with other paranormals. Dragons have survived for thousands of years and will continue to do so for another thousand years. Why is that so difficult for you to understand?"

Leia glared at the dark-haired shifter. "Why is it so difficult for you to understand that the old ways are dying? If we do not make changes now, our kind will not live to see another thousand years. You know as well as I do that fewer hatchlings are born every year. If we are to survive, we must adapt, Oben."

"Muddying the gene pool with other shifters is not the way to adapt," the dragoness on the other side of Oben said.

"If you believe allowing dragons to mate with a bear or a lion will not weaken our clans, then you are a bigger fool than I thought."

"Hold your tongue, Collette," Ryul said. "We are not here to discuss our hatchling problem."

Collette glared at him but fell silent as Ryul turned his gaze to Kaida. "What you have done was incredibly foolish, and you have risked the entire clan's safety."

"The fox shifter knows he must keep our secret," Kaida said.

"He knew you were a dragon?" Walter said.

"He did."

"Not surprising," Leia replied. "Our scent gives us away to most shifters. Even the ones who believe us extinct."

"This is the exact reason we avoid other shifters and humans," Oben said.

Leia snorted, a tiny bit of flame shooting out from her nostrils. "Humans cannot smell a damn thing. I could stand right next to one, and they would have no clue what I am."

"It does not mean we should invite them into our home." Ryul glared at Kaida. "As a yearling, your friendship with the grizzly shifter was tolerated because you were young and foolish. But you are an adult now. An adult who brought not only a shifter but two humans into our sacred space. Not only does one of them work for the human authorities, but they are the children of Senator Matthews."

Kaida's stomach dropped. She glanced behind her at Javee, who mouthed, 'I'm sorry.' She turned back to face the council. She didn't blame the dragoness for giving the information on Bren and Tyler to the council – it was her job, after all – but what were the odds that the human she rescued would be the son of the Senator doing everything in his power to subjugate shifters?

"Well?" Ryul said. "What do you have to say for yourself?"

She took a deep breath, the weight of the stares of most of her clan burrowing into the back of her skull. "The humans have no idea of our true nature. They believe we are bear shifters."

"So, that makes it better?" Collette said. "We should feel safer that humans know where our clan is because they believe us to be bears?"

"Many humans know where our clan is," Kaida said. "We may live in the woods and keep to ourselves, but there are humans and shifters in the city who know of us. How many times have hunters stumbled upon us? They, too, believe we are bear shifters. There is no reason that this may change."

"There is a difference between humans who stumble into our home and humans who are invited," Ryul said.

"They are only yearlings, and other humans had beaten them. I could not leave them to their fate," Kaida said.

"You could have, and you should have," Ryul said, sounding so much like Drago that Kaida glanced over her shoulder at the redheaded dragon. He stared at her with smugness and anger, and she resisted the urge to give him the finger. Acting like a yearling would not help her case with the council.

"The humans are below us," Ryul continued, "and your compassion toward them is weakness on your part."

"Compassion is never a weakness," Walter said.

Ryul shook his head. "It is when it will get you banished."

Her clan gasped behind her, and Kaida fought to keep the fear from spreading on her face. She knew they would bring up banishment, but hearing the words from an elder's mouth still brought tingles of panic down her spine.

"There will be no talk of banishment." Cadmus's low voice soothed her panic.

Ryul turned to Cadmus. "She brought humans into the clan, high elder. If they discover we are dragons, banishment is -"

"*If* they discover we are dragons," Cadmus said. "They believe us to be bears, remember? Humans are not the brightest species in the world. If we keep our flame to ourselves when the humans return, they will not suspect our true nature."

"When the humans return?" Ryul sputtered. "They are not returning to the clan, Cadmus."

Cadmus stared at Kaida, and a flush rose in her cheeks. How did he know?

"Kaida," Cadmus said. "What would you like to ask of the council?"

She swallowed down her nerves and kept her shoulders back. "I ask the council to grant the fox shifter mercy. He will keep our secret, and when you speak with him in the morning, you will see that what I say is true."

"We will take your request for mercy under advisement," Ryul said stiffly.

"Thank you, elder."

"If that is all, then we will -"

"Kaida," Cadmus's low voice interrupted Ryul, "what else?"

She licked her dry lips, knowing what she was about to ask was madness and cursing her dragon for getting her into this mess. "I ask the council for permission to train the yearling human and the fox shifter how to fight."

A smile broke out across Cadmus's face as the clan made more gasps of surprise and dismay behind her.

Ryul laughed. "You're kidding."

"I am not," she said. "The human believes we're bears, and the fox shifter will keep our secret. I will only need a week or two to train them. I'll take them to the training circle and keep them away from the clan."

"No," Ryul said. "Absolutely not."

"Ryul," Cadmus said. "That is not how this works."

Ryul sighed before sitting back in his chair. "Fine, we will vote on it. All council members in favour of allowing Kaida to bring a human and a shifter near our clan and thereby endangering all of our lives, raise your hands."

Her stomach a hot, twisted mess of bile, Kaida clenched her hands at her sides and scanned the council. When only Leia and Cadmus raised their hands, a small part of her was relieved. Bringing the humans into her world would only cause trouble.

I want the big human, her dragon grumbled to her. *Give him to me.*

Shut up. Christ, now was not the time for her dragon to get involved. She didn't know what the fuck was going on with her dragon, but its sudden crush on a damn human was a complication she didn't need.

"All those against?" Ryul asked.

The other four raised their hands. Kaida ignored her dragon's grumbling as Ryul said, "If we allow the fox to live, you will return him to his family immediately."

"Gram says he shouldn't be moved for a day or two," Kaida said. "It could make his injuries worse."

"That is not our problem," Ryul said. "As for the humans, if they show up to see the fox shifter, I would advise that you warn them not to return to our lands." He stood, gathering up his cloak. "The meeting is -"

"I'm overruling the council's decision."

Ryul froze and turned to Cadmus. "What did you say?"

"I said, I am overruling the council's decision. It is my right to do so as high elder," Cadmus said.

"Cadmus, be reasonable," Walter said. "I do not think the humans to be the problem that Ryul and the others do, but allowing them to be near our clan is madness."

"Why?" Leia said. "They think we are bear shifters. What is the harm?"

"What is the harm? Have you gone crazy?" Drago jumped up from his seat.

"Watch your tongue," Leia said to him. "You're speaking to an elder. Do not forget that."

"Forgive me," Drago said. "But we cannot allow the humans anywhere near our clan again. Humans are stupid and dangerous."

"Thank you for your input, Drago," Cadmus said. A serene look had dropped across his face again. "But as you are not yet a council member, your opinion is not asked for or needed. Return to your seat."

Drago's eyes flashed with angry light, but he returned to his seat.

"Kaida, do you believe we are in danger from these humans?" Cadmus asked.

"No, Cadmus," Kaida replied. "You are right in that they are not very bright. They will not discover our true nature in the short time it will take me to teach the yearlings to defend themselves."

"Cadmus, you cannot -"

"Hush, Collette," Cadmus said. "I can and I will. Kaida will train the yearling human and the fox to defend themselves. Will the adult human be joining them?"

Kaida's stomach clenched. "Some, I would imagine. He is the yearling's brother, and they seem close."

Both Oben and Ryul snorted in disgust, but Cadmus ignored them. "Very well. They are allowed in the training circle and Kaida's cabin only. I trust you will keep watch over them at all times, Kaida."

"Yes, Cadmus." She hesitated. "Will the council still require a meeting with the fox in the morning?"

"Yes." Cadmus smiled at her before heaving himself to his feet. "I cannot abolish every rule in one night, can I?" He looked out at the crowd of dragons. "The meeting is done. Return to your homes, my clan."

CHAPTER 5

"What did Dad say about your hand?" Bren turned off the highway and headed down the two-lane road toward the bear clan's land.

"He didn't even notice." Tyler stared morosely out the window. "I could have been wearing a cast, and he wouldn't have noticed."

Bren reached across and squeezed Tyler's shoulder. He wanted to ask Ty about moving in with him again, but he knew what his brother's answer would be. Tyler craved their father's attention and affection despite being rejected time and time again, and it killed Bren to watch him be disappointed repeatedly.

"Tyler, maybe you should -"

"Corey texted me this morning," Tyler said. "He's feeling better, he said."

"That's good news. Maybe he'll be able to go home today."

Tyler snorted and stared out the window again. "It's not a home. His foster parents didn't even text him last night. They don't give a shit. All they care about is getting their money. I told him he could stay with me."

"That's not a good idea," Bren said. "If Dad finds out he's a shifter -"

"He won't," Tyler said. "I'm dating Corey and didn't even know about it. He's good at hiding it."

"He shouldn't have to hide it, though, and if he lives with you and Dad, he will have to," Bren said.

"He hides it at his foster home," Tyler said. "What's the difference?"

Bren turned right onto the narrow dirt road. Tyler had a point, but it was still too dangerous for Corey to live with him. "If it came out that Dad had a shifter living in his home, it would ruin him politically. If that happens…"

"Yeah, yeah, he'd disown me," Tyler said. "I know Dad's career is more important to him than me. You don't have to keep reminding me."

The road grew bumpier and narrower, and Bren gripped the steering wheel tighter. As they crested the hill right before Kaida's home, his stomach made a funny little lurch that had nothing to do with the potholes they were driving over.

He followed the road – it was more like a dirt path at this point – past three cabins and parked in front of Kaida's. He shut the car off as Tyler unlatched his seatbelt.

"Ty, wait a minute."

"What?" Tyler stared impatiently at him.

"I'm not sure that having Kaida teach you and Corey how to fight is a good idea."

A scowl crossed Tyler's face. "It is, Bren. We need to know how to protect ourselves."

"I can show you some self-defence moves, and we can sign you and Corey up for some boxing classes at -"

"I want Kaida to teach us to fight." The familiar stubborn line had shown up between Ty's eyebrows. "And if you had seen her kicking Jeff's ass yesterday, you'd want her showing us how to fight too."

He opened the door and climbed out of the car before Bren could say anything else. He sighed and slid out of the car, slamming the door shut and studying the other cabins as Tyler bounded up the porch steps and knocked on Kaida's door.

Like yesterday, there wasn't a single person in the clearing surrounding the cabins. He studied the cabins, a crawling sensation on the back of his neck. His feeling of being watched was confirmed when a curtain in the cabin across from Kaida's home twitched.

He swung his gaze that way, keeping a friendly expression, but the curtain had already stilled. He knew that bear shifters could be standoffish and avoid humans, especially grizzlies, but this was bordering on ridiculous. It was a beautiful autumn day, and there wasn't one shifter outside raking leaves or -

"Human, come inside."

He turned around. Tyler had already disappeared into the cabin, and Kaida stood on her porch. His stomach made another of those funny lurches like he was hurtling down a steep hill on a roller coaster instead of standing on solid ground. She wore jeans and a faded pink t-shirt that clung to her full breasts. Sweat broke out on his forehead. He'd been one hundred percent accurate about what kind of body that cloak had been hiding yesterday, and the semi he was now sporting was about to turn into a full-blown erection if he didn't look away.

He dropped his gaze to the porch steps and climbed them slowly. He joined her on the porch, and when he glanced up, Kaida gave him an impatient look. "Come inside, quickly."

She glanced around the clearing, and he turned to study

the other cabins again. More curtains twitched and fell back into place, and he grinned at Kaida. "Looks like your neighbours are curious about the humans."

She herded him inside the cabin like a wayward child. Her hand grazed his lower back and sent a zinging sensation straight to his dick.

Tyler was already sitting on the couch beside Corey and holding the fox shifter's hand. An old man with pure white hair streaked with orange and hanging to his waist in a neatly made braid sat at the kitchen table.

"Bren, this is Cadmus, the high elder of our clan. Cadmus, this is Bren."

Bren walked forward and held out his hand. "It's good to meet you."

The old man stared at his hand, and amusement drifted across his face before he shook Bren's hand. "Hello, human."

He dropped Bren's hand and stood. He drifted across the room toward the door, stopping briefly beside the couch. "You did well with the council, young fox. Do not worry."

Corey kept his gaze on his lap as Tyler stared at Cadmus with frank interest. Cadmus smiled at him. "Enjoy Kaida's teaching, human yearling."

"Um, thank you. I will. It was nice to meet you, Mr. Cadmus," Tyler said.

Cadmus laughed, revealing straight white teeth, before moving to the door. "I will see you at dinner with the others, Kaida."

"Yes, Cadmus."

He left the cabin, and Corey slumped against the couch as Tyler said, "How old is that dude?"

"Tyler," Bren said, "don't be rude, please."

"Sorry. Hey, you okay?" Tyler asked Corey.

"I'm fine." Corey glanced at Kaida. "I'm ready to go home."

"Gram will be here in a bit," Kaida said. "You look much better this morning, and she may agree to send you home."

"That's great news," Tyler said. "I'll get you set up in our guest room."

Corey grimaced. "Ty, I don't think -"

"Holy crap! I forgot to show you what Julie Lesner posted on Facebook." Tyler yanked his phone out of his pocket. "She and Winston broke up, and she went nuclear on his page. Check it out."

As the two boys huddled on the couch and looked at Tyler's phone, Kaida pointed to the table. "Have a seat, human."

Bren sat down, and Kaida took two mugs out of the cupboard. "Coffee or tea?"

"Coffee if it isn't too much trouble."

She popped a pod into the machine and made him a coffee before brewing one for herself. She brought the coffee, milk, and sugar to the table and eased into the chair across from him.

Bren splashed some milk into his coffee before taking a sip. "It's good, thanks."

Kaida added a generous amount of sugar to her mug. Behind him, Bren could hear Corey and Tyler talking in low tones. Feeling awkward, he said, "Thank you again for keeping Corey overnight."

"You're welcome." She took a sip of coffee.

There was more awkward silence, and Bren cleared his throat. Typically, he had no problems talking to women, even ones as beautiful as Kaida. But for some reason, being around Kaida made his tongue twist into knots and his brain foggy.

It probably didn't help that he kept wanting to check out her rack like he was a horny teenager. He was a tits guy, always had been, and Kaida's looked perfect. Full and firm and probably as milky white as the rest of her skin. Were her nipples pink? He bet they were pink like her mouth. Or maybe they were –

Bren!

He realized he was sporting a semi again and shifted closer to the table, ensuring the wooden surface hid his junk. What the fuck was wrong with him?

Kaida stared at him like she knew exactly what he'd been thinking. She probably did. Shifters had great senses of smell, and as a bear shifter, hers was one of the best. No doubt she could smell his arousal.

Embarrassment heating his chest, he said, "So, how do you know Bishop?"

She toyed with the handle of her mug. "We have been friends since we were yearlings. Not much older than your brother and the fox shifter."

"Yearlings," he said. Cadmus had also used the word earlier, and it struck him as strange. "Is that what bear shifters call teenagers?"

"Yes," she replied before looking over at Tyler and Corey.

Tingles went down his spine. He had an excellent bullshit detector – he wasn't sure if that was from years on the force or if it was an innate trait – and he knew Kaida was lying. He tucked the little tidbit of info away in the Kaida file he'd created in his mind.

"So, was Bishop a part of this clan or…?"

"No," she said. "I found him in the woods one day. He'd been caught in a bear trap."

"Jesus," Bren said.

Kaida's face turned soft with the memory. "It had done incredible damage to his leg, and he'd lost a lot of blood, but he was still alive. Even as a child, he was one of the toughest shifters I'd ever met. I pried open the bear trap and brought him to Gram. She thought he might lose his leg even with his healing abilities and her healing poultices, but," another soft smile that sent a weird streak of jealousy through Bren's stomach, "my bear is stubborn and fierce. I believe he kept his leg by sheer willpower alone."

"Your bear?" Bren said.

Shit, did he *sound* jealous?

Pink tinged Kaida's cheeks. "My nickname for Bishop."

Unease settled in his stomach. Did Kaida have a thing for Bishop? Jesus, what was with him having the hots for every woman who wanted Bishop King? – Bren said, "You know that Bishop is getting married to his human girlfriend in two weeks, right? They have a kid together, too."

"I know. I've been invited to the wedding. Bishop and I are only friends, nothing more." She eyed him over the rim of her coffee mug. "Are you going to the wedding?"

"Yes."

He'd been a little surprised when he got the invitation. Despite saving Bishop's life, the grizzly shifter still wasn't fond of him. He'd wavered on going or not and, in the end, RSVP'd yes.

There was a knock on the door before it swung open, and a young woman stepped inside. She had long blonde hair with streaks of orange in it and she was about thirteen months pregnant by Bren's estimate.

"Kaida, do you have any eggs? We're out, and Jarvis is craving an omelet. How weird is that? I'm the one who's supposed to have pregnancy cravings, but Jarvis has been..."

She stopped dead in her tracks, sniffing the air before staring first at Tyler and Corey on the couch and then studying Bren at the table. Her hand rubbed her distended belly, and a smile of delight crossed her face. "Humans!"

Kaida stood up abruptly. "Sika, I don't have any eggs, but Gram probably -"

"Hi! I'm Sika!" The pregnant woman hurried over to the couch and grinned at Tyler.

"Hi, I'm Tyler, and this is Corey."

Sika was almost vibrating with excitement. "It's so cool to meet you."

"Sika, did you hear me?" Kaida glanced at Bren.

"I heard you." Sika walked toward them, smiling at Bren when he stood and shook her hand. "Hello, human!"

"Hello," Bren said. She pumped his hand rapidly and he grinned at her, making her smile widen. Her enthusiasm was weirdly infectious.

"Bren, this is my best friend, Sika. Sika, this is Bren."

"It's so awesome to meet you," Sika said. She was still holding his hand, her bright gold eyes with flecks of orange staring into his eyes intently.

Did everyone in their clan wear contacts?

"It's nice to meet you, too," Bren said.

"Sika." Kaida stared at their joined hands, and Sika dropped his with a soft giggle.

"I'm sorry. I've never touched a human before," she said.

"Seriously?" he said.

She nodded and, ignoring Kaida's grunt of protest, plopped down in the empty seat beside him. "Yeah. Our clan doesn't interact with humans very much. I rarely go to the city and it's not like I could touch random humans, is it? Besides, my mate Jarvis would have a fit if I started touching humans. He says they carry all sorts of diseases, and who knows what I would catch, which is silly because we have healing powers. We can heal ourselves of any of your gross human diseases."

She paused. "Not that you have gross human diseases. I'm sure you're very clean."

She leaned forward and inhaled deeply, her nose almost buried in Bren's throat. "You smell clean."

"Oh my God, Sika," Kaida said.

"What? He does. You smell really good, actually," she said.

"Thanks," Bren replied.

"Do all human males smell as good as you?" Sika turned to Kaida without waiting for a reply. "Have you smelled him, Kaida?"

She leaned forward to smell him again, making a squeak of surprise when Kaida's hand wrapped around her wrist. "Sika, enough. You are making the human uncomfortable."

"Am I?" Sika's expression was suitably chastised. "I'm sorry, human. I didn't mean to make you uncomfortable."

"You're not," Bren said. "I'm totally used to random women smelling me."

"Really?"

"No, not really."

Sika stared blankly at him before laughing. "You're making a joke, human."

"I am," Bren said.

"You're funny. You're funny, and you smell good. Do all humans smell as good as you?"

"It varies," Bren said. "Teenage boys – or yearlings as you call them – do not smell good."

"I smell fine," Tyler hollered from the couch.

Bren shook his head before leaning forward to say in a low, conspiratorial voice, "Don't believe him. Hormonal teenagers rarely smell good."

Sika giggled. "It is the same with our yearlings."

"I guess humans and bear shifters have something in common after all," Bren said.

Sika blinked at him. "Bear shifters?"

Kaida cleared her throat, and Sika sat back in her chair before saying, "Oh yes, bear shifters. Such as myself."

Bren's bullshit detector blipped out another series of high-pitched noises.

"You should probably go now, Sika," Kaida said. "Jarvis will be looking for his omelet."

"Yes, in a minute." Sika was still studying Bren. "May I ask you a personal question, human?"

"Sika…" Kaida said.

"Yes," Bren said. "If I can ask you one."

"Deal," Sika said.

"Sika, no," Kaida said.

"It's fine, Kaida. There's no harm in asking one question," Sika said. "Right, human?"

"Right," Bren said. He turned his smile to 'killer charm' and aimed it at Kaida. To his disappointment, it seemed to have zero effect on her.

"You're so handsome when you smile," Sika said. Her face beamed with delight as she grinned at Kaida. "Isn't he handsome for a human?"

Kaida's cheeks went bright red. "He's, uh, okay."

"I usually win the ladies over with my sparkling personality rather than my okay looks," Bren said.

Kaida blushed even more, and Sika giggled. "Do you have a girlfriend, human?"

"I don't." He took a quick look at Kaida. She was staring at Sika with murder in her beautiful golden-coloured eyes.

"I'm surprised." She examined Bren's hair and his shoulders before eyeing his body. "You are handsome, and, for a human, you have a pretty large body." She reached out and felt Bren's bicep. "Ooh, and you're muscular too. Why are you not mated? Do human females not enjoy a strong and muscular male?"

"Um, women seem to like it when a guy keeps in shape," Bren said.

"Hmm." Sika's gaze dropped to his crotch. "Is your," she pointed at his dick, "on the… smaller side?" She held her thumb and forefinger a few inches apart in case he couldn't figure out what she was saying.

"Oh my God, Sika!" Kaida's face was so red that Bren wouldn't have been surprised if he saw smoke coming from her ears.

He did a double take…wait, *was* that smoke coming from her nose?

Before he could look closer, she spun around and stared at the cupboards.

"Sorry, that was rude," Sika said. Her face was a little pink, and she rubbed compulsively at her belly.

Secretly amused by the bear's question but knowing that Kaida was upset and Sika was embarrassed, Bren said, "I have a busy job, so that doesn't allow me to date much."

Not a complete lie. Not the whole truth either, but he didn't need to try to explain to a bear shifter he'd just met about the intricacies of online dating and how horrifying it was.

"It's time to go now, Sika," Kaida said.

"But I haven't asked the human my personal question," Sika said.

Kaida spun around and sank into the chair, glaring at her best friend. Glancing over Sika's head at Tyler and Corey, she lowered her voice. "Asking the human his dick size is not a personal enough question for you?"

"I… well… it wasn't the personal question I meant to ask," Sika said.

"Too bad," Kaida replied.

Sika's face fell, and Bren said, "It's okay, Sika. Ask your question."

"Are you sure?"

He nodded, and Sika's smile returned. "How do you know when someone wants to mate with you?"

Bren stared at her.

Sika smiled encouragingly. "Well, human? For shifters, we know when someone wants to mate because we can smell their arousal for us. Humans have such a poor sense of smell. How do you know when someone wants you in their bed?"

"Uh, well, you ask them out," Bren said.

"Ask them out?" Sika cocked her head at him.

"On a date. Like to dinner or a movie. If they say yes, it generally means they're at least interested in you. And as you get to know each other better, it becomes easier to tell if the person wants to sleep with you. Maybe not by smell, but by how they look at you, or if they… flirt."

Sika grinned at him. "I do know what flirting is. I flirt with my mate all the time. But it's easier because I can smell that he wants me. What if you do all this flirting, and the human still doesn't want to mate?"

"Well, then you could just be friends, and you look for someone else to flirt with who you find attractive and hope they feel the same way."

"It seems like a lot of work just to sleep with someone," Sika said.

"It can be," Bren glanced at Kaida, "but it's worth it for the right person."

Kaida looked away. There was another knock on the door before it opened, and Kaida's grandmother stepped into the cabin. Today, she wore a burgundy velvet tracksuit with a matching velvet headband strapped around her forehead.

Bren hid his smile as Gram stopped beside Tyler and Corey on the couch and held out her fist. Tyler bumped it with his own. "You're looking ballin' today, Gram. I like the velvet."

"Thanks," Gram said. "Now, move out of the way for a minute so I can look at your boyfriend."

They all watched as Gram poked and prodded at Corey's head and ribs.

"Headache gone?" she asked.

"Yes, ma'am," Corey said.

"How's your ribs?"

"Sore, but my healing is starting to kick in."

"Still peeing blood?"

Corey blushed and took a quick look at Tyler before shaking his head. "No, ma'am. Not since last night."

"Good. You're a fast healer, little fox. Although I suppose you got youth on your side." Gram heaved herself to her feet.

"Can I go home?" Corey asked.

"I think so. You don't feel dizzy when you stand, do you?" Gram said.

Corey shook his head again. "No, I feel fine."

"All right then, you're free to go."

Bren didn't think he imagined that Corey and Kaida looked immensely relieved.

Corey hopped up from the couch and grabbed his sweater from the armchair. "C'mon, Ty, let's go."

Ty blinked at him. "Right now?"

Corey turned to Bren. "Can we go, Bren? My foster family is worried about me."

"No, they're not." Tyler stood and followed Corey to the door of the cabin. "You're coming back to my place, Corey. I'll look after you."

"No," Corey said.

Ty scowled at him. "Dude, c'mon."

"I can't," Corey said. "I appreciate the offer, but," he glanced at Bren, "with your dad, it's not a good idea."

"He's hardly home," Tyler said stubbornly. "He won't even notice that you're staying with us."

"I can't," Corey said again. "Please, Ty, I want to go home and sleep in my own bed. Okay?"

Bren could see the hurt on his brother's face, but Ty said, "Yeah, okay."

Tyler turned and smiled tentatively at Kaida. "We're still on for learning to fight, right?"

"Yes. How about Wednesday evening?" Kaida said.

"That long?" Tyler said.

"The fox needs to be completely healed," Gram said before patting Tyler's arm.

"Can you bring us here Wednesday night?" Tyler asked Bren.

Bren mentally reviewed his schedule. He was testifying in court that day for an ongoing case, but unless something got fucked up, he would finish in time. "Yes. Say around six?"

"Sure," Kaida said.

Gram joined them and smiled at Bren before putting her arm around Sika's shoulders and squeezing her. "How are you feeling, sugarpie?"

"Like I'm gonna explode," Sika said. "I'm so ready to hold our hatchling in my arms."

Hatchling?

"Soon," Gram said.

Sika took Gram's hand and pressed it against her belly. Gram's wrinkled face lit up, and she rubbed Sika's belly gently.

"Can we go, Bren?" Corey asked.

Bren glanced a final time at Kaida. She was staring at

Sika's belly with longing in her gaze, and he felt his own pang of want. He wasn't sure if a guy could have a biological clock, but if they did – his was ticking and had been for some time. He'd always wanted lots of kids, and as he neared his mid-thirties, he was painfully aware of how much faster time seemed to be moving.

He realized with embarrassment that he was staring at Kaida and that Gram was staring at him staring at Kaida. He joined Ty and Corey at the door as Corey took a tentative step toward Kaida and Gram.

"Thank you again," he said. "For everything. I really appreciate your help."

"You're welcome, little fox," Kaida said.

"We'll see you Wednesday," Ty said. He seemed oblivious to Corey's discomfort and tension.

"See you Wednesday," Kaida said. Her gaze flicked to Bren briefly before she gathered the mugs and turned away.

Feeling like a small child who'd been dismissed, Bren herded Corey and Tyler out of the cabin.

CHAPTER 6

W hat are you doing?
Kaida ignored her inner voice as she took the elevator to Bishop's office.

You don't even know he'll be there. For God's sake, you're acting like an idiot.

No, she didn't know whether Bren would be at the office. He had mentioned he would talk to Bishop on Monday, but she had no idea if he would. But that didn't matter because she absolutely one hundred percent was not dropping by Bishop's office in the hopes of running into Bren. She was stopping by because she was in the city and missed her friend. It would be good to say hello and see how the wedding preparations were going.

And why exactly are you in the city? Do you think Gram didn't know you lied when you said you needed tampons?

She cringed. God, she couldn't lie for shit, and when Gram had stopped in as Kaida was leaving, she'd said the first thing that popped into her head.

Gram hadn't said anything, just grinned and asked her to pick up some beef jerky – the old woman was addicted to it

– but Kaida had still felt like a yearling in the throes of its first real crush.

She couldn't help it, though. Her dragon was driving her crazy about seeing Bren again. It didn't matter that they would see Bren again on Wednesday. Her dragon was insistent on going into the city.

Unease trickled down Kaida's spine as the elevator doors opened, and she stepped out into the hallway. Her dragon rarely wanted to leave the clan. It found the city too loud and overwhelming, so for it to demand she go in the hopes of *maybe* running into Bren…

She shook off the unease and pulled open the door to BKF Securities. Bren wasn't in the reception area, and her dragon's excitement deflated. It growled unhappily, and she soothed it as Willow, the company's receptionist, smiled at her.

"Kaida, hello! How are you?"

Kaida smiled at the bubbly receptionist as her dragon immediately perked up and purred in greeting. As a general rule, her dragon wasn't fond of humans, but from the moment Kaida had met Willow, it had an instant soft spot for the perky and sweet human.

The fact that Willow knew she was a dragon was also oddly comforting. Although she hated that Willow only knew because Bishop's mate Ava had been stalked and nearly killed by an insane dragon, it was a relief not to hide who she was around Willow or Ava.

"Very well. How are you, Willow?"

"Good. You're here to see Bishop?"

"Yes. I don't have an appointment, though," Kaida replied.

Willow waved her hand. "Please, you don't need an appointment. You guys are practically besties."

Kaida's grin widened as Bishop's office door opened. Ava,

her curvy body clad in hospital scrubs and her red hair in a ponytail, stepped out into reception. Bishop towered behind her, holding a chubby, smiling, redheaded baby who looked exactly like her mother.

"Kaida, hey!" The scent of Bishop's happiness drifted to her, and her dragon made another happy purr. "What are you doing here?"

"I was in the city and thought I would stop by and say hi. Hello, Ava."

"Hi, Kaida." Ava smiled at her. "It's really good to see you again."

"You too. You're looking well."

"It's the excitement of the wedding," Willow said with a laugh.

"More like stress." Ava pulled her phone from her purse. "I swear, Bishop, I don't know what I was thinking when I agreed to plan a wedding in only six weeks."

Bishop kissed the baby's smooth cheek. "What's the point in waiting?"

"He wanted to go to the courthouse and get married by the justice of the peace," Willow said to Kaida. "Can you believe it?"

"There's nothing wrong with a small wedding, Will," Bishop said.

"That's not a small wedding," Willow said. "That's a 'my old lady is knocked up, and I need to marry her before her father comes after me with a shotgun' wedding."

Kaida's smile widened when Willow gave Bishop and Ava a suspicious look. "Hey, you two aren't having another baby and just not telling me, are you?"

Ava shook her head. "God, no. I am not pregnant, Willow, and if you start that rumour, I will murder you. So help me God."

Bishop joined Kaida, leaning down to press a kiss against her cheek. "It's good to see you."

"You as well, my bear." Kaida touched Lila's chubby thigh and the baby gave her a wide smile. "She's getting so big."

"Four months old now," Bishop said proudly. "She said daddy the other day."

"She didn't," Ava said with a laugh. "Honey, I know you want Lila's first word to be daddy, but she can't talk yet."

"It sounded like 'daddy'," Bishop said. He growled to Lila, and the baby kicked her feet happily and squealed excitedly before pulling on Bishop's short beard. He growled again and nuzzled her cheek.

I want to hold the hatchling!

Kaida soothed her dragon. She also wanted to hold the baby but asking would be rude. Still, she couldn't stop herself from running her finger along Lila's chubby thigh again.

"Honey, give Lila to Kaida," Ava said.

Kaida glanced at Ava, and the redhead smiled at her. "Only if you want to."

Bishop held Lila a little closer. Willow laughed. "Am I the only one who finds it adorable that Bishop never wants to share Lila with anyone?"

Bishop rolled his eyes before handing Lila to Kaida. Her dragon purred to Lila, and Kaida allowed the sound to escape her throat. The baby's eyes went wide. She stared at Kaida before looking at Bishop. He growled soothingly, and Lila turned her gaze back to Kaida. She touched Kaida's mouth, and Lila giggled when her dragon purred again.

"What is that noise?" Willow asked. "It sounds like purring, but...isn't."

Kaida cleared her throat. "Uh, that's me. My dragon, uh, makes that sound sometimes."

"Cool," Willow said.

Kaida kissed Lila's head as the chubby baby relaxed against her. Lila touched Kaida's hair, and Kaida pressed her nose against the top of Lila's head and inhaled deeply. God, she wanted her own hatchling. Her stomach ached, and her dragon made a soft noise of sadness.

Even if she found a mate from one of the other clans, the odds that she would conceive were incredibly low. The fact that Sika had conceived was a damn miracle. Her hatchling would be the first born to their clan in over a decade, and the entire clan was on pins and needles waiting for the hatchling to be born.

We might have a hatchling, her dragon said.

The hope in its voice made her chest ache.

Perhaps, she replied.

"You okay?" Bishop's voice rumbled, low enough that only she could hear.

"I'm good." The door behind her opened, and she smelled Bren's scent. Her dragon surged forward, purring and squealing and acting like an idiot. Her arms tightened around Lila, and the baby made a squeak of discomfort, which made Bishop immediately reach for her.

Kaida relaxed her grip and kissed Lila's head. "Sorry, Lila."

Lila stared over Kaida's shoulder at Bren as Bishop said, "Detective Matthews? What are you doing here?"

"Didn't I tell you?" Willow said with a slight grin. "Bren called this morning and asked to chat with you. He's your two-thirty appointment."

Taking a deep breath, Kaida turned to face Bren. He was staring at her and Lila, and she could smell both his lust and his happiness at seeing her. It made her dragon giddy – hell, it made her giddy – and she eyed the human with barely controlled lust.

He was wearing jeans and a blue dress shirt that complimented his eyes. The charcoal gray sport jacket he wore hugged the broad expanse of his shoulders. His tie was burgundy with small blue squares in a diamond pattern. She had a sudden vision of that tie wrapped around his wrists and her headboard while she rode him. What would he look like naked? Would he moan when he was in her pussy?

Bishop glanced at her, his nose twitching, and heat flushed her cheeks. Bishop could smell her lust for the human, and she had no idea how she would explain that. She swallowed hard as Lila let her head clunk against Kaida's chest. She giggled again before rubbing her cheek back and forth. No doubt the baby could feel the vibrations. Her dragon was purring so loudly that it was almost impossible to keep the sound inside.

"Hey, Kaida," Bren said.

Bishop grunted in surprise. "How do you know her?"

Ava joined them. "Hello, Bren."

"Hi, Ava. It's nice to see you again." Bren kissed Ava's cheek.

Her dragon protested immediately, the purr becoming a growl as Bishop's jealousy coated him in a thick scent. Her dragon hissed at Ava, and Kaida stiffened.

Stop it, she snapped.

Keep her away from the human. He's ours!

Oh my God, he's not ours. Besides, you know as well as I do that Ava is Bishop's mate. Her dragon was losing its mind.

"How do you know Kaida?" Bishop repeated.

"It's a long story and partially why I'm here," Bren said. "Why are you here, Kaida?"

"Oh, um, I was in the city and stopped by to see Bishop," Kaida replied.

"Happy coincidence then," Bren said. His gaze turned to

78

Lila, and Kaida's dragon purred again when his eyes softened, and more happiness drifted from his skin. "Hi, Lila. You're looking more and more like your mama every time I see you."

"Thank God," Willow said.

Bishop growled at her, and Willow laughed. "Hey, you literally said that to me yesterday."

Bren reached out to Lila, and the baby grabbed his hand. She examined his finger before trying to put it in her mouth, and he gently tugged his hand free before smiling at Kaida. Her cheeks flushed again – oh my God, she *was* acting like a yearling with her first crush – and she looked away.

She groaned inwardly when Ava looked at her and then Bren. Bishop's mate couldn't smell her and Bren's mutual attraction, but she was clever for a human. "I got your RSVP for the wedding, Bren. I'm so glad you could make it."

"Me too." Bren was still staring at Kaida, and she thanked God she was holding Lila. If she wasn't, the temptation to simply grab the human by the arm, take him outside to her car, and bang him until the ache in her pussy was finally gone, might have been too strong to resist.

The way he was looking at her – like he would be more than happy to join her for a quickie in her car, was doing things to her insides.

Yes! Please? Her dragon whined.

"You know," Ava smiled at Bren, "I realized I forgot to email you your invitation to Bishop's birthday party this Saturday. It's short notice, but any chance you can come? We're having it at the house. Nothing fancy, just a barbeque – if the warmish weather holds out – and a few friends and family."

"Oh, uh…" Bren glanced at Bishop.

The big grizzly shifter stared at Ava with undisguised shock, and Kaida almost laughed.

"Kaida will be there. Right?" Ava said.

Lila sat up, leaned forward, and pressed her mouth against Kaida's cheek. She licked and gnawed as Ava sighed. "Lila, no licking. Sorry, Kaida. This is something new she started doing a few days ago.

Lila giggled, and Kaida grinned at her before kissing the top of her head. "I don't mind. And, yes, I'll be at Bishop's birthday party."

"You have to come," Ava said to Bren. "Right, Willow?"

"Oh, totally," Willow said. "It's not a party if the cops don't show up."

Bren laughed. "Sure. I'll be there. What should I bring?"

"Just yourself," Ava said. "Mara and Roland are bringing enough food to feed an army. I'll text you the address. We're eating around six, but feel free to come by any time after five. Speaking of which," she glanced at her watch, "I need to get going. My shift starts soon, and I need to get Lila over to Mara."

Kaida handed Lila to Ava. The curvy human smiled at her and then Bren. "We'll see you both on Saturday."

She left the office, and as Willow returned to the reception desk, Kaida said, "I'd better go so you can meet with Bishop."

"Actually," Bren said, "if you have time, why don't you stay? You were kind of a part of this and can give Bishop a better idea of what they did."

"Sure," she said before she could stop herself.

Her dragon growled with pleasure. Bishop gave her another searching look before pointing to the boardroom. "All right, let's talk in the boardroom."

"Okay, so," Bishop scanned the tablet in his hand, "you want someone to keep an eye on Tyler as he's biking to and from school."

"Corey as well," Bren said. "He lives about ten minutes from Tyler, and Ty usually bikes to his place first, and then they bike to school. Whatever the extra cost is for Corey, I'll pay it."

"His parents don't know about what happened?" Bishop said.

"He lives with a foster family," Kaida said.

"Right." Bishop looked over his notes again. "You said that earlier."

"I'm pretty sure they're not going to pay to keep Corey safe, but he means a lot to Tyler, and I don't want him getting hurt again," Bren said.

"There won't be an extra charge for Corey," Bishop said. "He'll be with Tyler, and it's just as easy to keep an eye on both as it is on one."

"Thanks," Bren said with a glance at Kaida. "I'm hoping it will only be for a few weeks."

"You think this Jeff kid is gonna lose interest?" Bishop said. "Because from what you've told me, I doubt that'll happen."

"No, but Kaida has agreed to show Corey and Tyler some ways to protect themselves and how to fight if Jeff does approach them. Once they're better prepared, we'll ease off on the extra security."

Bishop's mouth dropped open, and he stared at Kaida. "You're teaching them how to fight?"

"Yes," she said.

"I'm bringing them by her place Wednesday night for their first lesson," Bren said.

She didn't think Bishop's jaw could drop further, but she was wrong.

"You're training them at your place?" Bishop said to her when he'd lifted his jaw off the boardroom table.

"What? What am I missing?" Bren said.

"Nothing," Kaida replied. "Bishop just knows how much our clan values their privacy."

"I know, and I promise that the boys will be respectful and not bother any of the other bear shifters," Bren said.

Bishop sat back in his chair, his gaze still trained on Kaida. "The council agreed to this?"

"Yes." She cut him a look that said *we will talk about this later.*

Bren was studying her and Bishop, and she tried to look nonchalant. She didn't know many humans, but Bren seemed weirdly attuned when she was lying or hiding something. And it had more to do with her just being shitty at lying.

You think? He's a cop, Kaida. He gets paid to know when people are lying to him.

"Okay, well, I'll look over the schedule and assign someone to Tyler and Corey starting this afternoon," Bishop said.

"Thanks, I appreciate it." Bren's surprise was written all over his face.

Bishop frowned. "Of course. Did you think I'd say no?"

Bren didn't reply, and Bishop looked over the tablet again. "It will likely be Davis with Ronin subbing in on his days off."

"All right. If they can, I'd prefer if Tyler didn't know he was being watched over," Bren said.

"Yeah, that shouldn't be a problem. I'll have Willow type up an estimate of the fees and email it to you in a few hours. Initial off on it and email it back. All right?"

Bren nodded and stood before holding out his hand. Bishop stood up and shook it firmly. "I guess we'll see you Saturday."

"You will," Bren said. "Kaida, it was nice to see you again."

"You as well," she said. "I'll see you Wednesday."

Bren left the boardroom. Bishop stared silently at her as they listened to him say his goodbyes to Willow. When the door to the office shut, Bishop skirted around the table and closed the boardroom door.

"What the hell, Kaida?"

She sighed and rubbed at her forehead. "I had no choice, my bear. The fox shifter was badly injured."

"I'm not talking about that." Bishop sat in the chair next to her with a heavy thud. "I'm talking about the fact that I can smell your lust for him. He's a human, Kaida."

"I am aware," she said. "I can't help it if my dragon is attracted to him. Just like you couldn't help being attracted to Ava."

"This is bad," Bishop said.

"It's fine. I'm not going to act on it."

"You *can't* act on it," Bishop said. "You're a dragon. He's a human. He has no idea that dragon shifters exist, and if he were to find out…"

"He's not going to find out."

"How the hell did you get the council to agree to let him and his brother back on your lands?" Bishop asked.

"They didn't. Cadmus overruled their decision," Kaida said.

"What? Why?"

"I have no idea," Kaida replied. "They're only allowed in my cabin and the training circle. It won't take long for me to train the two yearlings, and then I'll never see them again. It'll be fine, Bishop."

"Kaida," Bishop took her hand, "listen, Bren's father is -"

"I know who his father is," Kaida said. "And so does the council. Javee had all of Bren's personal information by the time I met with the council that night."

"Man," Bishop said, "we need to convince Javee to work for us. She could give Kat a run for her money when digging up information on people."

"We are well aware that Bren's father is the same Senator who's been trying for years to have shifters tagged and branded like cattle."

Bishop growled. "Not to mention all the bills he's tried to pass that would have vampires branded with ultraviolet light, witches banned from practicing magic of any kind, and the fae forced to wear iron bands around their wrists. He is a goddamn psychopath when it comes to the paranormal."

"I know," Kaida said. "But Bren doesn't seem to share his views about the paranormal."

"He doesn't," Bishop admitted. "He's helped us out more than once with clients and…"

"And what?" Kaida said.

"He saved my life once."

"What was that?" Kaida leaned forward and smiled teasingly at Bishop. "I didn't quite hear what you said."

He growled at her. "I said he saved my life once."

"A human saving the life of one of the strongest shifters I've ever known. Perhaps Bren is tougher than I thought," Kaida said.

Bishop rolled his eyes. "My point is, he may not be like his father, but it's too dangerous for you and the clan to be around him or his brother. What do you think would happen if Senator Matthews found out there were dragons?"

"War," Kaida said softly.

Bishop nodded, his face paling. "It's not worth the risk, Kaida."

"They won't find out," Kaida said. "They think we're bear shifters, and the fox knows he has to keep our secret."

"The fox knows that you're dragons?" Bishop said.

"Yes. He'd read a children's book that mentioned we smell like smoke. He guessed it fairly quickly."

"Oh my God," Bishop groaned before sitting back in his chair. "This is why you guys don't go around shifters and humans, Kaida!"

"I couldn't leave him and Tyler to be beaten by those boys, nor could I leave him to die in the forest. I had to take him to Gram," Kaida said. "Besides, I had no idea that my dragon would lose her shit over a human or that Cadmus would go insane and overrule the council's decision. Ever since Valen died, he..."

Bishop squeezed her hand. "He's still struggling with Valen's death?"

"Yes. He is so disconnected, my bear. From me, from the council... the whole clan. He still hasn't chosen a replacement for the council. Drago grows more impatient with each day that passes."

"Does he still think he will be the one Cadmus appoints?"

"Yes," Kaida said. "Just like he believes I will someday be his mate."

Bishop made a face. "God, I hate that guy. He's such a douche."

"Don't I know it." Kaida stood and leaned down to press a

kiss against Bishop's forehead. "It was good to see you, my bear. I'll see you Saturday, all right?"

"Yeah. Be careful with the cop. Will you?"

"I will," she said.

"Don't sleep with him," Bishop said with a grimace.

"I don't plan on it."

CHAPTER 7

"Tyler? Where are you?" Bren stepped into his father's apartment. He shut the door and headed down the hallway toward the kitchen.

He glanced in, groaning inwardly when he saw his father leaning against the granite covered island. "Hey, Dad."

"Hello, Bren." His father took a sip of wine before studying the tablet before him. "What are you doing here?"

"Picking up Tyler."

His father continued to look at the tablet. "How's work?"

"Fine. How's yours? Get any closer to your goal of branding shifters like beef?"

His father's head snapped up, and he stared coldly at Bren. "Watch your mouth with me, Bren. You might think you're better than me, but you're still my son and will respect me."

Bren held his father's gaze. He had stopped being afraid of his father a long time ago. "Respect is earned, not just given."

His father shook his head. "Everything I've done for you, and you're still a spoiled brat. You're exactly like your mother. Do you know that? Ungrateful and unhappy with everything you're given."

Tyler joined them in the kitchen before Bren could spit out a retort. He was wearing track pants and an *Iron Man* t-shirt, and he grabbed an apple from the bowl on the island. "Later, Dad."

"Before you go," his father's voice turned greasy, "I need a favour."

"What?" Bren said.

"There's a charity luncheon coming up. I'd like you to attend with me and Tyler."

"Why?"

"Because I want my family with me."

Bren snorted. "More like you want the press to see you with your family."

"It's for a good cause, Bren. Just once, you could think of someone other than yourself."

Bren glanced at Tyler. The teenager rolled his eyes and then twisted his body so his father couldn't see and made a wanking off motion.

Bren hid his grin. "What's the charity?"

His father paused. "It's raising funds for HAPI."

"No," Bren said. "I'm not going."

Humans Against Paranormal Influence, or HAPI for short, was an anti-paranormal group that he'd had more than a few run-ins with over his career as a detective. The group had been investigated a few times for brutality toward shifters. He'd never been assigned directly to a case, but he'd seen what happened with the cases that made it to court. They were almost always thrown out. Bren wasn't so naïve to think it was because the group was innocent rather than because of corruption in their legal system.

"Bren -"

"I'm not going, I said." He made his voice ice cold. "I don't feel the same about the paranormal as you do. Stop pretending that I do."

His father grunted angrily. Tyler glanced at Bren before saying, "I'm not going to it either."

"Like hell you're not," his father said.

"If Bren doesn't have to go, I don't either," Tyler said.

"You're living under my roof, and you'll do what I tell you," his father replied. "You're going to the charity luncheon, Tyler."

"Whatever," Tyler muttered. "Can we go, Bren?"

"Yes." Bren clapped his hand on his brother's shoulder, massaging the tension from it as they walked out of the kitchen.

"THIS IS GONNA BE GREAT, COREY," TY SAID.

"Right." The fox shifter stared out the window, and Bren watched him in the rear-view mirror.

"If you don't want to do this, Corey, you don't have to."

"He wants to," Tyler said.

"It can be intimidating to learn how to fight, Ty," Bren said. "Not everyone wants to learn."

Tyler twisted in his seat to study Corey. "You're not nervous, are you?"

"No," Corey said.

Bren had heard more convincing denials from guys he'd busted for breaking and entering while they were literally in the middle of breaking and entering.

"You don't have to if you don't want to," he repeated to Corey.

The fox shifter smiled faintly at him. "Yeah, I know."

"You're all healed up, though, right?" Tyler said. "Nothing hurts anymore?"

"No, I'm good."

"Man," Tyler twisted back around in his seat and resumed playing some game on his phone, "I would kill to have healing powers. My hand is still a little sore."

He glanced at Bren. "Don't tell Kaida I said that. It's not too sore for training."

Bren took a quick look at Tyler's hand. "You sure about that?"

"Yeah. It's not swollen or anything. Just still tender."

"Jeff and his friends haven't tried anything before or after school?" Bren said.

Tyler grunted. "Yeah, I already told you that. Jeff talked some shit to me in the locker room before PE yesterday, but considering his face still looked like roadkill, it was kind of funny. Wasn't it, Corey?"

"A little," Corey said.

"I wonder what he and his asshole friends told their parents about why they came home busted up so bad?" Tyler said.

"Language," Bren said.

Tyler rolled his eyes. "Okay, *Mom*. Asshole is, like, barely a curse. They haven't tried anything yet, but I know they will."

"He hasn't said anything to your other classmates about you and Corey dating?" Bren asked.

"No," Corey said. "It's weird."

"It is weird, but me and Corey decided we don't care if he tells the school. Right?" Tyler's gaze met Corey's in the rearview mirror.

Corey smiled. "That's right."

"Anyway, he hasn't said anything about Corey being a shifter or about us dating. He and his friends are telling the other kids that they got into a fight with some college frat boys over some hot girls who wanted to date Jeff and his friends." Tyler rolled his eyes. "Like college girls would have anything to do with those idiots."

He glanced again at Corey. "I wanted to tell them the truth – that they got their asses kicked by a woman, but Corey said I shouldn't."

"No, you definitely shouldn't," Bren said. "If parents or teachers find out, authorities will most likely want to speak to Kaida, and she and her clan want to be left alone. Don't say anything to anyone, Tyler."

"I won't," Tyler said. "I said I wanted to – not that I was gonna."

They were turning onto the road off the highway that led to Kaida's place, and Tyler crammed his phone into his pocket. His body vibrated excitedly, and while Bren wanted to tell him to relax, he didn't. He was vibrating a little himself.

Yeah, but from lust, not excitement.

He ignored his inner voice. His desire to see Kaida had only grown over the last couple of days. Seeing her on Monday had been a happy surprise, and he wondered if Kaida being there was what made Bishop agree to help him.

Probably. The bear shifter still thought he had a thing for Ava. Probably always would.

When you and Kaida start dating, he'll figure it out.

Bren took a right onto the dirt road leading to the clan's cabins. He was getting ahead of himself. Sure, he planned on asking Kaida out tonight, but that hardly qualified as they were dating.

If she even says yes.

She would. Bren wasn't blind, and he'd caught the occasional look she'd given his mouth and his crotch. She was interested in him, and he'd be an idiot not to ask her out.

The cabins came into view, and he drove to Kaida's and parked in front of it. Tyler was hopping out of the SUV before Bren had even shut it off. Corey followed more slowly. The door to Kaida's cabin opened, and Bren caught his breath.

She wore tight yoga pants and a long t-shirt, and her dark hair was pulled into a ponytail. She looked sexy as hell, and he pulled at the crotch of his jeans. The constant semi he sported whenever he was around Kaida was starting to get annoying.

He stepped out of the SUV and locked it before meeting Kaida and the boys in front of her cabin. "Hey," he said.

"Hello." She smiled briefly at him before turning her attention to the boys. Just that brief smile was enough to send a bolt of awareness to his dick. "You guys ready?"

"We totally are," Tyler said enthusiastically. "Right, Corey?"

"Yeah, we're ready," Corey said.

"Good." Kaida started toward a narrow path that ran through the woods beyond her cabin. "Follow me."

"Try again," Kaida said.

Panting lightly with a massive grin, Tyler ran full speed at Corey and grabbed for him. The smaller boy turned his body at the last moment, socking his hip into Tyler's body and wrapping his hands around Tyler's biceps. Tyler sailed into the air, landing with a thud on his back in the soft sand put down in a thick layer in the circular clearing.

"Good," Kaida said. "The easiest way to get a larger opponent down is to use his size against him."

Tyler popped up to his feet with the energy and grace of youth that Bren envied, holding his fist out to Corey. The fox shifter bumped it, and the two teenagers grinned at each other. Sand covered them, Tyler had a small rip in his shirt, and Corey's hair was sticking up, but they looked very pleased with themselves.

"Okay, what's next?" Tyler asked.

"That's enough for tonight," Bren called from the sidelines. "It's getting late."

"We've only learned a couple of things, and it's barely eight," Tyler said.

"You've got homework to finish, school in the morning, and," Bren glanced at the darkening sky, "it'll be dark soon."

Tyler glanced at Kaida, who nodded. "Your brother is right."

He sighed. "Fine. When's our next training session?"

"How about Friday night?" Kaida turned to Bren. "Unless you have plans?"

He grinned at her. "Nope, no plans. I'll bring the boys by around six again?"

A pink tinge covered her cheeks. "Sure."

"Sweet." Tyler took Corey's hand.

Bren followed Kaida down the narrow path that led back to the cabins. He was very aware of how amazing her ass looked in her pants as Tyler and Corey kept up a steady stream of chatter behind them.

When they were back at the cabins, Bren unlocked the SUV. "Get in, guys. I want to talk to Kaida for a minute."

"Bye, Kaida. Thank you," Tyler said as he climbed into the passenger seat.

"Thanks." Corey smiled tentatively at Kaida and slid into the back seat.

When the doors were shut, Bren turned to Kaida. "Thanks again, I really appreciate you helping them."

"You're welcome, human." Kaida's gaze flicked to his mouth before she looked away. "What is it you wanted to talk to me about?"

Here goes nothing.

"Would you like to have dinner with me tomorrow night?"

Kaida's body stiffened, and she took a step back. Her gaze landed on his lips again and then slid away. "I can't."

"Because you're busy or because you're not interested?" Bren said.

She hesitated. "I'm not interested."

Disappointment flooded his body. He'd been confident that Kaida was into him. "Okay. I'll see you Friday night with the boys."

She stared at a spot somewhere over his shoulder. "I'm sorry, Bren. It's not that I... I mean -"

"It's fine," he said. "You're not required to explain your decision. I'll see you Friday, all right?"

She nodded before finally looking at him. Was that regret in her eyes?

"I'm sorry," she said again.

"Don't be," he said. "See you Friday."

He climbed into the SUV, forcing himself to smile and wave at Kaida as he pulled away. She was staring at him, and it was no comfort to him that she looked miserable. He'd fucked up. Seen something that wasn't there, obviously, and now Kaida felt bad, and he looked like a fool.

She wants you.

He wanted to bang his hand on the steering wheel in

frustration. Kaida didn't want him. She just told him she wasn't interested.

"Dude," Tyler said.

"What?"

"Sorry the hot bear shifter turned you down for a date."

Bren jerked, and Tyler grabbed the dashboard when the SUV swerved on the narrow dirt road.

"Were you two eavesdropping on my conversation?" Bren said.

"No," Corey said quickly. "We weren't."

"It wasn't hard to tell you like Kaida," Tyler said. "It's never hard to tell when you like a girl. It's, like," he motioned to his face, "written all over you."

Bren didn't reply and Tyler reached over and punched him lightly on the thigh. "I swear we weren't eavesdropping. I figured when you said you wanted to talk to her, you would ask her out. You did, right?"

"Yeah," Bren turned off the dirt road and headed toward the highway.

"And she turned you down."

Bren didn't reply, and Tyler said, "You looked like you got punched in the gut. That's how we knew she said no. You need to get better at playin' the game with the ladies, Bren."

"Thanks for the dating tip, kid," Bren said. "Hey, do me a favour?"

"What's that?"

"Shut up."

Tyler laughed and snagged his phone out of his pocket. "I can't help it if I'm better at dating than you are."

BREN WALKED INTO HIS APARTMENT AND STARED AT THE CROW standing in the middle of the hallway. He shut the door, kicked off his shoes, and hung his jacket on the hook. "Hello, Lilianna. You're looking particularly evil this evening."

The crow cawed at him before turning and strutting down the hallway toward the kitchen. Her talons tapping on the wood floor sent an involuntary shiver down Bren's spine. He followed the bird into the kitchen, staring at Elora's ass as she rummaged through one of the lower cupboards.

Why couldn't he be attracted to her? She was good looking and intelligent, and he should have been attracted to her. Maybe if he asked her out on a proper date, there might be some sparks.

"Why are you staring at my ass?" Elora said.

"Trying to decide if I should ask you out," Bren replied.

Elora laughed and wiggled her butt at him. "You ingest another one of Helen's love potions or something?"

"No." He sat down at the table, the sight of Elora's wiggling ass not doing a thing for him in the libido department. "What are you looking for?"

"Barley," she said. "You got any barley?"

"Nope."

Elora straightened and closed the cupboard. Lilianna was investigating the narrow space between the cupboard and the fridge, and Elora skirted around the large crow before opening the refrigerator and grabbing a couple of beers. She twisted off the tops and handed a bottle to Bren, then sank into the chair next to him. "You're home late. Long day at work?"

"No. I had a thing with Tyler." He drank a swallow of beer, the cold liquid easing the dryness in his throat.

"What's wrong?" Elora asked.

"Nothing," he said.

"Bullshit."

"Nothing's wrong. Hey, did you ever hear from your sister?"

Elora nodded, relief crossing her pretty features. "Yeah. Sarina texted me this morning. Finally."

"Where was she?"

Elora drank some beer. "I don't know. All she said was that she didn't have cell service where she was. With my sister, that could mean she was torturing some bad guy in a dungeon in Mongolia or sunbathing on a remote beach in Fiji."

"Your sister leads an interesting life," Bren said.

"She does." Elora leaned forward and squeezed his hand. "Tell me why you're so sad, buddy."

"Tell me why I am an open book to you and Tyler, but everyone else in my life says I'm challenging to read," Bren said.

Elora smiled at him. "You show us the real you, honey. Plus, we love you, making it easier for us to see when you're sad. What happened?"

"Nothing happened," he said. "I took Tyler and Corey to Kaida's tonight to start their self-defence training."

"And?"

"And nothing. It went well. I'm taking them back on Friday night."

"And?"

He drank two large swallows of beer, the hops lingering on his tongue. "And I asked Kaida out, and she said no, that she wasn't interested."

Elora stared sympathetically at him. "I'm sorry, buddy."

"Thanks." He stared moodily at the beer bottle. "The thing is – I could have sworn she was into me."

"Maybe she's interested but a little shy about dating a human?"

"She said she wasn't interested. The words 'I'm not interested' came directly from her mouth."

"Ouch." Elora leaned back in her chair. "Well, at least she was honest with you. On a scale of one to ten – how awkward will it be to see her again on Friday night?"

"It won't be awkward. I'm a grown-ass man who can handle being rejected by a woman. It's just…"

"Just what?" Elora petted Lilianna's smooth back when the crow flew up and landed on her thigh.

"I thought she was interested in me. Maybe I'm losing my ability to read people," he said.

"So, you misread her. It happens," Elora said. "I know you're a detective and, like, one of your superpowers is reading people, but there's bound to be people here and there who are mysteries to you. Right?"

"Yeah," he said.

"Hey, it could be that she thinks you're a babe and wants to bang you, but her clan has a rule about not dating humans. Most bear shifters don't date humans," Elora said.

"I'm getting a weird vibe about the whole bear shifter thing," Bren said.

"What do you mean?"

"They don't act like they're bear shifters. I met Kaida's friend Sika on Sunday. She's pregnant and referred to the baby as a hatchling."

"Hatchling?" Elora said.

"Yeah. Don't bears normally call them cubs?"

"They do," Elora said. "Lizards call their babies hatchlings. Maybe they're lizard shifters who are pretending to be bear shifters."

"Maybe, but that seems weird. Plus, all of the women are

really large. Kaida is close to six feet tall, and her grandmother is over six feet tall. Sika was at least six feet as well. I've never met female lizard shifters that big before."

"I don't know what to tell you," Elora said. "Other than it's weird as shit."

"Yeah," Bren said.

Elora finished her beer and set it on the table. "I really am sorry she turned you down. But you're a great guy, and any day now, you'll find the right woman and start having that baseball team of babies you want. I know it."

He twitched, his eyebrows going up as he stared at Elora. She laughed and squeezed his hand again. "You're an open book to me, buddy. Get used to it."

"I TANKED THAT CHEMISTRY QUIZ," TYLER SAID AS HE RODE HIS bike beside Corey. "My dad's gonna kill me."

"Sorry, babe." Corey smiled at him. "If it's any consolation, I got an eighty-five on my Spanish test."

"Seriously?" Tyler leaned back and let go of his bike handles, steering the bike with his knees as he held out his fist to Corey. "That's awesome, honey."

"It's because of you." Corey bumped his fist before they turned right and headed toward downtown. "If you weren't tutoring me, I wouldn't...shit."

They both skidded to a stop before sliding off their bikes and straddling them.

"Hey, faggots." Jeff had stepped out between two parked cars and stood in the middle of the sidewalk halfway down the block.

Corey glanced at Tyler, the fear already written on his face. "Ty?"

"It's fine," Tyler said. "We're not that far from the school. Come on, we'll bike back, and I'll call Bren to come pick us up. Jeff won't catch us on foot."

Corey looked over his shoulder. "Too late."

Tyler followed his gaze. His stomach clenched, and his balls drew up tight. The same three guys who were with Jeff in the forest stood not five feet behind them. All of them were sporting black eyes or bruises on their jaws, and Tyler felt a moment of grim satisfaction that quickly disappeared when they moved closer.

"No bitch friend today. Guess she's still back in the woods, huh?" Jeff moved closer, and as the boys closed in around them in a rough circle, Tyler reached over and grabbed Corey's hand.

Jeff made a gagging sound. "You guys are fucking gross."

His heart banging against his ribcage, Tyler searched the street for an adult. It was empty, and his limbs trembled a little harder. Someone might hear him from inside their house if he screamed loud enough.

He opened his mouth, and Jeff said, "If you scream, I'll smash your faggot face in before anyone gets the chance to hear you."

"Stay away from him," Corey said.

Jeff sneered at him. "Aren't you the brave little faggot fox? You ready to get your brains rattled again?"

"Leave," Tyler said. "My brother is a cop, and if you touch us again, he'll arrest you."

Jeff bellowed laughter. "You think I'm afraid of a cop? My dad is a lawyer, asshole. He can get me out of anything."

"Maybe, but," Tyler glanced at Jeff's friends, "your friends won't be as lucky. You want to take that chance, dickheads?"

Jeff's friends glanced at each other, and Jeff snarled out, "Don't listen to the fucking faggot. Besides, he isn't gonna say a word to anyone. What do you think will happen if your dad finds out who you're dating, queer boy?"

Tyler's stomach dropped to his feet, and Corey squeezed his hand.

"That's right," Jeff said. "You think I don't know who your old man is? The world finds out you're dating a shifter, and 'poof,' there goes his career."

"I can't get in trouble with the cops again, man," one of the boys said. "My old man will beat my ass if I do. He threatened to send me to military school last time."

"Shut the fuck up," Jeff snarled. "Nothing is going to happen." He glanced behind him. "Grab those two faggots. We're going -"

"I suggest you listen to your friend, you sniveling little shit goblin."

All of them turned toward the sound of the man's voice. Relief swept through Tyler. He had no idea who the guy with the tattoos was, but he was as tall as Jeff and his friends, and while he might have been leaner than the bulky football players, his body was ripped. He silently thanked God for the Good Samaritan as the man leaned against a parked car with his arms crossed and raised one pierced eyebrow.

"Go on. Take your little gang of wanna-be thugs and head on home."

"Get lost, old man," Jeff said.

"Old?" The man straightened and stared at his reflection in the car window. He poked at the faint lines around his eyes before muttering, "Jesus, I gotta start using moisturizer or something."

"I said get lost before we fuck you up." Jeff glanced at his friends, who all raised their fists.

The tattooed man laughed. "Oh my God, you guys are

cute. Look at you with your tiny fists. Humans are so adorable."

Jeff stiffened and glanced at Corey. "You get a shifter friend to help you out, you little pussy?"

"I'm a friend of Tyler's brother. You have a problem with shifters?" the tattooed man said.

"You think you're tough because you're a what? Wolf shifter? Or maybe you're just a little fox, like that faggot." Jeff jerked his chin in Corey's direction. "We're not afraid of you."

"Me? Oh, I'm just a bird shifter," the man said.

Tyler's confidence waned. What could a bird shifter do against four football players?

Jeff laughed, and Tyler was reminded of a donkey braying. "A bird shifter? What a loser."

"C'mon now, don't be a big old meanie," the man said. "We gotta have something in common, right? You guys like Celine Dion?"

"Who?" The biggest of Jeff's friends said.

"Are you serious?" The man looked personally attacked. "Celine Dion. French Canadian songbird with the pipes of an angel and seven Grammys?"

The boys stared at him blankly and he heaved a sigh of exasperation. "*Come on*. Celine Dion! She won an Oscar, you guys. *My Heart Will Go On*? It was the number one song from *Titanic*."

"That movie with that old guy? Leo something? My mom has, like, the biggest crush on that guy. It's gross." Jeff's friend said.

"Old... are you kidding me right now?" The man made another harsh sigh of exasperation. "Okay, look, I don't know what the hell kind of music you *youth* are listening to today, but I have a Celine Dion CD in the car. Follow me, and I'll play you some of her hits, and you can hear how amazing she is."

"CD?" Another of Jeff's friends said. "Dude, seriously, how old are you?"

The biggest boy nudged him. "Old enough to break a hip banging your mom."

"Shut up, Dillon!"

"*Your* mom wasn't complaining about my hips last night, Dillon," the tattooed man said.

The two other boys burst into laughter. "Sick, man. Real sick. Your mom's banging a bird shifter."

"Shut up!" Dillon's face turned red. "My mom isn't banging a bird shifter, and if you say another word about her, I'll kick your ass."

"Whatever, man. Your mom's a whore, and we all know it."

"You fucking asshole!" Dillon snapped before shoving the other boy.

"Shut the fuck up," Jeff shouted. "All of you!"

Dillon glared at him. "He's talking about my mom."

"Who the fuck cares? She *is* a whore," Jeff snarled. He turned toward the tattooed man, and a shiver went down Tyler's back at the pure rage radiating from Jeff's gaze. "Last chance. Leave now, or I'll have my boys fuck you up."

"Will you, though?" The man cocked his head at Jeff, studying his black eye and split lip. "Because from what I heard, you and your boys got your asses handed to you by a girl."

Jeff's mouth dropped open, and a flush of red covered his cheeks. "Dillon, kick that fucking bird's ass."

Dillon rushed forward, and Tyler watched in stunned silence as the tattooed man, moving ridiculously quickly, grabbed Dillon's left arm and spun him around. He pushed him up against the car and yanked his arm up until Dillon screamed.

"Uh-uh," the man said as the two other boys approached him. He moved Dillon's arm again, and a fresh scream pealed from Dillon's throat. "I'll break his arm."

The other boys hesitated, and the man leveled his gaze at Jeff. "I don't want to break Dillon's arm, but I will."

"What kind of cop are you?" Jeff said.

Dillon drew in a ragged breath. "Mister, my arm, please. It hurts."

The man ignored him, keeping his gaze on Jeff. "Oh, I'm not a cop. Do you know why? Because I am not a good guy. In fact, I'm the type of guy who'll break a kid's arm. I hate bullies. You get it? So, if you and your homophobic bully friends keep bothering my boys here, things are going to get ugly."

His gaze turned dark, the humour completely gone from his face as he stared at Jeff. "You're going to play nice from now on. Stay away from Corey and Tyler. I'll be watching, and if you go anywhere near them…"

He tugged on Dillon's arm, and the boy squealed in pain. He released him, and Dillon staggered away, rubbing his arm and hitching in his breath.

"Let's go, Jeff," one of the other boys said nervously.

"We can take him," Jeff said.

"No, we can't. Have you lost your fucking mind? Let's go. The faggots aren't worth it," the boy replied.

The three boys walked away, and Jeff made a low snarl.

"Go on, Jeff," the man said, "don't make stupid life choices."

Jeff glared at him before shoving past Tyler, nearly knocking him off his bike. Corey steadied him, and they watched as Jeff stalked past their Good Samaritan.

"Oh, one more thing," the man said.

Jeff stopped, his back stiff and his hands clenched in fists before looking over his shoulder at the man.

"Say anything to anyone about Corey and Tyler dating, and I'll cut out your tongue."

The man's voice was pleasant, but Jeff's face paled, his black eye a dark and painful looking beacon against the white.

"Have a good weekend, sweetheart," the man said.

Jeff jogged after his friends. When they had turned the corner at the end of the block and disappeared, the man stuck his hand out.

"Hey, I'm Ronin."

"Tyler," Tyler said as he shook his hand. "This is Corey."

"Nice to meet you."

"Who are you?" Corey said.

"Are you seriously a friend of my brother's?" Tyler said. "Because if so, my brother is a million times cooler than I thought. What you did to Jeff and his friends was ballin'."

The man grimaced, and he looked a little sick to his stomach. "Yeah, well, threatening goddamn kids is not my thing, but sometimes bullies need to be bullied to get the message."

"How do you know my brother?" Tyler said.

Ronin hesitated. "Uh, through friends."

"What friends?"

"You should talk to your brother about that." Ronin clapped him on the back. "You guys head home now."

"Yeah, okay. Thanks, man."

CHAPTER 8

"Sika, what are you doing?" Kaida watched as her best friend crossed her cabin in lunging squats.

"Trying to bring on labour." Sika puffed her way across the room again.

"You're not due for another two weeks."

"I know, but I'm over this pregnancy thing."

Kaida laughed and caught Sika by the arm as she made another pass. "C'mon, sit down. I will freak out if that hatchling drops out of you right here."

Sika settled onto the couch with a loud groan. "God, my back hurts. My hips hurt, and my legs hurt. Hell, my ass cheeks hurt the other day. Why, Kaida? Why does my butt hurt?"

Kaida sat down next to her. "I have no idea."

Sika rubbed her belly. "Jarvis is so anxious to hold the hatchling. I am, too."

"The whole clan is," Kaida said. "The hatchling will never learn to walk."

Sika grinned at her. "It will be spoiled rotten."

"That's for damn sure," Kaida said. She glanced at her watch, and Sika poked her in the ribs.

"What time does the human get here?"

"Soon," Kaida said. "Why?"

"Just wondering. He's so handsome, isn't he?"

"I'm not attracted to him, Sika."

"No? So, you always wear makeup when teaching yearlings how to fight?"

Kaida blushed. "Shut up."

Sika giggled. "It's adorable that you have a crush on a human. Are you going to sleep with him?"

"God, no," Kaida said. "I'd probably hurt him. Besides, you know I like to be in control, and he's a cop. Cops have control issues. They want to be in charge all the time."

"Maybe," Sika said. "But Bren didn't seem like that."

"Please, you hardly know him. You talked to him for five minutes, and most of that time was spent talking about his dick."

"Like you're not interested in the size of his dick," Sika said with another giggle.

Kaida's dragon purred in agreement, and Kaida rolled her eyes. "I'm not sleeping with the human. I'm too strong for him."

"He was really muscular," Sika said. "He looked pretty strong. There's only one way to find out, right?"

"He asked me out Wednesday night."

Sika stared at her in delight. "Seriously? That's so cute. You said yes, right?"

"Of course, I didn't. I told him I wasn't interested."

"Liar."

"I had to. Look, I might be attracted to the human, but nothing can come of it," Kaida said. "It's not like we could ever have a relationship. If I did, the clan would burn me and the human to a crisp."

"They don't need to know." Sika's voice turned serious. "I want you to be happy, Kaida. I could smell how much you and your dragon liked him when the human was here. I'm not saying the clan and their needs aren't important, but just once, maybe you could put your needs ahead of the clan."

"I can't," Kaida said.

"You can. It isn't being selfish. The clan loves you, but you need to live your life, too. And I don't mean to be rude, but it's been a long time since you got laid."

Kaida glared at her, and Sika shrugged. "What? I'm not wrong. Unless you finally decided to bang Drago and didn't tell me?"

"No," Kaida said. "I will never mate with Drago."

"Thank God. I'll support your choice in mate, but that dragon is a total dink," Sika said.

"He really is," Kaida said.

"Anyway, you don't have to mate with the human for life or anything, but why not have fun with him? It would be cool to have sex with a human, don't you think?"

"Cool right up until the moment I break his fragile bones or set him on fire," Kaida said.

Sika rolled her eyes. "You won't set him on fire. And my God, how crazy are you when you have sex? Like, yeah, we're strong, but you think you're going to break a tall and muscular human by bouncing on his dick? Humans are fragile, but not *that* fragile. You're just using it as an excuse not to bang him."

"I'm not."

"You are." Sika rubbed her belly again before glancing at the door. "The humans are coming."

Kaida could also hear Bren's vehicle, and her stomach

twisted into knots. She jumped up and smoothed her sweaty palms over her yoga pants before helping Sika off the couch. Sika smiled at her. "You look gorgeous."

"I'm not trying to look gorgeous," Kaida said.

Her dragon purred loudly, and Sika laughed. "You might not be, but your dragon is."

The pregnant dragoness followed Kaida to the door, stepping out onto the porch with her as Tyler and Corey climbed out of the SUV.

Tyler slammed his door shut before glaring at Bren, who was walking around the front of the vehicle. "We don't need babysitters, Bren."

"You do," Bren said. "If Ronin hadn't been there today, you and Corey would have been hurt."

"We're learning how to fight," Tyler said.

"Exactly – you're learning," Bren said. "You don't know enough yet to protect yourselves. Until you do, the security detail stays."

"But -"

"This conversation is finished," Bren said.

"Fine, whatever," Tyler said.

Bren's phone rang, and he fished it out of his pocket. He glanced at the screen before turning away and answering the phone. "Matthews."

"Hey, Kaida," Tyler bounded up the steps and grinned at her. "How's it going."

"Good. Did you have some trouble today?"

"Yeah." Corey joined them on the porch, studying Sika for a moment before leaning against the porch railing. "Jeff and his friends tried to jump us a few blocks from school."

"But apparently, my brother hired a security firm to protect us," Tyler said. "He doesn't think we can handle ourselves yet."

"You can't," Kaida said bluntly. "And it was my idea that he hire someone to watch out for you."

"Oh." Tyler scuffed at the wood of the porch with his sneakers. "What are we learning tonight?"

"Ty?" Bren was standing near the vehicle again. "I'm sorry, but we have to go. I need to get back to work."

"What? We just got here," Tyler said.

"I know, but I have to go. Sorry, Kaida. I'll text you and see what will work for next week."

"Can't you pick us up when you're finished?" Tyler asked.

"I'll be late. Too late for you to stay here until I'm done," Bren said. "In the car, Ty."

Tyler stared at Kaida with a *do something* expression.

"I can drive the yearlings home after our training session," Kaida said.

"Awesome," Tyler said. "Problem solved. Later, Bren."

"Are you sure?" Bren asked. "Tyler's staying at my place this weekend and I don't live close to here."

"It's no problem," she said.

He hesitated. "Okay, well, thank you. Tyler – don't even think about drinking the beer in the fridge."

Tyler raised his hand in acknowledgement before looping his arm around Corey's neck. "See you later, Bren."

Bren waved distractedly and climbed into the vehicle. He drove off without looking at her, and her dragon pouted angrily.

Don't let the human leave.

"You ready, Kaida?" Tyler asked.

"Yes." Ignoring her disappointment that Bren was gone, Kaida followed Sika and the boys down the porch steps.

BREN SHUT THE APARTMENT DOOR. DESPITE THE COOL weather, he was hot and sweaty. And despite the coveralls he'd worn over his clothing, he could almost see the stink of garbage coming off him in tiny little waves. He grumbled out a curse, toeing off his shoes and shrugging out of his jacket.

Anyone who assumed that being a detective was glamorous work had never spent four hours combing through an overflowing dumpster looking for a goddamn murder weapon. He cracked his neck, tension making his shoulders and upper back stiff.

The stupid thing was, his mood had less to do with spending the last four hours wading through garbage and more to do with missing his chance to see Kaida when she dropped Tyler off at his apartment this evening.

Incredibly stupid, considering she wasn't interested in him.

"Ty? I'm back. Sorry, it's so late. I had to -" He stopped in the kitchen doorway, his heart knocking against his ribcage. "Kaida? What are you doing here?"

She set down the mug of tea and stood, wiping the palms of her hands on her thighs. A napkin with a few crumbs sat next to the mug. "Hello, human."

"Hey. Is something wrong with Tyler?"

"No, he's gone to bed," she said. "He had a bit of a headache, he said."

"Oh, okay." He leaned against the doorway, very aware of how bad he smelled. "So, uh, why are you still here?"

What the fuck, man?

Her cheeks tinged pink. "Tyler said I should stay until you got home. He said that you didn't like him to be left alone and…" Her cheeks went even pinker, and she groaned, "He's seventeen years old and does not need a babysitter. Oh my God, I'm an idiot."

Bren couldn't help but laugh. "Tyler can be very persuasive when he wants to be."

Her nose wrinkled, and he took a step back. "Sorry, I spent most of the night in a garbage dumpster."

She smiled, and he decided the dumpster diving had been totally worth it to see her smile at him.

"Did you find what you were looking for?" she asked.

"Yeah. Hunting knife covered in our victim's blood and, hopefully, the perp's fingerprints."

The smile dropped from her face. "Did they survive the attack?"

He shook his head and could almost feel the mask falling across his face. Talking about a dead body wasn't how he imagined spending time with Kaida.

"I'm sorry," she said. "Your job must be very difficult."

"Difficult but rewarding when we catch the bad guy." He waited for her to say she had to leave, and as the seconds turned into a minute, he finally blurted, "Did you want something a little stronger to drink than tea?"

She didn't reply, and he was berating himself for his stupidity when she said, "I could stay for one drink."

"Great." He pushed away from the doorway, embarrassed by how eager he sounded. "I'll have a quick shower, and I'll be back. Make yourself comfortable. Are you hungry? There's fruit in the fridge, or I think there might be some cookies in the pantry that Ty hasn't eaten yet."

"I'm good. Tyler gave me a muffin," she said.

"Great. Perfect. Be right back." He started down the hallway and turned, sticking his head back into the kitchen. "Don't leave, okay?"

"I won't."

"Okay. Good. Right. I'll be back." He practically sprinted to his bedroom, locking his gun away in the gun safe in his room before tearing off his clothes and quickly brushing his teeth. He showered in record time, afraid that if he took too long, Kaida would leave despite what she'd told him.

He yanked on his boxer briefs and jeans before brushing his hair. He hesitated, grabbed his cologne off the counter, and spritzed his chest before pulling on a t-shirt.

He smoothed his wet hair down and left the bedroom. He stopped in front of the guest room and eased open the door. Tyler was sprawled out on the bed with his earphones on. The faint music from his earphones competed with the loud snores emanating from his open mouth. Bren shut the door quietly and headed toward the kitchen. Tyler was a heavy sleeper, and with the earphones, he wouldn't hear anything.

What exactly is it you think he's going to hear?

He ignored his inner voice. Nothing was going to happen between him and Kaida. He'd asked her out, and she turned him down. That was that.

She was too warm. Much too warm.

She pulled at the collar of her t-shirt, pacing the kitchen back and forth as her dragon growled at her. *I want the human. Give him to me.*

Stop it. What is wrong with you? She had no idea what was wrong with her dragon, but she was starting to think that agreeing to stay for a drink had been a very bad – oh God, why was it so hot? She knew humans were fragile, but did they need to turn the heat this high in their homes? It wasn't even winter yet.

She wiped the sweat from her forehead and glanced at the doorway before blowing out a small puff of flame. The air shimmered in front of her, and she waved away the smoke drifting from her nostrils.

She was marginally cooler and fanned herself with her hand before grabbing a glass from the cupboard and pouring some water. She drank it in three swallows and wiped the sweat from her forehead again.

The human, her dragon whined, *give him to me.*

"Knock it off," she muttered.

Join him in the shower. Suck his cock. Fuck him.

Her eyes widened, and she backed up until her ass hit the edge of the counter. What the hell was going on? She was attracted to the human just like her dragon, but she couldn't fuck him. Forgetting that she'd be banished from the clan if they found out she fucked a human, like she'd told Sika earlier - Bren wasn't the type to give up control in the bedroom.

Only one way to find out.

Shut up, she snapped at her dragon. *Are you trying to get us banished?*

I need him. I need his cock.

She closed her eyes as lust flooded her body. Just thinking about Bren's dick was getting her going. She palmed her breast through her t-shirt, flicking at her nipple with her thumb as new desire made her growl deep in her throat. God, she wanted to see his cock.

She wanted to touch it. Taste it. Slide it into her pussy and ease this deep and maddening ache inside of her.

She closed her eyes, her other hand slipping between her legs to rub as she pictured pushing a naked Bren onto his bed, climbing on top of him, impaling herself on his cock and riding him until she'd taken what she wanted. Until he'd made her come repeatedly, and she was finally sated.

She would take the human as her mate, and he would fill her belly with his seed. When she was pregnant, she would –

What the fuck?

She pulled her hands away from her breast and her crotch, her heart hammering in her chest and little wisps of smoke puffing out of her nostrils with every breath she released.

He is our mate, her dragon said. *We love him.*

Her body jerked all over, and this time, flames shot from her mouth. She clapped her hand over her mouth, her eyes wide as she heard her mate's footsteps approaching the kitchen.

We love him, her dragon whispered.

She dropped her hand, a slow smile crossing her face as a new burning began in her belly. How could she have been so stupid? How could she even think of denying her dragon what they both wanted?

The human was her mate. She loved him, and it was time to take what was hers.

BREN STEPPED INTO THE KITCHEN. "OKAY, SO I DON'T HAVE much in the way of hard liquor, but there's beer in the fridge, and I think maybe a bottle of wine in the…"

He paused with his hand on the fridge door, inhaling deeply. "Were you lighting matches in here? It smells like –"

He grunted in surprise when Kaida's hand gripped his arm and, with surprising ease, whipped him around and slammed him back against the fridge.

"Kaida? What are you doing?" Every muscle in his stomach tensed, and his cock hardened when Kaida traced one finger down his stomach.

"I want you, human." She grinned at him, and he swallowed hard when he saw her sharp fangs.

"Um, maybe you should...oh fuck." His back arched, and a groan slipped out when she licked the side of his throat before sucking on his earlobe.

"You want me too," she whispered. "I can smell it." Her hand reached down and cupped his cock.

"Hey." He grabbed her wrist and yanked her hand away. "Kaida, wait, just a second."

She nipped his neck and then leaned back, pouting at him. "What's wrong, human? You want to fuck me. I know you do."

The usual golden colour of her eyes seemed weirdly dull, and the blue flecks had all but disappeared. Her pupils were blown out, and she had a look on her face that reminded Bren of the drug addicts who were always in lock-up at the precinct.

"Kaida, what did you take?"

She frowned at him before taking both his hands and pressing them against her breasts. Shit, her tits were amazing, soft and firm and... fuck.

He yanked his hands away, and she growled at him before reaching around and cupping his ass. "Do not deny me, human. You belong to me, and I will take what I want."

"What are you on?" he asked again. "What drugs did you take?"

"I do not take drugs." She squeezed his ass. "I love your ass."

"Thank you." He pulled her hands away and held them in his. "Are you sure you didn't take any medication today?"

"Of course not. I don't need medication, human." She brought his hand around her body and pressed it against one firm ass cheek. "Do you like my ass?"

"Yes, it's great."

"Good. Let's fuck."

She pressed her mouth against his, pushing him against the fridge again. Her tongue invaded his mouth, and he groaned and returned her kiss. She nipped his lower lip before kissing him again. He sucked on her tongue, her soft moan sending ripples of need straight to his aching cock.

"I want you, human," she breathed against his mouth. He could smell the mint tea she'd been drinking on her breath and, weirdly, the faintest scent of smoke.

"I want you too," he replied.

"I know. I can smell how much you want me." She grinned at him before giving him a sharp nip on his throat. "When we fuck, I want to be on top."

"Sure, whatever you want," he panted.

"Good mate," she said. She kissed his throat, and he lifted his head to give her better access.

Bren! Something is wrong. You need to stop.

Yeah, something was off, but fuck, Kaida's lips were so soft, and her body pressed against his felt terrific after months of celibacy. She wanted him, and he wanted her. What was the harm? They were two consenting adults.

Something is wrong with her. Very wrong.

He ignored his inner voice as Kaida kissed up his throat. He groaned when she licked his jaw and then sucked on his earlobe.

"I love you, my mate," she whispered into his ear.

He froze, his hands tightening on her waist. What the fuck?

"Do you love me?" She traced his stomach muscles through his t-shirt. "Say you love me. Right now."

With a loud grunt, he pushed her away. She scowled at him. "What's wrong with you?"

"*Me*? What's wrong with *you*?" he said. "I know you took something. What was it?"

"I told you, human, I do not take drugs." Her eyes were glowing, and he was pretty sure she was about to shift into her bear form at any moment.

Fear trickled into his belly, and she sniffed the air. "Do not be afraid of me, my mate. I won't hurt you. But I want what's mine. Will you give it to me?"

He scrubbed his hand through his damp hair as he scanned the kitchen. If he didn't figure out what... oh shit.

He stared at the foil-covered plate on the counter and then at the scattered crumbs on the table. He lunged past Kaida and peeled the foil off the plate. Kaida sidled up behind him, putting her arms around his waist and kissing his back. "My mate, come to bed."

He stared at the lone muffin on the plate, horror unfurling in his belly. "Kaida, did you eat a muffin from this plate?"

Her hands stroked his abdomen. "Yes. Tyler gave it to me. What's wrong?"

He turned around, trying to ignore Kaida's wandering hands as they roamed across his chest. "Fuck. This is bad. Kaida, that muffin was laced with a potion. A love potion."

She snorted laughter. "It wasn't. I would have smelled it."

She kissed his neck again, her hands sliding up over his shoulders. "Come to bed, my mate. Let me show you how well I can please you. My pussy is wet for you."

He groaned when she straddled his thigh and ground her pussy against him. "Kaida, you're under a spell. I swear."

"I'm not." She grasped his face in her hands and stared directly at him. "I love you, Bren. Do you love me?"

"This isn't real. What you're feeling isn't real. Do you understand?" he said.

119

Despair mixed with frustration crossed her face. "You don't love me."

Feeling weirdly guilty, he said, "No, it's not that. It's -"

"You do love me." Her smile made his heart do a weird stuttering thing in his chest.

"Okay, I need you to sit down for a minute. Will you do that?" Bren led Kaida toward one of the kitchen chairs.

She frowned at him. "I want to fuck you."

"I know, but I, uh, I have a friend coming over that I want you to meet."

She sighed but dropped into the chair. "Fine. Introduce me to your friend, human. But once they're gone, we are fucking. Do you understand?"

Bren yanked his cell phone out of his pocket. "Understood."

CHAPTER 9

"This is sooo bad." Elora paced back and forth in the kitchen. "I'm going to kill my grandmother."

"Get in line," Bren said.

"Oh God… this is really bad." Elora turned a little green and nibbled at the side of her nail.

Kaida was sitting at the table, staring intently at Lilianna, who was perched on the table. The crow returned her stare, its dark eyes unblinking.

"You're starting to freak me out a little, Elora." Bren had never seen the witch looking so unbalanced. "It is just a love potion, right?"

"Yes. But she's a bear shifter."

"So?"

Elora stared at him. "She's a bear shifter who thinks you're her mate, and she wants to have sex with you. What do you think she'll do if you deny her? Because I know a few female bear shifters from my yoga class, and they don't like being denied what they want. If you refuse to sleep with her, she might…"

"Might what?" Bren said.

"Shift to her bear form and rip out your throat," Elora said.

"Jesus." Bren wiped the beads of sweat from his forehead.

"You like her, right?"

"You know I do," he said.

"Then, maybe you could just…" Elora made a humping motion with her hips.

"I can't," Bren said. "She isn't actually interested in me, remember? I can't sleep with her while she's under the influence of your grandmother's damn potion. She's not thinking straight, and I'm not the guy who takes advantage of a woman like that."

"I know you're not," Elora said, "but you may have no choice. If she doesn't get what she wants, she may seriously injure you."

Kaida looked away from Lilianna's dark gaze. "I would never hurt the human. He's my mate, and if he is to give me a hatchling, he needs to be well. He can't put his seed in my belly if he's injured."

Elora's eyes widened, and a nervous giggle slipped out of her mouth as Kaida returned to staring at Lilianna.

"You can reverse the potion, right?" Bren said.

"Assuming that Helen tells me what potion she used, I can reverse it. But not until tomorrow," Elora said.

"What? Why?" Bren said.

"Because I'll need to go to the potions store, and it's closed for the night." Elora shoved her hands into her pockets and slumped against the wall. "I'm so sorry, Bren."

"It's not your fault," Bren replied.

"I'll find out from Helen what potion she used. The potion place opens at eight," Elora said. "I'll be standing outside the door waiting for them to open, I promise. It won't take me long to make up the reversal potion, so I should have it for you by nine-thirty at the latest. All you have to do is keep her distracted until then."

Bren glanced at the clock. It was almost midnight, and he grimaced. "Right, keep her distracted."

Elora straightened. "I'll stay the night with you guys, help keep her -"

"No." Kaida joined them and slipped her arm around Bren's waist before glaring at Elora. "You will leave now, little witch. I want to be alone with my mate."

"Do you like card games?" Elora said. "We could play cards and -"

"I said leave." Kaida's voice had lowered and sounded guttural and inhuman.

Elora made a soft sound of anxiety and took a step back. Lilianna cawed, loud and jarring in the silence, and flew to her shoulder. The crow stared at Kaida with what Bren swore was anger in her eyes. She cawed again, and a low, rumbling growl came from Kaida's chest. The air around them suddenly seemed too warm, and Bren armed the sweat off his face as the crow snapped her beak at Kaida.

Kaida growled again, and Bren quickly slipped his arm around her waist. The heat radiating from her was almost uncomfortably hot, but he didn't break his hold.

"It's fine," he said quickly. "Go home and get some rest, Elora. We'll be fine."

"Are you sure?" Elora said.

Bren nodded. He wasn't sure, but if Kaida shifted to her bear form, he didn't want Elora getting hurt. He briefly considered waking Ty and sending him home with Elora before discarding the idea. He didn't want to confuse or worry his brother, and the kid slept like a rock, anyway. Even if Kaida switched to her bear form and tried to murder him, Ty wouldn't hear a damn thing. Besides, call him crazy, but he believed Kaida when she said she wouldn't hurt him, even if he didn't have sex with her.

"Go home, Elora." Kaida leveled her gaze at the crow sitting on Elora's shoulder. "And watch yourself around the bird. It's more than just a crow."

"Um, yes, I know. Thanks." Elora inched her way toward the doorway and smiled faintly at Bren. "I'll be by in the morning as soon as I make the potion. Hang in there, okay? If she does change to her bear form, use your gun."

He frowned at her. "I'm not shooting Kaida."

"It won't kill her. Bears are fast healers," Elora said.

"I'm not shooting her," he repeated. "Good night, Elora."

He waited until he heard the front door shut before easing away from Kaida. "Do you want some more tea?"

Kaida shook her head and moved toward him. He backed away, cursing under his breath when his back hit the wall. She grinned predatorily at him, her fangs gleaming in the light. He wondered what was wrong with him that the sight of those sharp white teeth made his cock stiffen.

She placed her hands on either side of his shoulders, bracing them against the wall and penning him in before licking his throat. "Let's go to the bedroom, Bren."

"I don't want to have sex with you tonight," he said quickly.

She frowned at him. "Why not? Do you no longer find me attractive? Does your cock refuse to harden for me?"

She palmed his cock, and his semi turned to a full-blown erection almost instantly. He hissed out a breath as her smile widened. "Your cock wishes to fuck me."

He pulled her hand away from his dick. "No sex tonight, okay? I'm tired, and it's been a difficult day."

Her gaze softened, and she cupped his face before

stroking her thumb across his cheek. "My mate has a challenging job."

"Sometimes," he said.

She pressed a soft kiss against his mouth. "All right. We won't have sex tonight, but you will fuck me in the morning. Do you understand?"

Relief flooded through him. It disappeared when Kaida took his hand and led him out of the kitchen. "What are you doing?"

"We're going to bed," she said. "It's late and you need to sleep."

"We can't share my bed," he said.

She frowned at him and opened the door to the guest bathroom, peering inside before closing it. "Of course, we can. We are mates."

She reached for Tyler's door, and Bren said, "That's the guest room. Tyler's sleeping in there. My room is the last door on the left."

She pulled him down the hallway to his room. Opening the door, she stepped inside and glanced at the room before turning and pressing a kiss against his shoulder. "Time for bed, Bren."

She tugged her t-shirt over her head. He turned away, the image of her perfect breasts in the lacy white bra already burned into his head. "What are you doing?"

"Undressing," she said. "I sleep naked. Don't you?"

"Uh, how about you wear this?" He yanked his shirt over his head and held it out without turning around.

She sighed. "My mate, I don't want to wear your shirt. I want to feel your skin against mine."

"I know, but…" He was struck with sudden inspiration. "You're, um, hot, and we'll get sweaty if you're naked."

She sighed again and took the shirt from him. "Fine."

He kept his back turned as she changed, groaning inwardly when she wrapped her arms around his waist and kissed between his shoulder blades. "You will grow used to my warmth, my mate. I promise."

"Sure," he said.

"Come to bed." Her hand took his, and she tugged him toward the bed. He looked away from the bra and – *oh sweet Jesus, was that a thong?* – panties lying in a heap on the floor.

She looked way too good in his shirt. She was so tall that his shirt only fell to her upper thighs. He studied her long, tanned legs, his mouth going dry as an image of them wrapped around his hips flickered into his head.

Kaida smiled coyly at him, one hand reaching out to trace his abdomen muscles. She inhaled deeply. "Are you certain you do not wish to fuck tonight, human?"

"I'm certain." His voice was hoarse, and he cleared his throat as Kaida made a sound of disappointment. She dropped her hand and moved to the bed, pulling back the quilt and sheet and climbing in.

She patted the bed beside her. "Come, my mate."

She frowned when he pulled back the bedcovers. "Take off your jeans."

"Uh, I'm good with them on."

"Take them off," she insisted.

He continued to hesitate, and she glared at him. "I said I wouldn't fuck you tonight, Bren. Do you not trust your mate?"

"I trust you," he said automatically before realizing he meant it.

He stripped down to his boxer briefs, trying to ignore how Kaida's gaze narrowed in on his dick. He climbed in beside her and laid on his back. Kaida pulled up the sheet and quilt and threw one leg over his legs before resting her head on his chest. She played with the hair on his chest before kissing his sternum. "Do you like your job?"

"I do," he said.

"How many times have you been shot at?"

"More times than I'd like."

She snuggled closer, and he couldn't resist stroking her long, dark hair. He shut the bedside light off, plunging the room into darkness. She took his hand, linking their fingers together. "Do you fear your father like Tyler does?"

"Tyler isn't afraid of him."

"He is," she said. "I can smell it on him when he speaks of him."

His stomach clenched, and Kaida raised her head and kissed him. "I'm sorry, my mate. I didn't mean to upset you."

"I'm not upset," he said.

"You are, I can smell it. Are you afraid of your father?"

"No," he said.

"His position as senator makes him powerful," she replied.

"How do you know who my father is?" Bren's body stiffened, and Kaida made a weird but oddly soothing purring sound.

Bears can purr?

"Shh, my mate, do not worry," she said.

"How do you know who he is?" he repeated.

"Javee looked up information about you. It was for the clan's safety and the only way they would allow you and your brother to be in our home," she replied.

He relaxed against the bed as that rough not-quite-a-purr-but-almost-a-purr vibrated out of her throat.

This isn't normal, Bren. Bears don't purr.

"You're a bear shifter, right?" he asked.

"Why do you ask, my mate?"

"You're purring, sort of. Bears don't purr. Are you a tiger or a lion?"

The not-quite-purring cut out, and she lifted her head again to press another kiss against his jawline. "Have you slept with many shifters, Bren? Or did your father's beliefs keep you from them?"

He shook his head. "No, I don't feel the same way about shifters as my father."

"I know that," she said. "It's more than obvious. But sometimes, a parent's beliefs affect us in a way we don't realize. Have you slept with a shifter before?"

"Yes," he said. "In my early twenties, I pretty much only slept with shifters. Maybe it was my way of rebelling against my father."

"What type of shifters have you slept with?"

"Uh, a couple of rabbit shifters, a deer shifter…"

"Any predator shifters?"

"No," he admitted. "Most were casual hookups, but I dated a zebra shifter for a few months."

"Why did you break up?"

"She found out who my father was."

She kissed his chest. "Have you had any serious relationships?"

"Two long-term relationships with humans, never one with a shifter."

"Because of your father."

"Yes."

She raised her head and stared at him. He could barely make out her features in the dim light from the window but knew she had no issues seeing him. He forced a smile onto his face. "No big deal. Hazards of having an asshole racist for a father."

She touched his face. "He won't scare me away, my mate."

She rested her cheek on his chest again. He waited a beat and said, "Have you slept with a human before?"

"No. Only shifters." She stroked his chest, the touch more soothing than arousing. "But don't worry, I'll be gentle with you."

He grinned into the darkness. "I'm stronger than I look."

She laughed, the low sound making his cock twitch. "You seem strong for a human, but you're still fragile compared to me."

His smile turned to laughter. "Just so you know, calling a human male fragile can be a serious blow to his ego."

She lifted her head again. "Have I hurt your feelings, my mate?"

He squeezed her hip. "Nah, I'm good."

She traced his ribs with the tips of her fingers. "I don't think you're weak, but your human bones are fragile. It's so strange. I have never wanted to mate with a human until you."

Feeling guilty, he released her hip. "We should get some sleep now, Kaida."

"Yes," she said. She pressed her mouth against his, and unable to resist, he returned her kiss. She moaned into his mouth, and he pulled away, his heart beating hard against his ribcage.

"Good night, my mate," she said.

"Good night, Kaida."

⸻

KAIDA WOKE WITH ONE THOUGHT AND ONE THOUGHT ONLY – she needed to fuck her mate. She glanced to her left, her dragon growling when it saw the empty spot.

It's fine, she soothed. *We will find our mate and take what is ours.*

Finally, her dragon grumbled. *You should have fucked him last night.*

She climbed out of bed and headed to the primary bathroom. *He was tired and had a bad day.*

She ignored her dragon's grumbling and used the washroom. She washed her hands and used a new toothbrush she found in the medicine cabinet to brush her teeth.

She studied her reflection in the mirror. She'd been away from her clan for nearly eighteen hours. She should have been feeling discomfort and an urge to return to them. Instead, she was consumed by the need to be with Bren.

She smiled at the thought of her mate and left the bathroom. She headed toward the kitchen, halting in the doorway when she saw him sitting at the table with Elora.

Her dragon growled, and she tasted smoke in the back of her throat. She stalked forward, placing a possessive hand on her mate's neck, and stared at the witch sitting at the table. "Do you wish to have my mate as your own, little witch?"

Elora shook her head. "No, not at all."

"You spend a lot of time with him," Kaida said.

"We're friends," Bren said. "That's it, Kaida. I promise."

Her dragon surged forward to egg her on, and she bent her head and kissed her mate hard. She lifted her head, smiling at the scent of his lust before her gaze narrowed on the witch again. "He is mine, little witch. Keep your hands off of him."

"No problem," Elora said.

"Good. Leave. Bren and I need to mate."

"Uh, sit down and have some tea with us first," Bren said. He stood and took her hand, urging her to sit in the chair across from him. Glancing at Elora, he poured some tea from the pot on the table into a mug and handed it to her before returning to his seat. "Go on, drink."

"I don't want tea," Kaida said. She tried not to let her exasperation with him show. Her need to fuck him was growing by the second, and she was terribly afraid that if they didn't have sex soon, she would do something truly awful like force him into her bed.

You don't need to force him. Our mate wants us, her dragon replied.

"Just one cup. For me?" Bren said.

Unable to deny her mate, she sat down with a heavy thump into the chair and sipped the fragrant-smelling tea. It left a strange taste on her tongue, and she frowned as a weird tingling went down her spine. "What kind of tea is this?"

"My own blend," the witch replied.

"Drink some more," Bren said. He lifted his mug to his mouth, and after a moment, Kaida followed suit. She took three big gulps of the warm liquid to satisfy her mate and then set the cup down.

"There, I've drunk the tea." She turned and forced a smile at the witch. "Leave now."

"Why don't you have a shower first," Bren said. "Elora and I will finish our tea, and then I'll join you in the bedroom."

Her dragon hissed angrily, but Kaida decided it wasn't a bad idea. She felt a little weird and too warm, and the idea of a cool shower was appealing. "All right."

She stood, smiling at the way her mate's gaze dropped first to her tits and then to her legs. If the witch weren't here, she'd strip off her mate's t-shirt and show him exactly what he was missing out on.

Instead, she tugged at the hem of her shirt before kissing Bren again. She traced her fingers across the morning stubble on his jawline. God, she loved his lips. They were perfect. Everything about him was perfect.

She pulled back instead of straddling him in the chair like she wanted to and forced another smile at the witch. "Good-bye."

"Uh, bye, Kaida. Nice to see you again."

She returned to the primary bathroom, turned on the shower and stripped off Bren's shirt. He had a nice apartment, but he would still need to move in with her, she mused. She could not live so far from her clan, no matter how much she loved her mate. She stepped into the shower and stood under the cool spray of water. It sent goosebumps pinging to life on her heated skin, and her dragon purred happily.

She would have to move into one of the bigger empty cabins. Her small cabin was comfortable, but it would not be big enough for her and her mate. Especially if Tyler lived with them. Considering what a considerable dickhead his father was, it could happen.

She washed her hair with her mate's shampoo and used his body wash to lather her skin.

She would ask Cadmus if she could have the empty cabin next to Bones and Javee. It had three bedrooms. They were small, but at least that way, Tyler would have his own room, and they'd have a nursery as well.

Nursery?

She stared at her hand resting on her flat stomach. Nursery? Why would she need a nursery?

For when we are with our mate and....

Her dragon fell silent. She could feel its confusion and braced one hand on the slick shower wall.

Why would she and her dragon think Bren was her mate? She was attracted to the human, but the idea of her mating with a human was laughable. Even if she didn't set him on fire while they were fucking, she'd be kicked out of the clan if they ever found out she'd slept with a human.

But I want him as my mate. Her dragon still sounded confused and uncertain. *He said he was our mate and that he would...*

"Oh fuck!" Kaida's entire body stiffened, and she had to stop from smashing her fist through the wet tile. "The muffin! The goddamn muffin!"

She rinsed clean and shut the shower off, toweling dry and running her fingers through her wet and tangled hair. The tea she'd had earlier was swishing around in her belly, making her feel nauseous, and shame was flooding her entire body.

The things she had said and done to the human!

"It's fine," she muttered as she yanked her jeans over her hips and then stuck her panties into the pocket. "You were under the spell of a love potion, and the human knows that."

She slipped into her bra and pulled her t-shirt over her head, trying not to groan as everything she said to the human last night echoed in her head. How many times had she told him she was going to fuck him? Too many to count. She had touched him and kissed him and tried to...

"Shit, I'll be lucky if he doesn't arrest me for sexual assault," she groaned.

It wasn't our fault, her dragon growled.

"Why the fuck didn't you smell the potion in the muffin?" she said.

I was hungry! Her dragon pouted at her like a spoiled child. *Besides, all I wanted was to fuck the human. How was I to know he would try to trick us into being mates by feeding us poison?*

"Oh my God," she muttered. "One, it wasn't poison and

two, it obviously wasn't him. If it were, we would have fucked last night."

A little tingle of pleasure radiated from her pussy down her legs at the thought. She stared at her crotch, groaning inwardly as her dragon purred. She was *not* still attracted to the human.

Uh, yeah, we are.

"Shut up!" she snarled at her dragon before stomping toward the bedroom door. Now that the potion had worn off, her need to return to her clan was starting. A low buzz at the base of her skull that made her brain itch.

She moved down the hallway toward the kitchen, stopping outside the doorway when she heard her mate's – no, not mate, the *human's* – voice.

"How long will it take to kick in?"

"It shouldn't take too long. Hopefully, by the time she's finished showering. She didn't drink the entire cup, though, so..."

Kaida's hands clenched into fists. Was this the witch's doing? It had to be. But why? Moving quietly, she leaned forward and peeked into the kitchen. Bren was sitting at the table, and he reached out and squeezed Elora's hand.

She stared morosely at him. "When the WWC finds out about this, she'll be labeled a dark witch."

"I'm not going to tell the Witches and Warlocks Council," Bren said. "She didn't mean any harm, and I'll talk to Kaida, explain to her that -"

"I'm going to tell the WWC," Elora said.

Bren stiffened. "What? Elora, she's your grandmother."

"She also keeps trying to drug you with a love potion. It's illegal and dangerous."

"I know, but..."

"But what?" Elora crossed her arms over her chest. The

crow on her shoulder made a low and raspy caw and nestled its face into her neck. "What happened last night was dangerous, Bren. Kaida is a bear shifter who could have really hurt you."

"She didn't," Bren said. 'She listened to me when I said no."

Kaida's cheeks burned as Elora said, "Yeah, but what if she hadn't?"

"She did. Elora, if you tell the WWC what happened, Helen will be imprisoned."

"I know!" Elora's voice was loud, and Kaida could see tears slipping down her cheeks. "But what choice do I have? This is bad, Bren. I talked to her last night, and she was remorseful and promised never to do it again, but I'm not sure I can take that risk."

"Let me at least talk to Kaida first," Bren said. "Then, maybe -"

"Maybe what? Do you think that a bear shifter will be sympathetic to my grandmother drugging her?"

"It wasn't meant for her," Bren said. "It was meant for me."

"That doesn't make it any better," Elora said. "I mean, I don't even know how I will explain to Kaida why this happened. My grandmother is losing her marbles and -"

Feeling an odd sort of empathy with the witch, Kaida stepped into the kitchen. "You don't have to report your grandmother to the WWC."

"Kaida." Bren stood and stared nervously at her. "How, uh, do you feel?"

"Incredibly embarrassed, but the potion has worn off."

Relief crossed Bren's face. "Actually, the tea you drank this morning had a potion to reverse the other one. Elora made it."

Wishing she could leave, ignoring the itch in her brain to

return to her clan, Kaida sat across from him. "I'm sorry for last night."

"You have nothing to be sorry about," Bren said.

Kaida cleared her throat. "I said and did a lot of inappropriate things."

"Because you were drugged," Elora said. "By my grandmother. I'm so sorry. I can't even tell you how sorry I am. She wants Bren and me to be together, so she keeps giving him love potions in the hopes that we'll... but, I mean, we're not interested in each other that way. Right, Bren?"

"Definitely not," Bren said.

"Your grandmother must be a powerful witch," Kaida said. "I didn't even smell the potion in the muffin."

"Why did Kaida fall in love with me and not you?" Bren said to Elora.

"Because this one was a general potion. The first time, it was specifically tailored for you to fall in love with me, but I started locking up my hairbrush so she can't get strands of my hair anymore," Elora said.

"Wait, there can be general and specific love potions?" Bren said.

"Yes. A potion can be created so the person who ingests it only falls in love with a certain person. Like the first potion she drugged you with. You saw other people before you saw me, right?"

Bren thought back. "Yeah, I did."

"Right. So, if it had been a general one, you would have fallen in love with the first female, or male if she didn't specify the gender in the potion, you saw. But Helen stole some of my hair and used it in the potion, tying it to me and me alone."

"Holy shit," Bren said.

"This one from last night was a general one, meaning the

person who ingested it would fall in love with the first person they saw," Elora said. "She told me that she made sure to put walnuts in the muffins so that Tyler wouldn't eat them."

"Thank God," Bren said. He glanced at Kaida. "Tyler hates walnuts."

"But without access to my hair anymore, she was desperate enough to hope that I was the first person you saw after you ate the muffin. She said she was going to send me over to your apartment first thing this morning."

Bren suddenly blanched. "Kaida was here with Tyler last night."

"He went to bed before I ate the muffin," Kaida said.

Anger seeped into Bren's face. "But if he hadn't, and if you had tried to..."

"She wouldn't have," Elora said quickly. "Love potions are strong, but they're not so strong that they would make a person do something they know is fundamentally wrong. Even if Kaida had seen Tyler after eating the muffin, the potion wouldn't have worked because she's not interested in banging a seventeen-year-old."

"Definitely not," Kaida said.

"Anyway," Elora stared intently at Kaida, "I want you to know that I don't take this lightly and will report her to the WWC."

"I appreciate that, but don't do it," Kaida said. "I'm not excusing what your grandmother did, but I know something about meddling grandmothers. I overheard you say she was remorseful and promised not to do it again. Do you believe her?"

"I do. When she found out that a bear shifter had ingested the potion, it seemed to click in how crazy she was acting. She helped me make the reversal potion this morning. It wouldn't have been as effective so quickly if she hadn't," Elora said.

"Well, ultimately, it's your decision, but know I won't report her to the WWC. Family can be," Kaida paused, "difficult sometimes. Honestly, I would prefer if we pretended this didn't happen and never spoke of it again."

"I can do that." Elora stood, the crow on her shoulder flapping its wings to keep its balance, and she couldn't entirely hide the relief on her face. "It was nice to meet you, Kaida. I'm sorry it was under these circumstances."

"Nice to meet you as well," Kaida replied.

Elora squeezed Bren's shoulder. He smiled at her, and a weird feeling shot through Kaida's stomach. It was strong enough to obliterate the buzzing in her brain to return to her clan.

Oh shit. Was she… jealous?

Elora had left, and Bren was staring silently at her. She swallowed hard, shame making her cheeks burn hot. "I'd like to apologize again for last night. What I said and what I did was -"

"Stop," Bren said. "You don't need to keep apologizing. You were literally under a spell. I know you didn't mean anything you said or did."

"Right," she said. Her legs wouldn't stay still, and she was starting to feel sick to her stomach.

My clan, her dragon said. *I need them.*

"I should be apologizing to you," Bren said.

"It isn't your fault either."

"Living across the hall from a crazy witch isn't as much fun as it sounds," he said.

She forced a faint smile as he watched her.

My clan. Please.

"Did you want to stay and have breakfast?" Bren asked. "I promise it's just plain old eggs and bacon, nothing drugged."

She stood up so abruptly that she almost knocked the chair over. She grabbed it before it could fall, smiling uneasily at Bren as he stood. Sweat beaded along her hairline, and her dragon's insistence on returning to the clan was a deep and maddening itch in her brain. Her urge to shift was very strong, and she clenched her hands into fists behind her back.

"Kaida? What's wrong?"

"Nothing. I must return to my clan. I've been gone too long from them, and I can't... I need my clan."

She could hear the emotion in her voice. Normally, she hated displaying weakness in front of anyone, especially humans, but there was no pity in Bren's gaze. He stepped back as she almost ran for the doorway. "All right."

She paused in the doorway. "I... goodbye, Bren."

"Bye, Kaida."

CHAPTER 10

"Thanks, Will." Ava smiled at her best friend as Willow wrapped an elastic around the end of the braid and then smoothed back the sides.

"No problem." Willow examined Ava's head. "I'm getting way better at this French braiding thing."

"You are." Ava crossed her bedroom to the small vanity and checked her makeup as Willow sat on the edge of the bed.

Her feet dangled, and she grinned at Ava. "You guys have the biggest bed ever."

"You should see Rosalie and Hudson's bed," Ava said absently, picking through her jewelry box. "It's even bigger than ours."

"Uh, how do you know what Rosalie and Hudson's bed looks like?" Willow asked. "Do you and Bishop have some kinky partner swap thing going on?"

Ava turned bright red. "Willow!"

"No judgment if you are." Willow swung her feet. "You and Rosalie are both into bears, so…"

"Hudson is a polar bear, not a grizzly," Ava said.

"Still a bear."

Ava held up some earrings to her ears. "What do you think of these?"

"Cute. So, are you guys doing some kinky foursome thing, or what? You went on that double date together last weekend. Was it more than dinner? Wait..." Willow eyed her suspiciously. "Are you and Bishop cheating on me and Mal in the friendship department?"

Ava laughed, although her cheeks were still red. "We are not cheating on you and Mal with Rosalie and Hudson. Bishop and Hudson started to hang out a bit after he helped Hudson save Rosalie from the shifter who kidnapped her. I think Bishop likes having a friend who understands the annoyance of living in a world where everything is too small. Then we started doing some couple stuff together. Rosalie is super sweet, and I've considered inviting her to some of our girls' nights. I know Maggie wanted to, but Rosalie was worried that she was intruding."

"The more the merrier," Willow said. "Still haven't answered the sex question."

"Oh my God, you're like a dog with a bone," Ava said with another laugh. Princess wandered into the bedroom and jumped onto the bed. The cat purred loudly as it rubbed up against Willow.

"There is nothing sexual going on. Hudson and Rosalie are obsessed with and only with each other. It's adorable. And you know how Bishop is. Do you think he'd share me with someone?" Ava said.

"You make a good point." Willow petted Princess. "I'm no shifter but even I could smell Bishop's jealousy when Bren kissed your cheek."

Ava put the earrings on before sliding a bracelet onto her wrist. "Bishop knows that Bren and I are just friends."

"You could have knocked me over with a feather when you invited Bren to Bishop's party tonight," Willow said.

"You and Bishop both," Ava said.

"So, why did you? I mean, I get the wedding thing, Bren's your friend, but he and Bishop definitely aren't close."

"He saved Bishop's life when they had to rescue Ronin from that scientist, remember?" Ava said.

"Ronin brings it up at every staff meeting. It drives Bishop crazy," Willow said with a giggle.

Ava laughed before joining Willow on the bed. She sat cross-legged and toyed with the bracelet on her wrist. "I invited him because it was obvious that he likes Kaida, and I'm pretty sure she was into him too."

"Kaida's a dragon. She's not going to date a human," Willow said.

"No one ever thought Bishop would date a human," Ava said.

"That's kind of different," Willow replied. "Grizzly shifters are known for being loners, but dragon shifters are thought to be extinct by humans and shifters. Even if Kaida wanted to date Bren, she'd never trust him enough to tell him what she really was. And I wouldn't blame her, not with who his dad is."

"I know, but…"

"But what?" Willow said.

"I guess I'm just a romantic at heart," Ava said.

Willow smiled at her. "You are, and it's one of my favourite things about you. But didn't you tell Bianca you would set her up with Bren at the party? She's still single, right?"

"She is. They would be a cute couple."

"Super cute," Willow said. "Plus, she's a doctor. With

Bren's line of work, that could come in handy. He probably gets injured on the job all the time."

"I'll introduce Bren to Bianca and see where it leads," Ava said. "Besides, Kaida might not even show up. Bishop said in the past that she's cancelled for things like this. The dragons always have to be so careful about being around humans and shifters."

"God, that would suck so bad," Willow said.

They both looked up as Bishop walked into the room, carrying Lila.

"She hungry?" Ava asked.

Bishop kissed Lila's cheek. "Yep."

"When is that kid not hungry?" Willow asked as Bishop handed Lila over to Ava.

"Her dad's a grizzly, Will. She likes to eat," Bishop said.

"She certainly does," Ava said as she fed Lila. "How are party preparations going down there?"

"Good," Bishop said. "Mal and I have the barbeques going, and Mara texted. She and Roland are almost here with the food."

"Awesome," Ava said. "Thanks, honey."

"My in-laws are the best," Willow said.

"Yes, they are," Ava replied.

"Kaida texted me," Bishop said.

"Did she have to cancel?" Ava asked.

He shook his head. "No, but she will be a little late."

"It's good that she's still coming," Ava said.

"Yeah…" Bishop said. "You can't set her up with Bren."

"She's not interested?" Ava said.

Bishop hesitated, and Ava grinned at Willow. "Told you."

"They need to be kept apart," Bishop said. "Kaida's dragon is attracted to the human, and if we push them together, it will end badly. Bren can't ever know she's a dragon, honey."

He stared pleadingly at Ava, who said, "I know. I'll introduce Bren to a few other friends at the party."

"Thank you," Bishop said.

"I won't deliberately set them up," Ava stroked Lila's soft red hair, "but if there's an attraction between them, they may not stay away from one another."

"I know Kaida," Bishop said. "She won't endanger herself or her clan by dating a human."

"BREN, IT'S SO GOOD TO SEE YOU."

"Nice to see you as well, Kat." Bren kissed the jaguar shifter's smooth cheek. "How are you?"

"Good." Kat smiled at him as her mate, Ronin, joined them. If either of them looked surprised to see him at Bishop's birthday party, they hid it well.

"Detective." Ronin held out his hand, and Bren shook it.

"Here, let me add that to the table." Kat took the gift bag from Bren. "Ava told people not to bring gifts, but..." she pointed to the small table with presents.

"It's just a bottle of scotch," Bren said.

Kat laughed. "Bishop will be happy with that."

She headed across the small backyard, weaving around the shifters, talking in small groups of two and three. Ronin stared blatantly at her ass before turning back to Bren.

"How's it going, Detective?"

"Good. Thanks for looking after Tyler and Corey on Thursday. I appreciate it."

"You're welcome. Hey, do you know who Celine Dion is?"

Bren blinked at him. "Yeah, why?"

Ronin grinned. "No reason. You want a -"

"Holy shit."

Ronin followed Bren's gaze. A man had walked out of the house and into the yard. He was massive, standing over seven feet tall, and his body was thick with muscle. He joined a curvy dark-haired woman talking to a wolf shifter named Porter and Porter's human mate, Maggie and slid his arm around her waist before bending and kissing her briefly.

"That's Hudson. He's built like a brick shithouse, isn't he?" Ronin said with another grin.

"What kind of shifter is he?"

"Polar bear. He's a bartender over at Bud's Bar. I take it you've never been to the bar. Hudson's kind of hard to miss."

"A few times for work when I was a beat cop and then when the original owner, Bud, was murdered," Bren said. "I hear it's more friendly to humans now that Porter owns the place."

"Yeah, a little, but it's still mostly shifters who go there," Ronin said.

"So, heal anyone lately by crying on them?" Bren asked.

The phoenix shifter burst into laughter. "Not lately. It's been a slow few weeks." He clapped Bren on the back. "Can I get you a beer?"

"Sure."

"Be right back."

Ronin walked away. Bren stood awkwardly near the back fence, staring at the mixture of shifters and humans scattered throughout the yard. Kaida wasn't among them. Maybe she was in the house?

Do you think she actually came to the party? You saw the way she looked this morning after Elora reversed the potion. She looked sick to her stomach, didn't she? And she couldn't wait to get away from you. She's not going to show up.

No, she probably wouldn't, and that made him a complete idiot. He didn't want to admit to himself that he'd only come to the party hoping to see Kaida, but it was hard to ignore when he was nearly vibrating with anticipation of seeing her.

She's not going to show.

"Bren?"

He turned and held out his hand. "Happy Birthday, Bishop."

"Thanks." The grizzly shifter shook his hand before handing him a beer. "This is from Ronin."

Bren took the beer with a nod of thanks. "Looks like the party is going well. Lots of people."

Bishop glanced around the yard. "Yeah, that's because of Ava. I didn't have a lot of friends before I met her."

"Kaida mentioned you've been friends since you were kids," Bren said.

"Yeah," Bishop finally said after an awkward silence.

"Good, that's good," Bren replied, heat drifting up the back of his neck.

They drank their beer silently for a minute or two before Bren said, "So, I haven't seen Kaida. Is she, uh, still coming to the party?"

"You need to stay away from her," Bishop said.

Irritation painted the edges of Bren's vision a pale red. "Is that right?'

"Yes."

"So, you're Kaida's keeper. Is that what you're saying?"

Bishop rolled his eyes. "It's for your safety, human."

Bren took a sip of beer. "You know I'm a grown man, right? A grown man who is proficient with a gun?"

That earned him a grunt of irritation from Bishop. "Kaida is dangerous. Stay away from her."

"I thought she was your friend," Bren said.

"She is. And as her friend, I'm telling you to stay away from her. She won't mean to hurt you, but…"

Bren grinned at Bishop. "Aw, I didn't know you cared so much about my emotional state, big guy."

Bishop huffed out another grunt. "That isn't what I'm talking about. Look, I'm not trying to say you're weak or something, but Kaida is a very powerful shifter."

"Stronger than you?" Bren said.

"Yes."

"Interesting. I know female bear shifters are strong, but I didn't think they were more powerful than a fully-grown male grizzly shifter."

Bishop scowled. "She's not a ... can you stop being an idiot human for two seconds and listen to what I'm saying? Stay away from Kaida."

"I heard you the first three times, and I'll take your suggestion under advisement," Bren said.

"It's for your safety," Bishop said.

"So you keep saying. Hello, Ava."

Ava stopped next to Bishop. Lila was on her hip, and the baby made a low sound in the back of her throat that sounded remarkably like a growl. Bishop immediately responded with his own growl, and the baby giggled.

"Honey, Amos is looking for you." Ava pointed to an older man sitting near the food table. "He wants to have a drink with you."

Bishop hesitated, and Ava patted his chest. "Go on, my love."

The big grizzly shifter walked away, and Ava smiled at Bren. "I'm so glad you made it to the party, Bren."

"Me too. Thanks for the invite," Bren said.

Lila stared at him and made another growl. Bren laughed. "Did your baby growl at me?"

Ava kissed Lila's head. "Yes. Sorry."

"I thought she was human," Bren said.

"Oh, she is," Ava said. "But Bishop growls to her a lot and she started mimicking him about a week ago. Much to Bishop's delight."

The baby growled a third time, and Bren laughed again. "That is adorable."

He leaned forward and tugged lightly on Lila's sock-covered foot. "Hi, sweetie."

"Would you like to hold her?" Ava asked.

"Yes, if that's okay?" Bren said.

"Of course, it is." Ava handed Lila to him, and he held the chubby baby in the crook of his arm. She studied him solemnly, and when she growled, he growled back.

Her eyes widened, and she looked at her mother before looking back at Bren. Bren laughed. "I don't think she's impressed by my growling."

"Honestly, if anyone but Bishop growls to her, she looks at them like they're crazy," Ava said. "I can only imagine – oh, hey, Bianca! Come here for a second."

The woman walking past them pivoted and joined them. She was slender with sandy-brown hair and hazel-coloured eyes. She was gorgeous, and she smiled warmly at Bren. She wore eyeglasses that were sliding down her nose, and she pushed them up with one finger. "Hi there."

"Bianca, this is Detective Bren Matthews. He's a good friend of ours. Bren, this is Dr. Bianca Dartwell. She's a friend, and I work with her at the hospital."

"It's nice to meet you." Bren shook Bianca's hand.

"You as well," Bianca replied.

"Bianca is one of our best doctors in the emergency room," Ava said.

Bianca smiled at her. "That's very kind of you to say, Ava."

"It's true," Ava said. "She saved a woman's life yesterday after the woman came in with appendicitis. Bianca got her diagnosed and sent up to surgery just in time. Even an hour later, the woman's appendix would have ruptured."

"Impressive," Bren said.

Bianca shook her head. "It sounds cliché to say this, but I was just doing my job."

"Yes, but you do your job much better than most," Ava said. "Exactly like Bren. Did you know he's one of the youngest detectives in his precinct?"

"Wow," Bianca said. "Good for you, Detective."

"Call me Bren," he said as Lila reached up and grabbed his nose.

"Only if you call me Dr. Bianca," she replied.

He laughed, and Bianca grinned at him. "Just kidding. Call me Bianca."

"Ava?" A redheaded woman joined them. "We have a party emergency."

"Uh oh," Ava said. "Bren, this is my sister Amy. Ames, this is Bren."

"Nice to meet you," Amy said with a brief smile. "We're out of cheese, Ava. Like completely out of cheese."

"One – that's not a party emergency, and two – there's more cheese in the fridge," Ava said.

"There isn't," Amy said. "I looked twice."

"There is." Ava glanced at Lila, resting her head on Bren's chest with her eyes closed. "Bren, would you mind holding Lila for a bit longer?"

"Not at all," Bren said.

"Great, thanks. I'll be right back." Ava followed Amy into the house.

Bianca smiled at Bren. "So… human or shifter?"

"Human. You?"

"Human," she said.

Bren shifted Lila a little, and the baby made a soft, sleepy sound. He rubbed her back and inhaled her sweet scent as an awkward silence descended.

"Do you think it'll ever get less awkward when you're blatantly set up with another single person at a party?" Bianca asked.

Bren laughed. "I don't think so."

"Me either," Bianca said. "The perils of being single, I suppose. Although to be fair, Ava did mention to me ahead of time that she would introduce me to a handsome and funny guy at Bishop's party."

"Should I be jealous of this guy?" Bren said.

Bianca's laughter was soft and low and should have made Bren's dick take notice.

It didn't.

"Ava was being remarkably truthful about the handsome part," Bianca said as a flicker of movement over her shoulder caught Bren's eye. She stepped closer and placed her hand on his arm. "Would you like to have coffee sometime so I can investigate whether the funny part is true as well?"

"Kaida," Bren said.

"I'm sorry?" Bianca said.

Bren's pulse became a rapid, jittery beat as Kaida, looking gorgeous in a dark green dress, stalked toward them.

CHAPTER 11

Kaida smoothed her dress and knocked on the door of Bishop and Ava's home. Attending Bishop's birthday party was a bad idea, especially after being away from her clan the night before.

She shouldn't have come, but her dragon had driven her crazy all afternoon about seeing Bren again. It was almost as bad as her need to be with her clan. That realization both exhilarated and terrified her.

She should have still been craving the comfort of her clan. But only a few hours after she'd returned home, her dragon had started in on her about seeing Bren again.

She straightened her dress again as she heard footsteps on the other side of the door. Her dragon's need for the human was going to drive her crazy.

I want him.

I know, she snarled at her dragon. *You think I didn't hear you the first fifty times you said it?*

Her dragon growled as the door opened. Mal, a wolf shifter and Bishop's best friend, stared at the smoke drifting from her nostrils. "Hello, Kaida."

Sending a silent thanks that one of the few shifters who knew she was a dragon answered the door, she waved the smoke away and made herself smile. "Hello, Mal. Sorry."

"No problem. Come in."

She followed him into the house. She could hear Willow and Ava's voices drifting out of the kitchen as they walked down the hallway.

"See, Ames, cheese. Right there," Ava said.

Willow laughed. "In her defense, a giant container of breast milk blocked it from view."

"Everyone's out back," Mal said as he led her to the patio doors that opened to the backyard. "Head on out and grab a drink. I need to head to the kitchen for a minute."

"Thanks." She opened the door and stepped out into the yard. A table with a small pile of presents was to her left, and she added the small wrapped box she held to the pile. The scent of barbequed meat drifted to her. The yard was full of shifters and humans, and unease settled at the base of her spine. The humans would have no idea what she was, but the shifters...

It's fine. They think we're all dead, her dragon said. *Find Bren.*

We should leave, she said to her dragon. *If they smell smoke like the fox yearling...*

They won't. And if they do, they'll think it's from the food cooking. Find Bren.

She started to back up toward the patio doors. She needed to leave. There were too many shifters, and one of them was bound to –

There!

Her dragon made a loud purr of happiness, it had caught Bren's scent, and she swung her gaze to the right. Bren stood on the far side of the yard. He was – her dragon made another purr of happiness – holding Lila, and the sight of the baby in his arms intensified her desire for a hatchling until she felt almost dizzy.

He will be a good father to our hatchling, her dragon said. *Please, can I have him?*

"Be quiet," she muttered under her breath. "Just because he likes babies doesn't mean he wants a baby. Stop acting like -"

Mine!

Her dragon's roar was so loud it made her head hurt. A human woman stood with Bren, placing her hand on his arm. Her dragon snarled again.

She's trying to take what is ours!

Her dragon surged forward, and with fury and fire licking at her veins, Kaida stalked toward Bren. The woman with him was about to discover what happened to females who dared to touch what belonged to Kaida.

"Kaida," Bren said as she approached them. She barely registered the surprise in his voice or the happiness that immediately surrounded him. She knew her eyes were glowing and her body was starting to overheat, but she didn't care. The female was touching Bren, and if she didn't stop, Kaida would burn her to a fucking crisp.

"Who are you, human?" Her dragon pushed forward again and spat the question at the little female.

The female dropped her hand from Bren's arm, it only slightly mollified Kaida's dragon, and took a step back. Her dragon hissed angrily, and Kaida swallowed the smoke that wanted to drift from her mouth and nostrils.

"Kaida, this is Bianca. She's a friend of Ava's. Bianca, this is Kaida. She and Bishop have been friends for years," Bren said.

"It's nice to meet you." The woman pushed up her

eyeglasses. Kaida could still smell her anxiety, but the female met her gaze steadily enough before holding out her hand.

Kaida shook it briefly. The female's attraction to Bren still lurked between them, driving her dragon crazy.

"You as well," she said in a clipped tone.

Show the female he's ours, her dragon demanded. *Kiss him.*

She was tempted. God, was she tempted. Instead, she smiled at Bren, making her voice low and intimate. "Sorry I had to leave your place so abruptly this morning."

Bren's eyes widened, and he glanced at Bianca. "Uh, that's okay."

Disappointment coated the human female as Kaida's dragon practically sprinted around like a kid at recess. If Kaida let it, she was pretty sure the damn thing would be shouting "na-na, na-na boo-boo" at the poor woman.

A mixture of satisfaction and shame washed over her when Bianca said to Bren, "It was good to meet you, Bren."

She walked away, and Kaida's dragon shrank slightly at the look Bren gave her. "What the hell was that about?"

Before Kaida could reply, Bishop joined them. She hugged him briefly and kissed his cheek. "Happy Birthday, my bear."

"Thanks. Do me a favour? Stop scaring my party guests?" Bishop glanced at Bianca, who had joined a group of humans and shifters near the patio.

The smug satisfaction drained away completely, leaving only shame in its place. "I'm sorry," Kaida said. "I will apologize to the female."

"It's fine," Bishop said. "Just chill out, okay?" He held his hands out for Lila. "Bren, do you want another beer?"

Bren handed the sleeping baby to Bishop. Lila raised her head, blinking blearily at Bishop and growling. Bishop growled in return, kissing her soft cheek before the baby burrowed her face into his thick neck and made a few sleepy snores.

"I'm good, thanks," Bren said.

Bishop glanced at Kaida again. "Stop being… weird."

"I'm sorry," she repeated.

"Bishop?" Mal called from near the barbeque. "Come over here for a sec."

Bishop hesitated, glancing first at Bren and then at Kaida.

"Go, my bear. Enjoy your party," Kaida said. "I will behave."

With a final look at them, Bishop walked away. Kaida waited for a beat before looking at Bren. "I'm sorry."

"Sorry for scaring off a potential date or leaving so abruptly this morning?" he said.

"You're going to date the human?" Her voice was a low growl.

Bren shrugged, and her dragon pouted like a yearling banned from flying.

"Are you dating her or not?" she demanded.

"Well, considering you just scared the bejeezus out of her and made it seem like we had sex last night, probably not," Bren said.

She glanced around the yard. "Keep your voice down."

He grinned at her. "Don't want anyone knowing that a love potion took down the big bad bear, huh?"

She didn't smile at his teasing, and his tone turned somber. "Hey, I'm kidding. What happened was no big deal, all right?"

She shook her head, her embarrassment at the things she had said and done to him returning with a vengeance. Her need to apologize again was overwhelming. She glanced around the yard a second time. Most of the guests were shifters and, no doubt could hear everything she and Bren said if they chose to listen.

"Can we talk in private for a second?" she asked.

"Sure."

Bren followed her into the house. She'd been at Bishop and Ava's new home a handful of times and navigated her way to the spare room that Bishop used as an office. Bren shut the door behind them. She moved to the desk and traced her fingers across the framed picture of Bishop, Ava, and Lila sitting beside Bishop's laptop.

Bren joined her. He leaned against the desk and crossed his arms, pulling the material of his shirt taut across his chest.

Kaida looked away, her heart thudding and her dragon purring like crazy. Fuck, why did she have to be so attracted to him? Why did she have to remember exactly how he tasted, how he sounded when he moaned?

She took a deep breath and made herself look him in the eye. "I wanted to apologize again for last night."

Irritation flickered across his face. "I wish you wouldn't. It's not your fault you ate a love potion laced muffin. In fact, it isn't either of our faults. It's the fault of a crazy but well-meaning witch who lives across the hall from me."

"I guess," she said, "but I still need to apologize for the unwanted advances."

"You know damn well they weren't unwanted."

She flushed, and her gaze dropped to his mouth. God, his lips were so... inviting.

Those inviting lips curled up into a smile. "If I didn't know better, I'd think that maybe you were lying when you said you weren't interested in me."

"It was the love potion that made me do and say those things," she said.

"Oh yeah? So that's not sexual tension radiating between us right now?"

She lifted her gaze to his. His blue eyes danced with humour, and a smile crossed her face.

"You know what I think?" he said.

She shook her head as he leaned a little closer. God, he smelled so fucking good.

"I think you liked kissing me."

"Of course I did… love potion, remember?"

"Was it all love potion?" he said as he bent his head. She could feel his warm breath on her lips, and when she parted them, he made a low sound of need that sent shivers down her spine.

"All love potion," she lied.

"That's a shame." He straightened, and disappointment covered every inch of her body. "Was there anything else, or are we good now?"

"We're good," she said.

He lingered at the desk next to her. "All right. If you'll excuse me, I'm going to finish my conversation with Bianca, maybe ask her if she wants to – did you just hiss at me?"

She glared at him, her dragon growling and hissing and acting like a goddamn fool. "Stay away from the human female."

"Why?" His infuriating grin made her want to throw him down on the desk and fuck him until he was begging her to let him come.

Instead, she said, "Fine. Maybe *some* of my enjoyment from kissing you wasn't *entirely* because of the love potion."

"How much?"

"What?"

"How much was love potion, and how much was you being wowed by my stellar kissing abilities?" Bren asked with another grin. "We talking eighty/twenty? Sixty/forty? Fifty/fifty?"

"Seventy/thirty," she said.

"Seventy percent, not bad," he said.

"The seventy was the love potion."

"Ouch," he said.

She laughed, and he uncrossed his arms and rested his hands on the desk. "Honestly, I'll happily take the thirty percent. Although, if you want to kiss again and see if I can move that number up a little, I'm game."

"We can't," she said.

"Sure, we can," he said. "Wait, is that your way of saying I need a mint? Because I have that covered."

"No, it isn't..." she watched as he produced a package of mints from his jeans pocket and popped one into his mouth.

He sucked on it and then crunched it down before grinning at her. "Minty fresh."

Fuck it. One kiss wouldn't hurt.

She stepped toward him and pressed her mouth against his, swallowing his startled sound. He recovered quickly. She had to give him that. His arms slid around her waist, he spread his feet, and he pulled her in between his thighs, angling his mouth over hers and licking at the seam of her mouth.

She opened her lips, and he skimmed his tongue along the edge of her teeth before taking the kiss deeper. She returned his kiss, cupping his face in her hands and battling for control. He teased her tongue with his before retreating. She followed, sliding her tongue between his lips and tasting the cool mint in his mouth.

When his big hand cupped her ass and squeezed, she broke the kiss. He stared at her mouth, their breaths mingling. "That was nice."

She laughed. "Nice?"

He grimaced. "Sorry. I'm not exactly thinking straight. All the blood in my brain has drained south."

She could feel his erection hard and heavy against her belly. She rubbed against it, and he groaned, his hand tightening on her ass before he dipped his head and kissed her collarbone. "You wanna get out of here?"

"I can't," she said.

"Are you sure?" He tasted the soft skin of her neck.

She let her head fall back, moaning when he kissed his way up her throat to her jawline. "I'm mostly sure."

"What kind of percentage are we talking about?"

She laughed and ran her hands across his shoulders. "You're obsessed with numbers."

"I like to know what my chances of seeing you naked might be," he said.

She sighed. "I – we can't. Look, it's obvious that we're attracted to each other, but I can't sleep with you. You're fragile, and I don't want to hurt you."

"Could you knock it off with the fragile thing? I can take whatever you hand out, I promise," he said.

She skimmed her hands over the bulging muscles in his upper arms. "It's not just that. I like... control, and you're a cop, which means you like control, too. We wouldn't be compatible in bed."

"You don't know what I want," he said. "Maybe I'm perfectly fine with being handcuffed to the bed. How do you know if you don't ask?"

"Do you like being handcuffed to the bed?"

Fuck, she was not envisioning a naked Bren handcuffed to her bed.

Hell, yes, we are.

He grinned at her before pressing a light and much too

quick kiss against her lips. "A gentleman never kisses and tells."

Her brain on fire with images of Bren in her bed, she mashed her mouth onto his again. He let her kiss him hard, let her explore every inch of his mouth until they were both panting and breathless.

He didn't say a single word of dissent when she pulled him away from the desk.

He didn't make one protest when she pushed him into the leather chair in the corner.

He didn't utter a solitary rebuttal when she straddled him.

She rubbed her pussy against his cock, and he finally made a noise. A low groan that dampened her pussy and hardened her nipples.

She leaned over him and kissed him again, thrusting her tongue into his mouth as she rocked her pussy against his deliciously hard dick. His hands slid up under her dress, cupping her bare ass cheeks, his fingers playing with the silk strip between her cheeks.

"I want you, human," she said against his mouth.

"I want you too." He sucked on her bottom lip before sliding one hand out from under her dress. He cupped her breast, his thumb running across her beaded nipple. She moaned into his mouth. Her skin was heating up, a delicious fire of need and want rippling beneath her flesh.

He pinched her nipple, and she cried out into his mouth before kissing him hard. Their tongues dueled for control, and when he relented, her desire for him increased until she couldn't think straight.

"Can we go back to your place?" She reached between them and palmed his cock.

"Fuck," he moaned before nodding. "Yeah, let's definitely go back to my place."

She grinned at him and he kissed her again as the door to the office opened. They both froze, staring at Willow as she walked into the office with a large grey tabby in her arms.

"Don't give me that dirty look, Princess," she said before kissing the cat's head. "You're being locked in the office because you keep trying to escape into the backyard every time the door opens. This exile is your own doing, and I don't... whoa...whoa."

Willow stared wide-eyed at Kaida and Bren, her gaze dropping to Bren's hand that cupped Kaida's breast. She backed up, still holding Princess in her arms. "I am so sorry to interrupt. You two keep doing what you're... uh... doing, and I'll -"

Kaida pushed away from Bren, backing away as Bren stood up from the chair. "Shit. I'm sorry."

"It's fine," Willow said before giving them a bright smile. "NBD, right? I'm sorry for interrupting. I'll leave and -"

"No!" Her face burning... fuck, what had she been thinking? She couldn't sleep with a human... Kaida practically sprinted for the door. "I have to go. Um, I'm sorry. Can you let Bishop know I had to go?"

Without looking at Bren, she slipped out of the office.

CHAPTER 12

K aida stood at the edge of the training circle. She stretched her arms above her head before reaching behind her, grabbing her ankle and lifting her leg until her shoe-covered heel touched her ass. Her muscles groaned slightly in protest, but she ignored the slight burning before doing the same with her left leg.

Her dragon paced restlessly inside her, pouting, whining, and hissing at her until Kaida finally snapped, "Enough!"

She retreated retreated. Her feelings were hurt, and Kaida hated that she upset her, but the restlessness and discontent drove Kaida crazy.

She stretched some more, warming up her muscles for the training that was about to happen. It was Sunday afternoon. Tyler had texted her this morning asking if he and Corey could come by for another training lesson. Her stomach in knots, her dragon itching to see Bren again, she texted yes.

Ten minutes before they were supposed to arrive, she'd asked Gram to meet the boys at Kaida's cabin and send them her way. Then, she fled like a scale-covered chicken to the training circle. She was half-hoping that Bren would just drop the boys off. He had to, right?

He had to be pissed at her after what she did yesterday at Bishop's party. He hadn't texted her once, but that was good, right?

What guy liked a woman who ran hot and cold? It didn't matter if they were human or shifter. A guy didn't want a woman who couldn't make up her damn mind about whether she wanted to fuck him or not.

We want to fuck him, her dragon said with a sullen scowl. *You're just being difficult.*

"We can't," she muttered.

Allowing her lust to get the best of her on Saturday had been a mistake. One she couldn't make again. She would have to be firm and clear with Bren that while she wanted him, it wasn't a good idea, and they could only be friends.

What happens the next time you see him with another female?

Her stomach dipped and the yogurt she'd eaten for lunch suddenly felt like it was curdling. How her dragon reacted to seeing Bren with another female had been very bad, catastrophically bad, in fact, but she had to hope that once she stopped seeing Bren, her dragon's weird obsession with him would end.

Nope. Not going to happen.

She ignored her dragon. It needed to get used to the idea of never seeing Bren again. He wouldn't want anything to do with her after last night, which was good. It was a very good thing because if she kept seeing him –

"Hello, Kaida."

She spun around, her dragon purring with delight and the yogurt going full-on sour cream in her guts. She stared blankly at Bren as he joined her in the soft sand of the training circle.

"What are you doing here?" she asked.

He frowned. "Tyler said you were available for a training session this afternoon. Did that change?"

"No, I ... where are the boys?"

He glanced behind him at the path that wound through the woods. "With your grandmother in your cabin. I asked them to give me some time to talk with you before they came to the training circle."

She swallowed hard, ignoring her urge to retreat from the delicious smelling human. "Why?"

He arched one eyebrow at her, his eyes filled with amusement and maybe the smallest amount of lust. "Why do you think?"

"What happened yesterday at the party was a mistake. I'm sorry, but it can't happen again. I think it's best if we stay away from each other. All right?"

"Because you'll hurt me," he said.

"Yes." She could hear the impatience in her voice. "I'm strong, Bren. Stronger than you think."

He cocked his head at her. "Bishop warned me to stay away from you yesterday. He said you were a powerful shifter."

She didn't reply, and he studied her with a directness that made her nervous. "You know what I think?"

She remained silent, and he said, "I think you're lying to me, Kaida."

"I told you I wanted you," she said, "but I can't -"

"Not that," he said. "I think you're lying to me about what you are."

Her body stiffened, and her dragon squealed with excitement.

Tell him! Tell him what we are!

"I'm a bear shifter," she said.

"Are you, though?" he said.

"Yes."

"What kind?"

"Grizzly."

"Like Bishop," he said.

"Yes."

He continued to study her, and she looked away. "I'm a grizzly shifter, Bren."

"Fine. You're a grizzly shifter." His tone of voice said he knew it was complete bullshit. "A grizzly shifter who is too strong for me and would hurt me if we had sex."

She flushed. "That's right."

"You think I'm a fragile human," he slipped out of his jacket and left it in the grass outside the training circle, "so, let's fight. If you win, I'll stop asking you to explore whatever is happening between us. But if I win – you go on a date with me."

"You're joking," she said.

"I never joke about dating. Dating is a serious business."

She sighed. "I'm not going to fight you, Bren."

"What's the matter – afraid the puny little human will kick your – incredible, by the way – ass?"

She couldn't stop the grin from crossing her face. "Buddy, I would sweep the training circle floor with you."

He laughed before moving to the middle and bouncing on the balls of his feet. "Is that right? Why don't you show me what you've got then?"

Her dragon purred as her need to win and conquer reared its head. "You really will accept that we can't be anything but friends when I win?"

"*If* you win," he said, "and yes. I will accept that we can only ever be friends."

"Fine." She walked toward him, letting her fangs drop,

and her eyes glow as she grinned at him. "Don't worry, I'll go easy on you, puny human."

He gave her his own wide grin. "Ditto, pretty lady."

———

"ADMIT IT." PANTING LIGHTLY, BREN CIRCLED KAIDA. "I'M better at fighting than you thought."

"You're better at avoiding getting your ass kicked than I thought," Kaida said.

Bren laughed before making a little bow. "I'll take that as a compliment."

The last five minutes had passed in a blur as Kaida had attacked him again and again. He'd managed to fend off her blows and even attempt a couple of his own, but he'd be lying if he didn't admit she was much stronger and faster than he suspected.

Kaida's smile widened, and Bren's dick twitched against his jeans. The shifter was gorgeous in general, but when she was fighting? The flush of her pale skin, the way her eyes glowed... it was goddamn sexy as hell.

It was how she would look when they were fucking. The realization gave him an immediate semi. He grimaced at the pressure. He couldn't keep thinking about –

He grunted in surprise. Taking advantage of his momentary distraction, Kaida had hit him like a freight train. He was knocked backwards onto his ass, the air exploding from his lungs. The soft sand cushioned his head, and he grunted again when Kaida pounced on him. She straddled his hips, her hands yanking his arms above his head and pinning them to the ground as she leaned over him.

She smiled at him, her fangs flashing in the sunlight. "You lose, human."

"Did I?" he said with his own grin. "I've got a beautiful woman straddling me. That's always a win in my book."

She laughed and shifted a little. "Yeah, well, it's still losing in…"

She twitched as her pussy came in contact with his dick. Her gaze dropped to his crotch, where his semi had become a full-blown erection the moment he'd felt Kaida's soft weight. Surprise and lust crossed her face, and her grip on his arms loosened.

He used it to his advantage, heaving his body upward and knocking her off of him. She landed on her back, and he immediately threw his body onto hers, pushing his way between her thighs and pinning her arms above her head.

He grinned down at her. "What was that you were saying about me losing?"

She scoffed, her golden eyes flashing at him. "Using your dick to distract me doesn't count as a win."

"Hey, all's fair in love and war. If I have to use my dick to distract you, I will," he said.

She laughed again, that warm and throaty sound that made him feel dizzy, like he was speeding down the track of a roller coaster. His gaze dropped to her mouth, and without thinking about it, he pressed his erection against her pussy. Her pelvis rose, encouraging him to flex his hips again.

He studied her mouth, that full bottom lip that was begging to be sucked on. "I'd like to kiss you."

Her pelvis rose again, and when she ground her pussy against his stiff cock, he groaned. "Kaida -"

"Kiss me, human," she demanded.

He dipped his head and did what she asked, covering her mouth with his and sliding his tongue between her lips. She returned his kiss, sucking on his tongue greedily as she arched her body against his.

He released her arms, propping himself up on his hands as he kissed her neck and then nuzzled her earlobe. Her arms slid around his waist, her hands dipping under his shirt to roam across his back.

He groaned into her ear when she ran her nails teasingly down his spine before tracing the bumps of his ribs. They were dry-humping like they were teenagers, and he dug his fingers into the soft sand before kissing her again. He cupped her breast and grunted impatiently at the cloth barrier.

He shook the sand off his fingers and slid his hand under her shirt. She wore a sports bra, and he teased her nipple through the cotton before reaching for the band of the bra. He paused to check in with her, lifting his head to study her face.

Her eyes were glowing, and she was biting her bottom lip compulsively. She dug her nails into his waist. "Human, don't stop."

"Just wanted to make sure," he said before pressing a kiss against her mouth.

She scowled up at him, and he grunted in surprise when she reared up and flipped him over. He was on his back in the sand again, with Kaida lying on top of him before he knew what had happened.

"Jesus, you're fast and strong."

"I told you I was," she said as she lifted his shirt to expose his chest. He groaned when she kissed across his sternum. Her dark hair was in a ponytail, and the ends brushed against his ribcage like soft feathers as she licked around one flat nipple.

"Fuck!" He gripped the back of her head.

"You don't have to ask permission to touch my tits, human," she said with an impish grin. "You shouldn't expect me to ask permission to touch your dick."

She sat up and ground her pussy against his dick before tracing her finger around his belly button. "Or is that what you want? Do you want me to ask permission before I," her finger trailed down his zipper, "touch or suck or fuck your cock?"

She popped the button on his jeans and pulled down the zipper before sliding her hand under the band of his briefs. Her hand wrapped around his dick, and he groaned, his pelvis jumping and his hands squeezing her hips compulsively.

She leaned over him, a playful smile on her lips as her hand – her warm, incredibly soft hand – stroked his dick with long and lazy pulls.

"Well, human? Do I need to ask permission to take what is mine?"

He shook his head, pleasure drenching his entire system as Kaida ran her thumb through the precum that had collected at the tip of his dick. "Nope. It's all yours whenever you want it."

"Good." She rubbed a little harder. "Your dick is an impressive size. I expected a human to have a small dick."

"Glad I could surprise you." He reached for her breasts again, cupping their heavy weight through her shirt.

"Would you like to see my tits?" she asked. "Touch them? Suck on my nipples?"

"Yes, please," he said with a cheeky grin.

She laughed. "Then I guess -"

Her body froze, and she cocked her head, inhaling deeply before studying the path that led into the woods. "The boys are coming."

"Fuck," he muttered as she jumped off of him. He staggered to his feet, zipping up and buttoning his jeans as she straightened her shirt.

He could hear Tyler and Corey laughing and talking, and he grabbed Kaida's arm when she moved away from him. "What night works best for our date?"

"I won, human. There will be no date."

He grinned at her. "It was a tie at best. What about Tuesday night? I know a great restaurant on the west side. Say around seven?"

She glanced at the woods, and he tried to keep a neutral look on his face. If she said no again, he would have to ignore their obvious attraction and let it go. He wasn't into hounding a woman for a date, no matter how much he was into her.

"Seven-thirty," she said.

He wanted to do something idiotic, like fist pumping the air. Instead, he nodded calmly and said, "Seven thirty. I'll text you the restaurant address."

CHAPTER 13

"Thanks for driving me into the city, Kaida." Sika reached across and patted her arm. "Jarvis couldn't get away from work, and I really wanted to finish picking up everything we needed for the hatchling."

"It's no problem." Kaida turned left and headed for the outskirts of the city. They were close to Bren's apartment, and a little trickle of anticipation settled in her belly.

She hadn't told Sika about her date with Bren tonight. She wanted to, but her worry that Sika would accidentally tell the others in the clan kept her mouth shut about it.

"Hey, Kaida?"

"Hmm?" She made another left.

"Jarvis wants to join Avena's clan."

Kaida jerked, making the car swerve a little on the road. "What?"

"He's been talking about it for a while," Sika said.

"But Avena's clan is four hours away."

"I know. But it's still the closest clan to us."

Kaida stopped at a red light and stared at her best friend. "Why?"

"They're more progressive. Jarvis was there last year for a couple of weeks, remember?"

"Yes," Kaida said.

"Well, he and Norven became pretty good friends, and you know that Norven is on the council. He told Jarvis they were considering allowing some of their clan members to start working with and around humans and other shifters."

"You're kidding me." Kaida's mouth dropped open.

"I'm not. Norven talked to Jarvis last week and said they were close to convincing Avena it was the right thing to do. Once Avena is on board, the rest of the clan will follow. They do what their high elder tells them."

"I know, but... it's dangerous, Sika. If other shifters discover that we haven't gone extinct..."

"We *are* going extinct," Sika said.

The car behind them honked impatiently, and Kaida waved apologetically before driving through the green light.

"We're dying out, Kaida. You know that as well as I do. We need to change the old ways before it's too late."

"It might already be too late," Kaida said.

Sika looked out the window, her hand rubbing her belly. "Maybe."

"Cadmus would be open to changing our old ways," Kaida said.

Sika laughed. "He may be, but the rest of the council is not. Even if he demanded we change, the discord between him and the council would tear our clan apart. The council of elders for Avena's clan are all on board with the change."

"If you leave..." Kaida swallowed the lump in her throat.

Sika smiled sadly at her. "I will miss you terribly, my friend. But perhaps you could consider joining Avena's clan as well. I know the old ways do not sit well with you either."

"I can't leave Gram, and she will never leave our clan."

"I know. It was worth a shot."

Kaida smiled at her. "You are right. Things need to change, and perhaps Cadmus will convince the other council members of it someday."

"Perhaps," Sika said. "But someday will probably be too late. We need to start mating with other shifters and humans now if we want to survive."

Kaida stared at her in shock. "Mating with humans? Have you lost your mind, Sika?"

She shook her head. "No."

"A human woman would not be able to bear a dragon child."

"You don't know that," Sika said. "No one will know until it happens."

"It would kill her."

"Again, we don't know that," Sika said. "Humans are stronger than we think, Kaida."

An image of Bren surfaced in Kaida's mind. He hadn't been nearly as easy to defeat in their mock fight the other day as she thought he would be. Sika could be right, but –

"Kaida?"

Sika's voice had changed, and the scent of her fear filled the car. Kaida glanced at her. "What's wrong?"

"I – my water just broke."

Kaida dropped her gaze to Sika's lap. The crotch of her pants was wet, and Kaida muttered a curse under her breath. "All right, do not worry. We'll be home soon and -"

Sika shrieked, her hand clamping down on her belly.

"Sika!"

Kaida pulled over to the side of the road and grabbed Sika's hand. The dragoness squeezed it so tightly, Kaida thought her bones might crack. "What is it?"

"The hatchling is coming," Sika groaned.

"What? Right now?"

"Yes! Right now!" Smoke drifted from Sika's nose, and she frantically rolled down the window before blowing a puff of flame out into the cool air.

"You have to hold it," Kaida said. "We can't go to the hospital, and it's an hour before we get home."

"I can't hold it!" Sika shouted. "It's not like I have to pee, Kaida! The hatchling is coming! I need to push."

"Fuck! Don't push!" Kaida said as Sika moaned in pain again. "Is that another contraction already?"

"Yes," Sika hissed before blowing more flame out the window. "Help me, Kaida. Please."

Shit! What did she do?

Call Bren.

She winced when Sika squeezed her hand again.

"Kaida, I need a hospital," Sika said. "I am not having my hatchling on the side of the road."

"We can't take you to the hospital, honey. You know that. The baby will be born with scales, and its first breaths are smoke and flame. If the doctor sees that…"

"Fuck!" Sika shouted. "This cannot be happening." She started to cry. "I want Jarvis. Please, Kaida, I want Jarvis."

Call Bren.

They were close to Bren's apartment. If he was home, she could take Sika there. It would mean exposing their secret to Bren, but what choice did she have?

"Hang on, Sika. I have an idea." She grabbed her phone and called Bren, her stomach in knots and her pulse racing.

BREN'S STOMACH DID A DIP AND DIVE WHEN HE SAW WHO WAS calling. He'd been jittery and nervous since he woke up this morning, and while it was embarrassing at his age to be this excited about a first date, he couldn't contain it. Seeing Kaida's name on his phone screen only increased his anticipation.

Don't get too excited, buddy. She's probably calling to cancel.

Hoping that wasn't the case, he hit the answer button on the steering wheel. "Hey, Kaida, what's up?"

"Bren, are you at home?"

Kaida's voice was uncharacteristically shrill.

"No, but I'm close to home," he said. "What's wrong?"

"Shit. How close?"

"Five minutes," he said. "What's going on?"

"Are you working, or can you meet me at your place?"

"Technically, I'm working, but can meet you at my apartment."

There was a muffled groan of pain in the background, and Bren's hands tightened on the steering wheel. "What was that?"

"Sika," Kaida said. "It's okay, honey. Hold on. We're almost at Bren's place. Bren, please… can you meet us there?"

"I'm on my way."

"Thank you." She disconnected the call, and Bren flipped his lights on and stepped on the gas. Thanks to the lights, he made it to his apartment in three minutes instead of five. Kaida was parking in the visitor parking lot, and he parked in his spot and jogged over to her car as she opened the passenger door.

"Kaida, what's wrong?"

"Sika isn't feeling well," Kaida said as she helped her pregnant friend from the car. "Do you mind if she rests at your place for a few minutes?"

"Uh, sure, that's fine."

Kaida put her arm around Sika's waist and guided her

toward the front door of his apartment building. The woman was sweating profusely, and her face was pale.

"You sure she shouldn't go to the hospital?" Bren opened the door, and Kaida and Sika followed him to the elevator.

"I'm sure," Kaida said. Her voice was still on the shrill side, and she darted nervous glances at Sika as they rode the elevator to Bren's floor. He opened his front door, and Kaida practically dragged Sika into his apartment.

He shut the door and followed the two women down the hallway. Moving quickly, Kaida got Sika to his spare bedroom. "She needs to lie down for a few minutes."

She helped Sika stretch out on the bed. Bren studied the wet spot on the crotch of Sika's pants. "Kaida?"

Kaida refused to look at him. Instead, she sat on the bed next to Sika and took her hand. "Deep breaths, Sika. It'll be all right."

"I want Jarvis, please," Sika moaned.

"He's on his way." Still not looking at him, Kaida said, "I called Sika's mate and gave him your address."

"Kaida," Bren said again as Sika shrieked softly and grabbed her stomach.

"Breathe, honey," Kaida said.

"Kaida!"

She finally looked at him, and he gestured at Sika. "She's in labour. She needs a hospital."

"She can't go to the hospital, Bren," Kaida said. "Please trust me on this, okay?"

"Kaida, I'm so hot," Sika moaned.

"I know, sweetheart. Hold on." Kaida jumped up and opened the window. Cold air drifted in, and Sika made another moan.

"It hurts so bad. I want Jarvis."

"He'll be here soon, honey."

"She needs to go to the hospital." Bren stood at the end of the bed. "She can't give birth in my apartment."

"She's not going to give birth in your apartment," Kaida said. "As soon as her mate arrives, we'll take her back to the clan and -"

"Kaida, I have to push!" Sika suddenly shouted. She unbuttoned her pants and shoved them down her thighs.

"Not going to give birth, my ass," Bren said. He pulled his cell phone from his pocket. "I'm calling 9-1-1."

Kaida jumped off the bed and rushed toward him, grabbing his hand and holding her hand over his phone. "Bren, you cannot!"

"I have to," he said. "I don't know shit about birthing babies. Do you?"

Kaida swallowed heavily. "Gram has given me instructions and shown me pictures of how to birth a hatchling."

"Oh, fantastic," Bren said. "You've seen a PowerPoint presentation, so you're more than capable of helping Sika have her baby. Is that what you're saying?"

"She can't go to the hospital," Kaida said as Sika groaned behind them.

"Tell me why," Bren said.

Kaida bit her lip. "I can't. Please trust me. Leave Sika and me in the room, all right? Wait for Jarvis and -"

"No," he said. "Unless you tell me exactly why Sika can't go to the hospital, I call 9-1-1. I know your clan doesn't like humans, but this is an emergency."

"Bren." Kaida stared pleadingly at him, and he shook his head.

"Tell me why she can't go or -"

Sika shrieked in pain, and Kaida whirled around. Bren's jaw dropped when Sika's mouth opened, and flames shot out of her mouth. She sucked in oxygen and blew out another breath of fire.

"Better," she mumbled before collapsing against the bed.

Kaida turned to look at him, her eyes frantic with worry. "Bren, I…"

"I guess I know why she can't go to the hospital," he said.

"I can explain," Kaida said.

"Can you?" He stared wide-eyed at her. "So, when exactly did grizzly bears develop the ability to shoot fucking flames out of their mouths?"

"We're not bear shifters."

"No shit, Sherlock." Bren's legs were rubber, and if it hadn't been for the singed ceiling and the smell of sulphur in the air, he could almost convince himself that the pregnant woman lying in his guest bed wasn't breathing fire. "What are you?"

"Dragons," Kaida said.

He staggered backward, barely noticing when Kaida reached out and grabbed his arm to steady him. "Dragons are extinct, everyone knows that," he said through lips that felt like they'd been given a healthy dose of Novocaine.

"We aren't. We've only pretended to be," Kaida said. "I know this is a shock, but -"

His apartment buzzer went off, a long jolting buzz that made him jump.

"Are you expecting someone?" Kaida stiffened, and her hand squeezed his arm in a tight grip.

"No," he said.

"It's Jarvis," Sika panted. She was still trying to shove her pants down her legs.

"He couldn't have gotten here this quickly," Kaida said. "Honey, it isn't possible."

"He flew," Sika said.

"No," Kaida said as the buzzer went off again. "He wouldn't have, Sika. He knows it's against the rules."

"My mate is here. Let him in!" Sika growled. Bren watched in alarm as her chest glowed through her shirt.

"Stop making her angry," he said. "She'll set my goddamn apartment on fire."

Kaida spun around and ran out of the room. After a moment, Bren followed her. She pressed the button next to the front door. "Hello?"

"Kaida! Let me in!"

Kaida pressed the button and stared frantically at Bren as Sika made another shout of pain.

"Go," he said, "I'll wait for Jarvis."

Kaida ran back to the spare bedroom, and Bren opened his front door. Within less than a minute, a man was opening the door to the stairwell and running down the hallway toward him. He was about Bren's height, with long black hair tied back in a ponytail. Streaks of green ran through his hair, the colour matching the flecks of green in his golden eyes. He was wearing a pair of track pants and nothing else. His bare feet slapped against the wood floor as he pushed past Bren.

"Where is she?" he shouted. "Where is my mate?"

"Down the hallway, first door on the left." Bren closed the door and leaned against it as Jarvis ran toward the spare room. He looked at his phone before shoving it back into his pocket and heading to the bedroom.

He stepped into the room. Kaida had helped Sika remove her pants and underwear and draped a sheet from the linen closet across Sika's lower body. Jarvis, the muscles in his arms bulging, grunted as he pushed the bed across the room toward the wall with the open window. The heat in the room was intense, and Sika moaned again.

"Jarvis, I can't control my flame."

"I know, my love. It's not your fault," he said. He popped the screen and tossed it on the floor before sticking his head out the window and looking around. He smiled at Sika. "Blow your flame out the window, my sweet. Can you do that for me?"

"Yes," Sika groaned.

It was a smart idea, Bren had to give him that. The window faced a narrow alley that wasn't visible from the street.

"It hurts so bad," Sika said.

"I am sorry, Sika," Jarvis said. He climbed onto the bed and gently pushed Sika forward until he sat behind her. She rested against his chest, and he smoothed her hair away from her sweaty face. "I know it hurts, but soon you will be holding our hatchling in your arms."

He glanced at Kaida, who nodded. She was kneeling on the bed between Sika's legs. Taking a deep breath, Bren said, "What can I do?"

"Do you have any fans?" Kaida said. "It will help to cool her."

"Yeah." He hurried out of the room and grabbed the fan from his bedroom and the large one from the storage closet. He plugged them in and aimed the larger one directly at Sika. She moaned when the cool air washed over her, and Jarvis kissed her cheek.

"Better, my love?"

"Yes, I... fuck!" She turned her head and blew another short burst of flame out the open window. "Fuck, it hurts! The hatchling is coming! I have to push!"

Kaida looked under the sheet. "I can see its head. Push, Sika."

Sika turned her head and buried her face in Jarvis's neck

to muffle her scream as she pushed. Panting, she collapsed against Jarvis, her head lolling on his chest.

"Good, my love. You're doing so well," Jarvis said.

She blew out more flame as her body tensed. "There's another contraction starting."

"Push," Kaida said.

Sika pushed again, and Kaida said, "The head is free. Can you give me another big push?"

The heat intensified in the room, and Bren wiped away the sweat that made his eyes sting as Sika pushed again. Her chest glowed bright red, and she blew out another burst of fire before crying out in agony.

"Good, Sika!" Kaida shouted. "Good! Another push!"

"Jarvis!" Sika cried.

"You must push, my love. Right now. Bring our hatchling into the world." Jarvis's voice was calm. He kissed Sika's sweaty cheek. "Push, Sika."

She pushed again, her body straining with the effort, and Kaida shouted, "A towel, Bren. I need a towel!"

He ran for the linen closet, grabbing two large towels. When he returned to the room, he stopped dead in his tracks, staring at the baby that Kaida was holding.

"You have a son," she said to Sika and Jarvis.

Sika started to cry, and Jarvis hugged her tightly. Bren brought the towels over. He couldn't take his eyes off the baby. He was covered in a fine layer of green scales, and as Kaida took a towel from him and wiped the baby clean, his little face scrunched up.

"Step back, Bren," Kaida said.

He stepped back on his still-rubbery legs, the clean towel clenched tightly in his fists as the baby's mouth dropped open. He blew out smoke and a tiny puff of flame.

"Good, little one," Kaida rubbed the baby's scale-covered back, "do it again."

The baby blew out another breath of smoke and fire and then one more before he wailed his first sound.

Sika sobbed loudly, and Kaida held out her hand for the clean towel. Bren handed it to her, and Kaida set the baby on Sika's chest before covering him with the towel. Jarvis and Sika stared at their son, pressing kisses on his face and the top of his head. Kaida glanced at Bren. "I need a sharp and sterilized knife to cut the umbilical cord."

Bren tore his gaze from the baby. "Right. I'll, uh, go boil some water and sterilize a knife."

He backed out of the room and leaned against the wall, his legs shaking as violently as a shed in an earthquake. He'd just seen a dragon being born. A goddamn dragon.

CHAPTER 14

"Are you all right, Bren?" Kaida joined him at the table.

He honestly didn't know how to answer that. He settled on, "I think so."

She took his hand and squeezed it. "I'm sorry."

"How are Sika and the baby?" he asked, linking their fingers when she tried to release his hand.

"Good," she said. "She's tired, but the baby seems healthy, and he is already eating."

"That's good. So, dragon babies are born with scales, huh?"

"Yes. But they'll fall off in a few days," Kaida said.

"Are they always green?"

"No. The colour of the scales indicates what colour our dragon is. Just like the flecks of colour in our eyes and the streaks in our hair."

He made a soft snort. "And here I thought you all bought your contact lenses at the same place. Some detective I am, huh?"

"I'm sorry I lied to you," she said. "But I had to."

"Why don't you reveal yourselves to other shifters?" he asked.

"Honestly? I don't really know. Shifters have believed us to be extinct for as long as I can remember. They thought that even before they revealed themselves to the humans. Even if other shifters believed we still lived, we would never have allowed them to divulge our existence to the humans."

He stared at her silently, and after a moment, she said, "We must remain a secret, Bren. If the humans found out... can I trust you to keep our secret?"

"Are you kidding me?" He sat back in his chair, releasing her hand and running both hands through his hair. "I'll take this to my goddamn grave. If my father knew dragons existed..."

"I am sorry," she said. "I didn't mean to drag you into this, but we were shopping in the city, and Sika went into labour so quickly. There was no time to get her home."

"It's fine. You did what you had to do."

Jarvis walked into the kitchen and sat down next to Kaida.

"How is she?" Kaida asked.

"She and the hatchling are sleeping." Jarvis looked tired but extremely happy. "I have a son, Kaida."

She smiled at the dragon shifter and kissed his cheek. "You do. A beautiful, healthy son."

Jarvis held his hand out to Bren. "Thank you, human. I owe you a great debt for helping my mate and my son."

Bren shook his hand. "Congratulations."

"Can she travel, do you think?" Kaida asked.

"She says she can, but I don't want her to. She is exhausted and sore," Jarvis said.

"You're welcome to stay here for as long as you need," Bren said.

Jarvis smiled gratefully at him. "Thank you, human. We should be able to return to the clan tomorrow, but I know my mate would appreciate some time to recover."

"Do you want a beer?" Bren asked.

Jarvis nodded, and Bren grabbed three beers from the fridge. He opened them and handed a bottle to Jarvis and to Kaida. He raised his bottle. "To a healthy boy."

"A healthy boy," Jarvis and Kaida echoed and clinked their bottles against his.

They drank silently for a few minutes before Kaida said, "Does the clan know?"

"Yes. I called Walter and told him," Jarvis said.

"They must be freaking out," Kaida said.

"I had no choice. You know how everyone is on pins and needles waiting for the hatchling. They would have thought the worst if Sika and I didn't return tonight. I assured them the human would keep our secret," Jarvis said.

"Did they believe you?" Kaida glanced nervously at Bren.

"I think so."

"You think so, or you know so?" This time, there was no denying the anxiety in Kaida's voice.

"What's wrong?" Bren said.

Kaida shook her head. "Nothing. Everything's fine."

Bren stared at her in disbelief. Smiling faintly at him, Kaida turned back to Jarvis. "How did you get here so quickly?"

"You know how." Jarvis took two big swallows of his beer.

"That was a terrible risk, Jarvis," Kaida said.

"I had no choice. My mate needed me. Besides, it was overcast today. I flew above the clouds until I reached the human's home."

"You may have been seen," Kaida said.

"Wait, are you telling me you changed into your dragon form and flew here?" Bren said.

"I did," Jarvis said.

"It's forbidden," Kaida said. "We are only allowed to fly at night and only at certain times." She squeezed Jarvis' hand. "You will be banished if they find out, Jarvis."

"Only if they find out. I'm not planning on telling them. Are you?"

She shook her head and stared at Bren, who immediately said, "My lips are sealed."

"Are you returning to the clan tonight?" Jarvis asked.

Kaida hesitated. "I thought I would stay. In case Sika needed me. If that's all right with you, Bren?"

"Mi casa es su casa," he said. "Although we might have to order out for dinner, I wasn't planning on eating at home tonight and don't have any groceries in the house."

Kaida flushed as Jarvis finished his beer and stood. "I'm going to sit with Sika and the hatchling. Thank you again – both of you."

He leaned down and kissed the top of Kaida's head before shaking Bren's hand again. When he was gone, Kaida said, "I'm sorry about our date tonight."

"No big deal. We can reschedule."

She stared at him in surprise. "You still want to go on a date? Even after knowing what I am?"

"Yes."

"Why?"

"Why not?" he said.

"You do realize how dangerous I am to you, right?"

"I'm tougher than I look, remember?"

"Bren, I'm a dragon."

"Yep, I know." He drank another sip of beer as she stared at him in frustration.

"I could accidentally hurt you when we're in bed together," she said.

"Whoa, what's all this 'in bed' talk?" he said with a grin. "I don't care what you've heard about us humans. I don't put out on the first date, lady."

She didn't smile at his humour. "Bren, this isn't a joke. I could hurt you."

"How?" he said. "Explain to me how you could hurt me while we're having sex because unless you shift to your dragon form while we're banging, I don't -"

"Sometimes I lose control of my flame when I'm having an orgasm," she said in a low voice. "What if that happened? Is sex with me worth the risk of being burned alive?"

"I am pretty attracted to you," he said.

"Bren, be serious," she said.

He leaned forward. "Look, I don't think you'll hurt me. I think you'll have better control than you believe you will. Worse comes to worse, we make sure the bed is near an open window. If you need to let loose with a little fire, you can aim it toward the window. Problem solved."

She sighed and rubbed at her forehead. "It isn't that simple, human."

"It is," he said.

"I want to sleep with you," she said. "You know I do. Hell, every time I touch you, I lose my damn mind and start to think we could have sex, that everything will be fine. But if I hurt you, I couldn't live with myself."

"You won't hurt me," he said.

She closed her eyes and rubbed her forehead again. "You don't know that. And I can't take that risk."

"You should be sleeping." Bren was sitting at the kitchen table when she snuck quietly into the room. The light over the stove was on, casting a dim glow over his face. He looked tired and depressed, and she sat in the chair next to him, the guilt she felt worsening.

"I can't sleep knowing that you're sleeping on the couch in your own damn place," she said. "Let's trade spots."

"I told you before," he said. "I'm not making you sleep on the couch. You're my guest. You can have my bed."

"It's after midnight, and you look exhausted," she said.

He picked at a chip in the handle of the mug that sat in front of him. "I'll be fine."

"Are you always this stubborn?" she asked.

"Yes."

His blunt honesty made her smile. "Good to know. We could share the bed in a strictly platonic kind of way."

He stared at her, and she blushed. "Sorry. Forget it, that was a stupid suggestion and -"

"It wasn't." He stood up and set the mug in the sink before holding his hand out. "Let's go to bed."

"Are you sure?"

He nodded, squeezing her hand when she took his. "I'm positive. Honestly, I'm too tired and too thrown by the realization that dragons exist to be up for sex anyway. I'll behave, I promise."

"I'm not worried about that," she said in a low voice as they crept past the guest room. "I promise I won't do anything to you either."

He shut the bedroom door behind them and hesitated at the side of the bed. "Do you mind if I lose the t-shirt?"

She shook her head, ignoring her dragon's purring when Bren shucked his shirt and left it on the floor. He had a great body. An amazing body, actually, and she was itching to touch the light layer of hair that covered his chest. He was still wearing a pair of sleep pants, and for a moment, she hoped he would also lose them.

She berated herself internally as Bren climbed into the bed. For God's sake, she had just told him she wouldn't do anything to him.

She slid into the bed. His bed was queen-sized, big enough that there was an empty space between their bodies. That was a good thing, she told herself.

"Thank you for loaning me a shirt to sleep in." She smoothed his shirt down as she turned to face him.

"No problem." He was lying on his back, staring at the ceiling with his arms tucked under his head.

"*Are* you all right, Bren?" she asked.

"I will be. It's just a lot to… absorb," he said.

She stared worriedly at him, wondering if there was anything she could say or do to help him.

"Can I ask you a question?"

"Of course," she said.

"How do you guys survive? I mean, money wise. None of you work in the city, right?"

"Dragons have done very well with investments and stock," she said. "Each clan has its financial person who manages the clan's investments. The money we earn is split between the clan members depending on family size. But, if a dragon wants to earn money for additional things, they can get a job."

"Working online, I assume," Bren said.

"Yes. Jarvis and a few other clan members work in graphic design. Sika does editing and proofing of papers for university students. One of our council elders, Leia, has a surprisingly lucrative business designing and selling cross-stitch patterns. Another clan member, Finn, turned his hobby of making leather bracelets and other accessories into a successful small business."

"Interesting," Bren said.

"Material possessions and wealth matter very little to dragons."

"So, no hidden stashes of gold under mountains, huh?"

She was extremely relieved to see the small smile on his face as he turned on his side to face her.

"No, dragons liking gold is a myth created by humans. We live rather simply compared to most shifters and humans."

"How many dragons are in your clan?" Bren asked.

"We're a smaller clan with only twenty-five – twenty-six now – members."

"Are there other clans close to yours?"

"The closest one is about four hours from here. Their high elder is Avena, and they have almost seventy-five members."

"Have you met any of them before?" he asked.

"Yes. Many times. We have celebrations with them, and occasionally, clan members will live with another clan for a time. Before Sika and Jarvis were mated, Jarvis spent two weeks with the Avena clan. Other times, the council members will get together to discuss changes in how the clans are run or for other reasons."

She suppressed her shudder. The last time Avena's council had been here was to destroy one of their clan members. A dragon who had been banished, gone insane, and was stalking Bishop's human mate.

"You okay?" Bren asked.

She nodded, a little thrown by how easily the human could read her emotions.

"So, the clans are just big happy families."

She smiled. "We have disagreements like all families, but yes, it's an apt description."

There was silence for a few minutes. The only sound was the muted hum of the occasional car driving on the street below them. She was tired and knew Bren was, too, but she enjoyed the warm intimacy of lying in his bed in the dark and talking with him.

"Thank you again for allowing Sika and Jarvis to spend the night," she said.

"Of course," he said. "They're welcome to stay for longer. I'm not sure they should travel even tomorrow."

"They'll need to," Kaida said. "The clan will want to see the hatchling, and we'll feel the pull for our clan by tomorrow."

"What do you mean?" he asked.

"That morning after the love potion mess, when I left so abruptly," Kaida said, "was not only because I was embarrassed. I needed to be with my clan again. Dragons can only be separated from their clans for so long before they go…"

"Go what?" Bren asked.

"Insane."

"Are you kidding?"

She shook her head. "I am not. Our dragons will go crazy if we spend too much time away from our clans."

"How long can you be away from them?"

"It varies from dragon to dragon, but most cannot go more than forty-eight hours. Insanity sets in, and we," she hesitated, knowing how bad it would sound to the human.

"What?" Bren said.

"We kill ourselves."

"Holy fuck." He sat up on one elbow and stared directly at her. "That's a little extreme, don't you think?"

"It is our way. We cannot be separated from our clans.

Once the love potion no longer affected me, I needed to be with my clan again. My embarrassment at what I had done drove my need to be with my clan higher. Does that make sense?"

"Yes," he said. "Now I feel even worse about what happened."

"Don't," she said. "It wasn't your fault."

He settled back on his side, punching the pillow into a more comfortable position. Kaida studied his mouth and the strong line of his jaw, feeling a warmth and a need pooling in her belly.

Give me the human. Please?

She ignored her dragon's pleading. She had told Bren she wouldn't do anything to him and intended to keep that promise. It didn't matter how tempting she found his mouth or his half-naked body.

"Wait," Bren suddenly said, "you said earlier that Jarvis lived with that other clan for two weeks. How is that possible?"

"It doesn't necessarily have to be the clan you grew up with," Kaida said. "As long as your dragon is happy and feels accepted by the other clan members, being with a new clan is as soothing as your old one. Does that make sense?"

"As much as it *can* make sense."

She smiled a little. "Dragon ways are strange, I know."

"How do you go on vacation?" Bren asked.

Her smile widened. "If a dragon wants to vacation, we go in small groups. Last year, Gram and I went to Hawaii with Jarvis, Sika, Bones and Javee. Gram and I didn't spend every moment of our vacation with the others, but we had dinner together every evening. Our clan was smaller, but still our clan and our dragons were soothed. Do you understand?"

"Yes. What did you mean when you told Jarvis he would

be banished if the others learned he changed to his dragon form?"

She swallowed hard. "It's getting late, Bren. We should get some sleep."

"Tell me, Kaida."

She didn't want to. Christ, how she didn't want to, but from how Bren looked at her, he wouldn't be satisfied until she explained it. Her stomach churning, she said, "When a dragon breaks the clan's rules, they are punished. Sometimes, that punishment is banishment from the clan."

"Banishment from the clan," Bren repeated.

"Yes. The dragon is driven from the clan and not allowed to return."

"But you said that if a dragon is away from its clan for more than forty-eight hours, they'll go crazy and…"

He trailed off before sitting up. "Are you fucking kidding me?"

She sat up and hugged her knees to her chest. "I know how it sounds, Bren, but -"

"You know how it sounds?" He stared at her. "You banish them knowing that it's a death sentence."

"We do," she said. "The clans' elders are serious about keeping our existence a secret. Knowing we'll be banished for breaking that rule keeps us in line.

He snorted angrily. "I guess it's not a big, happy family after all."

She reached out and took his hand, more thankful than she could say when he didn't pull away. "It is a barbaric and outdated punishment that some dragons are beginning to question."

"Oh good," he said sarcastically, "it's nice to know that they're *beginning* to question it."

"Banishment doesn't happen very often," she said. "And it

has never happened in our clan. When Bishop learned of our existence, I should have been banished but wasn't."

"You were a kid," he said.

"I was a yearling and old enough to know better."

"So why weren't you banished?"

"Cadmus, the high elder of our clan, is… more lenient than some. It's why I brought Tyler and Corey back to our clan when the fox was injured. I knew that Cadmus would not banish me for it. I did not expect he would agree to allow me to train Tyler and Corey."

"Why did he?"

"I don't know," she said. "The council voted against it, but Cadmus has the power to overrule their decision, and he did."

"Does he do that often?"

"Only once before that I know of," she said.

"When you brought Bishop to the clan," he said.

She looked away. "Yes. The council voted to banish me. Cadmus said no."

"Jesus." Bren swiped his free hand through his hair. "Dragon clans are fucked up."

"They aren't," she said. "We are very protective of each other. Cadmus knows what we're doing is wrong, and he's been speaking with the other clan councils for years to try to change their minds. But they're afraid. If the humans discovered we existed, their fear of us could lead to war between us, Bren."

He didn't reply and she squeezed his hand. "The humans would not win that war."

"I know," he said.

He stared at their clasped hands for almost a minute before lifting his head to study her. A trickle of unease went down her back at the look on his face. "Does Ava know you're a dragon?"

"Yes, as does Mal and Kat and their mates," she said.

"Why?" he asked.

She looked away. "I spend time with Bishop. It would have been difficult to keep it a secret from his other friends."

"Is that right?" he said.

"Yes." Fuck, she hated lying to Bren. It made her feel awful and like she was betraying him somehow.

He let go of her hand, and she immediately missed the touch of his warm skin. "A year or so ago, I had a murder case. A woman who worked as an emergency nurse was being stalked by one of her patients."

"Bren -"

"That's how I met Ava. She was the nurse being stalked. She and her friend were out one night, and they were attacked. The friend – Brody – was killed. Do you know how he died, Kaida?"

He didn't wait for her reply. "He was burned to a crisp. Nothing but ash and fragments of bone. The medical examiner had never seen anything like it. I never caught the guy who did it. He just… stopped stalking Ava. Seemed a little odd to me, but what could I do? The case went cold, and Brody's murderer was never punished. There was no justice for his death."

"There was," she whispered.

He gently grasped her chin, lifting it until she stared at him. "The stalker that was after Ava. He was a dragon, wasn't he?"

"Yes. He belonged to Avena's clan. He believed a female in the clan was his mate even though she was mated to another. He murdered her mate. Avena and the rest of the council banished him. Only something went wrong. He went mad, but he didn't kill himself. He came to this city, discovered Ava, and decided she was his mate. He went after her a few times, but Bishop and Kat and Mal – they stopped him."

"What happened to him?" Bren asked.

"Once we realized it was a rogue dragon and which clan he belonged to, Avena and the others came to the city to destroy him. Only, he had gone after Ava again and was successful this time."

"Holy shit," Bren said.

"He took her into the woods, tried to hide her, but…" she hesitated, "we can sense the other members of our clan. If we concentrate hard enough, our dragons can find each other. His clan council searched for him. They found him and…"

"And killed him," he said.

"They had no choice, Bren. He had gone mad. He'd killed a dragon and a human, and he would have hurt Ava."

Bren released her chin and ran both hands through his hair. "Has something like this ever happened before? A dragon going mad but not killing themselves?"

"Never," she said. "But it has strengthened Cadmus's belief that banishing dragons from their clan is wrong."

"You think?" he spat.

She flinched, and he immediately reached out and took her hand again. "I'm sorry. This is a lot to take in, and I…"

"I know," Kaida said. She stared at their clasped hands as silence fell between them. After a few minutes, she said, "We should get some rest."

"Yeah." He released her hand and laid down, turning over until his back was facing her.

Her dragon growled unhappily, and she tried to soothe it. Truthfully, she was feeling rather miserable herself. Bren was disgusted by her and her clan, and there was nothing she could say or do to fix it. What they did was terrible, and there was no justification for it.

You have bigger issues than Bren no longer being into you.

She wanted to keep ignoring her inner voice, but it had grown steadily louder all evening and would no longer be ignored.

They will kill Bren when they find out he knows dragons exist. The council will vote, and they will vote to destroy him. It's bad enough that he's human, but his father...

She laid down, her pulse jumping and thudding and her dragon growling repeatedly. Bren had done them a favour by allowing Sika to give birth in his home. She would explain that to the council, and they would see they owed him a debt. If the hatchling had been born on the side of the road in plain sight of any human driving by...who knew what would have happened?

She would explain that to the council, and they would let Bren live. They had to.

And if they don't? If they vote to burn him alive? Her inner voice whispered.

Her dragon snarled with an intense fury that Kaida had never felt before.

We will burn them alive. If they go anywhere near our mate, we will set them ablaze with our flame.

Sick to her stomach, her heart knocking against her ribcage, Kaida stared into the darkness as her dragon growled and hissed.

CHAPTER 15

"Where is the hatchling?"

Kaida glared at Drago as he pushed past her. "What are you doing here?"

"What do you think?" he growled. "Is the human's stupidity catching? Is that why you're acting so fucking brain dead?"

"Watch your mouth." Bren joined them in the hallway, and Kaida automatically stepped in front of him. Drago bared his teeth at him.

"Stay out of it, human."

"This is my home, and you'll treat Kaida respectfully or leave," Bren said.

There was steel in his voice, and Kaida couldn't help but feel a trickle of pride mixed with lust.

Our mate is brave, her dragon crowed happily.

"You dare to speak to me that way?" Drago said.

"I repeat – my home. Mind your manners or leave," Bren said.

"Do not test my patience, human. I am in no -"

"Enough, Drago." Bones pushed past him, and Kaida

breathed a sigh of relief at the sight of the large dragon. Not even Drago would dare to challenge Bones, no matter how pissed he was. "Hey, Kaida."

"Hi," she said.

Bones held his hand out to Bren. "Hello, human. My name is Bones."

Bren shook his hand. "Nice to meet you. I'm Bren."

"Thank you for helping us with the hatchling. We are in your debt."

"We are not," Drago snarled. "Do not speak so foolishly."

"Watch your tongue, Drago," Bones growled without looking at him.

"Bones!" Jarvis came striding down the hallway, and he and Bones hugged roughly.

"Congratulations, Jarvis," Bones said.

Jarvis grinned at him. "I have a son."

"I heard." Bones clapped him on the back. "May I see the hatchling?"

"Of course." Jarvis glanced at Drago. "Come, Drago, meet my son."

Even Drago couldn't resist the lure of the hatchling. He followed Jarvis and Bones down the hallway. Kaida released her breath in a low rush before leaning against the wall. Bren eyed her carefully. "You okay?"

"Fine," she said. She wasn't, not by a long run, but she made herself smile at Bren. "You?"

"Was that guy's name really Drago?"

She nodded, confused when Bren leaned against the wall beside her and laughed. The sound was low and warm, and she felt a pull of longing in her belly as he laughed again. "Seriously? Drago is his name?"

"Yes, why?" She wasn't sure what was so funny.

"He's a dragon, and his name is Drago. You don't see why that's funny?"

"Not really. It's a family name," she said.

He laughed again, and she couldn't help but smile at him. "I like your laugh."

"Thank you." He moved closer and pressed a quick kiss against her mouth. Her dragon purred loudly, the sound slipping out of her mouth. He cocked his head at her. "There's that almost a purr again."

She cleared her throat. "It's not purring."

He traced his finger along her jawline, and her dragon purred again, louder and rougher.

"That was definitely a sort of purr," he said in a low voice. He was staring at her, his light blue eyes dark with need, and she arched her body toward him when he ran his finger down her throat and along the neckline of her shirt.

She absolutely could not do this, not with Drago and Bones in the apartment. So why was she leaning toward him? Why was she parting her lips and pressing them against Bren's?

He kissed her gently at first, the tip of his tongue sliding across her upper lip. She put her arm around his waist, drawing him up against her as she deepened the kiss. He sucked on her tongue before releasing her mouth. "Do you know how difficult it was to wake up with you in my bed this morning and not touch you?"

She ran her fingers across his broad chest. "I wanted to touch you too."

"You should have then."

She wanted to take Bren away from here. Go somewhere they wouldn't be interrupted, where her clan mates wouldn't find her, and she could finally take what she wanted and needed.

It's not that simple.

She sighed inwardly. Her inner voice was right. It wasn't that simple. As tempting as it was to fantasize that she and Bren could be together, the truth was – Bren was in terrible danger, and it was all her fault.

Her lust died immediately, and she stepped away from him, crossing her arms over her chest.

"What's wrong?"

"Nothing. I'm sorry. I shouldn't have touched you or kissed you."

"It's my fault," he said. "I kissed you first."

She laughed bitterly. "I wanted you to kiss me."

"Kaida?"

Bones was back and she scrubbed her hand across her mouth guiltily. "Hey. Did you see the hatchling?"

"Yes. He's beautiful. The clan is anxious to see him." If Bones could smell hers and Bren's lust, he didn't acknowledge it. He checked his phone before sliding it back into the pocket of his jeans. "It's almost noon. You've been away from the clan for nearly twenty-four hours. Do you feel all right?"

Surprisingly, she did. She supposed it had something to do with her dragon believing that Bren was her mate. Dragons with their mate could stay away from a clan longer than a single dragon could. "I'm fine."

"Good. Jarvis and Sika are feeling okay as well, but it would be better if they returned to the clan today. I spoke with Sika, and she said she could travel."

"Are you sure?" Bren said. "Maybe they should stay another day." He glanced at Kaida. "You should stay as well to help with the baby."

Bones studied her, and then Bren and Kaida licked her suddenly dry lips. After a moment, Bones said, "It would be better if you returned today. All of you."

"You're right," she said.

She could smell Bren's disappointment, but it was better for him – *safer* for him – if they left. The sooner she spoke to Cadmus and the rest of the council, the better chance she had to convince them that going to Bren and revealing their secret was necessary. She would make them understand that Bren wasn't a danger to them, despite who his father was.

If they touch my mate, I will destroy them, her dragon growled.

"We should return to our clan," she said to Bren. "Thank you for your help. I'll text you later about Tyler and Corey's training."

"Sure," he said.

They all turned when they heard Jarvis' voice. "Walk slowly, Sika. There is no need to rush."

"Jarvis, I'm fine," Sika said with a soft laugh. Jarvis held her arm, and she smiled at him. "My healing is starting to kick in, and I'm not nearly as sore."

"You should still be careful," he said.

Drago walked behind them, the hatchling cradled in his arms. He stared at the baby in reverent awe as Sika stopped in front of Bren.

"Thank you, human," she said with a sincere smile. "I am so grateful for your help."

"You're welcome, Sika," Bren said. "Congratulations on your son. He's beautiful."

Sika glanced at the baby, her smile widening. "He is, isn't he? You will have to come for his naming ceremony."

"Sika," Drago said with a frown, "do not speak such nonsense."

"Hush, Drago," Sika said and then hugged Bren.

He returned her hug, smiling at her when she kissed his cheek. "Thank you again, Bren."

Jarvis held out his hand. Bren shook it, and Jarvis clapped him on the back. "I will not forget my debt to you, human."

He reached for the hatchling, and Drago said, "Perhaps I should carry him to the car so you can assist Sika."

Jarvis grinned. "That's very kind of you, Drago."

Sika covered the baby's head and face with the light blanket. "Did you remember the car seat, Drago?"

"Yes. It's in the car." Drago followed Jarvis and Sika out of the apartment, gazing down at the baby even though he was completely covered.

"Are you ready, Bones?" Kaida didn't want to leave Bren, but she wanted to go before Bones said what she feared he might say.

"Yes." He turned to Bren. "The council wishes to speak with you, human."

Kaida's stomach dropped to her feet, and her dragon growled protectively. She calmed it as Bren said, "All right. When?"

"Tonight," Bones said. "Seven o'clock."

"Didn't you say you had plans?" Kaida said to Bren.

"It must be tonight, Kaida," Bones said.

"It doesn't *have* to be," she replied. "The council can wait a day or two."

"They won't," Bones said.

Her mouth bone dry, her fear making it hard to think straight, she said, "I'll talk to them, I'll -"

"It's fine," Bren said. "I can speak with them tonight."

Kaida's dread grew as Bones said, "Tonight, then. Goodbye, human."

"Bye." Bren was still staring at her, and she tried to smile at him, but her fear overwhelmed her.

"Perhaps I should stay with Bren for the day," she said. "Tell the council I'll return with the human tonight and -"

"No," Bones said. "You need to return, Kaida."

Her dragon growled at him, and smoke drifted from her nostrils.

Enough! she said to her dragon. *You can't challenge him.*

I can and I will, her dragon growled.

Holy fuck. Her dragon really had gone mad. She'd never defeat Bones in a challenge. His dragon was too large and too powerful.

Bones stared at her, waiting patiently to see if she dared challenge him. She pushed down her dragon and cleared her throat, tasting smoke in her mouth.

"Ready?" Bones asked.

She made herself smile at Bren. "I'll see you later, all right?"

"All right."

Ignoring her urge to kiss Bren, she followed Bones out of the apartment, shutting the door behind her.

"Bones," she said, "the council -"

"They will vote to kill the human," Bones said. "You know they will."

"He helped us," she said as they descended the stairs. "Surely they will show him mercy."

Bones shook his head. "He is the son of a powerful man who hates shifters."

"Bren is nothing like his father."

"The council will not see it that way."

"Cadmus will overrule it if they vote to burn him," she said.

Bones grabbed her arm before she could open the lobby door. "Kaida, listen to me. Do not believe that Cadmus's affection for you will save the human. This is bad, do you hear me? Really bad. They will kill him, and they will do it tonight."

Her dragon pushed forward and growled, "I will destroy them if they try."

Bones grunted in surprise, his dragon making a low growl. "You can't stop them."

"I will." Her dragon was so angry that her voice was barely understandable, but Bones made another surprised grunt.

"Are you in love with the human?"

"No, of course not," she said. "But I won't stand by and watch a good man lose his life. Not after he helped us. Many more humans would have discovered Sika and her hatchling if not for Bren."

"I know, but the council will not see it that way."

"I won't let them kill him," she repeated.

"You can't stop them, I don't care how pissed your dragon is," Bones said. "But there may be another way."

"What do you mean?"

He opened the lobby door and ushered her into the cool air. "We will speak with Javee when we return to the clan."

"HEY, MATTHEWS!"

Bren looked up from his computer. Jeremy was leaning against the cubicle wall, a pita wrap in one hand and a bottle of water in the other.

"What's up?"

"A hot chick at the front desk is looking for you."

"Thanks. I'll be right there." He turned back to his computer screen.

"She's seriously hot," Jeremy said. "Tits like you wouldn't believe, and these," he waved the pita in the air, "crazy looking eyes. They're like gold coloured with blue dots."

Bren stood up so abruptly that he nearly knocked Jeremy's waving pita out of his hand. What was Kaida doing here? Even though he'd just seen her this morning, part of him was thrilled to see her again. The other part was deeply uneasy. Kaida avoided humans and shifters as much as possible. To have her show up at the precinct couldn't be good news.

As Jeremy walked away, Bren hurried past the maze of cubicles and out to the front desk. The reception area of the precinct was full of people. Rodrigues, the admitting clerk, looked deeply annoyed and exhausted as he dealt with a man shouting indignantly about a parking ticket.

Kaida was standing near the door. He had an idea she was trying to blend in, but with her height, the blue streaks in her hair and her – his palms went a little sweaty – incredibly striking looks, blending in was a pipe dream. Bren scooted past a woman in a wheelchair and a man holding a wailing toddler.

"Kaida, hey. How are you?"

"Good."

She didn't look good. She looked pale and sick to her stomach.

"Are you feeling all right?" he asked.

"Fine. I'm sorry to come by without texting first."

"It's not a problem," he said.

She crossed her arms over her torso before studying the wailing toddler. "Is there somewhere private we can talk?"

"Sure. Follow me." He led her out of the reception area and past the maze of cubicles to one of the interview rooms. "Have a seat."

She sat down, her foot tapping the floor and her fingers pulling compulsively at the bottom of her leather jacket. He sat beside her and took her hand, stopping the frantic motion.

"Tell me what's wrong," he said.

She met his gaze, and for the first time, he could see how truly upset she was. His stomach tightened, and the hair on the back of his neck stood up. Not just upset – she looked afraid.

"Kaida? What is it?"

"You have to leave," she said.

"What do you mean?"

She pulled her hand out of his and reached into the inside pocket of her jacket. He stared mutely at the passport and envelope she held out to him. "What is this?"

She pressed them into his hands, and he flipped open the passport, shock making his body go still as he stared at his picture. He studied the name and the information next to it before looking up at her. "Richard Simpson? Why are you giving me a passport with my picture and the name Richard Simpson? Where did you even get my picture?"

"There's a birth certificate, a social security number, a driver's license for Richard Simpson, and fifty thousand dollars in that envelope. It's enough to get you away from here and start a new life. There's also a piece of paper with a phone number on it. Buy a burner phone, okay? When you have a bank account set up, use the burner phone to text that number with the bank account number. Another fifty grand will be deposited into the account. Once you've done that, burn the piece of paper, destroy the phone, and -"

"Kaida, whoa, stop." He set the passport and the envelope on the table and took her hands. "Take a deep breath and tell me what the hell is going on."

"You have to leave the country, Bren. I'm sorry, but you need to leave and start a new life."

His mouth dropped open, and he sucked in a gulp of air. "Are you kidding me right now?"

She shook her head, her hands tightening around his. They were almost uncomfortably warm, but he didn't let go. As she stared at him, a thin tendril of smoke drifted from her left nostril. "I'm not. You have to leave."

"A new life. With these?" He stared at the passport and envelope. "How the hell did you get these?"

She hesitated, and he squeezed her hand. "How?"

"There's a female in our clan - Javee. She is Bones's mate. She has a particular skill with computers that makes her valuable to certain people. The kind of people who can get these documents with very little notice."

He looked at the passport again. "Is that the picture from my driver's license?"

"Yes, Javee got it."

"How did she... you know what? Never mind. I don't want to know."

"You need to leave, Bren," Kaida repeated.

"Why?"

"It's for your safety. Please trust me."

He barked out harsh laughter. "I'm gonna need a little more than that, Kaida."

She swallowed hard. "The council wants to see you tonight to decide your fate, Bren. Humans cannot know about the dragons."

"I'm aware of that, and I'll tell them I'll keep your secret," Bren said.

"It won't be enough. They're going to vote, and they'll vote against you." More smoke drifted from her nostrils. This time, her hands grew so hot he had no choice but to release them.

She stared at his hands before saying, "I'm sorry. I didn't mean to hurt you."

"It's fine. So, when they vote against me, what does that mean? Death?" His voice sounded remarkably calm, considering his guts were churning so hard they were moving up into his esophagus.

"Yes."

He sat back in his chair, the blood pounding dully in his ears.

"I'm sorry," she said. "I'm so sorry. I should never have brought Sika to you, but I was panicking and I… I'm sorry."

"You brought Tyler to your clan," he said. Anger replaced the shock. "You brought Tyler and Corey to your clan, and if they had discovered you were dragons, Tyler would have been killed. Is that what you're saying? What the fuck were you thinking, Kaida?"

She didn't cringe at the fury in his voice, and a small part of him admired her for it.

"I was confident Tyler wouldn't realize what we were. He is in no danger from my clan if he continues to believe we are bear shifters."

"Did Corey figure it out?"

She hesitated, and he frowned at her. "Did he?"

"Yes."

"Fuck." He ran his hand through his hair. "If he tells Tyler -"

"He won't. Trust me on this, Bren. The fox yearling will keep our secret."

Unable to sit still any longer, Bren stood and paced the interview room. "Did Corey meet with the council?"

"He did," Kaida said slowly. "The council voted to let him live."

The tension eased a little from his shoulders. "All right, that's good news. If they let him live, then -"

"They let him live because he is a shifter," Kaida said. "They have no trust in humans. Especially a human whose father is…"

"A senator hell-bent on destroying shifters," Bren said.

She nodded, and he paced the room again. She picked up the passport and the envelope. "Bren, please, you must go. I know it's difficult, but -"

"Difficult?" He snorted in anger. "Don't, Kaida. If you think I'll leave Tyler, you're insane. I am not packing a bag and leaving my job and my brother and my goddamn life. I'll take my chances with your clan."

"If you die, Tyler will be alone anyway," she said.

"That's your argument?" Bitter laughter shot from his mouth. "Look, say what you want, but I am not running away like a scared little kid."

"Please, Bren." She stood and took his hands again, her face drawn and sorrow written across it. "It's the only way to save you. I can't watch you be burned to death by my clan. Do you understand? I can't. This is all my fault, and I'm so sorry, but I need you to do this. It's the only way."

"It isn't," he said. "I'll convince the council to let me live."

"And if you don't?"

"Maybe Cadmus will overrule their decision."

"We can't count on that." He could see her fear beginning to turn to anger. "I could make you leave."

"Oh yeah? You going to knock me out and then carry me away in the night in your dragon form?"

She scowled at him. "This is not a joke."

"Considering I'm the one who might be turned into a human torch by tonight, you can bet your ass I get that it isn't a joke," he said. "But I'm still not leaving Tyler. I will convince the council to let me live. Trust me, Kaida."

"Bren..."

"Trust me," he said. Even though Kaida was the reason he might be burned alive in less than six hours, he still weirdly wanted to pull her into his arms and assure her everything would be fine.

"I can't watch you die," she whispered.

"You won't," he said. "Everything will be fine."

THE CONFIDENCE HE'D HAD EARLIER AT THE PRECINCT WAS long gone. In fact, Bren didn't think he'd ever been this fucking scared in his life. He'd dealt with people who were high on PCP and crazy strong, he'd been involved in shootouts, hell, he had a fucking gun pointed at his head by a guy who could vanish into thin air, but it still didn't compare to the fear rolling through his guts right now.

He parked the SUV beside Kaida's cabin and shut off the vehicle. His hands were shaking, and he took a few deep breaths before grabbing his phone and studying the text from Tyler.

TYLER

Dude, thanks again for dinner. It was nice.
Later, loser.

He stared blankly out the windshield. He'd left work early and arrived at Tyler's school as Tyler finished for the day. He'd taken him for dinner, doing his best to make things seem natural and normal. He must have done an okay job. Tyler hadn't seemed to notice anything was wrong.

Instead of dropping Ty off like he usually did, Bren went

to his father's apartment with him. He had no respect for his father and hadn't for a long time, but he still loved him. If he was going to die tonight, he at least wanted to say goodbye to his father.

But, like so often, his father was in his office and on the phone. He'd waved distractedly at Bren but wouldn't finish the phone call so they could talk. Bren waited around for about half an hour before finally leaving.

He should have said goodbye to Elora but, in the end, couldn't do it. He might have fooled Tyler into thinking everything was fine, but he wouldn't have fooled Elora. He'd been afraid she'd pull the truth from him, and that fear had kept him away from her. Still, she would be pissed he just up and died without notifying her first.

He stared at his phone again before quickly texting Tyler.

BREN

You're welcome. I love you, kid.

The three little dots appeared immediately, and he waited even when Kaida's cabin door opened, and she stepped out on the porch. She wore a long blue cloak, and the moon's glow illuminated her face's paleness.

TYLER

Love u 2

He stared at the message for almost thirty seconds before shoving his phone into his pocket and climbing out of the vehicle. He met Kaida at the bottom of the porch steps. He wasn't sure how it was possible, but she looked worse than he felt. Her eyes were red and puffy, and she looked on the verge of throwing up.

"You okay?" he asked.

She shook her head. "I have never been less okay in my life, Bren."

"I'll convince them," he said with a confidence he didn't feel.

"No, you won't," she sighed.

He'd always admired her bluntness in the past, but now it was like a hard punch to the gut. "Then I guess this is my dead man walking moment."

Her body stiffened, and her eyes glowed bright. Smoke drifted from her nostrils as she cupped his face. Her touch was tender, but the voice that rumbled out of her throat was thick and inhuman and so disconcerting sounding that goosebumps erupted across his flesh, and his balls drew up tight against his body.

"I will not allow them to hurt you."

That thick, gargled voice was even more unnerving because he could hear traces of Kaida in it.

Her hand tightened on his jaw, and then she released him. She waved away the smoke that was almost obscuring her face and grimaced. "I'm sorry."

"That was your dragon, wasn't it," he said.

She hesitated and then nodded.

"Dragons can speak the human language?"

She nodded again, and even though he was most likely about to die, he couldn't help his fascination with the new information. "Can any other shifters do that?"

"No," she said. "It is unique to dragons. Come, they are waiting for us."

He followed her past the other cabins to the largest cabin in the clearing. Light glowed from the windows, and as they climbed the steps, he said. "Whose cabin is this?"

"It's the community cabin," she said. "We eat our meals

together, hold the mating ceremonies here, and the council has monthly meetings here."

They stopped at the door, and she smiled faintly at him. "Do not speak unless spoken to. Keep your answers short and try not to anger any of the clan council. All right?"

"No problem," he muttered.

His heart was threatening to beat its way right out of his chest, and his breath had turned short and shallow. He could feel the pulse throbbing in his temple, and his legs were rubbery. Kaida reached up and cupped the back of his neck, pulling his head down a little so she could rest her forehead against his.

He closed his eyes, breathing in her scent as she kneaded the back of his neck. "Kaida, I…"

Her mouth pressed against his, her lips cold and tasting like fear, before she said, "Be brave, my human… my mate."

CHAPTER 16

T he cabin was warm, brightly lit, and - Bren swallowed hard - filled with dragon shifters. He supposed filled was a bit of an exaggeration. Including the shifters sitting behind the long table at the front of the cabin, there were only about twenty shifters in the spacious main room.

Only? All twenty can burn you to a crisp with a single breath.

The main room had chairs in neat rows with a narrow aisle in the middle. Very aware of the dragons staring at him, he followed Kaida down the aisle toward the table at the front. Bones was sitting in an end chair near the back. A dark-haired woman with dark red streaks woven throughout her hair sat beside Bones, her hand clasped in his. Bones nodded to him and Bren returned his nod as the woman stared sympathetically at him.

Drago sat in the front row on the right. He gave Bren a barely concealed look of contempt before staring stiffly ahead. Sika and Jarvis sat in the front row on the left. Sika held the baby in her arms, and Bren glanced at him. He was still covered in shimmering green scales, and his tiny fist was curled against his face.

"Good evening, council." Kaida's voice was strong without a hint of anxiety as she made a short bow.

Bren studied the six dragon shifters sitting behind the table. Cadmus sat at one end, an empty chair between him and the female dragon shifter beside him. Cadmus smiled serenely at him as an ancient looking shifter with white hair streaked with light purple said, "Good evening, Kaida."

There was a moment of silence, and then a council member with greying hair and orange streaks said, "You have been brought to the council for the crime of revealing our true nature to a human." His gaze flickered to Bren and then back to Kaida. "You will be allowed to explain your actions before the council votes on banishment."

"Wait, what?" Bren stepped forward, his stomach flip-flopping like a fish in the sand. Kaida's hand curled around his arm and held him still as Drago immediately stood.

"Do not go near the council, human, or I will save us all the trouble and set you aflame right here and now."

"Enough, Drago," the ancient shifter said sharply.

"It is my duty to protect the council, Walter," Drago protested. He glanced around at the others. "It is all of our duty."

"We can protect ourselves," the dragoness sitting next to Walter said. "Return to your seat, Drago."

Smoke drifting from his nostrils, Drago sat down. Ignoring Kaida's *keep your mouth shut* look, Bren said, "You're banishing Kaida?"

The dragon named Walter said, "We will vote on banishment, human."

"She didn't do anything wrong," Bren said. "She saved Sika and the baby. You're going to banish her for that?"

"Hold your tongue, human!" the grey-haired shifter said. "You are not allowed to speak."

"Ryul," the blonde-haired shifter sitting at the far end of the table frowned at him, "the human will be allowed to speak just as Kaida will be."

"There is no need for the human to speak, Leia," Ryul said hotly. "We do not -"

"Enough, Ryul," Cadmus said. "He will be allowed to speak."

Ryul grunted in agreement, although Bren could see smoke drifting from his nostrils, and sat back in his chair as Bren said, "You can't banish her."

"Bren, enough." Kaida's hand squeezed painfully around his arm.

He turned toward her. "Why didn't you tell me you were also in trouble?"

She didn't reply, and some of his anger deflated. How could he have been so stupid? Of course, Kaida would be in trouble. Dragons were all sorts of fucked up. The fact that they had no difficulty banishing one of their own even when they knew it meant certain death... maybe it was better that they were going extinct.

She released his arm as Walter said, "Kaida, you may speak."

"Thank you," Kaida replied. "Council, my decision to reveal our true nature to the human was not made lightly. Sika's labour was sudden and fast. There was no time to return to our clan, and I knew we couldn't go to the humans' hospital. We were close to Bren's home, and my choices were to take Sika to his home to give birth or have her give birth on the side of the road in the car. I believe I chose wisely."

She glanced at Bren. "I have faith that he will keep our secret. He is an honourable human who understands that for our kind to live in peace with humans, our existence must remain a secret. I am confident he will never expose our secret."

"We will consider your words when voting," Walter said. He glanced at the other shifters sitting in the chairs. "Is there any other who wishes to speak on Kaida's behalf?"

Bren could see Sika starting to stand. Before she could, Drago rose to his feet and said, "I would like to speak, council."

Beside Bren, Kaida stiffened, and smoke curled out from her nose.

"Speak your piece, Drago," Walter said.

"Elders, I know in the past Kaida has proven difficult with her choices. As a yearling, she brought a grizzly shifter into our clan, and now she has exposed us to a fox shifter and humans. While I realize her actions are inexcusable, I do believe with time and discipline, she can be taught proper behaviour."

"Discipline?" Bren said. "Are you kidding me? She's not a dog, Drago."

Drago glared at him. "Speak again, human, and I will cut out your tongue."

A growl rose from Kaida's throat, and she said, "Take a single step toward the human, and you will regret it."

Drago stared at her, his unease obvious. She met his gaze unflinchingly, and after a moment, he looked away.

"Is that all you wish to say, Drago?" Walter asked.

"No," Drago said. "I wish to propose that I take Kaida as my mate. I will ensure that she behaves and is not a threat to our clan."

Sika burst out laughing, and Drago's face reddened. Ignoring Sika's giggling, he said, "Kaida needs a firm hand, council, and I am happy to provide it. As my mate, she will learn to put the clan above," he glanced at Bren, "everything and everyone else."

Jealousy was shooting through Bren's body like hot lava. The idea of Kaida being mated to the pompous dragon made his blood boil. He was pretty sure if he could shoot flame from his mouth, he'd be attempting to set Drago on fire in front of everyone.

Hey, Bren? You're about to die, remember? Maybe let go of the jealousy. Even if you could date Kaida, you're going to be dead.

Sika was still giggling, and Ryul scowled at her. "Hush, Sika."

"Council, will you agree to my proposal?" Drago said.

"We will consider it when making our decision," Walter said.

"We will not," Cadmus said. "It is Kaida's and only Kaida's choice who she takes as a mate." A small smile playing on his lips, Cadmus said, "Kaida? Will you accept Drago's mating proposal?"

"It will increase the odds in your favour," Ryul said.

Kaida fixed her gaze on Ryul. "I would rather be banished and go mad than mate with Drago."

There were a few gasps and muted laughter from the shifters sitting behind them. Drago growled and blew out a small blast of fire. "You'll wish you weren't so stubborn when the council votes to banish you."

Kaida stared icily at him. "I'll take my chances."

"Is there any other who wishes to speak on Kaida's behalf?"

Sika stood immediately, the baby still cradled in her arms. "I do, council. If it weren't for Kaida, my hatchling would have been born in a car on the side of the road. We would have been exposed to many humans, and who knows what might have happened. They could have taken our boy from me or simply killed him on sight when they saw him. Her decision to take us to the human's home was the right one, and to banish her for doing what she believed best for me and the hatchling is ridiculous. If it wasn't for her, our hatchling – the first one born to the clan in over a decade – could have died. I ask the council to show mercy upon her."

She sat down, staring at Jarvis, who kissed her forehead and put his arm around her.

"Thank you for your input, Sika," Walter said. "Is there any other who wishes to speak?"

Bren listened as, one by one, over a dozen more clan members stood and spoke on Kaida's behalf. Some told personal stories of Kaida helping them, and others shared more general examples of why Kaida was an integral part of their clan. All of them spoke with sincerity and respect for her. It was more than evident that Kaida's clan loved and supported her.

When the last dragon had finished speaking, thick silence filled the small space. Walter turned his golden-eyed gaze to Bren. "We will now speak of the human's fate. You may speak on your own behalf now, human."

Bren glanced at Kaida. She smiled encouragingly, although she still looked about three seconds from vomiting, and made a 'go on' gesture.

His hands were trembling, and for a moment, he wasn't sure he could even get any words out. He cleared his throat and glanced again at Kaida, taking courage in the calm way she returned his look.

He looked at each council member before saying, "I want to assure you that I understand how important it is to keep your existence a secret. I realize that with who my father is, your wariness of me is heightened, but as the senator's son, I am even more cognizant of keeping your secret. If men like my father discovered your existence, keeping peace between our kinds would be difficult. I want peace as much as you do. My job is to protect and maintain that peace among paranormals and humans. I want you to live your life without fear. I give you my word that I will never disclose your existence to anyone – paranormal or human."

He wanted to say more. His nerves practically screamed at him to keep babbling until the skeptical looks on the council members' faces changed. Instead, he took a step back and kept his mouth shut. He'd said what he could, and he had to hope they believed he was sincere.

"Thank you, human," Walter said. "is there anyone else who wishes to speak on the human's behalf?"

Kaida stepped forward, and Ryul said, "No. You are not allowed to speak on his behalf."

"Why not?" Kaida replied.

"Your friendship with the human is already troublesome," the second dragoness on the council said. "You will not be neutral when it comes to his fate."

"Sika is my best friend. She was not neutral regarding my fate, yet you allowed her to speak on my behalf. What is the difference, Collette?" Kaida said.

Collette shook her head. "There will be no argument on this point."

Kaida glanced at Cadmus, who made a slight shake of his head. Disappointment and hurt crossed Kaida's face, and she stepped back until she stood next to Bren again.

"Is there any other who wishes to speak on the human's behalf?" Walter said.

Jarvis stood, and Bren could have run over and kissed him. "I wish to speak, council. The human was very kind to me and Sika. He let us stay in his home, gave us food and drink, and allowed us time to bond with our boy. He didn't have to do any of that but didn't hesitate to make us feel welcome. I believe him when he says he will not speak of us to other humans, and he should be allowed to live."

He glanced at Sika and the baby. "For him to burn because he helped our hatchling, neither Sika nor I believe that is right. He shouldn't be punished for helping us. I ask the council to show mercy upon him."

He returned to his seat and took Sika's hand. The dragoness kissed his cheek as Walter said, "Thank you, Jarvis. Is there any other?"

Bren and Kaida jerked in surprise when Walter's gaze slipped past them, and he said, "Bones, you may speak."

Bren turned, staring at the giant dragon shifter as he stepped into the aisle. "The human should be allowed to live. Jarvis and Sika's hatchling does well because of his generosity. I ask the council to show mercy upon the human."

He returned to his seat, and Bren studied Kaida. The sick look on her face was still there, and he resisted the urge to take her hand. He had a feeling it wouldn't go over well with the other dragons.

"Any others?" Walter asked.

Silence filled the cabin, and after a moment, Walter stood. "We will return shortly with our decision."

Bren watched as the council members used a side door to file out of the cabin. When the door shut behind them, Jarvis jumped up and approached Bren. He shook Bren's hand. "Do not worry, human. They will vote to let you live."

"They won't." Drago had joined them. "Do not give the human hope, Jarvis." He took Kaida's arm. "Come, I wish to speak to you in private."

She wrenched her arm out of his hand and growled at him. "Touch me again, and I'll rip your balls off, Drago."

Sika laughed, and Drago's face flushed red. "I gave you a

chance, Kaida. Remember that when you're banished and going mad in the woods."

He stalked away, and Kaida smiled shakily at Bren. "Are you all right?"

"Never better," he said. "You?"

She grimaced. "It went as well as it could. Jarvis is right. The council may allow you to live."

"What about you? What if they banish you?" he said.

"They won't." Sika stood next to Jarvis and smiled confidently at them. "They won't banish Kaida, and they'll let you live. Because of both of you, our hatchling does so well."

Bren wanted to believe the dragoness, he did, but from the sick look on Kaida's face, it was apparent she didn't share the same confidence.

———

HER DRAGON WAS ON THE VERGE OF LOSING IT. THE SMOKE was thick in the back of her throat, and she had to swallow constantly to keep it from drifting from her nostrils.

Be still. You must calm yourself.

Her dragon hissed at her. *If they touch my mate, I will kill them.*

Bren being killed wasn't their only concern – she shared none of the confidence that Sika did that she wouldn't be banished – but her dragon didn't seem to care about that. All it cared about was keeping Bren safe.

She studied him as he rubbed a hand through his hair. He looked tired and unwell and... scared to death.

She couldn't blame him. If she were in his shoes, she'd be terrified, too. Hell, she *was* terrified. Her dragon might not care if they were banished, but the idea of being kicked out of her clan *and* knowing that Bren was dead... she shuddered. She'd go mad in less than an hour. She was sure of it.

Because you love him, her dragon said. *He is our mate, and you love him. Tell him!*

Enough. Now is not the time.

Her dragon believed it was the perfect time. It tried to push forward and take control so it could – *Jesus Christ* – confess its love to Bren. Her heart knocking against her ribs, sweat trickling down her back, Kaida used every ounce of her inner strength to keep her dragon from taking control.

Let me free!

No, stop it! The human is already freaked out. It will scare him even more if you tell him you love him. Humans do not take mates as quickly as we do.

Her dragon pouted but retreated with a soft hiss. The hiss turned to a purr when Bren touched her arm. "Kaida?"

"I'm fine," she said.

She took a deep breath, determined to put on a cheerful face for the human. It was all her fault he was in this mess, and while she might be seventy percent positive that they were both about to die, she wouldn't show that to him.

"It went well with the elders," she repeated. "Everything will be fine."

The look of disbelief on his face suggested she was doing a shit job of hiding her fears. She made herself smile at him. "It's the truth, Bren. You spoke well and -"

Anger flooded her when she saw the dragoness standing so closely behind her mate. She could smell Vorian's interest in Bren, and… was that the tiniest bit of lust?

Her dragon roared forward, and she didn't have a hope in hell of stopping it this time. She grabbed Bren's arm, pulling him closer to her before glaring at Vorian. The dark-haired dragoness's hand was still outstretched, and Kaida bared her fangs at her.

"Dare to touch him again, and I will burn you where you stand, Vorian." Her dragon growled out the threat, each word punctuating the sudden silence that had descended over the cabin.

Vorian's fear washed over her, and Kaida's dragon snarled her victory. "The human is mine. Do you understand?"

Vorian stumbled back and nervously exhaled a puff of smoke. "Yes, Kaida. God, you don't have to be such a bitch about the human."

"Leave," Kaida's dragon rumbled. Her chest was growing hot and she knew the others could see it glowing through her shirt. She didn't care. The human was hers. She'd kill any dragoness who tried to take him from her.

"Fine!" Vorian rolled her eyes and stalked away. The other dragons in the cabin – all of them had slowly been inching closer to Bren – backed away as well. The low hum of conversation began again. No doubt it was about her and her possessiveness over the human, but Kaida was too weary to care.

What did it matter if they knew she liked the human? She was about to be banished anyway.

"That was... unexpected," Jarvis said.

Sika elbowed him gently before smiling at Kaida. "She is only curious about the human, Kaida. They all are. You know how rarely they get a close-up look at humans without worrying about being discovered."

"He is not on display like an animal in a zoo," Kaida snapped. Her dragon had retreated, and she spoke in her normal voice.

"It's okay," Bren said. "I don't care."

"They need to learn manners," Kaida said.

231

"It's not that big of a deal," Bren said. He glanced at the other shifters behind them. "Is this your entire clan?"

"Almost," Sika said. "Some of our male yearlings are not here. They're probably playing video games. Even the chance to see a human up close won't tear them away from their stupid online games."

"Sounds like they're pretty similar to human teenagers." The look on Bren's face made Kaida's chest ache.

"Did you – have you seen Tyler?" she asked.

His eyes reddened, and he looked away. "We had dinner tonight."

She tried to swallow past the lump in her throat. It didn't work. "I'm sorry, Bren."

He stepped closer and lowered his voice. "If you're not banished, promise me you'll watch out for him."

"I will." She took his hand. "I'll keep him safe, Bren. I promise. And if I'm not around – Jarvis will look out for him. Won't you, Jarvis?"

"Of course. Do not worry, human. Your brother will always be safe. You have my word," Jarvis said.

"Thank you," Bren said.

They stood in silence for almost a minute before Bren said, "So, how long does it usually take the council to -"

The side door opened, and this time, Bren's hand squeezed around hers as they watched the council members file back into the room. The other dragons quickly returned to their seats.

Her dragon pacing restlessly within her, Kaida dropped Bren's hand but tried to smile at him. It came out as a grimace. Bren was incredibly pale, but he walked with her toward the council's table, his head held high and back straight. Her dragon puffed with pride at how brave their mate was.

"We have made our decision," Walter said when they were standing before him and the other elders.

Suddenly not caring what the elders or anyone else in the clan thought, Kaida took Bren's hand. He linked their fingers together, his gaze trained on Walter and the others, but his thumb rubbed along the length of her thumb.

Kaida glanced at Cadmus. Like the other elders, his face was serene and gave away nothing. He wouldn't allow her to be banished or for Bren to be burned. She had to believe that.

"Regarding Kaida's banishment, the council will allow her to remain with the clan. While involving humans is not ideal, the council believes she acted in the best interest of Sika and her hatchling and only involved the human out of necessity."

Bren's hand clamped down on hers, and his look of pure happiness made her chest ache again. It was her fault he was even here, but there was no animosity from him, only pure joy that she wasn't going to die.

He is our mate. The surety in her dragon's voice left no room for doubt.

The cabin was filled with the rough purrs of happiness from the rest of her clan members. She felt an overwhelming surge of love for her clan, leaving her weak and shaky. Bren glanced behind them at the clan before smiling again at her.

She took a deep breath and nodded to him. Her dragon was purring loudly to her clan, and her unease disappeared. The council would let Bren live. They would not sentence him to death when he'd played such a clear part in helping Sika and the hatchling. To allow her to live and condemn Bren to death would be grossly unfair.

Walter held up his hand, and the purring of her clan died out. "In the matter of the human, the council did not make this decision lightly. Our way of life is threatened when a human discovers who we are. In this particular case, the

233

threat is doubled simply by the nature of who this human's father is."

Walter's gaze landed on Bren, his golden eyes unwavering. "We appreciate what you have done for our clan, human. The support you offered to Sika and her hatchling was a gracious and generous gesture and quite unexpected from a human. We will never forget your kindness, but your continued existence threatens ours. Therefore, the council has voted to end your life."

Kaida stared in stunned silence at Walter. Behind her, she could hear the murmurs of her clan. The air had turned to molasses around her, and she slowly turned to face Bren. The colour had leeched entirely from his face, and a look of resignation covered his features.

He lifted her hand to his mouth and pressed a gentle kiss against her knuckles. "Remember your promise, Kaida. Keep Tyler safe."

Jarvis jumped to his feet. "Elders, I ask you to reconsider your decision. This man saved the life of my mate and my hatchling. If not for him, they would -"

"We are well aware," Ryul said. "You made your case earlier for the human, Jarvis. The council has made its decision, and it is final. Bones, take the human into the forest."

Her ears ringing and her stomach rolling, Kaida turned her gaze to Cadmus. The elder sat at the end of the table, his hands folded in front of him and that same serene look on his face.

"Cadmus!" Kaida's voice rose above the babble of other voices. "Cadmus, overrule their decision. Now."

Ryul's eyes widened. "You dare to tell the high elder what to do? Watch your tongue, Kaida. We may have spared you from banishment, but that does not mean we will allow you to speak without consequence."

Kaida ignored the older dragon. Still holding tight to Bren's hand, she said, "Cadmus, what is wrong with you? Killing the human is wrong. You know that! Do not -"

Her dragon growled out a warning, and Kaida whirled around. Bones was approaching Bren, and she immediately stepped in front of Bren, pushing her arm behind her body and hooking it around his waist. She pulled him forward until his chest pressed against her back, and she could feel his breath puffing against her hair. "Don't come any closer, Bones."

Bones stopped a few feet away. "You know this isn't what I want, Kaida. The human doesn't deserve to die. But I serve the elders, and as protector of the clan, I vowed to follow the council's decisions. I cannot and will not break that vow. Not even for you."

Her dragon surged forward, and there was a collective gasp of surprise from the clan when her chest glowed and she blew out a hot burst of flame. "We are friends, Bones, and have been since we were yearlings. But touch the human, and I will end your life."

A hard light shone in Bones's eyes. "Do you challenge me, Kaida?"

"She doesn't," Sika spoke quickly, fear making her usual low voice high-pitched. "Of course, she doesn't. Kaida, you must release the human now. Please, sweetie."

She fixed her gaze on Sika, and her best friend stepped back. "Kaida?" she whispered.

"Leave, Sika," Kaida's dragon demanded. "Take your hatchling and leave this place for your safety and his."

"Kaida." Bren's arm slipped around her waist, and he pressed his mouth against her ear. "Don't, honey. It's okay. You don't have to do this."

"You are mine." Her voice was thick and almost incomprehensible. "You are mine, and he is not taking you from me."

"Do you challenge me?" Bones repeated.

"Yes," Kaida said.

"Kaida!" Drago's voice rang out over the horrified gasps of her clan. "Do not speak so foolishly."

He moved toward her, stopping abruptly when she growled at him and blew another burst of flame in his direction. His face sweating from the heat, Drago said, "You cannot defeat Bones in a challenge. Hell, you'll be lucky if you survive. Bones will defeat you - probably kill you - and the human will die anyway. Step away and give the human to Bones."

"I always knew you were a coward, Drago," Kaida's voice rumbled out of her chest.

He flushed bright red, smoke pouring from his nostrils. "And I always knew you were an emotional fool."

She growled at him before turning her attention to Bones. "Come, old friend, it's time I taught you a lesson in manners."

Bones bared his teeth at her in a ferocious grin. "Are you sure this is what you want, Kaida? Does the human mean that much to you that you are willing to have your ass handed to you in front of the clan? To have the clan watch you beg for mercy?"

Her dragon roared with rage. "We will see who begs for mercy, Bones."

Bones's grin widened, and Kaida could feel the delicious fire of her dragon's fury in her very bones. Her dragon was itching to fight, and Bones would be a worthy opponent.

"Kaida, no," Bren said into her ear. "You're not doing this for me. You're not being injured or dying because of -"

The cabin door burst open, and Brandon and Matalis ran

into it. At fourteen and fifteen, they were the youngest of the yearlings. Still keeping her arm around Bren's waist, Kaida watched as Brandon staggered to his father.

"Brandon? What is it?" Rokan put his arm around the yearling's shoulders. "What's wrong?"

Brandon stared up at him, his lips trembling and his golden eyes huge in his face. "Dad, I... we..."

"What?" Rokan said.

His face a mask of shock, Matalis held up the tablet he carried in his right hand. "He was on TV and online. He outed us."

"What are you talking about, Matalis?" Javee moved toward Matalis, taking the tablet from his hand and scanning it.

His voice thin with fear, Matalis said, "The humans have proof that dragons exist."

CHAPTER 17

"What did you do, human?" Drago pushed forward and pulled Bren out of Kaida's grip. He swung Bren around, fisting his hands into his shirt as he exhaled smoke in a thick cloud into Bren's face. "What did you do?"

"I didn't do anything," Bren snapped.

Coughing, he shoved Drago away as Kaida growled out a warning. "Don't touch him again, Drago."

"Your stupid human has betrayed you," Drago said. "He has exposed us to the rest of his kind and -"

"I didn't," Bren said. "I haven't said a word to anyone, you asshole."

"Asshole?" Drago sucked in a gulp of air. His chest was glowing red beneath his shirt, and Bren was sure he was about two seconds away from being roasted alive.

"Drago, enough!" Cadmus's voice rose above the panicked hum of the other dragons.

Snarling under his breath, Drago turned away. Bren took Kaida's hand. She looked sick to her stomach, and her pupils were blown so wide only a thin golden ring surrounded them.

239

"What does it say, Javee?" Bones asked.

For the first time since he'd met the dragon shifter, Bren could hear unease in Bones's voice and see worry on his face.

Javee stared grimly at Bones before handing the tablet back to the teenager named Matalis. She pushed past the other shifters and opened a cabinet built into the cabin's wall. It hid a large screen TV, and Bren and Kaida joined the others as they crowded around the screen.

Javee turned the television on and flipped to the local news station channel. They watched silently as the local newscaster said, "Once again, here is the footage captured earlier this evening by multiple viewers in downtown Los Angeles. A note of caution – this unaltered footage contains graphic and unsuitable images for younger viewers."

The screen turned to the shaky and unstable video from a cell phone. The image was crystal clear, and Bren stared at the naked man standing at the top of an office building. The camera zoomed in on the man's pale face that seemed to glow in the setting sun's light.

Gasps of dismay and fear rippled through the dragons, and Kaida's hand grew so warm in his that his palm tingled.

"Well, fuck," Bones said.

"Is that Norris from Belinda's clan?" Sika asked.

"Yes," Walter said. Like the other elders, he had joined the dragons around the screen. He glanced at Cadmus, who was standing next to him. "We received word two days ago that he'd been banished from the clan."

"Why was he banished?" Sika asked.

"Holy shit!" Jarvis said.

Bren turned back to the television as more gasps of dismay reverberated through the clan of dragons. The naked man's body was bulging and changing, and they watched in horrified silence as he shifted. The person holding the cell phone swore in surprise, and Bren could hear screams of fear and disbelief from the people watching on the street.

A dragon, his orange scales gleaming in the sunlight, stood on the building. He was massive in size with a row of dark rust-coloured spikes running down the back of his neck, along his spine, and down to the end of his tail. He unfurled his wings, blotting out the sun above him, and more terrified screams could be heard from the crowd on the street below.

The dragon rose into the air with a heavy flap of his wings. The camera followed him, watching the dragon fly in a large circle before he dived and dipped through the air. He skimmed across the top of a neighbouring building and landed on the office building roof again.

He took a deep breath, his chest turning to a deep, rich reddish-orange before blowing out a terrifying blast of flame. The man holding the camera stumbled backwards, the dragon slipping out of view for a second as the lens was aimed at the people on the street.

They were staring up at the dragon with fear and confusion. When the dragon roared, the man swung the camera back up. Bren swallowed down the dizzying sense of vertigo, focusing his gaze on the dragon as it stomped back and forth on the roof.

The dragon stopped and blasted out another lungful of flame before shifting back to his human form. He stood on the side of the building and grinned at the crowd below him.

"There are many of my kind!" he shouted. "Those of us who are born of smoke and flame. We are... everywhere."

"What is Norris doing?" Sika said as the man stepped closer to the edge of the building. "What is he... oh no!"

Kaida made a low sound of pain as Norris, with a final grin to the crowd, swan dived off the building. He hit the sidewalk headfirst, the force of his impact smashing his skull apart and his brains splattering across the sidewalk.

"Oh my fucking God," Jarvis said as more screams echoed across the video. "Oh my fucking God."

The view on the screen switched back to the newscaster. His face and voice solemn, he said, "Today marks a momentous occasion. Long thought to be nothing more than an insane conspiracy theory by a few deranged individuals, we now have irrefutable proof that dragons exist."

"Oh shit, this is so fucking bad," Jarvis said.

The newscaster cocked his head, his hand coming up to touch his ear. "Folks, we've been given some new information. It seems the dragon posted a list on social media of what he refers to as 'dragon clans' with their locations."

The newscaster stared straight ahead at some unseen prompter, and Bren's stomach dropped when he said, "We have no idea how many dragons are in each clan, and local authorities are cautioning humans and shifters alike to steer clear of the dragons. The following clans have been identified: the Belinda clan of the city of Los Angeles, the Makeda clan of the city of San Francisco, the Avena clan of the city of New York -"

"Please, no," Sika whispered. She held her baby close to her chest, and she gave Jarvis a frightened look as he put his arm around her.

"The Borthala clan of the city of Cheyenne," the newscaster droned on, "the Havana clan of the city of Portland, the Cadmus clan of the city of -"

The horrified shouts filled the large cabin. The room was growing increasingly warmer, and Bren could see the chests of more than one dragon glowing bright red. Kaida's hand was squeezing his so tightly he'd lost all feeling in his fingers.

"Honey, ease up a little," he said.

She stared blankly at him before staring at their linked fingers. She relaxed her grip. "I'm sorry."

"They know where we are!" A wild-eyed dragon, his dark hair sticking straight up in short spikes, pushed through the crowd toward Walter and the other elders. "They know where we are, elders. We must prepare to defend our clan."

"They only said the city," Walter said. "You must be calm, Mateo. The humans don't know where our clan is, only that there is a clan in the -"

"They know." Javee approached with Matalis's tablet in her hand. She showed Walter the screen. "Norris posted the exact locations of over twenty clans online. Ours was one of them."

"Why would he do that?" Sika whispered.

"Because he went mad," Kaida said.

Walter was staring at the other elders with a look of blank shock on his face. The hum of excitement and fear grew louder in the room, and a few dragon shifters drifted toward the cabin door.

"Come, my clan!" Mateo shouted. "We must prepare ourselves for war with the humans. They will be here soon!"

He pushed his way toward the door, and Bren stared at Kaida in alarm when several shifters followed him.

"ENOUGH!"

The powerful voice stopped the dragons in their tracks and sent a shiver down Bren's spine. He turned to stare at Cadmus, who hopped nimbly onto the top of the table and clapped his hands sharply.

"My clan, be quiet and listen closely."

The dragons quieted down immediately, staring at Cadmus as the elderly dragon folded his hands behind his back. "We knew this day may come, and now that it has, it is important that we remain calm. Yes, the humans know we exist and where we are, but we cannot and will not panic. This is our new reality, and no one in this clan will do anything to humans or shifters who approach us. Is that clear?"

The dragons nodded, giving each other uneasy looks as Cadmus smiled down at them. "I know you are frightened, my clan, but it will be all right. We have walked this line for too long, and now our future lies before us – new and uncertain. But as long as we remain together, we will be all right."

"What if they attack us?" Mateo said.

"They won't," Cadmus said. "Not if we show them they have nothing to fear from us."

The elderly dragon spoke reassuringly, but Bren could still feel the nervousness of the crowd of dragons surrounding him.

"We all knew the risk of banishment and what a mad dragon might do or say. We must now live with the consequences of our choices. The council will speak with the other clans and formulate a plan. For now, return to your homes," Cadmus said.

"What about this human?" Drago pointed at Bren.

"What about him?" Kaida said.

"He's been sentenced to death," Drago said.

Bones rolled his eyes. "Are you kidding me? The entire world knows of our existence, Drago, and you're worried about one puny human?" He glanced at Bren. "No offense."

"None taken," Bren said.

"The human is not to be touched," Cadmus said. "He is free to go."

Kaida squeezed his hand, and he could almost see the tension leaking from her body.

"Go, my clan. Return to your homes," Cadmus said.

Kaida pulled him toward the door, pushing past the other

dragons until they were at the door first. "Time for you to go, Bren."

"I can stay," he said.

She shook her head as she opened the cabin door, and they stepped outside. "No, it's best for you to go."

He followed her to his vehicle. "Kaida, I -"

"Please, Bren." She glanced at the other dragons. "My clan is afraid, and sometimes, when dragons are afraid, they make choices they'll regret later."

"Like burning me to a crisp?" he said.

"Please go," she said.

"It'll be okay," he said. He wanted to kiss her but settled for awkwardly patting her arm. "The humans will get used to the idea of dragons existing."

She smiled wearily at him before backing away. "Goodbye, human."

"Goodbye, Kaida."

Kaida parked her car, grimacing when the reporters immediately blocked it in with their vans. They jumped out and crowded around her car, shouting questions at her through the glass as the flashes of the cameras nearly blinded her.

She stared grimly at the steering wheel. She'd made a mistake coming to Bishop's office. She should have known the reporters who descended on the clan this morning would follow her.

But she'd needed to talk to one of her best friends, needed to admit how afraid and confused she was, and guilt crept into her, she'd needed to be away from her clan for a bit. The entire clan had spent most of the day in the community

245

cabin, and their combined anxiety was making her dragon go a little crazy.

It kept asking for Bren and begging her to go to him, but after texting him this morning and not hearing back, she hadn't texted again. Maybe he was at work and busy, or maybe he wanted nothing to do with her ever again.

Her clan had, after all, voted to murder him last night.

"Hey!" She heard the muffled shout of the reporter pressing up against her door as he was pushed out of the way, and Bishop bent down to peer at her through the window.

Relief flooding through her, she opened her door and stepped out of the car. The steady click of cameras was an annoying buzz in her ears, and the microphones shoved toward her made her dragon growl in annoyance.

She soothed it as Bishop snarled at the half a dozen reporters crowded around them. "Get back, now!"

She realized that Mal and Kat were standing behind Bishop, and they pushed and shoved the reporters back as she and Bishop walked toward their office building.

"How dangerous are you?" A reporter shouted.

"How big are you? How many dragons are in your clan? Is it true that you can speak the human language when you're in your dragon form?" Another reporter spat rapid-fire questions at her.

"Who does your hair colouring?" A third reporter shouted.

Kat hissed at the reporter, who tried to dodge her. "Get any closer to her, and I'll kick your ass."

The reporter backed away. "God, lady, you don't have to be such a bitch."

"Go on and go home," Mal said calmly as he stopped in the office building doorway. "She won't be making any statements, and you're not going to get any footage of her turning into a dragon. You're wasting your time."

He shut the door, and, to Kaida's surprise, none of the reporters followed them into the building. As they took the elevator to their floor, Kaida said, "Thanks, you guys. I appreciate your help."

Kat squeezed her arm. "No problem. How are you doing?"

"Okay. It's still a little surreal."

"I bet. Did you know the dragon who outed you?" Kat asked as they stepped off the elevator and walked to the office.

"Knew of him," Kaida said, "but never actually met him. He was in Belinda's clan in Los Angeles. He was banished, went mad, and revealed our existence before committing suicide."

"Why was he banished?" Mal asked.

"I don't know. Cadmus and the other council members haven't told us, and with everything that's happened, none of us have thought to ask."

She followed Bishop into the office. "Cadmus has warned the other clans for years that this very thing would happen, but they wouldn't listen. Now..."

She trailed off as Willow hurried out from behind the reception desk and hugged her hard. "Hi, Kaida. I'm so sorry."

"Thanks, Willow."

"Will, would you mind getting Kaida a cup of tea?" Bishop asked.

"Of course not. I'll bring you one too." Willow smiled at Kaida before heading to the small kitchenette.

"Come into my office," Bishop said.

She sat in one of the comfortable leather chairs, and Bishop sat beside her. He took her hand. "How are you?"

"I'm sorry I didn't call before showing up," Kaida said.

"It's fine," Bishop said. "How are you?"

She could feel the sting of tears, and she blinked them back. "So much has happened in the last seventy-two hours. I don't even know where to start, my bear."

"Start from the beginning," Bishop said as Willow set two cups of tea on his desk and left, shutting the door behind her.

"You weren't kidding about a lot happening," Bishop sat back in his chair.

Kaida sipped at the now lukewarm tea. "I told you."

"How is the hatchling doing?" Bishop asked.

Kaida smiled. "Good. His scales are starting to fall off. The naming ceremony hasn't happened yet, but I expect it will happen soon. He's beautiful and healthy."

"Well, tell Jarvis and Sika I said congratulations," Bishop said. "Have you talked to Matthews since…"

Kaida laughed bitterly. "Since the council voted to burn him alive? Nope, haven't heard a word. Shocker, huh?"

"It just happened last night," Bishop said. "He's probably busy at work."

"Probably," she said.

"Look, if you tell anyone I said this, I'll deny it, but Matthews is a good guy, and he wouldn't be upset with you about what your clan decided."

"I challenged Bones." Kaida didn't look up from her hands, but she could feel Bishop stiffening in his chair.

"You challenged Bones? Do you have a death wish?" Bishop almost shouted.

"He was going to burn Bren alive. What did you expect me to do?"

"Kaida," Bishop took her hand, "are you in love with Bren?"

She refused to meet his gaze, instead studying their clasped hands. "It doesn't matter if I am. I'll never see him again. Even if he wasn't angry about the clan agreeing to murder him, he can't bring Tyler back to learn to fight. We have reporters all over our land, and if the senator saw Tyler and Bren with us…"

"Shit would hit the fan," Bishop said.

"Yeah. Anything I might have had with Bren is over. It ended the moment humans found out we existed."

"It doesn't have to be over," he said. "Bren isn't like his father."

"It's not only that," she said. "A dragon and a human cannot be together."

"I thought the same thing about humans and grizzlies," Bishop said.

She smiled a little. "My bear, it is not the same. Even with all of your strength and power, you would never hurt Ava when you mated with her. I cannot say the same. You know that."

"You never set me on fire when we were together," Bishop said.

She sighed. "I singed you a few times. The human does not have healing powers. If I lost control…"

"So open a window and point your flame in its direction," Bishop said.

She laughed despite her misery. "Good to know that all males think the same way."

They sat silently for a moment before she said, "Do you have any regrets about being with a human?"

"None," he said. "Ava is the best thing that ever happened to me. Without her, I'm nothing, Kaida."

Bishop squeezed her hand. "The detective is tough. I'll admit I have a lot of respect for the guy. He saved my life and he doesn't scare easily. I think you should give it a chance. It'll be easier now that humans know of dragons' existence. Right?"

"I don't know," she said. "Like I said, it doesn't matter anyway. I'll never see Bren Matthews again."

"You'll see him at the wedding on Saturday," Bishop said.

"My bear," she cupped his face and smiled, "I cannot attend your wedding."

"You have to," he said.

"I cannot," she repeated. "The reporters will follow me, and I am not ruining your wedding."

He growled in anger, and she stood and pressed a kiss against his forehead. "I wish I could be there, my bear, I do. I should get back to the clan. Give Ava my love."

He stood and took her hand. "I'll walk you to your car."

CHAPTER 18

K aida put the dishes in the dishwasher and checked her phone. She glanced around almost guiltily before pulling up Bren's Facebook profile. They weren't friends on Facebook, but it looked like he hadn't posted anything on social media in over a month anyway. She shoved her phone into her pocket before pouring herself a second cup of coffee.

It was Friday morning, and there was still nothing from Bren. No phone calls or texts. The acid clawed its way up from her stomach and settled in her chest as her dragon made a mournful cry.

Shh, it's all right.

My mate. I need him. Please? Her dragon said.

He is not our mate. You must forget him.

Her dragon made another sound of grief, and Kaida pressed a hand against her chest. The ache for Bren was a deep, physical one that had only worsened since Wednesday night. Straightening, she took a gulp of coffee that made her indigestion worse. Her healing powers were weakened, a side effect of her dragon's depression and misery, and for the first time in her life, she felt powerless and frail.

My sweet, it will be all right. She purred to her dragon, hoping to bring it out of its misery.

It burrowed down deep, refusing to acknowledge her comfort. Kaida sighed before heading to the front door of her cabin. She stepped onto the front porch and sank into one of the wooden rocking chairs next to the door.

She stared at the dirt road leading back to the main road. Yesterday, it was clogged with reporters' vehicles, and the reporters themselves roamed freely around the cabins, knocking on doors and peering through windows while the clan remained together in the community cabin.

About half an hour after she'd returned from Bishop's office, a half dozen police officers had shown up and herded the reporters off their lands. The reporters were still there, just below the crest of the first hill that led to their cabins, but the police had set up a barricade, and there were officers posted at the barricade and on a loose perimeter around their cabins.

Bones had spoken to a few of the officers guarding the perimeter, and, at one point yesterday evening, her grandmother had gone around handing out bottles of water and freshly baked cookies to the humans.

She could see Cadmus walking across the clearing toward her cabin, and she looked away as her dragon growled. It wasn't just her dragon that was pissed at the high elder. She could feel her own rage rising.

Cadmus climbed the porch steps and sat in the rocking chair beside her. She immediately stood, and he said, "Stay with me, Kaida."

Smoke drifted from her nostrils, but she sat down. Cadmus smiled at her. "You are angry with me."

"Yes," she said.

He pulled his cloak closer as a cold wind blew his long hair into his face. "Tell me."

"You would have let them burn the human alive. Bren saved the hatchling. He's a good man, and when the council voted to kill him anyway, you didn't say anything." The words tumbled out of her, hot, hurt, and dripping with fury. "He's a good man who didn't deserve the fate the council decided."

"Are you angry because he's a good man or because the council tried to destroy your mate?" Cadmus asked.

She glared at the old dragon. "Do not speak so foolishly, Cadmus."

She expected him to be angry with her. Instead, a smile crossed his face. "Valen and I once burned with the same fiery passion you and your human share."

"He is not my human," she said.

"I miss my mate," Cadmus said.

The grief in his voice dissipated her anger with him immediately. She reached out and took his hand. "I know. I'm sorry, Cadmus."

"Did I ever tell you that Valen and I had to seek permission from the council to mate?"

"What? Why?"

Cadmus stared off into the distance. "Even way back then, it was apparent that our kind was having more and more difficulty conceiving. The council at the time was desperate for hatchlings, and Valen and I mating would not have produced any."

She squeezed his hand. "Did you and Valen want hatchlings?"

"Oh yes. Very much," he said. "We even discussed going our separate ways and finding other dragons to mate with in hopes that at least one of us might have a hatchling. But in the end," a soft smile crossed his face, "we couldn't do it. He was my love and I was his, and our dragons would not be separated."

He set the rocking chair in motion, pushing back and forth as he stared at the sky above them. "It took some convincing for the council to allow us to mate, and if it hadn't been for Valen's father threatening to leave the council and the clan, we might not have received their permission."

He glanced at her. "Dragons are not so different from the humans sometimes when it comes to prejudices and bigotry. My life with Valen was not always easy, but I wouldn't trade our life together for something that would be easier."

"Your situation and mine are not the same," she said.

"It was kind of Bren to send officers to keep the reporters away," he said.

"We don't know it was him," she said. "I haven't heard a word from him since we voted to burn him alive."

She could hear the bitterness in her voice, and she pulled away from Cadmus when he squeezed her hand.

"It was him," Cadmus said simply. "I am sending Drago to join Belinda's clan."

She stared in shock at Cadmus. "What?"

"The council and I have been in discussions with Belinda and her council, and we have decided to send Drago to join their clan. They, too, have an open position on their council, and we believe Drago would be well suited to their clan."

"Does Drago know?"

"Yes. We spoke with him early this morning, and he agreed to join their clan. Although I did not speak of this with the other elders, I also felt that given Drago's constant pressure for you to mate with him, it would be best if he left the clan."

"I appreciate that, Cadmus, but I can handle Drago and his ridiculous notion that we are to be mates," Kaida said.

Cadmus smiled. "Yes, I know. Will you mate with Bren now that humans know of our existence?"

"Why did you not overrule the council's decision to burn him?" Kaida countered.

"I would have," Cadmus said. "But I wanted to give your dragon a chance to protect her mate. Which she did admirably."

"Yeah, challenging the biggest and strongest among us was real admirable," Kaida said.

Cadmus grinned again. "I would have bet money on your dragon to win the challenge, Kaida."

"You're a fool, Cadmus."

He bellowed laughter. "Perhaps. Will you mate with the human?"

"I can't mate with the human. Even now that they know of our existence, it's one thing to live peacefully with humans, another to have one join our clan," she said.

She stared moodily at the cloudy sky. "No one in the clan would accept Bren, and I can't leave the clan, no matter how much I want to be with him."

"I think you'd be surprised how many in our clan would accept the human. Especially since he helped Jarvis and Sika's hatchling be born."

"Have I mentioned how foolish you talk as of late, Cadmus?"

"A time or two," he said. "When do you leave for the grizzly's mating ceremony?"

"I'm not going," she said. "We need to keep a low profile."

"You must go. You need to live your life, Kaida."

"If I leave, reporters will follow me and ruin Bishop and Ava's wedding. I'm not doing that to my friend," Kaida said.

Cadmus rocked slowly back and forth. "There must be a way. We just need to be creative."

Her phone buzzed in her pocket, and she yanked it out, hoping against hope that it was Bren.

"Is it your human?" Cadmus asked.

She shook her head. "No, it's Bishop." She read the text before staring at Cadmus. "He has a plan so that I can attend their wedding."

"There, you see," Cadmus patted her hand, "it's all about being creative."

"OH, FOR GOD'S SAKE." MAL SLAMMED HIS HAND DOWN ON the horn as the reporters crowded around the car. "You just saw us drive in half an hour ago."

He rolled down the window and glared at the reporter closest to him. "Back off, idiot."

"How do you know the dragons? Are you a dragon?" The reporter shouted at him.

"I'm a wolf shifter, you moron." Mal bared his fangs at him, and the reporter and his cameraman shuffled back, giving each other uneasy looks. "I own a security firm and was here to speak with the dragons about a job. Not that it's any of your fucking business."

"What kind of job?" Another reporter shouted.

"What kind of..." Mal stared at Willow in disbelief, and she rolled her eyes.

"Obviously, it's a security job," Mal said. He could see some police officers pushing their way through the crowd of reporters and lookie-loos. "You're wasting taxpayer dollars because you won't leave some shifters alone to live their lives in peace. You get that, right?"

"How many dragons are in the clan?" The reporter said. "Did you know they were dragons before they were outed?"

Mal growled in frustration, and Willow pressed her hand on his arm as she leaned over and peered out the window at the reporter. "Hey, what about me? I'm a human who can see ghosts. Who cares about the dragons? You should be interested in me, right? Ghosts, people. I see ghosts!"

The reporter rolled his eyes. "Sure, you can, lady."

"I can," Willow said indignantly.

"Whatever. Ghosts were so five years ago," the reporter said.

"Get back. Go on now, move out of the way." A harried looking officer herded the mixture of humans and shifters away from the car as another opened the barricade.

Mal eased the car through the opening and stepped on the gas once clear of the crowd. Will clutched at the dashboard as the car rocketed down the dirt road back to the main highway.

"Slow down, honey."

"What a bunch of idiots," Mal said but eased up on the gas.

"Well, it's good that we can help the dragons with security," Willow said. "How many extra shifters will you have to hire?"

Mal calculated in his head as he drove down the road. "At least ten. Cadmus wants them all around the perimeter, and I don't blame him for that. Even with the cops there, a few reporters have snuck past and into the clan's area."

"How quickly can you find some extra men?" Willow asked.

"I'm going to make a few calls as soon as we get back," Mal said.

"You still need to shower and get dressed for the wedding," Willow said.

"I know. It won't take long to make the calls. Davis and Fenton have friends looking for work, and Porter said both Judd and Hudson wouldn't mind making a little extra cash. They can do a few afternoon shifts before they start work at the bar."

He checked the rearview mirror. "Think we're far enough away?"

"Yes," Willow said. "Pull over, honey."

Mal pulled the car over and shut it off. Willow hopped out of the car, and he followed his mate to the back of the vehicle. He popped the trunk, and Willow grinned at the dragoness curled up in the trunk next to a small suitcase.

"You okay, Kaida?"

"I'm good." Kaida took Mal's hand, and he helped her out of the trunk. "Thank you for your help. It was a good idea to sneak me out in the trunk."

"You're welcome." Mal slammed the trunk shut. "But it wasn't my idea."

"It was Ava's," Willow said. The three of them climbed back into the car. Mal started down the road, and Willow twisted around in her seat to smile at Kaida. "Bishop was moping around the house and being a real – well, bear – about you not coming to the wedding, so Ava devised the plan. It worked brilliantly!"

"It did," Kaida said with a grin. "Was it also Ava's idea to have us hire you for security?"

"Nah, that was Bren and Bishop," Mal said. "Bishop was about to text you about the security thing when Bren called the office."

"He was the one who sent the officers then?" Kaida said.

"Yeah, but the captain was only doing it as a favour to Bren, and it wasn't going to be permanent, so Bren called us to see if we could help."

"He's such a sweet guy and so handsome, don't you think?" Willow said to Kaida.

Mal grinned as Kaida, a pink tinge to her cheeks, looked out the window. "Thank you again for helping me attend the wedding."

"It's our pleasure," Willow said. "And we'll find someone to give you a ride home after the reception as well." She clapped her hands and beamed at Mal. "Our best friends are getting married today! This is going to be the best day ever."

BREN PARKED IN THE PARKING LOT OF THE SMALL CHURCH. THE lot was about half full, and he climbed out of the SUV, slamming the door shut and walking briskly toward the church. He pulled his tie out of the pocket of his suit jacket and looped it around his neck.

He wasn't proud of this, but he'd had to use his car's lights and siren to get to the church in time. He fumbled with the tie as he drew closer to the wide front doors of the church. The case the captain had dumped in his lap Thursday morning had been an absolute shitshow, and he'd worked eighteen hours both Thursday and Friday, as well as most of this morning.

He'd had less than an hour to get home, shower, shave, and get to the church.

"Shit," he muttered and stopped outside of the church. He wore a tie regularly and still couldn't tie one properly to save his life. It was embarrassing. He was about to say, 'fuck it' and go without the tie when he heard her low voice.

"Bren?"

He whirled around, staring at Kaida. "Kaida? What are you doing here?"

"I was invited," she said.

He grimaced. "Sorry, I meant – how did you get here without a bunch of reporters following you?"

A small smile crossed her gorgeous face. "Mal and Willow snuck me out in the trunk of their car this morning."

"That's great." He couldn't stop staring at her. She wore a form-fitting blue dress that perfectly matched the streaks of blue in her hair. Her long dark hair was pulled into a messy bun on the top of her head, with a few tendrils framing her face. He glanced at her breasts and then her hips before clearing his throat. "So, uh, what are you doing out here? The wedding is starting in less than fifteen minutes."

"I needed some fresh air." She glanced at the church. "Sometimes I get a little claustrophobic, and I'm used to keeping as far away from others as possible. The realization that I don't have to hide who I am around shifters and humans is still settling in."

There was an awkward silence, and he said, "You look beautiful."

The flush to her cheeks made him think of how she looked when they kissed. "Thank you. You look very handsome as well."

"Thanks. Can't get the damn tie right." He pointed to the tie draped around his neck.

"I can help you," she said.

"I'd appreciate that."

She stepped closer, and he inhaled deeply as she went to

work on his tie. She always smelled like - he smiled a little - vanilla and smoke, and he found it weirdly hot.

When she was finished with his tie, he took her hand before she could step away. "I'm really glad you're here."

"Are you?"

He held tight when she tried to tug her hand free. "What's that supposed to mean?"

She sighed and stared at their feet. "Why would you be glad to see me? My family tried to burn you alive. I know why you're avoiding me, I do, and I promise I'll leave you alone. But I wanted to say how sorry I am for -"

She made a low sound of surprise when Bren put his arm around her waist and tugged her against his body. He pressed a chaste kiss against her mouth. "I'm not avoiding you."

"You haven't texted or -"

"I know, and I'm sorry. I should have texted you, but I had a case dropped on my lap on Thursday, and I've been working crazy hours since then. I'm running late because I was working this morning."

"You don't have to use work as an excuse," she said. "I get it, okay?"

"It's not an excuse." He pressed his forehead against hers. "Yeah, it's been mostly work, but I thought maybe I should also give you some space. Lots of changes are happening in your world, and I assumed you wanted to be with your clan. I didn't want to intrude."

"You should hate me," she said in a low voice.

"*You* didn't want to burn me alive," he said. "In fact, I seem to remember you challenging the biggest, scariest looking dude in the room just to keep me safe. Thank you for that, by the way."

"You're not angry with me?" she said.

He shook his head. "Nope. Not even a little."

She cupped his face, and the fierce look in her eyes made his dick stir in his pants. "I would never let my clan or any other hurt you."

Jesus, did it make him weird to find her sexy as hell when she acted like he was hers to protect?

"I know," he said. "And for the record – I've got your back as well."

A smile crossed her face, and he grinned at her. "Yeah, yeah, I know. I'm a weak-ass human pretending a dragoness could need protection from him. I get how stupid I sound."

Her smile dropped, and she gave him another one of those fierce looks. "You are not stupid. You're one of the bravest humans I've ever met, Bren. It would be an honour to have you fight by my side."

When he kissed her, she parted her lips immediately. He tasted the sweetness of her mouth, one hand sliding down to squeeze her ass. She pressed herself against him, the kiss turning hungrier...needier.

With a low groan, he broke the kiss. Kaida's eyes were glowing and he could see the tips of her fangs between her parted lips. When she tried to kiss him again, he rasped, "Wait."

Her nostrils flared, and she took a deep breath. "I'm sorry."

"I'm not. But we're supposed to be attending our friends' wedding that starts in," he glanced at his watch, "six minutes, and I'm going to need at least two minutes before we go into the church."

She stepped away, tugging at her dress as he took a quick look around and then readjusted his aching dick. His erection was evident against his suit pants, and when Kaida stared hungrily at his crotch, he made a low groan. "You keep staring at my dick like that, and it's never gonna go down."

Her smile was both wicked and wanton. With another groan, Bren looked away and thought about the least sexy things he could imagine – changing his furnace filter, working on his taxes, catching up on the never-ending paperwork for his job.

After a couple of minutes, he held out his arm.

Kaida grinned. "Houston, we no longer have a problem?"

He laughed. "The mission is a go. Would you like to sit with me for the ceremony?"

Kaida slid her hand around his arm. "I'd love to."

"IT WAS A BEAUTIFUL CEREMONY, WASN'T IT?" MAGGIE, A human who – Kaida thought – might be mated to Mal's brother Porter, said with a tentative smile.

"It really was. Ava was gorgeous, and Bishop was very handsome," Kaida said.

Bren sat next to her, and he leaned forward to grin at Maggie. "He also looked incredibly nervous."

Maggie laughed. "Yes, he was definitely nervous."

Porter joined them, holding a beer in each hand, and sat in the chair next to Maggie. "Here you go, darlin'."

"Thanks, honey." She took the beer from him. "We were just talking about how lovely the ceremony was."

"It was nice. The food was fantastic." Porter patted his lean abdomen. "Shouldn't have been surprised, though. B was in charge of the food, and he loves eating."

Maggie took a sip of her beer. "I liked the church and the reception venue. We should talk to Ava and Bishop about who they booked through."

"Sure," Porter said.

"Are you getting married?" Kaida said.

Maggie's shy smile widened, and she held out her left hand. "We are. We got engaged last week."

"Congratulations. That's a beautiful ring," Kaida said as Bren shook Porter's hand and then Maggie's.

"I'm happy for you two," he said.

"Thanks, man. It wouldn't have happened if it wasn't for you. So, expect an invitation to the wedding," Porter said.

Bren tipped his beer to him. "I look forward to it."

Kaida glanced curiously at Bren. What exactly did the wolf shifter mean? Was Bren a secret matchmaker in his spare time?

A slow and familiar song filled the reception hall, and Porter groaned. "Oh my God, what do you want to bet Ronin asked the DJ to play Celine Dion?"

Maggie laughed. "He did. I overheard him talking to Rosalie and Hudson about it."

Porter stood and held out his hand. "C'mon, darlin'. Let's dance."

Maggie took his hand, and they joined the other couples. Kaida could see Bishop and Ava swaying in the middle of the dance floor. Bishop held Lila in one beefy arm, and the other was wrapped around Ava's waist.

Bren stood. "Would you like to dance?"

"Yes." She took Bren's hand, and he led her to the edge of the dance floor. He put his arm around her waist and pulled her in tight against him. Her dragon purred loudly, and her skin prickled with awareness. God, she wanted the human so much.

"What did the wolf shifter mean if it hadn't been for you, they wouldn't be getting married?" she asked.

"Maggie was being stalked by a hyena shifter who was also a cop," Bren said. "He kidnapped her, and I helped Porter and the others get her back."

She blinked at him. "I saw something about that on the news. The guy who kidnapped her was the hero cop who saved your father from the assassination attempt a few years back. Right?"

He nodded, a grim look passing over his face. "Yeah, that's the one. He regretted saving my father. He thought it was the mayor the guy was after, not my dad."

"I remember reading about the cop being killed." Her eyes widened, and she searched the dance floor until her gaze landed on Porter and Maggie. "I can't believe Maggie was the woman he kidnapped."

Bren didn't reply, and she stared at him in sudden horror. "Oh my God, you were the cop who killed him."

"I was," Bren said. "I didn't have a choice."

"I'm sorry," she said.

"Me too." He laughed bitterly. "My father did a fantastic job of keeping the name of the cop who killed Vaughn, hush-hush. He had to grease a lot of palms, but he got it done. My name was never released to the public, and they buried the story as quickly as possible."

They danced silently for a few minutes before, in a blatant attempt to change the subject, Bren said, "So, I know they're Ava's parents," he pointed with his chin at a redheaded man dancing with a curvy brunette, "but I didn't see Bishop's parents."

"Bishop's father died when he was still a yearling, and his mother is," Kaida hesitated, "difficult. She and Bishop have always had a strained relationship. She disapproved of Ava and made Bishop choose between her and Ava. Bishop chose Ava."

"That's a terrible thing to do to your kid," Bren said.

"Leslie is a miserable person," Kaida said. "After their hatchling was born, Bishop and Ava took her to see Leslie. It didn't go well. Leslie was rude to Ava and said some unkind things about the hatchling. She wasn't pleased that Lila was a human and said so to Bishop."

"Uh oh," Bren said.

"Yes, as you can imagine, it did not go well. They haven't seen Leslie since."

"Family can be difficult," Bren said. He stroked her lower back, and a throb of need started up in her lower belly.

"Do you speak with your mother?" Kaida asked. "Tyler told me he texts with her from time to time."

"That sums up our relationship pretty accurately. We text from time to time. She doesn't have much interest in Ty or me," Bren said.

"I'm very sorry."

"Thanks. I'm mostly over it… I think, but I worry about Tyler. Mom might not have been the greatest parent when I was growing up, but I at least had her in the house to occasionally show some interest in me. Dad was an absent father at best, and Mom wasn't exactly present either, but she at least pretended to care. Tyler didn't even have that. He spends so much time looking for our father's approval."

He turned her in a slow circle, and the pain on his face made her heart ache for him. "I've asked Ty a hundred times to move in with me, but he won't. He thinks that if he just tries hard enough, Dad will show interest in him. It isn't going to happen. All that matters to our father is his career. He drove my mother and me away, and eventually, he'll drive Tyler away, too."

"I like Tyler a lot," she said. "I'll miss our training sessions together."

Bren smiled. "He's already tried to convince me that he can keep training with you. He was beyond excited when he found out you were a dragon. He called me before I'd even left your clan on Wednesday night."

The smile faltered a little. "He's pissed about not getting to see you again, but with so many reporters there, it's impossible. Most of them know who he is, and the press would have a goddamn field day if they caught him visiting with dragons."

"You as well," Kaida said.

"Probably. But I'm not a kid. I can handle that kind of shit."

"What would your father say if he knew we were friends?" Kaida asked.

They were on the other side of the dance floor now. Bren stopped dancing and, ignoring the others who danced around them, said, "Let's get two things straight. One, I don't give a rat's ass what my father thinks or says about anything I do, and I haven't for a very long time. And two, you are more to me than just a friend, Kaida."

His gaze dropped to her mouth, and she said, "What am I to you, then?"

"A gorgeous, unbelievably sexy woman who I want in my bed," he said.

She blinked a little at his straightforwardness before admitting the truth. "I want to be in your bed."

"Then come home with me. Right now," he said.

"I can't," she replied. "If we have sex and I hurt you…"

"You won't," he said.

"I might."

"We'll be careful." He rubbed her back again, pressing her a little closer until she could feel the hard length of him against her hip. "Just thinking about you in my bed does this to me. I want you, Kaida. And although I don't believe you'll hurt me, I do believe that being with you is worth the risk."

He let go of her hand and cupped her jaw, rubbing his thumb along her cheekbone. "Take the risk, Kaida, just for tonight. Let's see how good it can be with us. What do you say?"

Her dragon demanded she say yes, its loud purring almost drowning out the rapid beat of her heart in her ears.

She wanted this man. Wanted him with a deep-seated ache she'd never felt before. His rock-solid belief that they could be together drowned her worry, leaving only desire in its place.

"Yes," she said in a low voice. "I want that very much."

His smile lit up his face, turning his already handsome features into something that resembled a god-like beauty. "Good. Let's get out of here."

CHAPTER 19

The human was nervous. Kaida could smell it drifting from his skin as he opened the apartment door and ushered her in. It was mixed with the stronger scent of lust, but her dragon still purred to the human, trying to soothe him.

"I really like that purring noise you do." They had grabbed her small suitcase from the trunk of Willow's car before they left the reception – Kaida flushed a little remembering the look of pure glee on Willow's face when she realized Kaida was leaving with Bren – and Bren set it down by the front door.

He took her hand and led her down the hallway, pausing at the kitchen. "Do you want a drink first?"

"No." She tugged on his hand, and this time, she guided him down the hallway. They entered his bedroom, and he flicked on the bedside lamp as she slipped out of her heels. By the time he'd kicked off his shoes and turned to face her, she had stripped off her dress and stood in front of him in her bra, panties, and stockings.

"Holy fuck," he said.

"Do you like, human?" she said with a small smile.

"Very much." He pulled her into his arms, and they kissed greedily. Kaida pushed Bren's suit jacket off his arms and loosened his tie. They broke apart, and she tugged on the tie. "Take off your clothes, Bren."

He stripped off his clothes, leaving them carelessly on the floor. She laughed when he hopped on one foot to remove his socks, but the laugh died in her throat when he pushed his briefs down his legs and stepped out of them.

"Do you like, dragoness?" he said teasingly.

His cock was long and thick, and her mouth watered, beautiful. She wanted to touch... she wanted to taste.

"I want it," she said. "Give it to me."

A smile crossed his gorgeous face. "Soon."

Her dragon growled in disapproval, but Bren was sliding his arms around her, and the way he trailed his fingers down her spine sent goosebumps popping up across her flesh. He bent his head and tasted her throat, his warm tongue licking a path up to her earlobe. He sucked on the lobe as he unhooked her bra. She wiggled out of it the moment it was loose, tossing it on top of Bren's clothes.

He sucked in a breath, staring hungrily at her tits. When he cupped one, she arched into his touch. "Beautiful," he said before plucking at one hard nipple. She cried out, arching her body against his until she could feel his cock pressing against her hip.

Before she could reach between them and touch it, his mouth closed around one aching nipple. He sucked hard, his hand teasing her other nipple with light pinches.

"Bren!" She clutched at his head, closing her eyes and losing herself to the sensation of his warm mouth and wet tongue as he kissed and sucked on each of her nipples.

She growled when he lifted his head. He pressed a kiss

against her mouth. "It's getting warm in here. Let's open the window."

She was making the room warm. The heat radiated from her body and would only get worse the more turned on she got. Embarrassment rolling across her in soft waves, she said, "Bren, maybe -"

"Nope." He kissed her again. "Worth the risk, remember?"

He crossed the room and opened the window wide, popping out the screen and leaning it against the wall. Cold air drifted in, and Kaida glanced at the bed as Bren joined her. "Do you want me to move the bed closer to the window?"

She shook her head. "No, it's close enough."

"Good." He stood behind her and kissed the back of her neck, cupping her hips and pulling her back against his dick. She ground against it as his hands slid up her flat abdomen and cupped her breasts. "Just so I know...how warm will your body get? Hot enough to burn me?"

"It shouldn't," she said. "As long as I release the flame."

"Perfect." He plucked at her nipples, making it difficult for her to concentrate on his words. "The window faces the alley, just like the spare room, so feel free to let loose with the fire."

She pressed her hands over his, stopping their movement. "Bren, are you sure you want to do this?"

"Yes. I'm not worried."

"Until I'm climaxing and accidentally set you on fire."

He laughed, the sound warm and rich and doing a remarkable job of soothing her fear. "I'll take my chances."

He nipped her neck, those big hands of his tracing the bumps of her ribs and making her forget why being with him was probably a bad idea. Hell, she was probably panicking for nothing. It would be fine. She was attracted to Bren, and she wanted to fuck him, but the orgasm had to be incredibly intense for her to blow fire. She'd only lost control of her orgasms a few times in the past, and she'd been younger then. She had better control now.

Yeah, well, you also haven't had sex with anything other than a vibrator for over a year, so...

Her inner voice made a good point.

"Kaida?" Bren's hands had stopped their roaming and were clasped loosely across her abdomen.

"Sorry," she said. "I was up in my head for a minute."

"Would you feel better if we had a safe word?"

She craned her neck to stare up at him. "Safe word?"

"Yep." His grin was adorable. "Let's see, if I start shouting 'marshmallow,' that'll be your cue to stop sexy fun times."

"Marshmallow?" A smile curved her lips upward. "Really?"

"What? I'll be a toasted marshmallow... you get it, right?"

She burst out laughing. "Oh my God, you're such a dork. But okay, marshmallow it is."

He slipped his fingers under the waistband of her panties, and her laughter was replaced with a low moan.

He kissed the sensitive spot below her ear and whispered, "Spread your legs, honey."

One hand cupping and teasing one breast, he touched the soft curls at the top of her mound with his other hand as she spread her legs. His fingers traced her wet pussy lips before dipping between them and rubbing delicately at her clit.

She hissed out a breath, smoke drifting from her nostrils as her skin heated up. She clutched at his arm as his fingers explored and teased. One thick finger probed at her opening, and when it slipped into her, she cried out with pleasure.

"I want to taste your pussy," Bren breathed into her ear. "You good with that?"

"Oh God, yes," she panted.

He helped her out of her panties and then rolled down her stockings, his tongue tracing a path from her thigh to mid shin as he crouched in front of her and pulled her stockings off her feet. He tossed them aside and stared at her pussy, a look of hunger on his face. She waited for him to kiss her pussy, but instead, he pressed another kiss on her thigh before standing. "Lie on the bed, honey."

She climbed onto his bed, lying on her back and watching as Bren took out a condom from the bedside table drawer. He set it on top of the table and walked to the foot of the bed. His hand stroked his cock lazily. She could see precum gleaming at the tip of it, and her mouth watered.

"Forget the pussy eating," she said. "I want to fuck you."

He grinned and shook his head. "No backsies."

"Human," she growled as more smoke drifted from her nose. "I want your cock."

"We have plenty of time. You can have it later," he said. He stretched out on his stomach between her legs and hooked his arms under her thighs. He kissed her inner thigh, and she let her legs fall apart wide. Bren was right. They had plenty of time, and just the thought of Bren's mouth on her pussy was making her wet.

When he didn't move, she tapped him on the back with her foot. "Human, eat my pussy."

"Yes, ma'am," he said with a soft laugh.

She cried out, her hands clenching around the bedsheets at the first touch of his tongue against her pussy. He licked slowly and delicately, cleaning away the moisture without going near her aching clit.

"Human!" Her voice was a low growl. "Enough teasing!"

"Enough?" His head lifted, and he smiled at her as his hands cupped her ass. "Honey, I haven't even started."

Her growl turned into purring as he dipped his head and licked up her slit. His tongue brushed against her clit, and she arched, her hand clamping down on the back of his head to keep him where he was. To her relief, he focused on her clit, licking and sucking and nibbling lightly until she was grinding her pussy against his mouth, and pleasure filled every molecule of her body.

"Kaida." Bren's voice was low and so sexy sounding it sent more pleasure licking up her spine. "Cool yourself down, honey."

She stared blankly at him before looking at her chest. It was glowing red, and the room was stifling hot, even with the open window. She rose on her elbows, turned her head, and blew a burst of flame through the window. The red glow in her chest dimmed and she fell back against the pillows as Bren smiled at her.

"Good. See... no problem."

"No problem," she gasped. Unease was trickling through her body. She hadn't even come yet, and Bren was making her so hot – no pun intended – that she needed to release the flame.

Maybe this isn't such a good idea, her inner voice whispered.

Her dragon snarled in disagreement, and the thought was lost anyway when Bren sucked on her clit again. She cried his name, her hands twisting and turning in his thick hair as he teased the swollen nub with gentle nips and licks.

Her body was heating up again, her chest glowing bright red as she drew closer to her orgasm. Bren's mouth was hot and wet, his tongue dancing feverishly over her clit, making the pleasure in her belly spike higher and higher.

He sucked her clit into his mouth again, and it pushed her over the edge. She shrieked his name and reared upward, her body on fire, the pleasure pulsing through every nerve ending. She sucked in a deep breath and turned her face toward the window, opening her mouth before the fire could consume her. It shot out of her mouth and out through the window, a giant blast of orange and red flickering heat that lit up the alleyway like a beacon.

She sucked in another breath, her body shaking wildly, and released another burst of flame. This one was smaller and less intense, and she moaned before falling back on the bed. Bren slid up beside her, turning on his side and resting his hand on her quivering belly.

"Are you okay?" she gasped out. Her hands trembling, she examined his mouth and face, looking for redness or burn marks.

"I'm good," he said.

"Are you sure? You're not burnt or -"

He pressed his mouth against hers, stopping the jumble of words. He cupped her breast, toying with her nipple as they kissed deeply.

She reached down and slid her hand around his cock, pleasure spearing through her belly when he groaned into her mouth. She jacked him lightly, rubbing her thumb across the slit at the top until his hips jerked uncontrollably.

He tore his mouth from hers. "Fuck, that feels so good."

She tightened her grip and stroked him some more as she kissed his chest. "Good. Roll onto your back. I want to be on top."

He immediately rolled onto his back, reaching for the condom. Her dragon growled with pleasure at her mate's obedience, and she leaned over and placed a path of kisses across his chest. She flicked her tongue against his flat nipple, and he muttered a curse, one hand cupping the back of her head. She sucked on his nipple and then broke free of his grip, smiling at him.

"Are you ready?"

"Condom," he muttered. Kaida took the condom from his hand. She rolled it down his cock, smoothing it into place and making a low sound of disapproval when he arched into her hand.

"Patience, Bren." She leaned over and kissed just below his belly button.

He cried out, his hips jerking upwards. "Kaida, please."

"I'll suck your cock later," she said teasingly before swinging a leg over him. "I want to fuck you."

"I want that too." His hands cupped her hips as she gripped the base of his cock. She pressed the head of his dick against her opening, and they both groaned when she lowered herself down. His head breached her, and she pushed against the thick length, moaning as he filled her.

She took all of him, her bottom pressing against his warm body as she sank down.

"So tight," he moaned as his hands dug into her hips.

She took a couple of deep breaths. "I love how thick you are."

"Glad you – oh fuck…" Bren cried out when she squeezed her pussy around his cock. "Honey, don't do that. You'll make me come."

She smiled down at him before taking his hands and placing them on her tits. He kneaded them roughly, his gaze trained on her pussy as she rose up and down slowly. His hips flexed beneath her, meeting each of her thrusts.

When she reached down and rubbed at her clit, he groaned and braced his feet on the bed, cupping her hips and thrusting into her harder and deeper. She let him control the pace as she brought herself closer to the edge.

"I want another one," she panted to him. "All right?"

"Yes," he groaned. "I want to feel you coming on my dick."

She moaned, hot pleasure spiking through her pelvis and lower belly at his words. As she continued to thrust, she concentrated on her clit, rubbing in hard and furious circles. Her chest started to glow, and she threw her head back, staring up at the ceiling as her orgasm grew closer.

When the pleasure washed over her, she faced the window and released the fire in her chest. Shuddering, she braced her hands on Bren's chest, riding each of his thrusts as he reached for his climax.

She reached for his hands, peeling them off her hips and yanking them over his head. She pressed him into the bed, pinning him down and riding him hard, squeezing her pussy around his cock with every downward stroke.

"Fuck!" The scent of his need intensified, and she watched in fascination as his eyes slammed shut and he shouted her name. His body reared up, the cords in his neck standing out as he came and came again.

She slowed the pace of her thrusts, rocking gently against him as he collapsed against the bed. She released his hands and eased off of him before removing the condom and tossing it into the garbage can next to the bed.

"Thanks," he gasped out as she lay on her side next to him.

He pulled her up against him, and she threw one leg over his, resting her head on his chest and listening to the rapid thump of his heart.

"You good?" she asked.

"So good," he panted, his warm hand stroking her back.

The room was smoky, and, a little embarrassed, she tried to wave the smoke away from his face.

"Hold on," he said. He leaned over and grabbed a small black remote on the bedside table. He pressed a button, and the ceiling fan above them whirred to life. The smoke started dissipating, and when goosebumps appeared on Bren's chest, she quickly pulled the sheet and quilt up to cover them both.

"Sorry about the smoke," she said.

"It's not a problem."

"Yeah, because having a bedroom that smells like a campfire is awesome."

He kissed her forehead. "I happen to love the smell of a campfire."

"Thank you for being so understanding."

"Thank *you* for not setting me on fire when you orgasmed."

Her smile turned into a laugh. "You're welcome."

They lay in silence for a few minutes. Bren stroked her back and said, "Can you stay the night with me, or do you need to return to your clan?"

Stay, her dragon growled to her.

"I can stay," she said.

"Are you sure?" He traced her spine with his fingers. "I understand if you need to be back with your clan."

She almost said *I need to be with you* before coming to her senses. "No, I want to stay."

"Good." He clicked off the light and yawned. "Because I'm dead tired, and I like the idea of falling asleep with you."

"I like it too," she said. "Do you have to work in the morning?"

"No, solved the case today because I am the world's greatest detective."

"That's good," she said with a soft laugh. She snuggled closer. It was nice to be in Bren's bed, to feel his warm body against hers and hear his even breathing.

"Bren?"

He didn't reply, and she was a little amused to realize he'd fallen asleep already. She kissed his chest and snuggled closer. "Good night, my mate."

HE LIKED WAKING UP WITH KAIDA IN HIS BED.

They'd fallen asleep with the window open and the ceiling fan on, and his room was cold. But even with the brisk fall air wafting through the window, he was toasty warm. He pressed a little closer to Kaida's warm back. There were benefits to having a dragoness in one's bed.

His morning wood pressed firmly against Kaida's ass. He kept his eyes closed and traced the pads of his fingers along her shoulder, down her arm, across the curve of her hip, and over her smooth thigh. She sighed softly and moved closer, pushing her ass against his dick.

He opened his eyes. The light spilling into his room suggested it was just after dawn. He kissed between Kaida's shoulder blades. Her hair was still piled on top of her head, and he kissed the back of her neck before cupping her breast.

She made a sleepy sound of need and arched her back, pushing more of her perfect breast into his hand. Last night had been incredible, and he didn't care what Kaida thought. The fact that she blew fucking fire when she climaxed was amazing.

He plucked at her nipple and kissed along the top of her shoulder. He'd spend the rest of his life sleeping in a cold bedroom if it meant waking up with Kaida in his bed.

Whoa, slow down there, buddy. You barely know this woman. Maybe don't start planning the wedding quite yet, what do you say?

His inner voice was right, but it was hard not to picture a long-term commitment with Kaida. She was intelligent and funny, and they had crazy chemistry. Why couldn't they at least date?

Maybe because she's a damn dragon? A human and a dragon have no future together. Don't be naïve, Bren. Kaida knows it won't work. You need to get on the same page.

Did she, though? She'd called him her mate on Wednesday night and nearly lost her shit when the other dragoness touched him. She was possessive of him, and he found that possessiveness extremely hot.

Still doesn't mean you have a future with her.

He shut his inner voice out and concentrated on Kaida's smooth skin. She was rocking her ass against his dick, and the sleepy sounds had become low moans. When he slipped his hand between her legs and cupped her pussy, he found her hot and soaking wet.

"Bren," she moaned.

"Good morning, Kaida." He nipped at the back of her shoulder. "How did you sleep?"

"Good," she panted as he rubbed at her clit. "Really good."

He pushed one finger into her, loving the way her smooth pussy gripped and squeezed. "You're very wet already."

"Fuck me," she demanded.

Her chest was starting to glow, and his dick hardened even more. He kissed her neck and whispered in her ear. "Stay right there, honey."

She moaned in disappointment when he slid his finger out of her pussy. He turned and fumbled another condom out of the bedside table, ripping open the foil and sliding it down his dick before rolling back to face her.

She was rubbing her clit, and her chest was glowing bright red. He cupped her breast – the heat radiating from her was enormous – and pinched her nipple. She cried out, and the tips of his fingers tingled from the heat when the red in her chest deepened.

He pushed her hand away from her clit and replaced it with his own. The heat intensified until his eyes were watering, and the air around them grew hot.

"Cool yourself down, honey," he said, stilling his fingers against her clit.

"Bren, fuck me," she moaned.

"I will, as soon as you cool down," he said.

She rubbed her ass against his cock, and he muttered a curse. His dick didn't care how hot she was, it wanted to be inside of her.

"Kaida," he said.

She drew a deep breath, and he watched in fascination as fire exploded out of her mouth. Her aim was slightly off, and he could see the singe marks on the windowsill. She craned her head to stare at him. "You will fuck me now, human, or I'll take what I want."

He loved it when she turned demanding. She'd said she liked control in the bedroom, and if it meant getting to bury himself deep inside of her tight pussy regularly, he'd happily let her take the damn reins.

He raised her leg, running his hand down her smooth thigh before sliding down a little and lining his cock up with her entrance. She pushed back immediately, sheathing him almost entirely, and they made identical groans of pleasure.

He squeezed her thigh and pushed in close, loving the way she gripped him so tightly right to the very base. "Fuck, you feel so good around my dick."

She moaned and pushed back, meeting each of his shallow thrusts. "Bren, harder."

He gripped her hip and pumped hard in and out of her. She cried out, panting loudly and reaching back to grab his ass as she stared up at the ceiling. He rubbed her clit before pinching it between his fingers.

She made another short cry, a small puff of flame escaping her mouth. "I'm sorry," she gasped.

He fucked her harder in response, burying his aching dick in her hot wetness over and over as she moaned his name. He pinched her clit again, and her pussy clamped down on his dick as she climaxed. Her chest glowed dimly, and smoke drifted from her open mouth and nostrils as she squeezed around him repeatedly.

The base of his spine tingled, and his balls drew up tight. Moaning her name, he pushed in deep, letting the pleasure wash over him as he pumped in and out of her tight pussy. His limbs shaking, he collapsed on top of her. She took his weight well, one warm hand rubbing his thigh as he kissed between her shoulder blades.

When he'd gotten his breath back, he moved back, easing out of her and disposing of the condom before lying on his side. She rolled to face him, and he pulled her in close, their legs entwined as she stared sleepily at him. "What time is it?"

"Early. Do you want breakfast, or do you want to sleep some more?"

She pressed a kiss against his mouth, the soft scent of smoke surrounding them both. "Sleep."

"Good," he said. "Because I'm gonna need at least half an hour before I can walk."

She laughed and snuggled in close. "Am I too warm?"

"Nope, you're perfect."

"You too," she mumbled as her eyes drifted shut. Bren stared at her face for a few minutes, tracing small circles on her back before closing his eyes.

CHAPTER 20

When he woke a second time, the bed was empty next to him. He sat up, the weird bubble of panic in his chest deflating when he saw Kaida's suitcase sitting open on the floor. He climbed out of the bed and headed to the bathroom.

Once done, he brushed his teeth, pulled on a pair of sweats and a t-shirt, and checked his phone for texts before opening the bedroom door.

"Shit!" He grabbed at his chest and glared at the large black crow standing in front of his bedroom door and staring at him. "Dammit, Lilianna."

The crow cawed loudly before turning and strutting down the hallway toward the kitchen.

"You know you have wings, right?" Bren said as he followed the bird. "You could just fly."

He walked into the kitchen. Elora and Kaida sat at the table together, half-eaten muffins and cups of coffee in front of them.

"Tell me your grandmother didn't make those muffins."

Bren grabbed a mug from the cupboard, poured himself a cup of coffee and joined them at the table, sinking into the chair next to Kaida.

"Ha, ha," Elora said. "Helen didn't make them, I did."

"Perfect." He grabbed one from the container and bit into it. He was starving and shoved another bite into his mouth before sipping coffee.

"Anyway," Elora turned back to Kaida, "before Mr. Worst Bedhead Ever interrupted us, I was saying that I couldn't imagine having to hide my true nature all the time."

"Honestly? It's weirder now, realizing that I don't have to hide who I am," Kaida said.

"I suppose," Elora said as Lilianna flew up to her lap and landed on her thigh. She handed the crow a piece of muffin and stared thoughtfully at Kaida. "How often do you change into your dragon form?"

"Once or twice a week," Kaida said. "We have designated times during the night when we can shift and fly for a bit."

"How awesome is it to fly during daylight?" Elora asked.

"We haven't yet. The council believes it's best to continue to keep a low profile for now, and with the number of reporters and humans milling about our home..." Kaida smiled at Bren. "Thank you for sending the police to keep the crowds back. It made a huge difference."

"You're welcome. Is Bishop's firm taking over on Monday?"

"Yes."

Bren took another sip of coffee. Elora was staring at him, and he almost spit out the coffee when she said, "So, you two are dating now, huh?"

There was a moment of perfect silence.

"Yes," Bren said.

"No," Kaida said.

"We're not?" Bren could hear the hurt in his voice and grimaced inwardly. He thought they'd had a great time last night and was anxious to get to know her better. But if Kaida didn't want to date him, he wouldn't beg.

Probably for the best, anyway. Once your father finds out you're dating her, the shit will hit the fan.

Like I care what my father thinks.

"Well, this is awkward," Elora said.

Kaida glanced at Bren. "I like the human very much, but we can't date. I can't leave the clan without being followed by reporters, and if Bren's father saw him with me..."

"I don't care about that," Bren said.

"I do," Kaida replied. "Dating the son of a man who holds great power and hates shifters isn't keeping a low profile. What do you think he'd do if he discovered we were dating, Bren?"

He didn't want to admit it.

"He'd lose his mind," he said.

"Exactly," Kaida said. "Honestly, my clan would not be happy about it either. They don't trust humans and probably never will."

"Dating Bren could show them that humans can be trusted," Elora said. "He's the most loyal, trustworthy person I know. Once they get to know him, they'll see it too."

He appreciated that Elora had his back but didn't think it would make a difference.

"You're a good man, Bren Matthews, and I wish things were different," Kaida reached out and took his hand, "but the timing is terrible. Yes, humans and shifters know about dragons, but that makes it worse. Perhaps when we are no longer a novelty, and the human's fascination with us has worn off, we could try dating?"

The hopeful look she gave him made his chest tight. He squeezed her hand. "I'd like that."

Kaida smiled with happiness. Bren wanted to be happy, too, but he had a feeling it would be months before he and Kaida could be together. The thought sent depression swirling through his guts.

"That could take forever," Elora echoed the thought in his head. "Your problem is finding a way for Kaida to sneak out so she can see you, right?"

"That's one of the problems," Bren said.

Elora nodded impatiently. "Yes, yes, your idiot father and the obsessed humans and the clan who will never trust you... but, look, you guys don't even know if you want anything serious yet, yeah? I mean, you just got together last night, right?"

Bren glanced at Kaida, a little amused to see the blush that graced her cheeks. "Right."

"Okay, well, let's forget about what your father might do if he found out you were dating or how obsessed the rest of the world would be with your sex life if they knew a dragon and a human were boning. Until you guys know you want to get married and have tiny little dragon-human hybrid babies together -"

"Our hatchlings would be dragon or human," Kaida said. "There is no such thing as a hybrid."

Bren stared at her. Did she want to have his babies?

Kaida cleared her throat and ignored the look he was giving her. "Go on, little witch."

"Until you know it's serious between you, there's no point worrying about the other two problems," Elora said. "We need to concentrate on the problem of Kaida leaving her clan without being followed by the reporters. We *could* wait until they finally decided to leave on their own, but I have a feeling that'll be at *least* a month. Dragons existing is the juiciest story to hit the world in years. So, we come up with a way for Kaida to leave the clan without being seen."

"How?" Bren said. "The reporters are all over the woods surrounding her home."

Elora grinned at him before holding out her hand and muttering a few incantations. A blue ball of light formed at her fingertips and then rose in the air, hovering above her fingers for a few seconds before it burst into a shower of glittery light.

"With magic."

LILLIANA CAWED SOFTLY FROM HER PERCH ON ELORA'S THIGH. Her beady black eyes studied the glowing bits of light as they slowly faded.

"Magic," Kaida said.

"Yes." Elora stared excitedly at her. "I'll make you an invisibility potion."

"You can do that?" Kaida asked. Her admiration of the little witch was rising by the minute.

"Sure can," Elora said. "It's ridiculously easy. I'll bind it to only you so that if someone else stumbles onto the potion and drinks it, it won't do anything. But that means I'll need a bit of your hair and a scale from your dragon."

"Why's that?" Kaida asked.

"I need something from your human form and your dragon form to make the invisibility potion work for both." Elora clapped her hands, making Lillianna caw in annoyance before flying off her thigh and out of the kitchen. "Oh, this is going to be so much fun. I haven't made an invisibility potion in ages. Bren, where are your scissors?"

"Are you forgetting something?" Bren said.

"What?" Elora smiled innocently at him.

"The WWC strictly regulates the use of invisibility potions. You have to first submit your request in writing to the council with your reasons for creating the potion. I'm pretty sure they won't believe 'so Kaida and I can date' is a valid reason to create the potion. It'll be denied, Elora."

"God, sometimes I hate that you're a cop and know all the rules," Elora said.

The hope that was growing in Kaida's belly disappeared. She'd woken this morning to find her dragon more content than it had been in years. Seeing Bren in the bed beside her made her dragon purr, and – she had to admit – it made her happy, too. She wasn't even feeling the pull for her clan yet, and she was certain she could spend another night with him before returning to her clan.

"It's my job," Bren said. "I appreciate you are wanting to help, Elora, but you could be labeled a dark witch if they caught you."

"Oh, please," Elora said. "They're not going to label me a dark witch for this. At most, I'd be reprimanded and have to pay a fine. Besides, do you know how many witches and warlocks break the rules daily regarding potions and spells, Bren? The WWC barely cares when someone like me breaks one tiny little rule. Just last week, my friend Janelle created a barrier spell that stopped her neighbour's dog from pooping in her yard. Her neighbour reported her to the WWC, and they didn't even send anyone to speak to her. They just sent her a form letter referencing the rules about barrier spells."

She rolled her eyes. "Honestly, the only time they care is if the spell or potion may potentially harm a human or paranormal. And with dark witches on the rise, they've got their hands full with them."

"Dark witches are on the rise?" Kaida said.

Elora blanched. "Shit, I shouldn't have said anything."

"Should we be worried?" Bren asked.

"No, no. It's fine. There's a bit of a… thing going on right now in the witch world, but it's fine. The WWC will handle it."

"What sort of thing?" Bren asked.

"I can't say," Elora said. "That will definitely put me on the WWC's shit list. Anyway, Kaida isn't using the invisibility potion for anything other than sneaking out of the clan to see you. Right, Kaida?"

"Yes," Kaida said.

"Then we're all good." Elora jumped up and started yanking open drawers. "Scissors, Bren?"

"Kaida, are you sure you want to do this?" Bren asked.

Kaida didn't hesitate. Now that humans knew about dragons and now that she'd successfully had sex with Bren without setting him on fire, she wanted to explore the possibility of a relationship with him. She *needed* to. Her dragon would go mad if she didn't.

"I am."

Your clan is going to freak out. They'll never accept him as your mate.

She ignored her inner voice and squeezed Bren's hand again. "Unless," God, she hoped he wasn't changing his mind, "you don't want to try dating?"

"I want to," he said immediately.

"Then we're good." She smiled at him, warmth flooding her belly when Bren returned her smile.

Elora waved the scissors and a clear plastic baggie in the

air and slammed a drawer shut. "Got them. This is going to be so great for you two."

She stood beside Kaida and snipped off a small lock of her hair before placing it in a plastic baggie. "I've been watching a ton of the dragon stuff online and on television, and the good news is, I haven't seen Kaida once, so you guys should be able to go out and do couple stuff without people realizing you're a dragon."

Kaida scowled. "How often have they shown my clan members on TV?"

"Not that often," Elora assured her. "It mostly happened before the police set up the barricade, and even then, the dragons weren't that clear because the damn vultures were trying to record you through the windows of your houses. God, people suck."

She smiled tentatively at Kaida. "Okay, so I'll need a dragon scale now."

Kaida held out her arm and concentrated. She heard Bren's sharp breath when the scales appeared on her forearm. Hoping he wasn't freaking out, she plucked out a scale – her dragon grumbled a complaint – and handed it to Elora.

Elora held the shimmery blue scale up to the light. "It's beautiful. I would kill to see you in your dragon form." She stared hopefully at Kaida.

"I can't," Kaida glanced around the kitchen. "I am much bigger in my dragon form, and I'm pretty sure Bren doesn't want his apartment destroyed."

"Definitely wouldn't get my security deposit back after that," Bren said.

Elora laughed. "Yeah, okay." She dropped the scale into the plastic baggie next to the hair. "Lilianna, let's go."

"How long will it take to make the potion?" Bren asked.

Lilianna flew back into the kitchen and landed on Elora's

shoulder. She preened Elora's hair before cocking her head and staring at the bag with the scale in it.

"Not that long," Elora said. "I should have it done by tonight."

Bren glanced at Kaida. "Can you stay that long?"

"I think so," she said.

We stay with our mate, her dragon growled.

"You sure?"

"Yes. I'll let you know if it changes," she said.

"Okay. I'll text you when I'm done." Elora, her body nearly vibrating with excitement, left the kitchen.

Kaida and Bren stared silently at each other before Bren leaned forward and pressed a kiss against her mouth. "Hi."

"Hi." She had a big stupid grin on her face that was matched by the one on Bren's.

"I had a great time last night," Bren said.

"I did, too."

"Are you hungry? A muffin isn't much for breakfast." He stood and opened the fridge door. "I could make us some pancakes or eggs and toast."

She joined him at the fridge, sliding her arm around his waist and kissing his neck. "I'm not hungry. Not for food."

"Oh yeah?" He wiggled his eyebrows at her. "What are you hungry for?"

She purred to him and slipped her hands under his shirt to stroke his lean abdomen. "Do you need to ask?"

"Not really," he said with a cute grin, "but I like hearing how hot you are for me."

She groaned, and he laughed. "Unintentional bad pun, I promise."

She kissed his neck again, liking how it made his stomach muscles quiver against her fingertips. "Why don't we go back to bed?"

He shut the fridge door. "I am one hundred percent into that idea."

The front door opened, and Kaida stared at Bren when they heard Tyler say, "Whatever, Dad. My chemistry test is more important. God, why can't you be like a normal dad for once."

"Shit," Bren said in a low voice. "Sorry, Tyler has a key to my place."

"Bren? Hey, Bren! Are you awake?" Tyler's voice moved down the hall. "Can you please tell Dad that I'm not... holy crap! Kaida! Hi!"

Kaida pulled her hands out from under Bren's shirt and stepped back. Shit. She was wearing one of Bren's t-shirts and yoga pants, and her hair was a rat's nest on top of her head. Telling herself it could have been worse – she could be braless - she smiled at Tyler. "Hey, Tyler."

Tyler glanced at her and then at Bren, his gaze taking in Ben's bedhead and her disheveled look. A huge smile crossed his face. "Oh my God, are you guys, like, together?"

Bren grimaced. "Ty, don't -"

"Hello, Bren."

A tall man with dark hair and blue eyes stepped into the kitchen. Despite never meeting him before, Kaida knew who he was. She'd seen the senator on TV and online enough times.

"Hello, Dad." Bren's voice had turned ice cold.

There was an awkward silence, and when Bren didn't introduce them, the senator stepped forward and held out his hand. "Robert Matthews."

"Kaida," she said and gave his hand a quick shake.

The senator stared steadily at her. His eyes might have been the same colour as Bren's, but they held none of the warmth that Bren's did. Her dragon growled out a warning, and she swallowed the smoke drifting up her throat.

"You didn't tell me you were dating someone, Bren," the senator said.

"I didn't know it was any of your business," Bren said.

His father's smile didn't thaw the ice in his gaze. "You're my son. Your life is always my business."

Bren didn't reply, and Robert looked her up and down. "You're big for a female."

"Dad!" Bren snapped. "Are you fucking kidding me right now?"

His father ignored him. "Are you a shifter? Is that why you're so tall?"

Heat was rising in her chest. Her dragon paced restlessly, growling at her to show the ignorant human what she could do to him.

"Oh please," Tyler scoffed. "Like Bren or I would ever date a shifter. We're not stupid. You'd lose your shit and end up in a damn mental hospital or something."

His father glared at him. "Watch your language, Tyler."

"Whatever." Tyler rolled his eyes in the universal language of teenagers and started texting on his phone.

"Why are you here?" Bren said to his father.

"Can't I visit my son without an interrogation?" Robert replied. He smiled his icy smile at Kaida. "I assure you I'm not the monster Bren has undoubtedly told you I am."

"Don't flatter yourself," Bren said. "I don't talk about you at all."

The icy smile turned a few degrees colder. "We need to speak about tomorrow. I've spoken to the captain of your precinct, and he's agreed to give you a few hours off work so you can join me."

Bren's brows creased. "What are you talking about?"

Annoyance flashed across his father's face. "Do you even look at your email, Bren? I had Theresa send you the email on Friday."

"I was busy with my job," Bren said. "If you need to discuss something with me, try reaching out yourself instead of having your assistant email me."

"If you responded to my texts, I might," Robert said. "The charity luncheon is tomorrow. It starts at eleven thirty and goes on until three. Wear a suit."

"I'm not going," Bren said.

"I need your support on this one," Robert said. "I'm announcing the introduction of the bill to the Senate. I want my family with me."

Kaida's stomach dropped as Bren said, "You're actually doing it. You're putting forward that ridiculous bill."

"It isn't ridiculous," Robert said. "It's a necessary step to protect humans from the paranormal."

"Forcing the paranormals to be tagged like animals and registering on a list isn't protecting humans," Bren said. "There is no point to this bill, and you won't get it passed. There are paranormals in the Senate, for God's sake. They'll never vote for it."

"I don't need them to," Robert said. "Both the House and the Senate have more humans than paranormals."

Bren scoffed. "It still won't work. Hell, it won't even make it past the subcommittee and you know it. You'll never have it passed into law, Dad. Stop wasting your time."

Bren's father's face was a deep dark red that made Kaida think of wine that had long gone sour. "You're wrong, Bren. The discovery that dragons exist has made humans nervous."

"What's the big deal?" Tyler looked up from his cell phone. "I think dragons are cool and so does everyone else at my school." His gaze drifted briefly to Kaida before returning to his dad. "They're, like, super chill."

"You have no idea what they're like, Tyler," Robert said. "They're dangerous. They're monsters who are a danger to the very fabric of our society. The fact that they lied about their existence speaks volumes about their character. They need to be monitored and controlled for our safety."

"Maybe they didn't say anything because of people like you," Tyler said. "Besides, they're not dangerous."

"See if you're still saying that when they burn everything you love," his father snapped.

Tyler rolled his eyes and returned to looking at his phone.

"This bill is important to me, as is having my family there to support me when I make the announcement," Robert said. "You will be there, Bren. You and Tyler both."

"I can't." Tyler's tone teetered on exasperation, leaning toward outright disrespect. "Oh my God, I told you how many times I have a chemistry exam tomorrow afternoon. I can't miss it. It's my hardest class."

"You can do a make-up exam," Robert said.

"No!" Tyler glared at him. "I'm not missing the exam."

"Is a chemistry exam the hill you want to die on?" his father snapped.

Tyler folded his arms across his chest. "Guess so."

Robert's cell phone rang, and he snatched it from his pocket. "For God's sake." He jabbed at the answer button. "Theresa, what is it?"

He listened before muttering a curse and ending the call without saying goodbye. "I need to go into the office. Bren, make sure you're there by -"

"I'm not going." Bren's voice was low but firm. "I don't support the bill, nor do I support the HAPI group. They're doing some illegal shit, Dad, and if you align yourselves with them -"

His father slammed his hand down on the kitchen table. "Enough, Bren! You know, just once, it would be nice if one of my children would look past his nose and support my efforts to fix this mess the world is in."

"Paranormals don't make the world a mess," Bren said. "It's the people who work for and volunteer with HAPI that are fucking everything up."

"Your bleeding heart sentiments are getting old," Robert said. "Neither of you want to be there tomorrow? Fine, don't be there. I don't need my constituents seeing what utter failures both of my sons are. Tyler, let's go."

"I'm staying with Bren tonight," Tyler said. "Right, Bren?"

The look he gave his brother was almost pleading. Without hesitating, Bren said, "Yes."

"Whatever," Robert said. He glanced at Kaida. "It's unfortunate my children's thoughtlessness marred our first meeting. It was a pleasure meeting you, Kaida."

Her hands in tight fists behind her back, Kaida said, "Goodbye, Senator Matthews."

He left the kitchen, and when the front door slammed behind him, Tyler said, "God, what a douche."

"Tyler," Bren warned.

"What? He is," Tyler said.

"He's still our father," Bren said.

Tyler shrugged before grinning at Kaida. "Can you imagine the look on his face if he knew Kaida was a dragon?" He snorted loud laughter. "He was going on and on about how dangerous dragons are, and one was standing right beside him. He's lucky she didn't torch him when he started talking shit about dragons."

"I wouldn't torch a human," Kaida said quickly.

"I know," Tyler said. His phone buzzed, and he glanced at it. "It's Corey. Can he come over and hang with us, too, Bren? Please?"

Bren glanced at Kaida. "Sure. Does he need a ride over?"

Tyler texted Corey and read the screen when his phone buzzed again. "Nah, his foster dad will be near here. Said he'd drop him off."

He stuck his phone into his back pocket and sniffed at his armpits. "I'm gonna take a quick shower. Oh, shit. I didn't wash the clothes I left here the last time I stayed over."

"I washed them and the other clothes, too," Bren said. "The amount of clothes you leave here is staggering. Do you have any left at home, buddy?"

"Some. Thanks for washing my stuff, dude." Tyler fist-bumped Bren before grinning at Kaida. "It's cool you and my brother are dating."

"Go have your shower, Ty," Bren said.

Tyler sauntered out of the kitchen, typing again on his phone. Bren waited a few seconds before turning to Kaida. "Well, you've met my father. Still want to try dating?"

She wrapped her arms around his waist and kissed his chest, her dragon purring softly to him. "Yes. You are not your father, Bren."

He rubbed her back. "Sorry about Tyler joining us for the day. If I didn't let him stay, Dad would have harassed him all afternoon about not going to the charity event, and -"

She pressed her lips against his, stopping the words. When she drew back, he smiled at her. "What was that for?"

"I love that you put Tyler's needs ahead of your own. You're an amazing brother, and Tyler is lucky to have you," she said.

His smile made her dragon purr again. He kissed her and then said, "Thanks for understanding. But if you want to return to your clan rather than hang out with the boys and me, I get it. I'll ask Bishop to bring the potion to you tomorrow and -"

"I want to stay," she said.

"I want that too." He kissed her again. "When Corey arrives, why don't the four of us go for lunch? I know an amazing diner that isn't very busy. There shouldn't be too much worry about a shifter smelling your scent and discovering what you are."

"That sounds perfect," she said.

CHAPTER 21

B ren set the suitcase on the bed and stripped out of his work clothes. He took a quick shower and threw on a pair of jeans and a t-shirt before heading to the kitchen. He grabbed a beer from the fridge and opened it.

Kaida would be here any minute, and he couldn't wait. She'd spent the entire day with him, Tyler, and Corey yesterday, and even though Elora had brought the invisibility potion to them by dinner time, Kaida had stayed until almost nine. They'd watched a movie with the boys, and he didn't think he imagined that Tyler was starting to glom onto her like a baby duck imprinting on a human. His younger brother wanted a mother figure, and while technically, Kaida wasn't old enough to be his mother, she had a calm and almost motherly energy that Tyler couldn't resist.

She'll be an excellent mother.

Yes, she would be. He allowed himself to imagine Kaida carrying his baby for a few brief moments before shaking his head and drinking some beer. He was being ridiculous. He appreciated that Kaida wanted to try dating, but he knew how it would end. His father would never accept her, and while he didn't give a shit what his father thought, her clan would never accept him, and Kaida wouldn't leave her clan. It was a no-win situation.

So why are you torturing yourself? End it with her now. Is the heartache worth it just so you don't have a case of blue balls?

He gulped down another swallow of beer, the bitter hops coating his tongue. It was more than just the sex. He liked Kaida a lot, and the thought of not seeing her made him anxious and pissed off.

It's only going to get worse if you don't end it now.

"Yeah, well, I'm not ending it with her, so shut it," he muttered.

There was a knock on his door, and he set the beer bottle on the counter and walked toward the door, unlocking it and swinging it open. "Since when do you knock, Elora? Or for that…"

The hallway was empty.

"What the hell?" he said.

"Bren, it's me."

He startled back, his heart knocking in his chest, and he made an unmanly squeak of surprise when he felt Kaida brush past him.

"Kaida?"

"Hi there." The door swung shut on its own, the deadbolt turning as if with magic.

"This is super weird," Bren said. "How did you get into the building?"

"Followed one of your neighbours in." Kaida's hand brushed across his chest. At least, he thought it was her hand. "Is that okay?"

"Yeah, it's no problem," he said. "Jesus, this is weird."

Her low laugh went straight to his dick. "I know. Hold on, I'll take the other potion."

Her voice was growing fainter, and he walked slowly to the kitchen. "Are you in here?"

"Yes. I'm about to take the potion," Kaida said.

"How come I can't see the bottle?" Bren asked.

"Whatever non-living stuff I'm holding when I drink the invisibility potion turns invisible with me," Kaida said.

"Oh. Cool."

"Very." There was silence, and then she said. "Okay, it takes a couple of minutes to kick in."

"Do you feel different?" he asked.

"No," Kaida said. "It does tingle a little when you disappear and reappear."

The air shimmered in front of him, shimmered and wavered, and then Kaida appeared, materializing in the kitchen like an actor on the Star Trek series.

His plans to throw out a glib, "Beam me up, Scotty," died in his throat.

Kaida was naked – gloriously naked – and her long hair flowed down her back in soft waves. She leaned against the counter, setting a small bluish-coloured bottle on the countertop. His gaze dropped to her breasts, and his cock hardened immediately. She really did have the most amazing tits he'd ever seen.

"How was your day, Bren?"

He blinked at her. "What?"

"Your day? How was it?"

"You're naked," he said.

"I know," she replied.

"Why? I mean, not that I'm complaining," he moved closer to her, but when he reached for his beer, she scooped up the bottle and took her own drink, "but I wasn't expecting you to be naked."

"I don't shift with my clothes on," Kaida said. "It would destroy them."

She handed him the beer bottle, and he took a long drink, his gaze still on her delectable tits. "No clothes when shifting. That makes sense."

She laughed. "Did Bishop bring my suitcase to you today?"

"He did. It's in my bedroom. What did you have to promise him to get him to do that favour?"

She took his beer and drank another swallow as his gaze dipped down her body. "Nothing. He did it because we're friends. Was it too presumptuous of me to leave some clothes and toiletries here? Bren?"

Her hand reached out and poked him in the chest. He dragged his gaze from her pussy. "What was that?"

Her smile was wicked and sweet. "Is it a problem if I leave some clothes and toiletries here? I can't wear clothes when I'm in my dragon form, and it's a pain to carry them in my mouth or talons when I'm flying here."

"It's not a problem," he said. "But I'm also perfectly fine with you walking around my apartment naked."

She laughed again. "Until Elora and her crow show up, or Tyler drops by with Corey."

"Good point," he said. He told himself to be a gentleman and lifted his gaze to her face. It was flushed with happiness and maybe a touch of desire, and he cupped her naked hip, tracing his fingers over her warm skin. "You look beautiful."

"Thank you. It was so amazing flying in the daylight, Bren." Her eyes sparkled, and she couldn't stop grinning. "Do you know I have never flown in the light before?"

"Really?"

"We've only ever been allowed to fly during the night. It

was," she paused, "a little terrifying, a lot exhilarating. I have never felt my dragon so happy and content."

"I'm glad," he said. "Are you hungry?"

"Maybe. Are you?" Kaida asked.

"I could eat… something." His gaze dropped to her pussy again.

She purred to him and pressed her naked body against him. "Let's go to your bedroom."

He pressed a kiss against her warm throat. "I like that idea."

He followed her to his bedroom, knowing she could smell his eagerness and not giving a damn. He started stripping off his clothes the minute they were in the room. She laughed as she opened the window, then crossed to the bed and sat on the side.

When he was naked, she crooked her finger at him. "Come here, human."

His pulse thudding and his lungs already fighting for oxygen, he joined her at the bed, standing in front of her. "Lie back, Kaida." His need to taste her, to bury himself between her smooth thighs and listen to her cries of pleasure were too intense to ignore.

"No," she said with a devilish smile as she eyed his erect cock. "It's my turn to taste you."

Her hand slid around the base of his dick, and he moaned when she licked away the bead of precum at the tip of his cock. His hands slid into her hair, gripping tightly and urging her forward before she could lean back.

Her warm laugh washed over his dick, and he groaned when she licked around the ridge and kissed her way down the heavy shaft. Her lips were soft and warm and felt fucking amazing, but he needed more. He gripped her skull tight and made a low pleading noise that made her purr loudly.

"Do you want my mouth, human? My tongue?"

"Christ, yes," he muttered. "Kaida, please. Suck."

Her warm wet mouth surrounded his aching dick, and he was in heaven. He forced himself not to drive forward into her mouth as she sucked in a slow and steady rhythm. Her tongue traced the vein below before cleaning away the precum that had collected at the tip. When her soft hand cupped his balls and tugged, he groaned harshly, his pelvis bucking forward.

"Such a good human," she said before closing her mouth around the head of his cock and sucking hard.

"Fuck!" He pushed forward, sliding his cock deep into Kaida's mouth, his hips driving back and forth as she sucked. She hummed, the vibration travelling down his cock and straight to his aching balls. She gave his balls another tug and a squeeze that wavered on the knife edge between pleasure and pain.

She hummed again, and he knew he was going to come, knew he couldn't hold back. He cried out with frustration when Kaida released his cock with a loud pop. Her hand gripped the base, squeezing tight and preventing him from coming as she smiled up at him. "Not yet, human."

"Oh fuck, please," he groaned. "Kaida, I need to fucking come."

Her teasing look and the way her fingernails of her other hand scraped across his lower abdomen would be the fucking death of him.

"I know you do, but I want you to fuck me," she said.

He took a deep breath, trying to think of anything other than how fucking good Kaida was at sucking his cock. Kaida released his dick and leaned around him to open the night-stand drawer. He kept his eyes closed, sucking in lungful after lungful of oxygen as Kaida opened the condom.

When her soft hands rolled the condom over his dick, he groaned in pleasure and agony.

"Good, human," she praised, rubbing his upper thighs. "Now, fuck me."

He didn't open his eyes right away. He needed a few more minutes to regain control. But when Kaida made a sound of impatience, he took a deep breath and opened them.

"Fuck me," he said.

"Isn't that supposed to be my line?" she asked with a grin.

She was on her hands and knees on his bed, her head pointed toward the window, her delectable ass pointed straight at him. She widened her thighs until he could see her perfect pink pussy. It gleamed with wetness, and before she could stop him, he bent and licked her wet slit from her clit to her tight entrance.

"Bren!" Her voice was breathless, her thighs already starting to shake as he stiffened his tongue and probed inside of her. "Oh my God! Bren, please!"

He licked his way to her clit, sucking at it lightly as she made another pleading moan. He loved hearing her sound this way. She liked to be in control during sex, and he was one hundred percent good with that, but he couldn't deny that hearing her pleading and begging was also a turn-on for him.

His cock rock-hard, he straightened and pulled Kaida back by her hips until her ass pressed against his pelvis. She wiggled against him, trying to slide his dick into her pussy, and he squeezed one firm thigh. "Patience, honey."

"Fuck me, human!" She glared at him over her shoulder, her eyes glowing and the glow from her chest filling the room with reddish light. "Before I lose my patience and take what is mine."

He grinned and lined his dick up at her tight entrance,

sliding into her with one hard push that made them both cry out with pleasure. Kaida fit him like a glove, tight and warm and perfect. He would never tire of being with her, of fucking her until they were both sated and weak.

Kaida made another harsh cry before blowing flame out the window. The glow in her chest died out, and she rocked back and forth on the bed, fucking him with short, hard strokes. He gripped her ass in his hands, letting her take the lead as he watched her pussy slide back and forth over his cock.

When he couldn't take it anymore, he drove into her, meeting each of her thrusts, turning her short strokes into long ones that sent pleasure skating down his spine. Kaida cried out, her hands clenching into the bedsheets, and she didn't resist when he reached down and took her arms. He lifted her until she was kneeling on the bed, her spine against his chest and her pussy impossibly tight around his cock.

He cupped her tits, playing with her nipples as the heat radiating from her chest made his fingertips tingle. She turned her head and palmed the back of his skull, kissing him hard on the mouth. Their tongues dueled as he tugged on her nipples, and their lower bodies rocked back and forth.

When the heat began to burn his fingers, he pulled back. She immediately turned away and released another lungful of flame. Thin smoke drifted in the room, and he kissed the side of her neck as he trailed his fingers down her flat abdomen.

His balls were tightening, and he knew he couldn't hold out much longer, not with the warm slick grip of Kaida's pussy surrounding his entire dick. He cupped her pussy, kissing her neck and the top of her shoulder as his other hand toyed with her breasts. When his fingers skated across her clit, her purring filled the silence in the room.

He rubbed firmly before sliding her clit between two knuckles and giving it a firm pinch. She shouted his name, her pussy squeezing around him as she climaxed. He fucked her hard and rough as Kaida's final burst of fire soaked the room in bright light.

He drove deep one more time, his release strengthened by the way Kaida's pussy milked his throbbing cock. When he'd emptied himself, he rested his forehead against Kaida's damp back. Both of them were panting harshly, and the acrid smell of smoke was thick in the room.

He straightened and kissed the back of Kaida's shoulder as she waved the smoke away from their faces. "Sorry."

"You know I don't mind." He pulled out of her and disposed of the condom as Kaida stretched out on the bed. He joined her, cupping her breast and kissing the top of her shoulder as she threw one leg over his and rubbed his thigh.

When his heartbeat had finally slowed to a normal pace, he said, "That was incredible."

"You're welcome," she replied.

He laughed, and she smiled at him before cupping his face. "It's good with us. Isn't it, human?"

"Yes," he said.

She kneaded his thigh. "I'm glad that I haven't crushed your fragile bones or accidentally set you on fire."

He burst into laughter before planting a kiss on her mouth. "Me too. You hungry? I can make us some dinner."

"Starving," she said with a soft smile. "Feed me, human, and in return, I'll take you to my bed again."

"Technically," he kissed her throat, "it's my bed, but I like where you're going with this. Come on. I'm about to make you the best boxed macaroni and cheese you've ever tasted."

"Do you want jam or peanut butter or both?" Bren juggled two pieces of hot toast onto a plate in front of Kaida.

"Just jam, please." Kaida was scrolling through his iPad.

"Did you sleep okay last night?" He placed the jam before her and sat down, spreading peanut butter across his toast.

"Yes, thank you." She smiled at him. "I like spending the night in your bed."

"I like it too."

"What time do you need to leave for work?" She was wearing just his shirt, and her morning bedhead was sexy as hell.

"Half an hour, forty minutes. You're welcome to stay in my apartment as long as you want. I can leave my spare key for you."

"Thank you, but I'll leave when you do," she said.

She turned back to his iPad, and he said, "Did you find it yet?"

"Found it." Kaida propped his iPad up against the jar of peanut butter and hit play on the video. The image of his father, standing at a podium with a few men and women in suits standing behind him, popped up on the screen.

His father smiled at the sizeable crowd sitting at the round tables in the hotel conference room. "Thank you again for joining us today. Your donation to the HAPI group is much appreciated. I'm honoured to work with such a fantastic organization dedicated to keeping humans safe."

He waited for the polite applause to die down before gripping the podium. "As you know, we've recently confirmed the existence of dragons."

There were some scattered boos throughout the crowd, and the senator put up his hands, nodding in agreement. "The existence of these creatures puts us all in grave danger. While it is harmful enough to have predator animals such as grizzlies, lions, and wolves walking among us, the dragons living in the forest outside our city pose an immediate threat to every man, woman, and child."

The senator paused, his hands gripping the podium, his gaze solemn as he stared at the crowd. "Many of you know that I have spent almost my entire political career fighting for the rights of humans. Humans who deserve to live without fear of the monsters who walk among us. I promise you that I will never stop fighting. And, as many of you also know, I've been working on a bill for the Senate. One that will require paranormal creatures to register with the government and wear an identification tag so that we can better identify threats to us and our loved ones."

He paused again, a greasy smile crossing his face. "Today, I'm happy to announce that, very soon, I will be introducing the bill to the Senate."

The room erupted in applause. Some people stood up, clapping and cheering as the greasy smile on his father's face widened.

Feeling sick to his stomach, Bren hit the stop button on the video and flipped his iPad face down on the table. His appetite was gone, and he pushed his toast away, watching Kaida do the same.

"You okay?" he asked and then could have smacked himself. What a stupid question. Of course, she wasn't okay. "Sorry, that was a dumb thing to say."

She reached out and took his hand. "It wasn't. I'm all right. It's … gross to watch a bunch of people cheering over having my kind tagged and registered."

"It won't happen." He squeezed her hand.

"It might," she said. "There were a lot of people in that room."

"It is only a fraction of the people in this city," Bren said.

"Even if the bill gets past the Senate and the House, the President will still need to sign it into law. She'll never sign it. She's pro-paranormal. It'll be fine, Kaida. No one's being tagged and registered."

"I hope you're right, Bren," Kaida said, "but we both know the discovery of my kind changes everything."

CHAPTER 22

Kaida set the potion bottle on the table and waited. A few minutes later, her entire body tingled, and she stared down at herself as she reappeared out of thin air. She grinned as she walked to her bedroom and dressed in jeans and a thick sweater. It had been two weeks of taking the invisibility potion, and she still got a thrill from disappearing and reappearing.

She returned to her small kitchen and made herself a cup of coffee. She and Bren had slept in this morning, and there'd only been enough time for Bren to shower quickly before they left. She had a key to his apartment and could have stayed longer, but without her mate there, her dragon's urge to return to the clan appeared quickly.

She sank onto the couch, sipping at her coffee. Her dragon, always grumpy in the morning, made a disgruntled hiss when there was a knock on her door.

"Come in," she called.

"Hey, honey." Sika joined her on the couch, sitting down and tucking her legs under her.

"Hi. Where's Kova?" Kaida asked. They'd had the naming

ceremony for the hatchling a week ago, and Sika and Jarvis had named the baby after Jarvis's father.

"He's with Jarvis," Sika said. "I finished feeding him, but he was fussy, so I handed him off to Jarvis." She laughed. "I feel a little guilty, but Jarvis does love spending time with our hatchling, so…"

Kaida smiled at her. "You and Jarvis are wonderful parents, Sika."

"Thanks, honey. How are you?"

"Good," Kaida replied.

"You look good. You look happy," Sika said.

"Do I?"

"Yes. Is it because of how much time you've spent with the human the last couple of weeks?"

"Who says I've been with Bren?" Kaida said.

Sika rolled her eyes. "Please. You've had dinner twice with the clan in the last two weeks, and I've come by every night this week, but you haven't been here. Also – you're covered in the human's scent."

"Shit," Kaida said.

Sika laughed. "How are you sneaking past all of the reporters? Are you hiding out in the car trunks of the security firm like the other clan members when they need to go into the city?"

"Yeah," Kaida said. She hated lying to her best friend but couldn't tell her about the invisibility potion. Elora was doing her a favour, and she didn't want the affable and sweet witch to get in trouble.

Kaida stared at Sika over her coffee cup. "Are the other clan members talking about me behind my back?"

"Some," Sika admitted cheerfully. "But most of them think it's just a fling or a phase you're going through."

"Seriously?"

"Yep," Sika said. "Honestly, Kaida, you're not the only clan member who has started," she paused, "socializing with the humans."

"What?" Kaida sat up abruptly, coffee sloshing over the side of the cup to burn her fingers. She set the mug on the coffee table and wiped her fingers on her jeans. "Are you joking?"

"I'm not," Sika said. "Finn has been going into the city almost every night, as has Savina and Atticus. All three of them return smelling like humans."

"What has the council said?"

"What can they say?" Sika said. "They are grown dragons and free to do what they want."

"They could be banished," Kaida said.

"Didn't you hear?" Sika said. "The council elders across the country had a Skype meeting. They decided to, at least temporarily, stop the banishments."

"Holy shit," Kaida said.

"Cadmus was the one who suggested it, and the other council elders agreed to it. Bones was there when Cadmus told the other council members. He told Jarvis that Ryul just about lost his mind."

"I can't believe they stopped," Kaida said. "Is it the councils everywhere?"

"The councils in Canada and Europe have agreed to stop as well, but the Russian and Asian councils flat out refused to end the banishments," Sika said. "No one's heard a word from Australia and New Zealand."

"It's good that they've ended the banishments," Kaida said.

"It is," Sika replied. "In Europe, they also allow their dragons to fly during the day. There have been videos all over the internet. However, Cadmus said it's best if we hold off for a while longer. I think mostly because of Bren's father."

She wrapped her arms around her knees. "I can't wait until we're allowed to fly during the day. I have never flown in the light before."

Kaida stared guiltily at her coffee mug as Sika said, "I'm very happy for you, Kaida. Will you and the human try for hatchlings sooner than later?"

"It is not serious between us, Sika," Kaida said. "It can't be."

"Why not?"

"Do you believe the clan would allow a human to live with us? They think it's a phase, remember?" She stood up and paced back and forth angrily. "They believe I will come to my senses soon and mate with someone like Drago. They don't care that Bren is my mate, or -"

She shut her mouth with a snap as Sika smiled gently at her. "Not serious, huh?"

Kaida rubbed at her temples. "Am I making a mistake, Sika?"

"No," Sika said. "If you love him and he is your mate, you should be with him. Do you love him, Kaida?"

Kaida stared at her best friend. "I think – ye -"

The knock on her door sent her already racing heart into overdrive. She walked to the door and yanked it open, frowning when she saw who it was. "What do you want, Drago?"

He pushed past her. "We need to speak."

"Good morning, Drago," Sika said.

"Hello, Sika. How is the hatchling?"

"He's good," Sika said.

"Will you leave us? I want to speak to Kaida alone," Drago said.

Sika glanced at Kaida. Feeling more than a little annoyed, Kaida nodded. Sika stood gracefully and kissed Kaida's cheek before leaving the cabin.

"Why are you here, Drago?" Kaida carried her coffee cup to the kitchen and dumped the coffee down the sink.

"We need to speak about our future," Drago said.

She stuck the coffee cup into the dishwasher and then turned to face him. "We don't have a future."

A scowl deepened the lines on his forehead. "I am aware of your indiscretions with the human, Kaida. We all are. You stink of him."

"What's your point?" she said coolly.

"My point is that despite your," Drago paused, "infatuation with the human, I'm willing to overlook your foolishness so that you may take your proper place at my side."

She stared in silent shock at the redheaded dragon. He couldn't actually believe that she would be his mate, could he?

Taking her silence for acceptance, he said, "We leave for Belinda's clan tomorrow. You should spend time with your grandmother today. She's been missing you the last couple of weeks."

"Have you gone mad, Drago? Is that it?" Kaida said.

She thought her dragon would be angry at Drago's assumption that they would simply bend to his will, but her dragon wasn't even remotely angry. Amusement was its sole emotion and she had to fight to keep the smile off her face as her dragon's amusement grew.

"Have *you?*" he asked. "You barely spend any time with the clan now. You are with the human all night, and when you are here, you're distant. The human is not your clan, Kaida. We are. If you think he can replace us, you are mistaken."

"I know exactly who my clan is," Kaida said. "And it's not

you. You are not my mate, my friend, or my clan member. You are nothing to me, Drago, and I'm tired of your insistence that I be your mate. I will never mate with you, and you'd be wise to stop insisting that I do. Both my dragon and I are weary of your attention."

"You're making a mistake," Drago said as smoke drifted from his mouth and nostrils. "You think the clan will accept the human as your mate? They won't. You'll spend the rest of your life alone. You will never have a mate or a hatchling."

"Leave, Drago," she said. "I wish you well on your journey to Belinda's clan."

He glared at her, the sparks practically spitting from his mouth and his golden eyes glowing brightly. She crossed her arms across her chest and stared pointedly at the door.

"You will regret turning down my offer to be your mate," Drago said before yanking open the door. With a low growl, he left her cabin, slamming the door behind him.

———

KAIDA TASTED THE SAUCE BEFORE STIRRING IT AGAIN AND adding more onion powder. She placed the lid on the pot and checked the time. Bren would be home soon, and she drained the pasta and left it at the back of the stove before placing the garlic bread in the oven.

She reached for the pasta bowls in the cupboard when she heard the door open. She smelled Elora's scent, and her dragon purred happily. It liked the little witch and made another low purr as Elora walked into the kitchen.

"Oh my God, Bren, that smells delicious. Tell me you made enough for me – oh, hey, Kaida. Sorry, I should have knocked."

"It's fine," Kaida said. "How are you, Elora?"

Elora dropped into a kitchen chair. "Good. Is Bren home yet?"

"Not yet. Do you need to speak with him?"

Elora picked at her nail. "No, not really. Helen is at her monthly poker night and I was feeling bored."

"Would you like to have dinner with us?" Kaida asked.

"I don't want to intrude," Elora said.

"You're not."

"In that case, I'll gladly accept the dinner invitation," Elora said. "What can I do to help?"

"You can finish setting the table," Kaida said. She stirred the sauce again as Elora placed the pasta bowls on the table.

"Where is your crow shadow?" Kaida asked.

Elora laughed. "Lilianna was sleeping, and she's a real dick if you wake her up. I left her at home. I'm thrilled you and Bren are dating. I don't think I've ever seen him this happy."

"Well, it's only possible because of you and your potion," Kaida said. "So, thank you."

"Not a problem. Do you need some more?"

"It's getting a bit low," Kaida said. "Do you mind?"

"Nope. But I will need more of your hair and another scale," Elora said. "Remind me to grab them from you before I leave."

She added silverware to the table before rooting through the cupboard for napkins. "Did you hear about the big rally this afternoon in Hyde Park?"

"I watched a bit of it online," Kaida said.

Elora rolled her eyes. "I was at the potions store, which is only a few blocks away, so I went to the rally. It was so ridiculous. Bren's father is an asshole. He was working the crowd up into a frenzy. He has no idea how much damage he's causing by trying to pit humans against paranormals."

Kaida didn't reply, and Elora patted her arm comfortingly. "Don't stress about it, though, okay? There have been plenty of pro-dragon/paranormal rallies the last two weeks to counter the negative ones."

"I know," Kaida said. "My friend Willow – her mother-in-law organized one two days ago. Willow invited my clan to go. The council thought it would be better if we didn't go, but Willow said many humans and paranormals supported allowing us to live our lives as we've always done."

"I went to that one, too," Elora said. "It was great. The woman running it – it must have been your friend's mother-in-law – gave a fantastic speech. She seriously should consider running for mayor."

"I thought the mayor was pro-paranormal," Kaida said.

"He's pro whatever he thinks will get him re-elected," Elora replied. "Anyway, my point is, I know it's stressful, and rallies like the one the senator held are terrible and stupid, but I'm confident that most people in the city don't hold his views."

Kaida stirred the sauce and didn't reply. She wanted to believe that Elora was right, but she hadn't watched only a bit of the senator's rally. She'd watched all of it, feeling more and more sick to her stomach the longer Bren's father spoke.

"Has the pressure eased off your clan yet?" Elora asked.

"No, not really. Fewer reporters try to sneak onto our lands, but not enough to make a difference. We still require security around our land, and clan members still have to be snuck out by Bishop and his team members if they want to avoid being followed all over the city."

"That sucks," Elora said. "People will calm down eventually. Something new will come along and be the next big thing." She looked over Kaida's hair. "Did you see that putting streaks of colour in your hair is trending right now for humans?"

"Yes. The clan has been closely monitoring anything related to dragons that's popping up on the internet."

"Does it bug you that they're mimicking your look?"

"No," Kaida said. "It's a good thing. It makes it easier for us to blend in."

Elora laughed. "You make a good point. Hey, were you born with that colour in your hair, or do you dye it?"

"We are born with it," Kaida said. "It matches the colour of our scales when we are in our dragon forms."

"Same with the flecks of colour in your eyes, huh?" Elora said.

"Yes. Most dragon's eyes are gold with flecks of colour, but a few are born with their irises the colour of their scales rather than gold."

"That's so cool," Elora said.

The front door opened, and Kaida's dragon purred so loudly that she couldn't contain it. Elora grinned at her as Bren yelled out, "I'm home! Holy God, that smells good."

She could hear him heading down the hallway as he continued to talk. "So good that I'm going to put my plan to take you straight to bed on hold and instead eat some dinner before I eat your puss- Elora, hey."

Bren stopped in the kitchen doorway, his face turning a cute shade of tomato.

"Hello, Bren," Elora said with a grin. "How was work?"

"Uh, good." He hesitated and then crossed the kitchen to press a kiss against Kaida's mouth. "Hey, that smells delicious."

"The garlic toast will be ready in about thirty seconds. I've invited Elora to have dinner with us tonight."

"Cool. I'll change and be right back." Bren kissed her

again and left the kitchen, bumping his fist against Elora's as he walked by.

Elora grinned at Kaida as she grabbed three beers from the fridge. "Oh my God, you two are friggin' adorable."

KAIDA STOOD IN THE DOORWAY OF THE KITCHEN AND STARED at Bren's ass as he loaded the dishwasher. He straightened and closed the dishwasher, then set the pots in the sink to soak. As he ran hot water into the pots and added soap, she moved behind him and put her arms around his waist.

"Hey," he turned and kissed the tip of her nose, "I'm almost done cleaning up. Did you and Elora pick out something to watch on Netflix?"

"Elora said thanks for the invite, but she headed home."

Bren grinned at her. "Perfect."

Kaida laughed and squeezed his waist. "She's your friend, Bren."

"She is, which is why she took off. She could tell I wanted some alone time with you."

Kaida pressed a kiss against his shoulder "I don't want you blowing off your friends for me."

"I'm not." He turned and slid his arms around her waist. "I promise."

He kissed her. It was slow and deep, and immediately made her want more.

"The bedroom," she said. "Now."

He grinned and took her hand, following her without complaint to his room. He had already opened the window and the room was cold. It felt amazing against her overheated skin and she smiled at him. She loved how thoughtful and considerate Bren was.

"Thank you for opening the window," she said. "I'm sorry it needs to be cold."

He tugged her shirt over her head and reached to unclasp her bra. "I've told you before, you don't need to apologize. The room heats up quickly even with the window open."

He took off his shirt and added it to her shirt and bra on the floor before unbuttoning her pants. She shimmied out of them and her panties, enjoying the way his eyes darkened when he saw her pussy.

"Soon it will be too cold for you to keep the window open," she said.

He shoved his pants and briefs down his legs, stepping out of them before pulling his socks off with a couple of hard tugs. "I'm not worried about it."

She sat on the side of the bed and removed her own socks as Bren took out a condom and set it on the nightstand. Maybe he wasn't worried because he didn't plan on still being with her when the weather turned below freezing.

Her dragon growled angrily at the thought and she could feel the smoke drifting from her nostrils. *The human is mine. Mine!*

Enough, she said sternly. *Bren agreed to dating, nothing more. This will never work out between us so be happy with what it is now.*

He is my mate. Her dragon sulked like a toddler. *He is my mate and I will not allow anyone else to have him.*

He isn't a toy for you to play with. He has his own thoughts and wants. You cannot simply demand he be your mate.

Yes, I can.

Arguing with her dragon was pointless. Bren was standing at the end of the bed, staring thoughtfully at her.

"Sorry," she said. "I was, um, talking to my dragon."

He smiled a little. "What did she have to say?"

"Nothing of importance." She relaxed on the bed, smiling at Bren when he joined her. They faced each other on their sides, and she pressed against him as they kissed. God, the human was a good kisser. He held nothing back, always letting her taste and feel his need for her with every brush of his mouth against hers. She sucked on the tip of his tongue, his low moan vibrating against her breasts.

Her dragon purred to him as he cupped one breast and toyed with her nipple. Her chest was already beginning to glow red. Even his gentle caresses made her desire grow and her flame build in her chest. If she wasn't careful, one day she really would set him and his damn room on fire.

"Hey," he pressed a kiss against her throat, "stop worrying about it. You haven't burned me yet, right?"

"How do you know that's what I was thinking about?" She gasped when he pinched her nipple before trailing his fingers over her abdomen and down one thigh.

"You get the same look on your face." He tasted her throat, then teased her collarbone with his tongue.

"What look is that?" Her hand dug into his side and she threw one thigh over his hip when he touched the top of her pussy.

"The one that says, 'Oh my God, he's the best lover I've ever had, I'm worried I might set him on fire.'" Bren grinned at her when she laughed. "What? That's the look."

She cupped his jaw, her face turning serious. "You are the best lover I've ever had, Bren. I mean that. Before you, I rarely lost control of my flame and now…"

She waited for a smug smile to cross his face. What man wouldn't get one? To her surprise, his smile was unbelievably sweet. "I feel the same way about you. Minus the losing control of my flame part."

She studied his warm blue eyes and the face that had

become so important to her in so short a period. She wanted to tell him how loved and safe she felt when she was in his arms, but his fingers were sliding over her clit and the thought was lost under a wave of pleasure.

She squirmed in his embrace, pumping her pelvis against him as he rubbed her clit. Her pussy ached, squeezing uselessly around nothing as he teased her with soft strokes.

"I need you. Now," she moaned.

She reached for his dick, growling at him when he pulled away. He kissed the palm of her hand. "Just a minute, honey."

He rolled the condom onto his dick, then pushed her lightly onto her back. She shook her head immediately, sitting up when he kneeled between her thighs. "No, Bren. I can't – my face, that is… I shouldn't be facing you so close. Just in case."

"I'm not worried." He continued to kneel between her thighs, his hand stroking lightly between her breasts. "You won't hurt me, Kaida."

"I might," she whispered.

"You won't," he said. "Lie back."

She chewed at her bottom lip. Her favourite position was being on top. She loved looking down and watching her partner's face as she rode him, but it didn't mean she never wanted to switch things up. But with Bren… if she lost control of her flame and couldn't move away in time…

She shuddered all over, staring mutely at Bren as he stroked her still-glowing chest. "You won't hurt me," he repeated. "I want to be on top, honey. Let me."

She turned her head and blew out a short burst of flame toward the open window before taking a deep breath and lying back on the bed. Bren smiled at her, and her feelings of trepidation disappeared when he bent his head and sucked her nipple into his mouth. He teased both nipples, cupping and kneading her breasts until her nipples were hard, her chest glowed again, and liquid dripped down her inner thighs.

"Bren, please!" She didn't often beg, but he was rubbing the head of his cock up and down her pussy, teasing her clit, pausing at her entrance but not slipping in.

He propped himself up on his hands above her. "Look at me, honey."

She stared up at him, her hands clinging to his waist, her thighs pressing against his hips, as he slowly entered her. Her loud purrs filled the room as he slid into her, filling her to an uncomfortable fullness as her walls stretched around his thick length.

"Fuck, you feel so good," he muttered.

"Please," she moaned again.

Bren dropped a kiss against her mouth. Her chest was glowing, and she could feel the heat rising in her, but she kept it at bay as Bren drove in and out of her with slow and deep thrusts. He moved in a steady rhythm, refusing to speed up even when she urged him on with soft cries and her fingernails down his back.

"Please!" she cried out. She needed more. She needed it to be harder and faster.

"Soon," he said before dipping his head and sucking on her nipple. It had to be too warm, she could feel the heat rising from her body, but it didn't seem to bother him. He teased her nipple with his tongue as he continued to drive in and out with that same slow and maddening pace that made her want to scream and beg for more.

"My mate, please," she moaned.

He stopped and stared down at her. She needed to take back what she said, but when Bren said hoarsely, "Again," she didn't hesitate.

"My mate, please fuck me. Give me what I need."

He touched her face before fucking her hard and deep. She wrapped her thighs around his waist and raked her nails down his back as he drove in and out. The sound of her purring drowned the slap of their bodies as her mate thrust into her repeatedly.

The heat grew in her chest, and the desire to release the flame before she burned was almost impossible to hold in.

Keep our mate safe.

She swallowed down the smoke, ignored the flame. She wouldn't – *couldn't* – hurt her mate.

"My mate!" she cried. "Please!"

When his hand slipped between their bodies and skated across her clit, she couldn't hold back her orgasm. It washed over her, the heated pleasure sparking the flame inside of her into a fierce fire that threatened to consume her.

She sucked in a breath, the air hot and dry between her and her mate, the fire in her lungs fighting to be free. She watched Bren as his pleasure washed over him. He closed his eyes, pumping his hips as he came deep within her.

The trust her mate showed, his belief that she would never hurt him, extinguished the flame in her chest. She released her breath, a small plume of smoke drifting from between her lips to rise lazily to the ceiling.

Bren collapsed against her and kissed her throat before rolling off of her with a groan. He stared dazedly at the ceiling, small beads of sweat sliding down his torso.

"Oh my God," he muttered.

She curled into him, smiling a little. She had pleased her mate.

Kaida traced her fingers along Bren's forearm. She loved being curled up with him in the bed, loved the feel of his warm body against hers. The bedroom was cold, but Bren hadn't asked her to shut the window after their lovemaking was done. Eventually they would have to close the window, winter would be too cold for Bren to sleep with the window open even with the warmth of her body. But for now, she would enjoy it.

How quickly you forget. You won't be with the human by winter.

Her dragon growled at her inner voice. It didn't plan on ever giving up Bren, and as each day went by, her dragon's claim on him grew stronger. It fully believed that Bren was their mate.

As if he'd read her thoughts, Bren kissed the back of her shoulder and said, "Can we talk about the mate thing?"

"It was my dragon who said it," she replied quickly.

It wasn't just her dragon who said it. Her voice would have been different if it was, but she'd been more than happy to give in to her dragon's wishes and call Bren her mate. She waited for Bren to call her out on her lie.

Instead, he kissed her shoulder again. "I know. But is it only your dragon who believes it?"

"My clan knows I'm spending time with you," she said. "They believe it's just a fling. I'm not the only dragon in the clan socializing with humans."

"Okay," Bren said. "But that isn't what I asked you. We agreed to try dating, and it's been a couple of weeks. I know how your dragon feels. I want to know how you're feeling about us."

"Does it matter?" she asked. "My clan will never allow you to live with them, and I can't be away from them."

"You spend every night away from them," he said.

"And every day with them." She stared out the window at the brick wall of the building next to them. "I can't be away from my clan, Bren. I'm sorry, but -"

He squeezed her waist and spooned her even closer. "You don't have to say sorry. I get it. You can't be away from your clan, so we need to figure out how to make your clan accept me. Maybe I should get an invisibility potion from Elora and spend time with you and your clan on my days off. We can ease them into it."

"It isn't just my clan." The topic she'd been avoiding and denying even to herself finally reared its ugly head. "You want hatchlings."

"I do. You don't?" He had tensed behind her.

"I want them very much, but I'm not sure I can have them."

He tugged on her arm until she rolled over to face him. He pulled her into his embrace again. "Have you seen a doctor about it?"

"No, it's not that. It's... dragons are going extinct, Bren. We're going extinct because our females rarely become pregnant. Jarvis and Sika's hatchling is the first to be born in our clan in over a decade. The odds that I will ever be a mother are incredibly low."

"But not zero," he said.

She cupped his face. "You want hatchlings. I cannot promise to give them to you."

"No woman can *promise* to give me a kid, just like I can't promise to give her a kid," Bren said. "Having difficulty getting pregnant is not the same as knowing you absolutely can't have kids. It's worth the risk to me."

Her dragon purred with happiness, and Kaida could feel warmth spreading through her entire body. Her mate was perfect, and she had no idea how she'd gotten so lucky.

You're going to disappoint your mate.

She wanted to tell her inner voice to shut up, but it made a point that she couldn't ignore. It might be worth the risk to Bren now, but after a few years, when it became evident that she would never conceive, then what?

Bren stroked her cheek with his thumb. "Look, I know we have a lot of hills to climb with this relationship, but I think it's working for us so far. You're important to me, and I don't want to give up on us. Do you?"

"No," she admitted.

His smile radiated happiness. "Good. So, should I start hanging out with your clan?"

"Let's give it a bit more time," she said. "Do you mind?"

"No." He pressed a kiss against her forehead. "We have all the time in the world."

CHAPTER 23

B ren stepped out of his apartment building. It was a cool and overcast day, and he could smell rain in the air. He'd only taken two steps toward his parking spot when the door opened behind him, and Kaida called his name.

He turned around, smiling when Kaida threw her arms around his shoulders and pressed a kiss against his mouth. She was wearing just a pair of panties, and a shirt of his that fell mid-thigh on her. He squeezed her ass through her shirt and grinned at her. "What are you doing out here? It's freezing."

"You're not allowed to leave for work without saying goodbye to me."

"You were snoring so sweetly that I didn't want to wake you," he said with a grin.

She wrinkled her nose. "I don't snore."

"You don't *not* snore," he said.

She poked him in the back, and he laughed and squeezed her ass again. "Sorry, I will never again leave the apartment without saying goodbye."

"Thank you," she said. Despite the cold air, she was soft

and warm against him. He pressed his mouth against hers and couldn't resist deepening the kiss. She moaned into his mouth, and he sucked on her bottom lip before releasing her mouth.

"Maybe I should take the day off," he said.

"Maybe you should." She wiggled her eyebrows at him.

"I would if I didn't have a court appointment this morning."

She growled, and a puff of smoke came out of her mouth, drifting upward. "Fine, abandon me and go to work, but someone's being handcuffed to the bed again tonight as punishment."

She rubbed her pelvis against his erection, and he groaned out a curse. "I want to agree that's a punishment, but I can't quite find the words."

"Good," she said with a wicked grin. "Now, if you'll excuse me, I'm going to crawl back into your bed and masturbate."

"Evil. You are truly evil," Bren said. He slapped her on the ass as she walked back to the apartment door, letting herself in with the keys she carried.

She paused on the threshold and wiggled her ass at him. "See you tonight, detective."

He adjusted his dick through his jeans, trying to relieve some of the pressure as he watched Kaida's delectable ass all the way to the elevator.

Christ, it would be a long day at work.

"HOLY SHIT, MATTHEWS. YOU'RE BANGING A DRAGON shifter?" Jeremy stood up and stared over their shared cubicle wall at Bren.

"What?" Bren blinked at him. "What did you say?"

It was midmorning, and he'd returned to the precinct after his court appointment. Despite the paperwork on his desk, he couldn't stop thinking about Kaida and everything he wanted to do to her tonight. For a second, he wondered if he'd been talking out loud to himself.

"You're banging a dragon!" Jeremy's voice was carrying across the big open room, and Bren made a shushing motion.

"Keep your voice down, for God's sake," Bren said.

"Everyone probably already knows anyway," Jeremy said.

"What are you talking about?" Bren said.

"Bren?" His captain, a quiet man named Morales, had stopped in front of his cubicle. "Can I see you in my office?"

His stomach in knots, Bren followed him to the office. Morales shut the door and sank into the leather chair behind his desk. "Have you seen the news?"

"I just got back from court. What's going on?" Bren said.

Morales turned his computer screen to face Bren. He had a local TV station website on the screen and hit play on the video.

A reporter popped up, standing in front of his father's office building downtown. Bren's stomach dropped to his feet when she said, "As of yet, there has been no official statement from Senator Matthews regarding the news that both of his children are dating shifters. In fact, it seems he had no prior knowledge of this when we questioned him about it. We're standing outside his office, but it appears Senator Matthews has left. We'll continue to monitor the situation and let you know if and when he returns to the office."

The screen switched to the news anchor in the studio. "Thank you, Carol," the news anchor said. "Channel Five was the first to report this breaking news. We are also the only studio to have exclusive videos of Senator Matthew's sons, who both appear to be in intimate relationships with shifters."

Nausea running rampant through him, Bren watched as the grainy video appeared. It was of Tyler and Corey sitting on a park bench, holding hands and talking. The camera zoomed in just as Tyler leaned in and kissed Corey.

"We know the young man on the right is a fox shifter," the newscaster's voice droned, "thanks to more anonymous footage sent to our studios."

The view switched to show the forest outside of the city. Bren clenched his hands into fists as the camera swung to the right and caught the image of the small red fox running past a few trees. The fox stopped next to a pile of clothes at the base of a tree and sniffed the air before studying the forest around him. After a moment, the fox's body rippled, and he shifted into Corey. He grabbed his clothes and started to dress.

Bren's hands clenched into fists. "He's a kid, captain. They recorded a naked kid who -"

"They blurred him out," Morales said.

"That doesn't matter. It's still an invasion of privacy."

Morales grimaced. "He's on public land. We've already had a few calls from concerned citizens demanding we arrest him for public indecency."

"Are you fucking kidding me?"

"I wish I were," Morales said. "There's more."

He tapped the screen, and Bren watched as another video popped up. His chest tightened when he saw Tyler and Corey surrounded by reporters outside their school. "What the fuck? Where the fuck are the teachers?"

As the reporters screamed questions at Tyler and Corey, his nails bit into his palms. Both boys looked upset and frightened, and Bren muttered another curse as a man pushed his way through the crowd and stood in front of the boys.

"Get the fuck back," he roared at the crowd of reporters.

"Who are you? What's your name? How do you know the boys? Are you the fox shifter's father?" A reporter shoved a microphone into the man's face.

Fur sprouted on the man's face, and he bared his fangs at the reporter. "Get that microphone out of my fucking face, or I'll make you eat it."

The reporter skittered back, clutching the microphone as the shifter took Tyler and Corey's arms. "Let's go, boys."

Bren sagged with relief when Davis got both boys into his car and drove away from the school. A few reporters jumped into their vehicles to follow them, and Bren rubbed at his temples as the video switched back to the newscaster.

"Any idea who that guy was?" Morales asked as he hit pause.

"Yeah. It's a shifter named Davis. I hired a security firm to keep an eye on Corey and Tyler because they were being bullied at school for being gay. They were attacked in the forest a few weeks ago by a bunch of football players."

"Jesus," Morales said. "Did your father know Tyler was gay and dating a shifter?"

"What do you think?" Bren said. "I gotta go."

"Wait." Morales held up his hand. "It wasn't just Tyler they caught on video."

Bren sank back into his chair as Morales typed on his keyboard. He stared grimly at Bren. "This video is all over social media."

Bren read the title on the screen. "Senator's Son Heats Up with Dragoness"

"Shit," he groaned as the video played. Someone had captured his and Kaida's moment in front of his apartment building this morning. He watched as the shaky but perfectly clear video captured their kiss, him grabbing her ass, and – he groaned again – the puff of smoke that came from Kaida's mouth.

"Shut it off," he said.

Morales turned the video off. "So, that's shitty for you."

"Yeah," Bren said. "Do you mind if I take the day -"

His cell phone buzzed, and he pulled it out of his pocket. It was Tyler, and he said to Morales, "Sorry, I need one minute."

He answered the phone. "Ty? Buddy, are you -"

"Bren?" Tears clogged Tyler's voice. "Bren, can you come over? Dad's really mad at me, and he's, like, freaking out. He won't stop screaming and -"

Bren winced when he heard his father's voice. "Get off the goddamn phone, Tyler! We are having a fucking discussion! Hang up the phone now, you little shit! I swear to God if you don't -"

"Tyler, I'll be right there," Bren said quickly. It was too late – the connection had been broken.

Bren jumped to his feet. "Captain, I need -"

"Go," Morales said. "Take care of your brother."

HE COULD HEAR HIS FATHER'S ANGRY SHOUTING IN THE hallway outside the apartment. Bren dug the key to his father's place out of his pocket and unlocked the door, letting himself in and closing the door before stalking to the kitchen.

Tyler, his face red and streaked with tears, stood near the doorway as his father paced and slammed his hand repeatedly on the marble-topped island.

Bren slipped his arm around Tyler's shoulders, squeezing him tight. "It's okay, buddy."

"I'm sorry," Tyler said. "I didn't know what else to do. Dad is losing it."

"It's okay," he repeated.

"I cannot believe you would do this to me. You ungrateful, inconsiderate asshole!" His father hadn't even noticed Bren's arrival. "Do you have any idea what you've done? Do you?" He whirled to face them. "My career is – oh, look who fucking shows up. My *oldest,* ungrateful, inconsiderate son. What do you have to say for yourself, Bren?"

"Calm down," Bren said.

His father's face went a new blood pressure spiking shade of red. "You did not just tell me to calm down."

"I know you're upset, but yelling at Tyler isn't –"

"Shut up!" His father was nearly apoplectic with rage. "You will shut up and listen to what I have to say for once in your goddamn life, Bren!"

"Fine," Bren spat. "Say what you need to say. Tyler, go to your room and pack a suitcase."

"No!" his father shouted. "He stays right here. You know, I expected this type of shit behaviour from you, Bren. You've spent your entire life pushing back against me, defying every rule I ever gave you. I knew that bitch in your apartment was a shifter the second I saw her. You'll do anything to poke at me, to make me look like an idiot, and to get under my skin. Even if it means you have to fuck a shifter."

He laughed bitterly. "But getting a goddamn dragon to fuck you just to stick it to me? Brilliant, you asshole."

"It has nothing to do with you," Bren said. "I don't know how many ways I can say this – but I don't think of you at all. None of the decisions I make in my life ever take you into consideration."

"That's pretty fucking obvious," Robert said.

"You haven't earned that consideration," Bren said.

"You don't care about anyone but yourself," his father said.

"You're wrong," Bren said. "I care about Tyler and -"

His father's gaze swung to Tyler the moment Bren said his name. "You know, I might have expected this from Bren. He's been a disappointment his entire life, but you?" Robert shook his head. "I had dreams for you, Tyler. Dreams that you fucking destroyed because you're as selfish as your brother. It's bad enough that the entire goddamn city knows my son is sticking his dick in another man's asshole, but a shifter? You've ruined my career. Is that what you wanted? To destroy the one thing I loved?"

Fresh tears spilled down Tyler's cheeks. "Dad, I'm sorry. I didn't mean -"

"It's too late for apologies," his father said. "You're sick in the head, Tyler. You need help. What you're doing isn't normal. Do you understand that?"

Tyler staggered back, his face the colour of old porridge. His anger a fiery inferno raging through him, Bren stomped forward and shoved his father up against the island. He grabbed him by the collar, shaking him roughly and snarling, "Shut the fuck up!"

"Bren, don't!" Tyler shouted.

"Don't you say another fucking word," Bren said to his father. His hands still fisted in Robert's collar, he said, "Tyler, go pack a suitcase. Right now."

"Bren..."

"Go, Tyler. Now."

He could barely hear his younger brother's footsteps fading down the hallway over the blood pounding in his ears.

"Let go of me."

For the first time in his life, Bren heard fear in his father's voice. He released him, stepping back and taking a deep breath as Robert straightened his shirt. "How dare you speak to me that way. I am still your father and -"

"I said, shut the fuck up," Bren's voice was low and deliberate. "You'll keep your mouth shut and listen to what I say. If you don't, I will handcuff you to the chair and gag you with a fucking towel."

His father took a step back. "You've lost your mind."

"Do you know what impact your words have on Tyler?"

"He's sick!" his father snapped. "He's sick, and he needs help."

"No, he doesn't!" Bren roared. "He is a perfectly normal teenage boy who was just outed in front of the whole goddamn world! He needs our support and love right now, not accusations that he's sick or ruined your career. For once in your miserable life, can you look past your needs and do the right thing? Tyler needs you. He needs you to step up to the plate as a goddamn father and support him. Tell this fucking city and the rest of the world that you love him and support him and his choices, no matter what that does to your career. He needs you, Dad. Don't let him down like you let me and Mom down."

His father shook his head. "I haven't let anyone down. You think I'm a terrible father, but maybe I'm just unwilling to settle for anything less than the best from my children. It isn't my fault you and Tyler are too weak to meet my expectations. I set the bar low for you and even lower for Tyler and both of you repeatedly disappoint me. You ask for support from me, but neither of you show an ounce of support or respect for what I'm trying to achieve."

"Because you're trying to suppress and control the paranormal," Bren said. "You're a racist, and neither Tyler nor I will -"

"I am doing what's best for us!" his father shouted. "The paranormal are a threat to our existence. You're a cop! You see the harm they inflict on humans every day, and you still want to give them the same basic rights as humans. How can you be so naive? So weak?"

"Believing everyone deserves equal treatment is not a weakness," Bren said. "Tyler needs you. Can you be there for him or not?"

His father lifted his chin, the familiar stubborn look landing on his face. "I love you and your brother, but I will not accept nor support Tyler's failings. *Because* I love him."

"That isn't love, Dad," Bren said. "And if you think it is, then we have nothing left to say to each other."

He turned around. Tyler was standing in the doorway, a small suitcase in one hand and his backpack flung over his shoulder. "Bren?"

"Let's go, Tyler."

He and Tyler headed toward the front door, his father trailing behind them. Tyler stopped with his hand on the doorknob when his father said, "If you leave now, don't bother coming back. Either of you."

Bren stared at the key in his hand before tossing it at his father's feet. "Goodbye, Dad."

"I'M SORRY. I'M SO SORRY, BREN." TYLER SWIPED AT HIS TEARS as Bren drove away from their father's apartment.

"Buddy, stop. You have nothing to be sorry about," Bren said. "You haven't done anything wrong. Do you understand?"

"I've ruined Dad's career," Tyler whispered.

"No, you haven't. He'll figure out a way to spin this whole thing. He'll come out smelling like a rose, just like always."

"They kicked me and Corey out of school," Tyler said. "The principal called us into the office and told us we needed to take the rest of the week off. Said that there were too many reporters at the school because of us. He made us leave. The reporters were everywhere."

"Yeah, I saw," Bren said grimly.

"This guy – he said his name was Davis, and he was from the security firm you hired – got us to his car, drove Corey home, and then took me home. If it hadn't been for him, Corey and I…"

"Trust me," Bren reached across and squeezed Tyler's leg, "your school will be getting a goddamn earful from me about how they handled this."

"Dad doesn't want me to come back home." Tyler's voice caught in his throat.

"You can live with me, Ty," Bren said.

"But you're dating Kaida, and I don't want to wreck that."

Bren frowned at him. "You won't. Kaida likes you a lot. And even if she didn't, you are what matters to me. You will always come first, buddy."

Tyler sniffed loudly before staring out the window. "What about the rest of my stuff?"

"Dad will go into the office tomorrow, I'm sure. While he's gone, we'll use your key to return and get the rest of your things. Okay?"

"Okay. I'm sorry, Bren."

"Again, you don't need to be sorry. I'm sorry all of this is happening to you."

Tyler's phone buzzed, and he pulled it out of his pocket. He read the screen before looking up at Bren. "It's Corey. His foster family is really mad at him because he didn't tell them he's a shifter. He's locked in his room, and his foster dad is threatening to break down the door and kick his ass. We gotta help him."

Bren flicked the switches that turned on the lights and the siren on his car and stepped on the gas. "Hold on, Tyler."

———

BREN HAD BARELY HIT THE ANSWER BUTTON ON HIS STEERING wheel when Kaida's voice, frantic with worry, filled the car. "Bren, where are you?"

"I'm with Corey and Tyler. We just picked up Corey from his foster home."

"Are they okay?" Kaida asked.

"My dad kicked me out, and Corey's foster dad tried to kick his ass, but, yeah, we're okay," Tyler said.

"Oh, mostoirín," Kaida's voice turned grave. "I'm sorry."

"Thanks," Tyler said.

"Are you with your clan?" Bren asked.

"No, I'm still at your place. I fell back asleep after you left. I was getting ready to leave when Elora came by and told me what was going on."

"Okay. I'm about ten minutes away. Sit tight, all right?"

"See you soon," she said.

He disconnected the call and took a right, heading toward his place. He was tempted to turn his siren and lights on again, but instead, he took a few calming breaths and drove the speed limit.

"You should have arrested Corey's foster dad," Tyler said. "He tried to hurt him."

"No," Corey said before squeezing Tyler's hand. "I didn't want him arrested."

Bren stared at him in the rearview mirror. "As soon as we get to my place, we'll contact your social worker and tell him what happened. Okay?"

"Yeah, okay," Corey said.

"Then what?" Tyler asked.

"Group home, probably," Corey replied. "There aren't many foster families that'll take kids my age."

"Bren," Tyler stared worriedly at him. "He can stay with us, right?"

"We'll talk to the social worker, buddy. He may have to go to a group home temporarily, but we'll figure something out. I promise."

"It's fine," Corey said. "You don't have to take me in."

"Corey -"

Corey squeezed Tyler's hand. "I'm not your brother's responsibility. Don't worry about it. Everything will be fine."

They pulled into Bren's parking spot, and he shut the SUV off before opening the back hatch. Corey and Tyler grabbed their suitcases and backpacks and followed him across the parking lot toward his apartment building.

"Maybe we can ask them to let you temporarily stay with us until they find a foster home," Tyler said. "Maybe -"

"Shit!" Bren stopped, holding his arms out. "Back, you guys. Back to the car."

"What's going on?" Tyler glanced up as a crowd darted out of the building's lobby. "Are those...reporters?"

"Yes. Back to the car. Now!" Bren whipped around and cursed angrily when he caught sight of the crowd running up behind them. In seconds, a horde of reporters surrounded them, shoving microphones into their faces and shouting questions.

"Bren!" Kaida was fighting her way through the crowd of people toward them. There was a moment of perfect silence as the reporters realized who she was before questions were screamed at them again.

"Bren!" Kaida hooked her arm around his waist as cameras flashed. The lights were blinding, and they covered their face with their arms.

"We need to go," Bren said.

"How long have you been dating?" A woman, her long dark hair in a ponytail, thrust a microphone into Bren's face. "Is your relationship with your father on the rocks because of this?"

Bren shoved the microphone away. "No comment. Excuse us, please. We have no comment. Let us pass."

"Bren!" Tyler's voice was scared. Reporters had surrounded him, and Corey and Bren could barely see him.

"Tyler!" he shouted.

The air was heating up, and he turned toward Kaida. Her face was pale, and smoke drifted from her nostrils as she glared at the humans surrounding them.

Shit. Any minute, she was going to flash fry them.

"Kaida!" He cupped her face, ignoring the flash of cameras going off around them, and made her look at him. "Honey, it's okay. Don't shift, and don't breathe fire."

"Too close," she growled out. "Too close to my mate."

Her voice was the voice of her dragon, and a shiver went down his spine. She was closer to losing control than he thought.

"I'm okay," he said. "Don't shift, honey."

"Tell them to leave," Kaida growled.

The woman standing closest to Kaida made a small squeal of panic and backed away when more smoke emerged from Kaida's mouth. Bren didn't think it was his imagination that Kaida's body was getting bigger or that her skin was taking on a shimmery blue tinge.

"Kaida, don't," he said.

"Bren!" Tyler shouted. "Bren, help us!"

Fuck! His heart thumping against his sternum, Bren grabbed Kaida's arm. It was like touching the side of a hot woodstove, and he dropped her arm and shook his hand out.

"Kaida, please, you need to -"

"MOVE!" The deep voice rang out, reminding Bren of ancient gods casting down fire and brimstone on unsuspecting humans.

The crowd of people froze, and the voice shouted again. "Get the fuck out of here! All of you!"

The man from Bishop's birthday party – Bren searched his memory, Hudson, his name was Hudson, and he was a polar bear shifter – strode toward them. The ground seemed to shake beneath his feet as he scowled menacingly at the reporters surrounding Tyler and Corey.

"Move," his low voice was a deep growl, "before I make you move."

The reporters backed away. A camera flashed from somewhere in the crowd, and Hudson bared his teeth and let loose with an angry growl.

"You guys, swear to God, I'll do my best to hold the big guy back, but he's got a real short temper." Ronin peered around Hudson's giant body. "I can't be responsible for the bloodshed if you keep pissing him off."

He stepped around Hudson and grinned at the reporters. "I know what you're thinking. He's Canadian, they're super nice, they're always polite, and they're too full of cheese and gravy to be angry. But that's where you're wrong."

He leaned forward and said in a conspiratorial whisper to the reporters closest to him. "I've seen Big White rip the spine right out of a dude because he mocked his love of Canadian bacon."

When the reporters stared silently at him, Ronin laughed and turned to Tyler and Corey. "Boys. It's good to see you again. Staying out of trouble, I see. C'mon over here with me and the big guy."

As Tyler and Corey moved toward Ronin and Hudson, there was another growl. Relief swept through Bren. Bishop, Mal close behind him, pushed through the reporters surrounding him and Kaida. Kaida still vibrated beside him, smoke leaking out of her nostrils at an alarming rate and her eyes glowing brightly.

"Kaida." Bishop brushed past him and took Kaida's arm. If it burned his hand, he made no indication. "Kaida, look at me."

She turned her gaze upward. "I will kill them all, my bear."

"No, you won't," he said. "Control your dragon."

"They're too close to my mate. I must protect him."

"He can protect himself," Bishop said. "He's strong for a human, remember?"

She turned her gaze toward Bren, and he smiled reassuringly despite how his skin prickled with fear that Kaida would shift and kill the reporters. "He's right. I'm fine, honey. I don't need help."

To his relief, Kaida's body relaxed and returned to its normal size. Her skin lost the shimmery blue colour, and the glow in her eyes faded. She took his hand. "I'm sorry."

"It's fine."

"Time to go," Mal said. "More reporters are arriving."

"Jesus, what a shit show," Bishop growled as he shoved aside some reporters. "Get out of my way, assholes."

"Holy shit," Bren said as more and more reporters piled out of cars and vans. "What the hell is happening?"

"You two are the flavour of the month," Ronin shouted from where he and Hudson stood protectively next to Tyler and Corey. "I can totally see why – you make a hella cute couple."

"We won't get them back to Bren's apartment without Kaida losing her shit," Bishop said.

"I'm fine," Kaida growled.

"No, you're not," Bishop said. "You're about ten seconds from roasting them alive."

Mal scanned over the crowd of shouting reporters. "Willow's car is closer than the apartment building. You, Hudson, and Ronin hold the crowd back as best you can while I get them to her. She can take them to my parents' place. They won't look for them there."

"They'll just follow us," Bren said as the reporters, keeping a close eye on Hudson and Kaida, started to shuffle forward again.

"You haven't seen Willow drive," Mal said. "Let's go. Hudson, clear us a path to Willow's car, would you?"

Bren winced when Hudson opened his mouth and roared deafeningly. Tyler and Corey cringed, and Ronin pushed them toward Bren and the others. The reporters screamed and stumbled back, clapping their hands over their ears as Hudson stalked toward them.

"Fucking hell, it's like magic," Ronin shouted as he followed the enormous polar bear shifter. "We have got to hire this guy full time."

"Ronin, help Bishop and Hudson keep the crowd back," Mal said as he pushed Tyler and Corey through the opening. He took Tyler's suitcase and Corey's backpack. "Move, boys. Quick."

Bren took Kaida's hand, and they squeezed their way through the narrow open path. Bishop brought up the rear, pushing back against the tide of reporters as they tried to follow.

"Willow! Pop the trunk!" Mal shouted.

Willow popped the trunk of her car, and the boys threw their stuff in the back. Mal whipped open the doors. "Everyone in."

Bren pushed Kaida toward the front passenger side as he followed Tyler and Corey into the back seat. It was a tight fit, but he crammed up against Tyler as Mal slammed the door shut behind him.

He heard Bishop bellow, "Get the fuck back!" as Mal leaned down to Willow's open window.

"Will, get them to Mom and Dad's. Lose the reporters."

"You got it!" Willow blew him a kiss, and Tyler and Corey made startled shouts when she stomped on the gas.

Bren grabbed the handle at the top of his door as Kaida braced her hands on the dashboard.

"Hang on to your giblets!" Willow shouted as she drove down the street and turned the corner on what felt like two wheels.

"Fuck!" Bren said.

"Oh shit!" Tyler shouted. "We're gonna die!"

Laughing hysterically and driving so fast the cars were coloured blurs around them, Willow weaved in and out of traffic, eyeing the rearview mirror.

"Red light!" Kaida shouted. "Red light!"

Tyler and Corey screamed in unison as, with the precision of a race car driver, Willow twisted the wheel to the right. They slid by a stopped Honda Civic in the thin gap between the car and the sidewalk, narrowly missing its front bumper as Willow stomped on the gas again and careened through the intersection. Cars honked, brakes squealed, and

Willow slipped past a silver SUV with another practice turn of the steering wheel.

She glanced in the rearview mirror and eased up on the gas, blending in with the traffic flow as Kaida collapsed against the front seat.

"Lost 'em," Willow said with a happy smile. "Easy-peasy."

"I think I wet my pants a little," Corey said.

"Me too," Bren said.

"I wanna do that again," Tyler said.

Willow laughed and headed toward the freeway. "I like you, kid."

CHAPTER 24

"But how did Pudding even know to come rescue you all at Bren's place?" Mal's mother, a tall, gorgeous wolf shifter named Mara, placed another cup of tea in front of Kaida and pushed the plate of cookies toward Ty and Corey. "Have some more cookies, boys."

"Pudding?" Tyler said.

"Oh, that's my silly little nickname for my Malcolm," Mara said. She smiled at Willow. "How did he know, honey?"

Willow ate the last bite of her cookie. "Once the news broke about Bren and Kaida, Mal had a feeling that reporters might show up at Bren's apartment. I volunteered to keep an eye on the place, and if reporters showed up, I'd call Mal so he could warn Bren."

A scowl marred her pretty face. "Only, I didn't realize that a bunch of them were already hiding in the building lobby. Some other reporters showed up just as Bren and the boys arrived. I called Mal as soon as they started swarming them and luckily, he and Bishop were meeting a client at a coffee shop near Ben's apartment. Ronin and Hudson were heading to Kaida's clan for their morning shift. I assume Mal called them and asked them to come help."

"Thank God you guys were there," Bren said.

He looked tired and a little pissed, and Kaida pushed her cup of tea away. It was her fault he was upset. If she hadn't gone downstairs this morning like an idiot, the entire city wouldn't know about the two of them. To make matters worse, she had almost lost control in front of him. She'd been so close to shifting to her dragon form and burning the reporters alive.

He's probably scared of you now.

She shuddered all over as her dragon made a mournful cry. Bren hadn't spoken to her since they arrived at Mara and Roland's place, but he'd been focused on Tyler and Corey and making sure they were all right. He was probably just preoccupied.

Or he hates you and wants nothing to do with you.

Her dragon made a second grief-filled cry, and she soothed it as she tried to focus on the conversation around her.

"Well," Mara was sitting on the other side of Corey, and she reached out and took Corey's hand and Tyler's hand in hers, "I'm so sorry for what you've gone through. You didn't deserve to be blasted all over social media and the television like that. Poor, sweet boys. No one deserves to feel bad for loving someone. It's terrible that your classmate sent those videos to the media."

The wolf shifter radiated kindness and a motherly instinct that Kaida could only hope to replicate with her hatchlings. Tyler and Corey were already fixated on her. She could smell their fascination. Knowing they were both starved for a mother type role model, she wasn't surprised in the least by their immediate affection toward her.

"Did Jeff admit he did it?" Bren asked.

"No," Tyler said. "But we know it was him. Who else would have done it?"

Kaida's phone buzzed, and she looked at the screen. A low growl slipped out her throat, and Bren said, "What's wrong?"

"It's Sika. I know how they got the video of us this morning." Her anger grew, and smoke drifted from her nostrils.

"That's so cool." Tyler stared in fascination as Kaida waved the smoke away.

"How did they get the video?" Bren said.

"Drago," she replied.

"Drago?" Tyler turned to Corey. "A dragon named Drago. Hilarious."

The two boys' snickering turned to outright laughter, and Bren said, "Enough, you two. Why would Drago take that video, Kaida? More importantly – why would he release it to the press?"

She rubbed the back of her neck. "He is being sent to Belinda's clan to join their council. He asked me to go with him as his mate, and I refused."

"Ah, the old spurned lover bit," Willow said.

"Drago and I were never lovers," Kaida snarled.

Willow held up her hands. "Sorry."

Kaida slumped against her chair and grimaced apologetically at the tiny human. "No, I'm sorry, Willow. I didn't mean to snap."

"You've had a hard day," Willow said. "It's perfectly understandable."

"When they saw the video online, Sika and Jarvis went to Cadmus with their suspicions that it was Drago. Other than Bones, Sika, and Jarvis, he's the only one in the clan who knows where Bren lives," Kaida said.

"It could have been a human," Tyler said. "Someone walking by at the right moment."

Kaida shook her head. "It was Drago. He told me I would regret refusing to be his mate."

"What did Drago say when Cadmus confronted him about it?" Bren asked.

"Drago has already left for Belinda's clan. Cadmus called him, but Drago denied it was him. He said that they had no proof he did it."

"Bren's a cop," Tyler said. "He can find the proof. It's, like, what he does."

"It's not worth it," Kaida said. "What's done is done."

She wanted to reach out and take Bren's hand but resisted. Sika had also texted Cadmus's request that Kaida return to her clan immediately and bring Bren. She couldn't refuse the high elder's order, but she also couldn't force Bren to return to the clan with her. Now that his father knew the truth and Bren and Tyler's lives had been completely upended, she was pretty sure it was over between her and Bren.

Her dragon wailed in misery, and she shuddered again when pain sliced through her chest at the thought of losing her mate.

The front door slammed, and Mal and Bishop joined them in the kitchen.

"Hi, honey." Willow smiled at Mal as he bent and kissed her.

"Hey. Good job with the driving."

"Thanks!" She beamed at him and hopped up from her chair so Mal could sit in the crowded kitchen. He pulled her into his lap, and she draped her arms over his shoulders as Bishop leaned against the counter.

"What's the situation like at my apartment?" Bren asked.

Bishop grimaced. "Reporters camped out everywhere. Doesn't look like they'll go anywhere for a while. I wouldn't go back for a few days."

Bren rubbed wearily at the back of his neck. "Shit. Okay, looks like it's a hotel for us."

"Nonsense," Mara said. "We have plenty of space. You can bunk down with us until this blows over."

"That's incredibly kind of you," Bren said, "but I don't want to intrude and -"

"You aren't." Mara reached out and took Tyler's hand and Corey's hand. "We're happy to have you stay with us."

Tyler and Corey were staring at Mara with something already a little close to love. "Can we, Bren? Please?" Tyler asked.

Before Bren could reply, Kaida said, "Cadmus is asking that you return to the clan with me, Bren."

"Sweet," Tyler said. "Can we see you in your dragon form when we're there?"

"You're not going," Bren said.

"What? Why not?" Tyler said.

Bren glanced at Kaida. "You're staying here with Mara and Roland."

"But -"

"No arguing, Ty," Bren said.

"Come, my loves," Mara said. "Let me show you to your rooms. Grab your stuff."

She herded Tyler and Corey out of the kitchen. Kaida cleared her throat. "Will you come with me, Bren?"

"Do I have a choice?"

There was no anger in Bren's voice, but she winced like he'd shouted the question. "You always have a choice, my ma -"

She cut herself off abruptly, glancing at Bishop. She

wanted to speak to Bren alone but didn't know how to say it without being rude. She turned her gaze to Willow, hoping against hope that the little human would pick up on her request.

Relief filled her when Willow immediately slid from Mal's lap. "C'mon, guys. Let's give them some privacy."

She tugged Mal to his feet and led him to the doorway before making a 'come here' motion to Bishop. "Bishop, come with us."

The big grizzly crossed the kitchen but paused in the doorway. "If you want me to go to Kaida's clan with you, I will."

A grin cracked Bren's face. "You offering to protect me, Bishop? Because I appreciate the offer but unless you promise to, at some point, pick me up in your arms and carry me away *Bodyguard* style, I'll have to pass."

Bishop rolled his eyes, but a small smile crossed his face. "You've got balls of steel, Matthews."

"My clan isn't going to hurt him, my bear," Kaida said.

Bishop shrugged. "Let me know when you're ready to go, and I'll drive you back to your clan." He followed Mal and Willow out of the kitchen.

Kaida stood and paced back and forth, staring at the floor as she spoke rapidly. "You don't have to come with me, Bren. Cadmus is requesting your presence, not demanding it. I know that with what's happened, your interest in me has… waned, and I understand. If I were in your place, I wouldn't -"

Her brisk pacing faltered when Bren stood in front of her.

"Hey," he said. "Look at me."

She stared at him, her dragon purring excitedly when Bren put his arm around her waist.

"If you were in my place, you wouldn't what? Wouldn't want to keep dating me? Wouldn't want to stick around?" he asked.

She shook her head. "No. My dragon can't – won't – leave you."

A soft smile crossed his face. "Then don't act like I can leave you. Because I can't, Kaida. I want to be with you no matter what. My... *interest* in you will never wane. Never stop. Ever."

He kissed her, and she breathed in her mate's scent, her body trembling with the sheer volume of how much she loved him.

Yes. Love. Her dragon purred happily at her acceptance of her true feelings. *We love our mate. Tell him.*

Before she could, Tyler rushed back into the kitchen. "Bren, you gotta talk to Corey's social worker. He called, and Corey's trying to tell him what's happening, but... please, can you talk to him?"

"Yes." Bren kissed Kaida's temple. "Give me five minutes, and then we'll leave."

"YOU OKAY, HUMAN?" SIKA ASKED.

"Yes. Eating dinner with a couple dozen dragons who may or may not be contemplating setting me on fire is my favourite way to spend a Tuesday evening," Bren said.

Bones snorted laughter. "The human is funnier than I expected. Javee, pass the salad, would you?"

Javee passed him the salad as Sika said earnestly, "We won't set you on fire, human. Cadmus has overruled the council's decision."

"Not to mention," Kaida's grandmother was sitting to his

left, and she gave him a toothy grin, "the smell of burnt human is a bitch to get out of our clothes."

"Gram!" Kaida was on his right, and she stared in horror at her grandmother as Bren burst into laughter.

"Relax, mostoirín. The human knows I'm only kidding." Gram patted Bren's hand before eating a bite of potatoes. "Cadmus made it clear to all of the clan that we are to treat you with respect and that you and your brother are welcome to stay with us for as long as you need."

"That's very kind of Cadmus and your clan," Bren said. "Thank you."

"I still think if the council would let us do interviews with the press, it would get them to back off," Jarvis said. "It's worked for Avena's clan."

"What do you mean?" Bren said.

Jarvis was holding Kova, and he shifted the sleeping baby to his left arm before saying, "Avena's clan in New York allowed a reporter into their home. They gave an interview and explained a bunch of stuff about dragons, how our clans work, that sort of shit. They even switched to their dragon forms and flew for them."

"What? When?" Bren said.

"This morning," Bones said. "They've been playing the interview on a loop all over television and the internet since then."

"There are rumours that Belinda's and Makeda's clans will do the same," Javee said.

"The reporters have already stopped surrounding Avena's clan," Jarvis said. "If we do the same -"

"The press may be backing off, but there are still plenty of humans gawking and trying to get onto Avena's land," Bones said. "It will take more than an interview and some pictures to ease their curiosity."

"But it could help a little," Jarvis continued doggedly. "If the reporters left, then maybe the humans would grow tired of -"

Bones slammed his fist down on the table. The hum and flow of conversation stopped, and the rest of the dragons sitting in groups around the half dozen long tables all stared at Bones.

"I will not be a monkey in a cage for the humans' amusement," Bones growled. Smoke curled from his nose, and Bren could see the tips of his fangs protruding from between his lips. "We are not zoo animals for them to look at and marvel over our uniqueness, Jarvis."

Javee placed her hand on his arm. "Be calm, my love."

Bones took a deep breath and released it, the thick cloud of smoke emerging from his lungs, nearly obscuring his face. "Cadmus and the other elders are right not to do interviews with the humans. We owe them nothing. Not an explanation of how we live nor a glimpse into our lives."

"All right," Jarvis said. "You don't have to be a dick about it, Bones. It was only an idea."

He glanced down at the baby in his arms before holding him out to the large dragon. "Here, hold Kova for a while. It will help calm you."

Bones cradled the baby in his arms, and Javee stroked the baby's round head and kissed his forehead. Bren was a little amused to see that holding the baby did seem to calm the big dragon.

He slipped his hand under the table and rested it against Kaida's thigh. Despite his assurances and the polite way the dragons treated him, she'd had a pinched and worried look since they joined the clan.

She slipped her hand under the table and took his, holding it tightly. They were both staring at the baby, and after a moment, Sika said, "Bren, you haven't held Kova yet, have you?"

He shook his head, and she motioned to Bones. "Give Kova to the human, Bones."

Bones hesitated before standing and reaching across the table to hand the baby to Bren. "Do not drop him, human."

Sika rolled her eyes. "It is because of Bren that Kova is safe. He's not going to harm him."

Bren took the baby, sliding his right hand under his neck to support the baby's head until he cradled him in his left arm. The baby was the spitting image of Jarvis, and Bren smiled at Kaida when she leaned against him and traced the baby's soft cheek with one fingertip.

"He's a beautiful hatchling," she said.

"He is," Bren replied. His breath caught in his throat when the baby made a soft snort, and his eyelids fluttered open. His irises were a brilliant shade of gold with flecks of jade. Bren stared in fascination at them as the baby stared back unblinkingly.

Sika was sitting on the other side of Kaida, and she leaned closer, smiling at Bren. "He likes you, human."

Kaida kissed the baby's foot, clad in a dark orange sock, and stroked his tiny leg. Bren glanced at her. The look of yearning on her face matched his own. He was sure of it. The idea of having a baby with Kaida almost felt like an obsession now.

She met his gaze and smiled at him, and not caring that the other dragons were there, he leaned down and pressed a kiss against her mouth. Instead of pulling away like he half-thought she might, she returned his kiss.

When they broke apart, Gram was grinning widely at them. She held her arms out. "Give the hatchling to me, human, and return to Kaida's cabin so you two can start making your own hatchling."

"Gram!" Kaida's face turned a bright red as the other dragons around them laughed.

Gram took the hatchling and kissed his forehead. "Oh please, it's not like we don't already know you're sleeping with the human. Just remember to be gentle with his fragile human bones."

BREN SQUINTED INTO THE DARKNESS. HE COULD HEAR KAIDA dressing, but she had pulled the blinds in the bedroom, and the room was pitch black. He fumbled for his phone on the nightstand, turning on the flashlight and aiming it in her general direction. Kaida raised her hand to block the light shining in her eyes.

"Sorry." He flicked on the bedside lamp before sitting up. "What time is it?"

Kaida wore the blue cloak that matched the blue in her hair and eyes. She fastened the cloak and slid the hood up over her head. "Almost three. I'm sorry I woke you. Go back to sleep, Bren."

"Where are you going?"

"It's my night to fly," she said and then purred so loudly her entire body seemed to vibrate. She rolled her eyes. "Sorry, my dragon gets super excited about flying."

"I bet. Can I come with you?" he asked.

"What?" She stared at him in obvious surprise.

"Can I come with you?"

"I… that's not a good idea."

He slid naked out of bed and crossed to her, secretly amused by the way her gaze immediately dropped to his dick. He put his arms around her. "I'd like to join you. I'd love to see you in your dragon form."

"Why?"

"Because it's a part of who you are, and I want to see that specific part. I want to see *all* of you."

She continued to hesitate, and he kissed the tip of her nose. "Look, I'm not asking to go all *Dragonriders of Pern* on you here, okay? I just want to see you in your dragon form and watch you fly. But if you don't want me there, I won't go."

"I want you there," she said. "But I'm worried that seeing me in my dragon form will…"

"Will what?" he asked.

"At best, kill your attraction for me. At worst, scare the shit out of you," she said bluntly.

"I think you underestimate how strong my attraction to you is, and I don't scare easily. You should know that by now."

She relaxed against him. "You're the bravest human I know."

He laughed. "Even though you don't know that many humans, I'll still take it as a compliment."

She studied him for a moment. "Are you certain you want to do this, Bren?"

"Yes," he said with no hesitation.

"All right. Get dressed."

His worry that it would be too dark to see Kaida change was unfounded. The moon was out, nearly full, and so bright that the world shone in cool blue light. He followed Kaida through the trees. Her hand was hotter than usual. He imagined that it was because of her excitement about flying. He was excited, too, and the chance to see Kaida in her dragon form made his skin tighten with anticipation.

They were deep in the forest now. They'd been walking steadily for nearly twenty minutes, and he could hear the rustle of the smaller animals as they passed. Unease settled in his stomach. He'd left his gun in Kaida's cabin, and he regretted that. While he wanted to see Kaida in her dragon form, he didn't fancy being a late-night snack for a bear or a wolf.

"What's wrong?" Kaida was inhaling deeply, and she looked over her shoulder at him. "Have you changed your mind?"

She had smelled his nervousness. He squeezed her hand. "No. But I'm not looking forward to a bear or wolf deciding to taste test me while you're out flying."

She smiled. "The creatures of the forest do not go near this place."

"Because of you?"

She started walking again. "Yes. My scent and that of my clan's is... off-putting to them. You will be safe while I am flying, my mate. I would not leave you alone if I did not believe this to be true."

She spoke absently as she picked her way through the trees, but his stomach tightened, and he had to swallow the urge to giggle like a little kid. It was the first time that Kaida had called him her mate outside of the bedroom, and –

Not true. She called you her mate the night they were going to burn you to a crisp and when the reporters surrounded you.

That was true, she had. But both times, he hadn't thought much of it. He'd been more concerned about the real possibility of dying the night he met with the council and of Kaida firebombing the bunch of reporters. Tonight, though, he was entirely focused on her and being called her mate was a shot of pure happiness. Maybe her feelings for him were growing as strong as his feelings for her. She had told him earlier that she couldn't and wouldn't leave him.

Not entirely accurate. Kaida said her dragon couldn't leave you. Ever stop to consider that only her dragon is really into you? Kaida's always insistent that her dragon calls you her mate, not her, remember? Also, you've known each other for less than a month. Maybe chill out on the 'we're going to be together forever, and I want her to have my babies' thing.

He cringed inwardly. He was acting a little on the desperate side, and if only Kaida's dragon felt strongly toward him, his obvious desperation to be with her would turn Kaida off. She liked him, and they had a great connection and mind-blowing sex, but all they'd agreed to was trying dating. That didn't equate to love. Her dragon might be weirdly attached to him, but he didn't know who had more control – Kaida or her dragon. He suspected that it was Kaida, and with all the battles their relationship was facing – scaring her off by pushing for more was a real possibility.

Let's not forget that your father is trying to force her clan to be branded like animals. Do you think she'll let this go on much longer, no matter how attached her dragon is to you?

"Bren? What's wrong?" Kaida had slowed to a stop, and she stared worriedly at him.

He pushed all the questions and the fears out of his head. This might be his only chance to see Kaida in her dragon form, and he wouldn't waste it worrying about a future that was too soon to consider.

"Nothing," he said. "How much further?"

"We're here." She led him past a large pine tree, and he stared at the clearing before them.

It was man-made and about a hundred and fifty feet long

and two hundred feet wide. Stumps dotted the clearing here and there, but most had been completely removed. Grass seed had been planted in the clearing, and with no trees to block the sun, it grew in a thick, soft green mat that was calf-high.

"It's a landing pad," Bren said.

Kaida smiled a little. "Yes."

She dropped his hand and pointed to one of the larger stumps at the edge of the clearing. "Sit there, Bren. All right?"

"Sure."

She hesitated before pressing a kiss against his mouth. "Are you certain you wish to see this?"

"I am," he said.

She still looked a little worried. "Once I've changed to my dragon -"

"Let me guess, don't come near you or touch you," he said.

She blinked at him. "No, you may touch me if you wish. My dragon will be," she adopted a long-suffering tone, "pissed if you don't touch and admire. She wants to show off."

He laughed. "Okay, cool."

"I was going to say that once I've changed to my dragon, make sure you are well clear when I'm about to fly. I don't want to hit you with my wings or something accidentally."

"Right," he said. Things suddenly seemed surreal, and Kaida must have sensed it because she stared at him worriedly.

"Bren?"

"I'm fine," he said. "It's just suddenly... a little weird, you know? I'm about to see a real-life dragon."

"I can wait a bit to shift if you'd like," she said.

He shook his head. Her little glances upward, the smoke curling out in a steady stream from her nose and mouth, and the nervous energy surrounding her showed him clearly that she was itching to shift.

"No, go ahead and shift." He kissed her and then walked away toward the stump. He sat down, sticking his hands into the pockets of his jacket, the wood cold against his ass despite his jeans. He watched as Kaida moved to the middle of the clearing. He noticed the other cloaks lying in heaps in the clearing for the first time. There were five of them, and he immediately scanned the sky, but there was no sign of the other dragons.

He returned his gaze to Kaida, his mouth going dry when she unfastened the cloak, and it slid from her shoulders. She was completely naked beneath the cloak. Half her body was in shadows, the other half lit into stark awareness by the moonlight. The curve of her hip and the lean length of her thigh made his cock immediately hard. He was suddenly aching to take her right there in the clearing with the light of the moon bathing both of their bodies.

He stood, his desire to see her in her dragon form completely overtaken by his need to make her his. Before he could take a step, Kaida's body began to swell. He could hear the cracking of her bones as her head fell back and her spine arched. She dropped to her hands and knees, her face obscured by the smoke drifting from her mouth. Her pale skin turned blue, he blinked, and now shimmery blue scales covered her body.

Her body was distorted to an impossible size, and he flinched when he heard more bones cracking. Even across the clearing, he could feel the heat radiating from her body. The air around him shimmered, and sweat dripped down his face. His eyes watered, and he squinted them shut against a particularly fierce blast of heat.

When he opened them, a dragon stood in the clearing. He

stared in silence at Kaida. She was close to twelve feet in height in her dragon form, and he estimated that she was at least forty feet long. Her scales were a shimmery dark blue, the wings folded against her body a lighter shade of blue. A double row of bony spikes started behind her head, growing larger as they followed the length of her spine, then waning in size as they travelled down her long tail to the tip. Her legs were large and powerful, each foot tipped with four black talons at the front and one at the back. Each talon was thick and razor sharp.

He walked toward her. His legs were shaky, but it wasn't nerves that made him feel like he was using rubbery noodles to propel himself forward. It was excitement and pure adrenaline.

He stopped before her, smiling when she bent her head toward him, and that great rumbling purr erupted from her chest. It was almost deafening in sound. The heat that radiated from her was so intense he wondered for a moment if it would burn him to touch her.

His worry was dispelled when Kaida nudged him with her large head. He stumbled back – Christ, she was strong – and then reached out and rubbed the space above her nose. She was hot but not painfully so, and her scales were somehow both rough and smooth at the same time.

Remembering what she'd said about her dragon, he said, "You're beautiful."

The dragon purred again, her golden eyes glowing with delight. She nudged him a second time, this time knocking him clean off his feet. Her purr turned to embarrassment – was it weird that he could recognize her different purrs? – and he jumped to his feet before rubbing the side of her face. "I'm okay. Are you ready to fly?"

The dragon opened her mouth, revealing long and pulse-pounding rows of sharp white teeth. Bren swallowed hard when she said, "Fly."

The voice was thick and more gargled than when the dragon spoke while in her human form, but that undercurrent of Kaida's voice that still ran through it made the proverbial shivers run up and down his spine.

He took a deep breath and smiled at her. "Have fun."

He returned to the stump and sat down. Kaida stared at him for a moment before unfurling her wings. His pulse, which had slowed to normal, immediately ratcheted again, pushing the blood through his body in hot and throbbing waves. Her wings were a combination of leathery membrane and tough bone supports. They were massive in size, and as she spread them out completely, he guessed her wingspan to be at least seventy feet.

"Holy shit," he breathed.

Kaida was staring at the sky, her broad chest heaving in great gulps of moonlit air as her powerful legs crouched. With almost magical ease, she leaped upward, her enormous wings beating the night air so hard that the wind from it nearly knocked him off the stump.

He grabbed the stump's sides, watching with awe and disbelief as Kaida rose quickly and steadily into the sky. When she was almost forty feet above the tree line, she flew forward, her body gliding through the air, the beat of her wings echoing in his ear drums. She did a few dips and dives, her body swooping gracefully across the sky before she flew toward the mountains in the far distance. She grew smaller and smaller until not even the bright moonlight was enough to help him see her.

"Holy *fucking* shit," he said.

He was still clinging to the stump, and he released his grip, his fingers aching from the pressure. He stared at the moon, his heart rapping against his rib cage like an impatient butler knocking on his master's door, processing what he'd just seen.

He unstuck his tongue from the roof of his mouth and said, "I saw a dragon fly."

When nothing replied, he studied the night sky and waited for her to return to him.

CHAPTER 25

The others returned before Kaida. The first dragon who dropped from the sky to land in the clearing with a ground shaking thud was bright orange. He was larger than Kaida, and he stared curiously at Bren before shifting with a low pop to his human form.

Bren didn't recognize the shifter. His short blond hair had streaks of orange throughout it, and he was well over six feet tall and had a lean and muscular body. He picked up his cloak, not bothered by his nakedness, and draped it around his body before nodding to Bren and walking out of the clearing.

The next two that arrived, landed in the clearing together. The bigger one was a rich dark green, the smaller the colour of emeralds. Bren turned away hastily when they shifted to their human form, and the smaller one was a woman. He waited a few minutes and then turned around. The dragons were in their cloaks and already at the edge of the clearing. Without looking at him, they disappeared into the trees.

Ten minutes later, a dark shadow blotted out the moon. Bren looked up, his eyes widening as the dragon coasted silently to the ground. It was midnight blue and so colossal that when the tip of one massive wing brushed against a tree as the dragon landed, the tree cracked with the sound of a gunshot and landed on its side as though felled by an invisible axe.

"Holy fuck," Bren said as the dragon turned its golden gaze toward him. The dragon growled, its teeth shining in the moonlight as smoke drifted out of his mouth. Every muscle in Bren's body went slack.

Shit. This had been a terrible idea.

There was a low pop, and the vast dragon turned into the vast human body of Bones. Bren choked in a breath, pressing his hand against his chest. "Jesus Christ, Bones. You scared the shit out of me."

The dragon laughed and smoothed his goatee down as he reached for his cloak. "You didn't piss your pants. I'm impressed."

"I came pretty fucking close." Bren stood up, taking a few steps toward Bones. A dragon, much smaller in size and with its scales a deep, rich red colour, landed behind the dragon shifter. "You have to be at least what? Sixty feet in length in your dragon form?"

Bones twirled his finger in a circular motion. "Turn away before my mate shifts, human. Unless you want to know what it feels like to have your flesh melted off."

Bren turned around immediately. Behind him, he heard the now familiar pop and then Javee's soft voice. "Don't be a dick to the human, honey."

"You know it's my go-to." Bones' voice was thick with amusement.

Javee laughed. "Indeed. You may turn around now, human."

Bren turned, nodding to the pretty dragon shifter as she

fastened the last button on her cloak and pulled the hood over her head. "Hello, Javee."

"Hello, human." Javee took Bones's hand. "Your mate was not far behind me. She will return soon."

"Thanks."

"Come, my love," Javee tugged on Bones's hand. "Let us leave before Kaida arrives and mates with her human."

Bones made a face before following Javee toward the trees. "Gross."

Javee laughed. "As if we're not going home to do the same, my love."

The grin on Bones's face widened, and he grabbed a handful of Javee's ass as they left the clearing.

The heat from the dragons quickly faded, and the cold air returned. Bren blew on his hands and stuck them under his armpits to warm them. It'd been almost two hours since Kaida had shifted to her dragon form, and he'd grown steadily colder while waiting. He stomped his feet as he paced back and forth in front of the stump. He was having a hot shower when he returned to Kaida's cabin. A scorching, steaming shower with a cup of coffee afterward that was hot enough to scald his tongue.

The soft thud behind him made him turn quickly, his breath steaming out in front of him in the cold air. Kaida stared at him but made no move to shift to her human form. He walked toward her and stroked her face when she bent her head. "Welcome back."

She purred loudly and then shifted to her human form. Her pale skin was still a soft shade of blue, but it disappeared as she reached out and traced a hand across his chest. "Hello, human."

"Hello, Kaida."

She purred again, the sound softer and a bit sweeter when

she was in her human form and tugged down the zipper of his jacket. "Did you miss me?"

"Yes."

"Good." She pushed his jacket off his shoulders and then moved closer, frowning at the goosebumps on his arms. "Are you cold, my mate?"

"A little," he said.

She leaned in and kissed his neck, her tongue tasting his skin as she slid one arm around his shoulders and used her other hand to unbutton and unzip his jeans. "My mate needs to be warmed, doesn't he?"

He moaned when her warm hand slipped into his briefs and wrapped around his dick. His semi turned to a full-on erection, and she purred happily before nipping at his earlobe.

"Are you always this... oh fuck, that feels good..." He thrust into her hand as she pumped him firmly.

"Always this what?" She kissed his jawline and nipped at his throat.

"Uh... affectionate after you fly?"

She laughed. "If by affectionate, you mean horny, then yes. Flying makes me want to fuck. Do you have a problem with that human?"

"No, ma'am," he said as she tugged his shirt over his head. "But maybe we should head back to the cabin. It's a little cold and someone might see us if we – shit!"

Kaida had hooked one foot behind his legs and with a gentle shove, tripped him as neat as could be. He landed on his back on the ground, the blow softened by Kaida's grip and the thick grass below him.

She straddled his thighs and pulled the opening of his jeans apart, pushing down the front of his briefs until his cock popped free. She rubbed him with one hand, long firm strokes that made his hips rise and his breath puff out of his chest in low moans and groans.

She cupped one breast, toying with the nipple until she made her own soft moan.

"Kaida," he said hoarsely. "Please."

She rubbed her thumb across the top of his dick, smiling in approval when she felt the moisture gathered there. She rubbed across the slit and then traced the ridge before tugging lightly on the head.

He cried out, his hands reaching to clamp on her thighs, his fingers digging into her smooth skin. "Fuck, Kaida!"

"Do you know what I was thinking about while I was flying, Bren?"

He shook his head, his gaze glued to her perfect tits, to the way her nipples had hardened as she teased them with her fingers.

"I was thinking about you waiting for me to return. I was thinking about your," she bent over and he sucked in a hard breath when her warm mouth surrounded the head of his cock and she sucked lightly for a few seconds before releasing him, "beautiful cock and how it belongs to me and only me."

She straightened, her terrible, wonderful hand still stroking, pulling, teasing. "Only me. Is that not right, human?"

"Yes," he said. "That's right."

Her thumb traced the thick vein that ran along the underside, her smile both sinful and sexy. "You are my mate, human. Say it."

"I'm your mate," he groaned out.

She scooted forward and when her wet pussy rubbed along the length of his shaft, they both moaned. She reached down and rubbed her clit, parting the lips of her pussy and showing him the swollen nub that gleamed in the moonlight. "Do you see how wet you make your mate?"

"Yes," he whispered.

She rubbed a hand across his bare chest, flicking one flat nipple with her finger, before tugging lightly on his chest hair. "Are you ready to be fucked, my mate?"

He muttered a curse, his hands cupping her hips and squeezing. "We can't."

She growled at him, smoke drifting out of her mouth. She grabbed his hands and yanked them above his head, pinning them into the grass as she leaned over him, letting her tits rub against his chest.

"Fuck," he moaned when she rubbed her pussy up and down the length of his aching dick.

She growled again, her eyes glowing, before she kissed him hard on the mouth. Her tongue thrust between his lips, tasting and teasing and taking. He returned her kiss, just as hot and eager as she was.

They broke the kiss, both of them gasping for air. She growled again and said, "Your cock is mine. Do not deny me what is mine."

He nipped at her throat. "I'm not denying you. But I don't have a condom on me and I'm pretty sure you don't have one in that cloak of yours. So, what do you say we head back to your cabin and finish this… oh fuck, that feels good."

Kaida's warm pussy slid down his cock and any lingering cold he felt disappeared completely. He hadn't taken a woman bare in years, and the feel of her hot wet warmth surrounding his dick was almost overwhelming.

"I want you like this," she whispered into his ear. "When you are close, tell me and I will finish you with my mouth. Do you agree to this, my mate?"

"Yes," he said as his body arched. "Fuck, yes."

"Good." She brushed her nipple across his mouth. He captured it between his lips, licking and sucking it into a stiff and swollen peak. Moaning, her pelvis rising up and down in slow thrusts, she tugged away before giving him her other nipple to tease. He gave her what she wanted until she was crying out with pleasure.

She pulled away, sitting up and bracing her hands on his chest as she rode him hard. He gripped her smooth hip with one hand and used his other to tease her clit. Her head fell back, her long dark hair tickling his thighs as she moved hard and fast. He rubbed her clit with the ball of his thumb, using the firm steady pressure he'd discovered she liked. Her chest was glowing bright red, the air around them growing steadily hotter as her internal temperature rose. He was no longer cold, the sweat sliding down his skin as he watched Kaida's chest grow a deeper red.

She sucked in a deep breath, her body stiffening and her pussy squeezing around him as she came. Her face pointed to the sky, her pussy squeezing and releasing him as she came again and again, she opened her mouth and released a burst of flame. It was larger and hotter than he'd ever seen her release and he watched in fascination as the fire lit up the clearing.

She blew out another burst of flame, this one a little smaller, before collapsing on his chest. Her warm body shook, and he could feel her heart pounding against his. She moved her pelvis in slow gentle motions, squeezing his dick with every downward stroke as his hands slid down and gripped her ass.

He squeezed lightly and met each of her thrusts, pressing hot kisses against her shoulder as the ache in his dick grew. He pumped harder, relishing the feel of Kaida's blunt nails digging into his shoulders, the nip of her sharp teeth against his throat. She was soaking wet and so fucking warm… he could feel his balls tightening and the base of his spine was tingling.

He didn't want her to finish him with her mouth, he wanted her pussy. He wanted to feel her squeezing around him as he drove in deep and emptied himself inside of her. Wanted her to take every last bit of his cum into her soft and supple body.

Before he lost his mind and just came inside of her, he gasped out, "Kaida, I'm close. Honey, I'm so close."

She slowed to a stop and he bit back his groan of disappointment as she pressed a kiss against his neck. His body stiffened, his cock going impossibly hard when she whispered into his ear, "I don't want to finish you with my mouth."

He groaned, his fingers squeezing the soft flesh of her perfect ass. "Kaida…"

"I want you to come inside me, my mate. Do you want that?"

"Yes," he moaned.

"It's what you're supposed to do, isn't it?" Her voice was low and hypnotic. "We are mates, aren't we?"

"Yes." He thrust hard, Kaida's warmth surrounding him down to the very base of his dick.

"I want to please my mate," Kaida licked the curve of his ear. "What do you want, Bren?"

"I want to come in you," he gasped out.

"I want that too," she breathed.

He flipped her over so quickly, she didn't have time to react. He was back inside of her, his dick surrounded by her hot warmth before her gasp of surprise had died out. Her thighs squeezed his hips and she smiled up at him as he propped himself up on his hands above her.

"Fuck me, my mate," she demanded.

He drove into her, hard and fast, her hips meeting his stroke for stroke. Her soft hands were everywhere, his chest, his ribs, his back, stroking and teasing and driving his need higher. He was so damn close, balancing on the razor thin edge of his control.

He was fucking Kaida. He was fucking her bare and when he was done, she'd be pregnant with his baby. She'd be his forever. A vision of Kaida, her belly round with his baby, flashed through his head and he shouted her name as he climaxed, straining and pumping as he emptied himself deep inside of her. Her muscles clamped around him and he collapsed on top of her, breathing harshly against her neck as her warm hands stroked his back.

He rolled to his side, worried about crushing her, and brought her with him. His cock was still softening inside of her and she kept herself close against him, kissing his neck and chest as he stared up at the moon.

The pleasure of his orgasm was fading, leaving him feeling a little sick inside. What the fuck was wrong with him? He'd just had some sort of...of breeding fantasy about Kaida, and he'd let himself come inside of her. Had he gone crazy?

As if she sensed his discomfort, she said, "All my tests are clear, Bren. I promise."

"Mine are too," he said. "Are you on the pill?"

She didn't reply and he smoothed her hair back from her face. "Kaida, are you on birth control?"

"No," she said before rolling out of his embrace. She climbed gracefully to her feet and walked across the clearing to her cloak. He sat up and tucked his dick away, buttoning and zipping his jeans before grabbing his shirt and putting it on.

He stood and snagged his jacket from the ground before walking to where Kaida waited for him at the clearing.

"Come, human," she held out her hand, "we need to get you home before you freeze to death."

"Kaida, wait." The tone of her voice was normal, but she wouldn't look at him. He tugged on her hand. "Look at me."

She took a deep breath before raising her gaze to his. "What's wrong?"

"What's wrong?" He frowned at her. "We just had sex without a condom and you're not on birth control. We need to talk about what we do if you get pregnant."

She shook her head. "It's not going to happen."

"You don't know that," he said.

"I do." She pressed a quick kiss against his mouth. "Dragons have a hard time getting pregnant, remember?"

"I remember, but…"

"It isn't possible," Kaida said. "We have to try for years to have a baby. One instance of unprotected sex isn't going to result in a baby. I promise."

"And if you're wrong?" Bren said.

"I'm not." She kissed him again. "Look, I wouldn't have asked you to come in me if I thought there was even a small chance it would result in pregnancy. I'm not trying to trap you into anything, if that's what you're worried about. I am not going to get pregnant from this."

"I didn't think you were trying to trap me. I'm a big boy, I could have said no." He could hear the anger in his voice, and she smiled apologetically at him.

"You're right. I shouldn't have said that. I'm sorry. C'mon, you're freezing, I know you are."

"But what if you're wrong," he persisted as he followed her into the woods. "What if you are pregnant?"

"I'm not wrong," she said. "Trust me, Bren."

"Go home, Bren."

Bren glared at Morales. "I can do my job, Captain."

"You were followed to that break and enter I assigned you this morning, weren't you?"

Bren didn't reply and Morales said, "They followed you back to the precinct. We've got reporters camped out in front of the building."

"They'll lose interest soon," Bren said.

"Probably. But it won't hurt for you to take the rest of the week off. Hell, it'll probably be good for you. You work too much anyway. Give it a few days for shit to calm down and come back to work on Monday."

"Captain, I don't -"

"Not a choice, Matthews." Morales' voice was calm but there was no compromise in it. Once he'd made up his mind about something, there was very little chance of changing it.

Bren shut down his laptop. He started to pack it up and Morales shook his head. "Time off, Bren. The precinct will survive without you for a few days."

"My caseload is -"

"Will still be waiting for you when you come back. If there's anything that's an emergency, I'll get another detective to cover for you."

Pissed, but knowing that there was nothing he could do, Bren left his laptop on his desk. Morales clapped him on the back. "You get your vehicle yet?"

"Yeah," Bren said. "The security company that I hired to protect Tyler got my keys from me this morning. They picked up my car and grabbed me some clothes and stuff from my apartment. Said there was still a pack of reporters hanging around."

"Fucking vultures," Morales said. He squeezed Bren's shoulder. "This'll blow over eventually. You got a place to stay?"

"Yes," Bren said.

"Good. Text me if you need anything, yeah?"

"I will. Thanks, Captain."

Bren grabbed the ballcap he'd stuffed into the bottom drawer of his desk and jammed it onto his head before heading out the back door of the precinct. His SUV was parked close to the door and after taking a look for reporters, he jogged over to it and climbed in. He put his sunglasses on and took the back alley out to the street, easing behind three news vans and the crowd of reporters milling on the sidewalk – Christ, how many reporters did this city have? – and making his escape down the street.

He checked his rearview mirror repeatedly and made a few unnecessary turns before being satisfied that he wasn't followed and heading toward Mara and Roland's house. He'd given his cell number to Mara before he left with Kaida last night, and Mara had texted him this morning to tell him both boys were doing fine but that, as per the school's original request, she was keeping them home with her for the rest of the week.

He pulled into the driveway of the wolf shifter's home and shut the SUV off before checking his phone. There was no text from Kaida. Not that he expected there to be. After they returned from the clearing, they'd crawled into bed. Kaida had fallen asleep immediately. He laid awake until just after six then had a quick shower. She'd mostly woken when he kissed her goodbye but was asleep again before he even made it to the door of the bedroom.

He still felt uneasy about having sex without a condom. He knew Kaida was right – the odds of her being pregnant were low, but what if she was? It'd be one hell of a mess they'd gotten themselves into, if she was.

Like you wouldn't be thrilled if she were pregnant.

He couldn't argue with his inner voice. He would be over the goddamn moon if Kaida was carrying his baby. She wasn't, he knew she wasn't, but he couldn't help the little thrill he got just thinking she might be.

They needed to sit down and talk...really talk. But Kaida was spooked about everything that had happened with his father, and he had the bad feeling that she would bolt like a startled deer if he even pushed a little to talk about where their relationship was going. He wanted to clear the air with her, wanted to find out if she loved him or if she was just going along with her dragon's infatuation with him because it was easier, but the thought that it might push her to drop him entirely from his life, made him feel sick to his stomach. Worse – it scared the shit out of him.

He stared at himself in the rear-view mirror before yanking his sunglasses and ballcap off and leaving them on the passenger seat. "Some fucking tough guy you are," he muttered and headed toward the house, locking his car behind him.

He knocked on the door and smiled at Mara when she opened it. "Hi, Mara. Sorry to drop by without texting first."

"Don't be silly," she said. "Come over whenever you want. The boys and I are about to have lunch. Have you eaten?"

"No," he said as he followed her into the house and down the hall to the kitchen. Tyler and Corey were sitting at the table, both of them looking at Tyler's iPad. Bren dropped into the seat next to his brother and Tyler held out his fist without looking away from the iPad.

"Dude."

"Hey, buddy." He bumped Ty's fist with his own.

"Why aren't you at work?" Ty asked.

"I'm taking a few days off."

"Because you want to or because you have to?" Tyler finally looked at him.

Bren didn't reply and after a moment, Mara said, "The soup is almost ready. You boys wash up and then set the table for me, would you?"

"Sure," Corey said.

He and Tyler left the kitchen and Mara smiled at Bren. "Your brother and his boyfriend are lovely young men."

"Thanks again for letting them stay here. I appreciate it," Bren said.

"We don't mind at all. Actually," Mara tasted the soup again, "I chatted with Corey's social worker this morning, and he agreed to let us temporarily foster Corey until a more permanent solution could be found."

"Seriously?" Bren said.

"Yes. Neither Roland nor I could stand the thought of him going to a group home when we have so much space here. It's just our Becky at home now and it's been nice having more than one teenager again," Mara said.

Bren laughed. "You might be the only person I know who is actively looking for more teenagers. Are you sure you know what you're getting into?"

Mara grinned at him. "We have six children, Detective, and four of them were hormonal teenage boys at the same time. It was complete and utter chaos, and I miss that chaos tremendously."

Bren laughed again. "Well, thank you again. I know Corey is grateful to you."

"He is a sweet boy," Mara said.

The front door slammed, and heavy footsteps trod down the hallway. Bishop poked his head into the kitchen. He was holding Lila in his arms and the baby squealed with excitement when she saw Mara. "That smells good, Mara. Any chance there's enough for – Matthews, hey."

"Hey," Bren said as Bishop crossed the room to kiss Mara's cheek.

"There's plenty of soup, Button," Mara said as Lila squealed again and reached for the elegant wolf shifter. "Hi, sweet Lila. Come here, my darling girl."

She took Lila and kissed her cheek. Lila growled happily, and Mara laughed. "Oh, you are the sweetest thing."

"Thank you again for watching her," Bishop said as the boys joined them in the kitchen again. Tyler and Corey set the table, moving around the kitchen as comfortably as if they'd lived there for weeks, not a day.

"It's never a problem. You know I love my Lila girl." Mara laughed again when Lila chewed and licked at her cheek. "I see she's still in her chewing phase."

"Yes," Bishop said. "Ava will be by after her shift to pick her up. Around four, she said."

"Perfect," Mara said.

Bishop sat down beside Bren, studying him silently. "How'd it go with the clan last night?"

"Fine," Bren said.

"No problem with the other," Bishop glanced at Tyler and Corey, "clan members?"

"He wants to know if any of the dragons tried to set you on fire for dating Kaida," Tyler said with a snicker.

"Everyone was very welcoming," Bren said. "In fact, I was about to call your office, see if there was someone available to sneak me back to the clan."

"Why sneak in?" Tyler said. "Everyone knows you and Kaida are a thing. Who cares?"

Bren supposed Tyler had a point, but the dragons were

already being inundated with reporters. If they saw him, it would only make it worse. "True, but we're still going to keep a low profile for now."

Tyler glanced at Corey. "Corey says we should do the same thing. I don't want to hide anymore though."

"It's not hiding," Corey said.

"He's right," Bren replied. "Keeping a low profile is not the same as hiding a relationship."

"I guess." Tyler was standing near Mara and he reached out and touched the top of Lila's foot.

Bren was feeling as dejected as Tyler looked. He masked it with a smile. "It'll get better, Ty. It's only until the press finds a new story to fixate on. They'll lose interest in us, I promise."

Tyler continued to stare at Lila. "Will they? Dad's in the news, like, all the time and everyone knows how much he hates shifters. What if they never get tired of following us?"

"They will," Bren said with a confidence he didn't feel.

Mara leaned forward and kissed Tyler's forehead. "Your brother is right, sweetheart. They'll move on, they always do."

God, Bren hoped the wolf shifter was right. He couldn't stand the idea of his brother always needing to hide who he loved. It wasn't fair to him.

Or you.

"Bren?"

He glanced at Bishop. "Sorry, what did you say?"

"I said I can take you to Kaida's place after lunch."

"Thanks, I appreciate it," Bren said.

CHAPTER 26

"Bren? What are you doing here? What's wrong?" Kaida was sitting at her kitchen table with Cadmus when Bren let himself into the cabin.

"Hey. Everything's good. My captain told me to take the rest of the week off. Reporters are following me."

She rubbed at the back of her neck. "Shit. I'm sorry."

He shook his head. "It's not unexpected. Hello, Cadmus."

"Hello, human." Cadmus pointed to the chair beside him. "Join us."

Bren sat down in the chair. Cadmus leaned over and inhaled deeply before reaching out and poking at Bren's shoulder. He had the happy look of a small child just learning to walk, and a grin cracked Bren's face when the old dragon leaned forward and sniffed him again.

"Humans smell so strange," he said to Kaida. "Although I imagine your mate smells good to you."

Kaida's face flushed and she made a strangled sound that Bren guessed was meant to be an agreement to Cadmus's statement. He nearly fell off his chair when Cadmus stood and said, "The council is meeting. I'd like you and Kaida to join us."

Cadmus walked toward the door, raising his eyebrow when neither Bren nor Kaida followed him. "Come. The council waits for us."

The three of them walked to the main cabin without speaking. Tables had already been set up for the evening meal and the other council members were seated around one. The one named Ryul frowned when he saw Bren and Kaida. "What are they doing here, Cadmus?"

"I asked them to join us." Cadmus sat down, waving his hand at the two empty seats beside him.

Bren and Kaida sat. Bren glanced at Kaida, but she seemed as confused as he was about why they were joining the council meeting.

Cadmus folded his hands in front of him and said, "Earlier this morning, Senator Matthews sent word that he would like to meet with the head of our clan to discuss the growing tension between us and the humans and to see if we can find peace."

Bren jerked in surprise. Kaida dropped her hand below the table and squeezed his thigh as he stared at Cadmus. "He did what?"

"What growing tension?" Walter said. "There is no growing tension and if there is, it is the humans who caused it."

"More aptly, the senator," Collette said. "That asshole has been holding protests all over the city about what a danger we are." She glanced at Bren but didn't apologize for calling his father an asshole.

She didn't have to. He knew better than all of them what kind of man his father really was.

"Perhaps he is ready to try to learn more about us,"

Cadmus said. "He has assured me there will be no press or reporters there, and I have hope that the meeting will help reassure him that humans have nothing to fear from us."

"No," Bren said. "This isn't a good idea, Cadmus. No matter what you say, you will not change his mind. Whatever reason my father has for meeting with you – it isn't a good one. The fact that he doesn't want press there – that's a huge red flag. He *always* wants the press around for shit like this."

Cadmus didn't reply and Kaida leaned forward. "Listen to Bren, Cadmus. He knows his father better than us. If he says you shouldn't meet with him, you shouldn't."

"You would let a human tell our high elder what to do?" Ryul snorted. "We have looked past your infatuation with the human, Kaida, but do not ask us to start taking his advice."

"Enough, Ryul," Leah said. "Kaida makes an excellent point. The human knows his father best. If he says it's a bad idea to meet with him, then we should listen to him."

"Not we," Cadmus said. "I would be the only one to meet with him."

The council members protested vigorously, and Cadmus held his hand up to silence them. "The Senator wants to meet with only me. I believe if we all show up, it will only cause more distrust between us."

"You are not going alone," Walter said. He banged his hand down on the table for emphasis, smoke curling out of his nostrils. "I do not care that you are the high elder. None of us will allow you to meet with the human alone."

"I will take Bones with me," Cadmus said.

"Cadmus, let me speak to my father first," Bren said. "Once I've talked to him, I'll have a better idea of what his angle is for this meeting."

"He wishes to discuss peace," Cadmus said. "To refuse the meeting with him would be telling him I do not wish to have peace. I must do this, Bren. For the safety of the humans in this city."

"I know. But if peace really were what my father wanted, he would have the press there. Believe me," Bren said. "Let me speak with him first before you set up a meeting. All right? I'll call him tonight."

He reached under the table and took Kaida's hand. She squeezed it tightly as everyone stared at Cadmus. After a moment, the old dragon nodded. "I will consider the merits of meeting with your father a little longer before making my decision."

"THIS," SIKA SCOOPED OUT KAIDA'S PHONE FROM THE LARGE bowl of dry rice, "is not the way to start a weekend."

"Tell me about it," Kaida said.

"Did you drop it in the toilet?"

"No!" Kaida took the steaks out of the fridge and seasoned them. "I dropped it in the sink this morning when it was full of water."

"Shitty," Sika said. "Think it still works?"

Kaida returned the steaks to the fridge and sank into the chair next to Sika. "No. I tried turning it on half an hour ago and nothing."

"Super shitty." Sika kissed Kova's head. The hatchling was strapped to her chest with some kind of harness and sleeping soundly. "What are your plans for this glorious Friday evening?"

"Not sure yet," Kaida said.

"Where's your human?"

"He's with his brother. He'll be home in an hour or so... I think." She glared at her phone. "I can't call or text him."

Sika fished her phone out of her pocket. "You can call him on my phone."

"I don't know his number," Kaida said.

Sika laughed. "Ah, modern technology – isn't it marvelous?"

"Yeah." Kaida lapsed into silence, and Sika poked her in the shoulder.

"Tell me what's wrong."

"Nothing's wrong."

Well, except that you're in love with Bren but too afraid to tell him because you know the senator will make it his mission to destroy you and your clan if you claim his son as your mate. Oh, and also – you had unprotected sex with Bren... on purpose. You want to be pregnant with his hatchling.

She hadn't done it on purpose. She'd just been caught up in the moment, that's all. With her dragon egging her on to keep fucking Bren and how good it felt to have him inside of her, it wasn't surprising that she hadn't wanted to stop.

Besides, Bren agreed to it.

That was a real shitty and manipulative thing you did to him. It wasn't fair, and you know it. You need to apologize. There's a reason he's been acting distant the last couple of days.

Her dragon whined unhappily. Bren had been acting weird and a little distant. He'd spent most of Thursday with her, but they hadn't spoken much. They'd spent most of their time in bed.

Her face flushed. Bren had been very careful to use a condom each time they were together. She should have apologized yesterday but couldn't seem to form the words. She couldn't shake the feeling that their time together was ending and that by this time next week, Bren would be gone, and she'd be alone.

That nagging certainty had her reaching for Bren, had her

nearly frantic to touch him, to take her pleasure from him as often as possible. Spending yesterday with Bren in her bed was what she'd needed. But it wasn't solving the growing tension between them, so she'd vowed to talk to him tonight over dinner.

"Hey, you still in there?" Sika gave her another poke in the shoulder.

"Sorry, I'm …"

"Tell me what's wrong, honey," Sika said gently. "Maybe I can help."

"It's… I don't even know where to start or -"

The knock on her door made them both jump.

"Come in," Kaida called.

Javee stepped into her cabin. Her face was pale, and Kaida could smell her anxiety from across the room. "Javee, what's wrong?"

"Sika, would you give me a minute alone with Kaida?" Javee asked.

"Sure." Sika left the cabin.

The minute the door shut, Kaida said, "What's wrong?"

"Has your human spoken with his father?" Javee asked.

"No, at least not as of this morning. Bren tried to contact him a few times yesterday, but his father wouldn't return his calls. He said he would go to his father's office today, but I wrecked my phone and don't know if Bren talked to him. Why?"

"Bones is with Cadmus at the main cabin. They're going to meet with the senator. They're leaving in five minutes, and I don't have a good feeling about this."

Kaida immediately grabbed her jacket, shrugging into it and heading for the door. "Me either."

The two of them jogged to the main cabin. The door

opened as they reached the porch steps, and Cadmus and Bones stepped outside.

"Cadmus, you said you would wait until Bren spoke to his father," Kaida said.

"No, I said I would consider the merits of meeting with him a little longer. I have considered it and believe meeting with Senator Matthews is wise," Cadmus said.

"I'm coming with you then," Kaida said.

She waited for Cadmus to say no and was already mentally preparing her argument when Cadmus said, "All right."

"You need me. You and Bones going alone isn't... wait, what?"

Cadmus snorted laughter. "I said all right. You may come with us."

A large black SUV pulled into the clearing and stopped in front of the cabins. A blond man with a long, lean body stepped out. Kaida could smell that he was a cheetah shifter as he approached them.

"Mr. Cadmus?" The cheetah shifter held his hand out to Cadmus. "My name is Fenton. I understand you need a ride past the reporters."

Cadmus shook his hand. "Myself and my two companions. Can you get all of us out without the reporters seeing us?"

Fenton looked Bones up and down. "Should be able to."

"We have a vehicle parked in the woods not far from the reporters," Bones said. "We'll only need you to drive us to it."

"Sure. Whatever you want," Fenton said.

"Cadmus," Kaida took his arm as he walked by her, "I don't think this is a good idea. Bren will return soon. We should wait and -"

"It will be fine, Kaida. Do not worry." Cadmus pulled away and followed the cheetah shifter to the SUV.

Bones was kissing Javee goodbye, and the dragoness gave him a fierce look. "Be careful, my love. Promise me."

"I will. I'll see you soon," Bones said.

Kaida followed Bones to the SUV. "Bones, can you not talk him out of this?"

"I tried," the large dragon said. "He's determined."

"Shit. This is a really bad idea," Kaida said.

"Probably," Bones replied. "But he is our high elder."

"Do the other council members know he's doing this?"

"I don't think so," Bones said.

"Come, you two," Cadmus called cheerfully. "We do not want to be late."

"Javee," Kaida looked over her shoulder at the dragoness, "can you find Bren's cell number? Call him, tell him what's happening, and give him Bones's number. Tell him my cell is dead. Okay?"

Javee nodded, and Kaida, her stomach churning, climbed into the cargo area of the SUV with Bones.

"You still haven't heard from your father?" Mal sat down on the couch next to Bren.

Bren shook his head. "No. They said he was out when I went to his office this morning. When I went back this afternoon, he was in meetings all afternoon. When I returned just before five, he'd left for the day."

He was pretty sure his blood pressure was at stroke levels. He made himself take a few deep breaths. "He knows exactly why I want to talk to him.

"Maybe he really does want to talk about peace," Willow said. She was sitting cross-legged on the floor, holding Lila.

"He doesn't," Bren said.

He rubbed his forehead as he scanned his phone. When he'd arrived at Mara and Roland's, Mal and Willow and Bishop and Ava were there for dinner. He'd quickly filled them in on the details surrounding his father's request.

He could hear Tyler, Corey, and Mal's youngest sister, Becky, in the dining room down the hall. They were joking and teasing each other as they set the table.

"And you haven't talked to Kaida at all today?" Ava said from her spot next to Bishop on the loveseat.

"No," Bren scanned his phone again, "nothing. I've sent multiple texts, and I've called her. It goes straight to voicemail."

"I tried her earlier," Bishop said, "and I also got her voicemail."

"Can you try someone else in the clan?" Willow suggested.

"No, I don't know anyone else's number." He could hear the frustration in his voice as he glanced at Bishop. "Do you have anyone else's number in the clan?"

The big grizzly shifter shook his head. "No, sorry."

Bren's phone buzzed in his hand. He stared at the unfamiliar number before answering. "Hello?"

"Bren, it's Javee."

The anxiety in the dragoness's voice made Bren's scalp tighten, and dread seeped into his chest. "Hey. What's wrong?"

"You're a hard guy to get a hold of," Javee said. "It took me forever to find your cell number."

"A cop's number is usually more difficult to track down,

even for a hacker like you. What's going on? Have you talked to Kaida today? She isn't answering her phone."

"Her cell died," Javee said. "It's why I'm calling. Cadmus is meeting with your father tonight, and he took Bones and Kaida with him."

"What?" Bren exploded off the couch and paced the living room as the others quit talking and stared at him. "When? Where?"

"They left almost two hours ago, but I don't know where the meeting is."

"Shit," he said.

"I'll text you Bones's number. Call him, and he'll give you their location," Javee said.

"Yeah, okay. Thanks, Javee."

"Bren?"

"Yeah?"

"Something doesn't feel right about this. I know the guy is your father, but…"

"I know. Send me Bones's number."

He ended the call and waited impatiently for Javee's text, ignoring the others in the room. His phone dinged, and he immediately called Bones's number, his free hand clenching into a fist when it rang and rang in his ear.

It clicked to voicemail, and he said, "Bones, it's Bren. I need you to call me back immediately and tell me where you're meeting with my father."

He disconnected the call and muttered a loud curse.

"What's going on?" Mal asked.

"Cadmus, Kaida, and Bones are meeting with my father right now. No one knows where, Kaida's cell is dead, and Bones isn't answering his."

"Can you call your father's office and ask?" Ava suggested.

"They wouldn't tell me even if the office was still

open," Bren said. He slammed his hand against the wall. "Fuck! Something isn't right. I can feel it. My father doesn't want peace, and if he did, he sure as hell wouldn't meet with Cadmus without the press around to document it."

"You're a cop. Can't you get your IT guy to track your dad's phone?" Willow asked.

"I need a warrant for that, and no judge will give me one without probable cause." He hammered his hand against the wall again as Tyler walked into the room.

"What's wrong?" Ty asked.

"I need to know where Dad is, and he isn't answering my calls," Bren said. "Have you talked to him today?"

Tyler snorted. "I haven't talked to him since he was such a dickhead at his place." He glanced at Ava and Willow before smiling sheepishly. "Uh, sorry about the language."

Bren tried to calm down. His usual levelheadedness and ability to think through a crisis had utterly abandoned him. Which was stupid because he didn't even *know* it was a crisis. Maybe his father really did want peace.

You don't actually believe that. If you did, you wouldn't be freaking the fuck out right now.

"You okay?" Tyler gave him a cautious look. "You seriously look like you're freaking out, dude."

"I am, a little." He didn't have the energy to lie to his brother. "I'm worried about Kaida. She and a few other clan members are meeting with Dad, but no one knows where, and they're not answering their phones."

He had a sudden idea. "Do you still have Dad's assistant's number in your cell?"

"Yeah," Tyler said.

"Can you call her? Tell her there's been an emergency, and you need to know where Dad is."

Tyler pulled his phone out of his pocket. "If you need to know where Dad is, I can track his phone."

Bren's pacing slowed. "I – seriously?"

"Yep. Dad insisted I let him do that stupid find my phone thing with me. I said fine, but if he got to track my location, it would only be fair for me to track his. I can find his location for you."

Bren rushed over, grabbed Tyler's head between his hands and planted a loud smacking kiss on his forehead. "Jesus, I love you, kid."

Tyler grinned at him. "Everybody does."

CHAPTER 27

"You're sure this is the place?" Kaida stared out the windshield.

"Yes," Cadmus said. "It's the address that was texted to me."

"He wants to meet at an abandoned airfield?" Kaida shook her head as she studied the black Lincoln parked beside the largest hangar. "I don't like this."

"What's there to like?" Bones replied.

"We should leave," Kaida said. "The Senator is up to something."

"We're not leaving," Cadmus said. "Come, we have nothing to fear."

He opened the door and climbed out of the car, leaving Kaida and Bones no choice but to follow them.

They slammed the doors and started after the high elder as he walked briskly toward the hangar. Bones was sniffing the air, and Kaida said, "It's a trap."

"No shit, Admiral Ackbar," Bones said.

"We need to force Cadmus back to the car and go," Kaida said.

Bones laughed dryly. "Like we can force Cadmus to do anything. If we piss him off enough, his dragon will kick both our asses. The old man is tough as fucking nails."

"Shit," Kaida muttered as they drew closer. The only car visible was the Lincoln, but she could smell the scents of many different humans drifting out from the open door of the battered and weather-aged hangar. "There's more than just the senator inside there.

Bones shrugged. "Look, the senator obviously has some plan that won't end well... for him. No matter how many guys he brought with him, they're no match for us. We don't like what they say or do, we shift to our dragon forms and burn them to a crisp, or we fly out of there. Right?"

"Right." Kaida followed Cadmus and Bones into the concrete and steel hangar.

To her complete lack of surprise, Bren's father was there with, she counted quickly, fifteen other humans. The hangar was cold. Most of the windows that made up the far wall of the hangar had been broken by vandals or bored teenagers, and the enormous rusted doors at the front of the hangar were pulled back and half hanging off the hinges, exposing the inside to the elements. Their footsteps echoed on the concrete floor as they joined the senator in the middle of the building.

"What are you doing here?" Senator Matthews said coldly.

"What are they doing here?" Kaida pointed to the men standing around him in a loose cluster. "I thought you wanted to meet with our high elder alone."

"These are my associates," Senator Matthews said. He glanced to his right. "This is Martin Grimes."

Kaida studied the man standing to the right of Bren's father. He was over six feet and heavily muscled. He had pale skin and light blue eyes, and his blond hair gleamed in the beams of sun peeking through the holes in the roof of the hangar. He stroked his thick beard as he returned Kaida's look. He looked vaguely familiar, but she couldn't place how she knew him.

"I know who your associates are," Bones said. "You bringing the leader and members of the HAPI group to this meeting isn't exactly setting a tone for peace."

Kaida's dragon growled out a warning as Martin laughed. "You're wrong, dragon. We want peace with the paranormals. It's why I created the HAPI organization."

"You literally have the words 'against paranormals' in your name," Bones growled. "We are not stupid, human."

"You sure about that?" One of the other men said under his breath.

Bones growled again, smoke drifting out of his mouth, and the men glanced uneasily at each other.

Cadmus held up his hand. "Enough. We are here in good faith to speak about peace with you, Senator Matthews."

"That's right," Senator Matthews replied. "And how we achieve peace is by your... *clan* leaving my city."

"Are you serious?" Bones said.

The senator ignored him, training his gaze on Cadmus. "Before your clan leaves, we want you to agree to be tagged and monitored by the HAPI group. It's a simple procedure. A small chip is embedded in the back of your skull and -"

Bones barked out a laugh. "Enough. High elder, it's time to leave."

Cadmus held out his hand. "One moment, Bones."

"Cadmus -"

"A moment, I said." A growl rose from the old dragon's throat, and Bones and Kaida took a step back, giving each other a troubled look.

Bones hadn't been joking when he said Cadmus could kick their asses. In his youth, the high elder had been the clan's most powerful dragon and despite what appeared to be a fragile appearance now, his dragon was still powerful and dangerous. Even Bones, with all his power and strength, would be no match for an angry Cadmus.

"Senator, while I appreciate that you have your concerns about my kind, I want to assure you that we have no wish to harm the humans. We will continue to live as we did before, quietly and with little contact with humans."

"Is that right?" Senator Matthews turned his dark gaze toward Kaida. "Because a member of your clan is in a relationship with my child. That doesn't seem like the dragons are keeping their distance."

Cadmus glanced at Kaida, a soft smile crossing his face before he turned back to the senator. "We cannot choose who our children fall in love with, Senator. You may disagree with your son's choices, but I will not deny Kaida her mate."

"Mate." The Senator's voice held a thin note of disgust in it. "Your dragon whore seduced my son to drive a wedge between him and me and to weaken the faith my constituents have in me. I will not -"

"Call her a whore again, and you will be nothing but ash on the floor," Bones snarled at him.

Kaida put a hand on Bones's arm as Cadmus said, "Insulting my clan will not get you what you want, Senator. Peace can only be achieved through -"

"The only way to achieve peace is if you disgusting animals leave. You are a threat to every human in this city, and it's my job to protect them," the senator said. "Revealing yourself to humans was a mistake. They're frightened, and their fear will push my bill through the Senate. If everything goes according to plan this evening, every paranormal on the planet will be tagged and registered by this time next year. No longer will you be able to hide your true nature in the shadows. We will know exactly who and what you are."

The Senator lapsed into silence, his face red and his hands clenched into fists. Kaida could almost hear the heavy thud of his pulse as he glared at Cadmus.

A weary look of resignation on his face, Cadmus said. "I want peace between our kinds, Senator Matthews. I want paranormal and human alike to live without fear of the other. But with men like you in charge, there can be no peace. We will not leave our home or allow ourselves to be tagged by your group, and you will not accept anything less. Our conversation is done."

A triumphant look passed over the senator's face. "Understood."

The senator held out his hand, and Cadmus walked forward to shake it.

Her dragon growled a warning, and beside her, Bones stiffened. "Cadmus, return to me. Now!"

Martin stepped closer as the senator took Cadmus's hand. Kaida and Bones growled a warning as something in the man's hand glinted in the light.

"Cadmus!" Kaida shouted as Martin stuck the hypodermic needle into Cadmus's neck and injected its contents.

Cadmus jerked back, his hand clapping down on his neck as he stared at the big blond man. "What have you done?"

Bones and Kaida charged forward, and, moving quickly, Martin yanked Cadmus closer, whipping him around as he pulled a gun from his belt and pressed it against Cadmus's temple. "Any closer, and I'll blow his brains out. Think your high elder can survive that?"

They stopped, and Bones snorted harsh laughter as the

other men pointed guns at them. "You stupid asshole. You're fucking dead, and you don't even know it."

Kaida waited for Cadmus's scales to appear. Even if he didn't fully shift immediately, the scales of his dragon would be thick and heavy enough to stop any bullet from piercing his skull. When he remained in his human form, she took a step forward. "Cadmus?"

The senator laughed, an ugly sound that echoed in the abandoned hangar. "What's wrong, bitch? You didn't think we're this stupid, did you?"

"Cadmus, shift," Bones said.

"He can't," Martin said. "How's that for fucking bananas? We just injected your precious high elder with a serum that suppresses his ability to shift."

Horror infused every molecule in Kaida's body as she stared at Cadmus. The old dragon's face was pale, and she could see fear in his eyes for the first time in her life.

"Cadmus, you must shift," she whispered.

"I cannot," he said.

Her dragon screamed with fury and pushed forward. She would turn the pathetic humans to ash for what they had done. She would set the city on fire with her flame, and the world would finally know a dragon's real power. They would cower and beg for mercy before she finished with them.

Beside her, Bones was swelling, his bones cracking and scales appearing on his flesh as he began to shift.

"Stop!" Martin shouted. "If either of you shift, I will put a fucking bullet through the old man's brain. I swear to fucking God, I will."

Her dragon screamed again, its wrath rising. With the last of her willpower, Kaida pushed it back. She grabbed Bones's arm. His body was still swelling, and he'd be in his dragon form any moment now. "Bones, stop!"

He growled at her, and she balled her hand into a fist and punched him in the face, shouting out a curse as her hand connected with hard scales and the fragile bones cracked under the pressure.

"Stop! They'll kill him! Stop, Bones!" she shouted as she held her broken hand against her chest.

He pointed his face at the ceiling and roared in rage, red hot flames shooting out of his mouth and illuminating the hangar with flickering light. His entire body trembled, but he was shrinking to his normal size. Kaida breathed a sigh of relief as his pupils turned normal and the scales disappeared.

Senator Matthews was staring at him, the terror evident on his face, and the other men had huddled together in a tight circle, their guns all aimed at Bones.

After a moment, the senator loudly cleared his throat and ran a shaking hand through his hair. "And that, gentleman, is why paranormals are dangerous to humans."

"Fucking animals," Martin muttered.

"What have you done?" Kaida said as she stared at the senator.

His smile was chilling. "Do you know how long it's taken Martin to create that serum? Do you know how many failures we had? The fourth version we tried? It was... bad. We tested it on some shifters without their knowledge, of course. We have volunteers across the world committed to our cause. It was simple enough for them to drug unsuspecting paranormals. A few drops of the serum in a drink and down the hatch... instant suppression of their shifting abilities. Only that fourth version was a real doozy of a fuck up. It didn't suppress their abilities. It changed them. It attacked them like a virus and turned their bodies against them. Four of the five shifters we drugged died within twenty-four hours of receiving the serum."

He glanced at Martin, his grin widening. "We almost said fuck it, this will work, didn't we, Martin?"

"Yes, sir."

"It wasn't the outcome we wanted, but dead shifters weren't so bad either. Only," the Senator pulled at the knot on his tie, "the fifth shifter didn't die. She was a police officer. We didn't plan on drugging an officer of the law. She just happened to be at the wrong coffee shop at the wrong time. Left her drink unattended long enough for one of our volunteers to drug her drink."

"What happened to her?" Kaida said.

"It was quite astonishing. Her body mutated and changed like the others, but instead of dying, she … became stronger. She became a monster." He grinned at Kaida and Bones. "You'll love this part – her husband was a scientist. A bear shifter named Wyatt. Not long after she fully turned and it was obvious that it was permanent, he locked her in a cage and spent every moment of his life trying to find a cure for the 'virus' she'd been infected with."

"How do you know this?" Bones asked.

"I told you. We have people everywhere. That includes the labs of mad bear scientists. Wyatt tried to cure his wife with a phoenix shifter he found somewhere, but the phoenix escaped the lab and disappeared. Wyatt moved his infected wife here to our city, and we continued to keep an eye on him. We were still working away like busy little bees on our serum, but imagine our surprise when the mutant creatures showed up outside the lab. That idiot scientist had allowed his wife to infect other shifters."

The senator made a snort of disgust. "We monitored it closely, of course. My son was the detective who took the case of a squirrel shifter murdered by one of the infected shifters."

Kaida stared at him in shock. "There are mutant shifters in the city infecting other shifters?"

"Oh God no. One thing about that bear shifter scientist is that he knew how to clean up his mess. He caught the mutant and returned him to his lab. Our last communication from our man inside was that they had also caught the phoenix shifter again, and Wyatt was using him to try to cure his wife."

"What do you mean last communication?"

"The lab was blown apart shortly after that. Our man was a member of the security team, and his body was one of the bodies found in the rubble. Burned horribly and a bullet in his brain, but they identified him through dental records," the senator said.

"Who blew up the lab?"

"I don't know, and I don't care. It also killed Wyatt and his monster of a wife, and the serum mess was finally behind us."

The senator glanced at his phone before putting it back in his suit jacket inner pocket. "It was the thirteenth version of the serum that finally worked. It isn't perfect. It only suppresses a mutant's ability to shift for about twelve hours, but our boys are already close to creating a longer-lasting version. One that will suppress for a few days, maybe even a few weeks. Eventually, we'll create one that will permanently suppress a shifter's ability, and we will go down in history as the men who saved humankind."

"You are fucking batshit insane," Bones growled.

"No, we're saving the world from monsters," Martin said. Still holding the gun to Cadmus's head, he said to the men behind them. "Bring in the body."

Three of the men left the group and jogged out of the hangar. A few minutes later, they returned, and Kaida stared in horror at the body of the dark-haired man they carried.

"What the fuck?" Bones spat when the men dumped the body in front of him and Kaida.

"Who is this?" Kaida stared into the man's lifeless eyes.

The senator cleared his throat again. "A volunteer who understands the importance of what we're trying to achieve."

"You killed someone," Kaida said. "You're a – a murderer."

"Well, I didn't kill him," Senator Matthews said. "But that doesn't matter. Because as far as our city and the rest of the world are concerned, the dragons killed this poor man."

"What are you talking about?" Kaida said.

Senator Matthews smiled at her. "Kaida, that's your name, right? Well, Kaida, unless you want to see your elder's brains splattered all over the wall, you'll set this man on fire."

"You're fucking insane," Bones said.

One of the men was approaching him, a needle in his hand, and Bones bared his fangs at him. "Come anywhere near me with that, and I'll melt the flesh from your bones."

Martin pressed the gun against Cadmus's temple. "I'll kill him. Don't fuck with me, dragon. You don't ever want to fuck with me. You're going to be a good little asshole and let the nice man inject you."

"Bones," Cadmus said. "Do not allow them to inject you. My life doesn't matter."

Bones stared at their high elder as the man holding the needle approached him. With his big hands in fists, Bones turned his head and exposed his throat. "It matters, Cadmus."

"Inject the motherfucker. Now," Martin said.

Kaida watched as Bones was injected. Her dragon snarled and hissed, but she stopped it from surging forward as Bones curled his lip at the man. The human skittered back, licking his lips nervously.

"Bones?" Kaida said.

Bones closed his eyes, his hands clenching and unclenching. "Fuck."

Martin laughed. "You think it wouldn't work?"

Another man approached Kaida, and the senator held out his hand. "Wait. She has to burn the body first."

"I won't," Kaida said.

"You will or your giant asshole buddy dies," Martin said. "I'm itching to put a bullet right through his ugly face."

Bones stared steadily at him, and red rose up Martin's neck and across his face. "Fucking animal. Stop staring at me."

"Enough," the senator said. "Burn the body, Kaida."

"Just do it yourself," she snapped.

The senator cocked his head at her. "My dear, you know that won't work. We need the body to be ash and bone and," he grinned at her, "without access to a crematorium... it's all up to you. Go on, show us what you can do to a human body."

With her stomach roiling and her heart hammering a frantic beat against her rib cage, Kaida drew a deep breath and released her flame. The heat rushed over her, and her dragon tried to make a bid for freedom. She blew more flame onto the body, holding her dragon back with grim determination as the smell of burning flesh assaulted her nose.

Wincing, she continued to blow flame until the body was nothing but ash and a few fragments of bone.

"Astonishing," the senator whispered. He held a handkerchief in front of his nose and waved it in the air as a look of disgust crossed his face. "God, that smell really lingers, doesn't it?"

Kaida flexed her broken hand, wincing when pain shot up her arm. It was already starting to heal, but it would take a few more hours before it returned to normal. The man holding the needle approached her, and a growl burst from her throat.

"Jesus, enough," Martin said. "You know the deal by now. Get injected or watch your friends die."

Kaida eyed the needle, her heart a loud bass beat in her eardrums.

No, please.

The pleading and fear in her dragon's voice broke Kaida's heart.

I'm sorry, my love, she told her dragon as she tilted her head, exposing her throat. She stared at Cadmus, the sorrow and love that radiated from his gaze, as the needle slid into her neck with a sharp pinch.

The liquid was cold and alien, and her dragon made another wailing cry. She took a deep breath, trying not to let her panic get the best of her as the cries of her dragon grew quieter and quieter. She was still there. Kaida could feel her, could feel her sorrow and her fear and her rage, but it was like there was a thick wall of glass between them. Her dragon threw herself at it to get to Kaida, but the glass stood solid.

I'm so sorry, she repeated to her dragon. *Forgive me.*

"Well, now that that's taken care of, let's get down to business," the senator said. "Obviously, we're framing the three of you for the murder. Once the people of this city realize you lured their senator to an abandoned hangar under the ruse of peace talk, when they're told you killed a man and almost killed me, support for my bill will skyrocket. We'll save humankind, and you will be a part of that. You should be proud of yourselves."

"Go fuck yourself," Bones said.

The senator laughed. "It's not the most elegant phrase, but it gets right to the point. Here's the thing: you know we can't let the three of you live, right? There are enough bleeding hearts in this city that they might believe the shit you tell them. So," he shrugged, "this is the part where you die. Sorry about that."

Martin grinned at the senator. "Jesus, look at their faces. It's like they thought they all might live through this." He turned to Bones, the lunatic grin widening. "Guess you should have shifted when you had the chance, huh? Now you're going to die because you wanted to save this old man who's gonna die anyway. Stupid fucking animals... dumb as shit."

"Get on with it," the senator said with another glance at his phone. "we don't have all night."

"Right." Martin's finger tightened on the trigger of the gun pointed at Cadmus's head. Before he could squeeze the trigger, a roar pierced the inky darkness outside the hangar.

"You sure this is right?" Mal asked.

Both he and Bishop had volunteered to go with him once he had his father's cell location. Bren had accepted gratefully. He hoped he was overreacting, hoped his suspicion wasn't true, but that tingling sensation nagging at the base of his skull wouldn't let him quite believe it. Realizing his father's cell was pinging at the abandoned airfield outside the city only strengthened his suspicion.

"Yeah, that's my dad's car parked by the hangar," Bren said. "Kill the lights, would you?"

Bishop shut off the headlights and drove slowly toward the hangar. He stopped the truck when it was still sixty feet from the building and shut off the engine.

The three of them studied the hangar. The rusted enormous doors were wide open at the front of the hangar, but from their angle, they couldn't see inside.

"Pretty fucking creepy," Bishop said. "No way this is just a goddamn meeting."

He rolled down his window and inhaled deeply before looking at Mal. "Shit, you smell that?"

"Yeah." Mal was unclicking his seat belt and opening his door. "Hurry."

"What do you smell?" Bren climbed out of the truck after them. "Bishop? What the fuck?"

Bishop and Mal were already stripping off their clothes, and fear slithered down Bren's spine. "Bishop?"

Bishop shoved his jeans and briefs down his legs. "I can smell at least a dozen humans and Cadmus and Bones."

"What about Kaida?" Can you smell her?" Bren said as Mal made a low grunt and shifted to his wolf form.

"Yeah, I can smell her. She's…"

"She's what?" Bren pulled his gun from his belt and clicked off the safety. "She's what, Bishop?"

"She's afraid," Bishop said.

He shifted to his grizzly form and ran toward the hangar, Mal loping behind him.

"Fuck!" His body shaking with adrenaline, Bren ran after them.

"Shoot it!" The senator shouted as the massive grizzly ran into the hanger, his paws slapping down on the concrete with booming thuds.

Screaming, Martin shoved Cadmus to the ground and aimed his gun at the grizzly.

"Bishop!" Kaida screamed as Martin fired. The bullet hit

the grizzly in the right shoulder, and Bishop roared angrily before slamming one paw into Martin's side. The force of the blow drove Martin back, the gun flying from his hand as he crashed into the side of the hangar and dropped to the floor.

One of the other men aimed his gun at the snarling grizzly. Barking and growling, the grey wolf leaped onto the man, knocking him to the ground. The man screamed and fired his gun, the bullet ricocheting off the metal roof. His scream turned into a gurgling moan when the wolf sunk his teeth into his throat and tore it open.

"Cadmus!" Bones charged forward, growling with pain when the gunshot echoed in the hangar and blood appeared in a bright bloom on Bones's shirt. He clapped a hand to his ribcage and bared his teeth at the man who had shot him before stalking forward.

"I-I'm sorry," the man whispered. "Please, I didn't mean…"

He threw the gun down on the floor and turned and fled toward the back of the hangar, slipping out through a side door.

"Say goodbye, you stupid dragon bitch!"

Kaida froze. Her dragon screamed behind the glass wall, throwing herself at the glass with renewed frenzy as Kaida stared at the barrel of the gun pointed directly at her chest.

"Ain't no way you'll survive a bullet to the heart." The man about to kill her was small and unremarkable looking. Freckles were scattered across his nose, and his pupils were huge. She could smell the fear and adrenaline rolling off him like mist on a lake.

Faintly, she could hear Bishop's angry roar and feel the floor trembling as he bolted for her. He wouldn't make it in time. She was going to die today in this cold hangar. She was going to die, and she'd never told Bren how much she loved him.

She flinched back at the gunfire, waiting for the pain in her chest and the agonizing screams of her dragon.

There was nothing. No pain or weakness. She watched in numb shock as the man about to kill her crumpled to his knees and fell forward, his face hitting the concrete with a harsh smacking sound that reminded her of rubber soles on wet pavement.

There was a large bloody hole where the back of his head used to be, and she stared at the bloodied bits of grey matter oozing out of his skull with a numb sense of shock.

"Kaida!"

Bren was standing a few feet behind her. She stared at him as he lowered his gun. Her dragon sang with happiness, the sound muffled behind that terrible glass wall. "Bren?"

He tried to smile at her, but it was more of a grimace. "Sorry, I'm late. I can't run as fast as a grizzly and a wolf."

She started toward him, her relief turning to horror when his father stepped up behind him. "Bren, watch out!"

She froze in place, the heat that always burned within her turning cold when Bren's father pressed the gun against his temple.

Bren stiffened, his hand tightening around his gun. "Hello, Dad."

"Drop the gun, Bren." The senator's gaze darted around the now quiet hangar as Bishop and Mal changed to their human forms with low popping sounds.

"It's over, Senator," Mal said. He held his hands up in a non-threatening manner. "Your men are dead or have run away. You're the only one left."

"Martin," the senator said. "Martin, get your ass over here."

"He's gone." Bishop pointed to the far door. "He ran out of here just like everyone else. You're done."

"Shut the fuck up!" The senator's voice was panicked.

"Let him go." Kaida moved slowly toward them. From the corner of her eye, she could see Bones step in front of Cadmus, shielding the high elder with his body.

"Don't you dare say a fucking word to me, you - you animal." The senator turned his empty gaze toward her. "This is all your fucking fault. You seduced my son. You -"

"She didn't. I asked her out first," Bren said. "You want to be pissed with someone, be pissed with me."

"Shut up, Bren," his father snarled. "For once in your fucking life, just shut up."

"It's over, Dad," Bren said. "Whatever you had planned? It's finished. Give me the gun."

"It isn't over," the senator said. "We can - we can help each other, Bren. I'm your father, for God's sake. If you back me up and tell your captain that these dragons burned a man, he'll believe you."

"I won't lie for you," Bren said. "Give me the gun, and maybe, just maybe, you won't go to prison for the rest of your life."

The senator laughed, a bitter sound that set Kaida's teeth on edge. "You have no fucking idea what you've done, Bren. You and your fucking animal friends have wrecked everything. My entire life, everything I've worked for, gone just like that because you couldn't stop from sticking your dick in her!"

He sneered at Kaida. "Brainwashing my son into turning against his father was your plan all along, wasn't it? You stupid, lying whore! You -"

Kaida cried out when Bren drove his elbow into his father's stomach. His father jerked back, retching and coughing, but when Bren reached for the gun in his hand, he stumbled back, aiming the weapon at Bren's face. "Don't."

413

"It's finished," Bren said. "Give me the gun, Dad."

"I'm not going to prison," his father said. "I'm walking out of here and getting in my fucking car and driving away."

"You know I can't let you do that," Bren said.

Kaida's stomach dropped when the senator put his finger on the trigger of his gun. "I'm your father."

"I'm your son," Bren said softly as he took another step forward. "You may not be a good man, but even you wouldn't shoot your own son."

The senator stared at him for a few seconds before lowering the gun, his body slumping. Kaida released her breath in a harsh rush, adrenaline still singing through her veins, her dragon still snarling and growling in her glass prison.

Bren reached for the gun, and Mal shouted a warning as the senator shoved Bren aside and pointed his gun at her. "You don't get to have my son, you stupid bitch!"

The senator's body jerked wildly at the gunshot. He staggered back, catching his balance as the gun fell from his hand and landed with a clatter on the cement. He clapped his hand against his shoulder as he stared at his son. "You shot me. You shot your own father."

"It's just a flesh wound. You'll live." Bren holstered his gun and grabbed the handkerchief sticking out of the front pocket of his father's suit jacket. He pressed it against the wound in his father's shoulder. "Put pressure on it."

"You shot me," his father whispered again.

"Stay still, Dad." Bren, pale and grim looking, pressed hard against his father's shoulder before glancing at Mal. "Call 9-1-1."

CHAPTER 28

"Oh, you are the sweetest little hatchling. Yes, you are. Look at that beautiful red hair." Gram lifted Lila into the air, studying her in the sunlight that filled the cabin. "I could just eat you up."

She brought Lila down to her chest, kissing her cheek before grinning at Ava. "That's only a saying, human. I don't mean a harmful thing by it."

"I know," Ava said with a smile.

"My goodness, you are so sweet," Gram said as Lila stared at her. "The clan members would go crazy over you."

Ava glanced at Kaida and then at Bishop before standing. "Why don't we introduce Lila to a few other clan members."

"Oh, bless you, they'd love it," Gram said. "Most of them are in the community cabin right now."

Ava kissed Bishop. "You and Kaida stay here and get... caught up."

"Sure," Bishop said.

Kaida smiled at Ava when the curvy redhead took her hand and squeezed it. "You have a lovely home, Kaida. I'm so glad to visit your clan finally."

Kaida nodded but didn't say anything. She couldn't. Her throat was too tight, and the compassionate look Ava gave her was threatening to break loose the flood of tears Kaida had been holding back for the last two days.

Her dragon made a plaintive cry before falling silent. Kaida wasn't sure what was worse – her dragon badgering her constantly to go to Bren or the melancholy and misery it kept lapsing into.

She realized Gram and Ava had left the cabin with Lila, and Bishop stared silently at her from across the table.

"My bear," she said. "How is your shoulder?"

"Fine," he said with a dismissive shrug. "Healed in a couple of hours. Can the three of you shift again?"

"Yes. The suppressant wore off by mid-morning yesterday. There seem to be no lingering side effects for me, Bones, or Cadmus."

Bishop muttered a curse. "I can't believe the fucking humans. To think they can control us by suppressing our ability to shift. This is so bad, Kaida. Really fucking bad."

"I know," she said. "Did they find Martin?"

Bishop shook his head. "No, he's gone. They already have someone new in charge of the HAPI group, and they're denying any knowledge or involvement with the drug Martin was trying to create. It's complete bullshit, they're lying through their goddamn teeth, but there's no proof that any of them knew. Bren had a search warrant by Saturday afternoon for the organization, but if they had anything on their computers or in their office, they'd already gotten rid of everything. They said they haven't heard from or seen Martin or any members who ran on Friday night."

Kaida rubbed at her forehead. "Jesus, what a mess. Bren's captain came by this morning. He met with Bones, Cadmus, and me, and we went over everything that happened again. Gave more official statements, as he put it. He said that the senator is insisting he had no idea the HAPI group had created the suppressant and that he believed they were meeting to talk peace with us."

Bishop snorted angrily. "Does he think he can get away with the lies? He confessed everything to the three of you."

Kaida traced her finger along the grain of the wood table. "Yeah. Morales said if he's smart, he'll admit to his involvement and try to get a plea bargain out of it. If he isn't, we'll have to testify in court."

"That won't be for a while if it even happens," Bishop said.

They lapsed into silence for a few minutes before Bishop said, "What does Bren say about all of this?"

"I don't know. I haven't spoken to him since Friday night."

Bishop sat forward in his chair, shock written on his face. "You what?"

"Why would he, my bear? He was forced to kill one man and shoot his father because of me," Kaida said.

"The guy was going to kill you, and it's Bren's job to stop people from killing each other," Bishop said. "And as far as his father – he *barely* shot him."

Kaida scowled at him. "Not helping, my bear."

"It's true," Bishop said. "The bullet went right through. He didn't even need surgery, for fuck's sake. Bren was freaking out when he realized you were at that meeting with his father. He's into you. Hell, he might even love you."

"My clan will never accept him," Kaida said.

"Bullshit," Bishop replied. "He saved your life, Bones's life, and the life of your freaking high elder. What more must he do to prove to your clan that he's worthy? Fuck your goddamn clan, Kaida. You deserve to be happy, and if your clan doesn't see that being with Bren makes you happy, then tell them to go fuck themselves and live your life with Bren."

She laughed bitterly. "It's not that simple, my bear, and you know it. I cannot live without my clan."

"But you can live without Bren?" Bishop said.

Hot and painful tears fell as her dragon made another heartrending wail of suffering.

"No," she whispered. "I cannot live without my mate either."

Bishop reached across the table to grab her hand. "Kaida, you have -"

The knock on the door made them both jump. She squeezed Bishop's hand before wiping her cheeks and crossing the room to open the door.

Bren was standing on the porch, and her dragon purred with a sweet and joyful pleasure that couldn't be contained. A small smile crossed Bren's face at the sound. "Hello, Kaida."

"Hello, Bren."

"Can I come in?"

She stepped back, holding back her urge to throw her arms around him as he stepped inside her cabin. "Hello, Bishop."

"Hey." Bishop stood and shook Bren's hand. "Good to see you."

"I never did say thanks for your help on Friday night," Bren said.

"You don't need to." Bishop pressed a kiss against Kaida's cheek. "I'm going to find Ava and Gram."

Kaida waited until the door was closed behind the big grizzly before giving Bren a nervous look. "How are you?"

"Good. You?"

"Fine. I can shift again, and my hand is completely healed."

"I'm really glad to hear it," he said.

There was an awkward silence, and Kaida said, "How's Tyler?"

"Doing as well as he can. It's a lot to take in for a kid. We're still waiting for the reporters to leave my place and now Dad's place. Once they're gone, we'll move the rest of his stuff from Dad's to my apartment. He and Corey are going back to school tomorrow."

"Good, that's good," Kaida said.

Bren picked at his nail. "Mara and Roland are applying to be Corey's permanent foster home."

"You're kidding?"

"I'm not. I guess they talked it over with Corey, and when they suggested applying for it, he all but started crying. He really likes them both."

"He deserves to be with good people," Kaida said.

"He does."

More silence. Kaida could barely hear herself think over the purring of her dragon. It wanted her to go to Bren, wanted her to touch him and kiss him and tell him that she loved him.

"Kaida?"

Her mouth trembling, the tears catching in her eyelashes, she stared mutely at him.

"I love you."

She blinked away the tears, bringing Bren back into focus. "What did you say?"

"I love you," he said simply. "I don't care about my father or your clan. Hell, I'll take Elora's invisibility potion and sneak into the clan every night if that's what needs to happen to spend time with you. But I promise I'll do whatever it takes to win your clan over and make them realize I'm not going anywhere."

He stepped closer, his voice steady and calm as he said, "I love you, Kaida. I want to spend the rest of my life with you and only you."

A sound came out of her mouth that was half-laugh and half-sob. She lunged for him, throwing her arms around his neck and taking his mouth in a hard kiss. He returned her kiss before pulling back and grinning at her. "So… does this mean you love me too?"

"I love you, my mate," she breathed against his mouth before kissing him again. "I love you."

He rested his forehead against hers, his warm hands stroking her lower back. "I need to ask – is it both of you who love me or just your dragon who's infatuated with me? Because I -"

"It's both of us," she said immediately. "It's been both of us for weeks, but I was afraid to say anything. I was afraid it would scare you off."

He laughed. "Jesus, we really should have sat down and had a damn conversation. I was worried about scaring *you* off."

She kissed him quickly. "I do not scare easily, my mate."

"No, you don't," he said. "I'm sorry I haven't been by or called the last couple of days. I thought maybe you'd need some space and to be with your clan after what my father did to you. And I've been spending a lot of time either at work or with Tyler and -"

"I know," she said. "I know, and I'm so sorry you had to shoot your father for me. I can't even imagine what -"

"Eh, it was barely a shooting," Bren said. "He didn't even need surgery."

She laughed long and hard before kissing Bren's neck. "Now you sound like Bishop."

"I think that grizzly is starting to like me," Bren said. "My natural charm is finally winning him over."

"Have you spoken with your father since Friday night?" she asked.

"He agreed to see me at the hospital last night," Bren said.

"How did it go?"

"He used the opportunity to tell me again what a disappointment I was to him. That he should have shot me and been done with it."

"Oh, Bren." She stared horrified at him. "I'm so sorry."

"I'm not," he said. His voice was devoid of emotion. "It was a good reminder that cutting him out of my life, cutting him out of *Tyler's* life, is the right choice. He's a monster and he'll spend the rest of his life in prison."

"Your captain said if he was smart, he'd accept a plea deal."

"I doubt he will. He's still adamantly denying he had anything to do with it. That it was all the HAPI group's idea and he was an unwitting pawn." He sighed and rested his forehead on hers again. "Morales is getting warrants to go through everything of my father's."

"Do you think they'll find something that connects your father to what the HAPI group was doing?"

"If my father was smart, no. But you never know. If they don't find anything, my father will never accept a plea bargain and you'll have to testify. He seems to think he'll win a trial, that no one will believe the word of shifters and his own son over him. He's an idiot."

"I'm sorry for the choice you had to make," she said.

He cupped her face and stared at her. "Kaida, I'm not. I don't know how many ways I can say this but choosing you over my father was simple. I love you."

She hugged him tight. "This isn't going to be easy. My clan is -"

"Your clan is wary, I get it," he said. "But if I can win over a grouchy eight-hundred-pound grizzly, I can win over your clan. The good news is *my* clan already loves you. I told Ty I was coming over to confess my love to you, and he could barely contain his excitement. I was half-certain he would text you before I even got here to welcome you into the family."

"Your brother is important to me too," Kaida said. "He's a great kid and I'm looking forward to getting to know him better."

"You won't be saying that when you find his dirty socks stuffed between the couch cushions," Bren said solemnly.

She pressed another kiss against his mouth. "If it means I get to see you every day, it will be worth it."

He squeezed her hips, his look somber. "If you want to continue on the way we were for a while, I'll understand. We can fly under the radar until things quiet down a bit. Your clan doesn't need to know that -"

"No," she said. "You are my mate and I won't hide that from my clan. You're a part of our clan now and they'll just have to accept it. At least to our faces. Prepare for them to gossip about us behind our backs."

He grinned at her. "I can handle some gossipy dragons."

There was another knock on the door and, holding tightly to Bren, she said, "Come in."

The door opened and Bones stuck his head into the room. "Hello, human."

"Hello, Bones."

"We saw you drive in and the council has requested to see you both."

Kaida took Bren's hand, smiling confidently at him even

though the nerves were kicking up in her stomach. "Come, my mate."

They followed Bones to the main cabin. "You doing okay, Bones?" Bren asked.

"Yes, why wouldn't I be?" Bones asked.

"Oh, I don't know, maybe because you were shot in the side not two days ago?"

Bones shrugged. "Javee removed the bullet for me and kept the wound clean until the suppressant wore off and my healing abilities returned."

"Must have been a painful few hours," Bren said.

Bones grinned at him. "That, human, is why your kind so cleverly created whiskey."

He opened the main cabin door and motioned for them to go in. Still holding Bren's hand, Kaida stepped inside. Her entire clan, as well as Ava and Bishop, were in the cabin. The council stood at the front of the room, lined up in a neat row as her clan members turned and faced Kaida and Bren.

"Step forward, human," Cadmus said.

Bren's hand squeezed hers and she squeezed back before releasing him. Bren took a couple steps forward, staring calmly at the clan as they returned his look. It didn't matter what her clan said or did, she would not give up her mate, no matter the consequence or the cost. She wouldn't...

The thought died in her head as, one by one, each clan member bowed to Bren. Her dragon purred loudly at their show of respect to her mate. Cadmus, with a serene smile, was the last to bow.

Ryul stepped forward, his hair gleaming in the light. "We thank you, human, for saving not only the life of our high elder, but for saving the lives of Bones and Kaida."

He took a deep breath, glancing at the clan members again before saying, "My clan, welcome Kaida's mate, Bren

Matthews, formerly of the human clan, but now a member of our clan."

The clan erupted into cheers. They pounded their feet and purred loudly until the entire cabin was filled with the sound. Kaida joined Bren, taking his hand and smiling at him as he gave her a slightly dazed look.

"So, did what I think just happen, happen?" he said.

She laughed and pressed a kiss against his mouth. "Welcome to the clan, my mate."

There was a loud whistle and the cheers and purring died out. The clan turned to face Cadmus as he walked slowly across the cabin to stand in front of Kaida and Bren.

"Congratulations," he said. "But there is one more announcement to make."

He took Kaida's hand, holding it firmly, as he turned to face the clan. "My clan, long have you waited for me to choose the new member of our council." He squeezed Kaida's hand. "My choice is Kaida."

He turned and kissed both of Kaida's cheeks. "Welcome to the council."

She stared at him in shock, barely hearing her clan's fresh cheering and purring. "Cadmus, are you... are you certain?"

He laughed and squeezed her hand. "I have never been more certain of anything in my life, Kaida." His gaze fell on Bren. "Take your mate home and celebrate."

He walked away, and Kaida turned to stare up at Bren. "I... did that just happen?"

He pulled her up against him, a large smile crossing his handsome face. "Welcome to the council, my mate. I love you."

She pressed a kiss against his mouth. "I love you too, my mate. Always."

"DUDE, ALL I'M SAYING IS THAT IF WE'RE LIVING IN THE wilderness, I need a car to get to school. I know you and Kaida are tired of driving me in every day. Plus, I could get a car with tinted windows, and those stupid reporters still camping out wouldn't even know it was me." Tyler grinned at Bren before flopping down on the couch.

Bren rolled his eyes. "And where will you get the money for insurance, gas, and repairs? Cars are expensive, Ty."

"I know. But, like, Corey and I got it all figured out. Roland said he would help us find a cheap second-hand car and we'll get both our names on the insurance and split the costs."

"Did Corey get that job?"

"He did," Tyler said proudly. "He's working weekends and one night a week at Walmart. Shit… since I'm working at Target, does that mean we gotta be, like, arch enemies?"

"Oh, how will your love ever survive," Bren said dryly.

Tyler threw a pillow at him. "Whatever, dude. Think about the car thing, okay? I need a small, minuscule loan toward my half of the cost of the car. And I'll pay you back in three months tops, I promise."

"I'll think about it," Bren said as he unloaded the dishwasher. "Now, how about you get over here and sweep the kitchen like you promised Kaida you would."

"Sure. Where did she go anyway?"

Bren put the mugs in the cupboard. "She ran over to Sika's for a bit. Ty, are you sure you like living here with the clan?"

"Are you kidding me?" Tyler stopped sweeping the floor for a moment. "The last three weeks have been awesome. We live with dragons, man. My coolness factor at school has jumped exponentially. Everyone wants to be my friend."

He started sweeping again. "And Bones said he'd shift to his dragon form for me and Corey this weekend. How cool is that? I mean, I know Kaida shifted so I could see my first dragon, but Bones is like," Tyler waved his hand in the air, "super effin' badass, you know?"

"He is," Bren said with a grin.

The door opened, and Kaida walked into the cabin. The smile on his face died when he saw her face. "Kaida? What's wrong?"

"Nothing," she said. "Nothing's wrong." Her gaze flickered to Tyler. "Ty, would you mind giving your brother and me a minute alone?"

"No prob," Tyler said. "I gotta call Corey and tell him Bren agreed to the car thing anyway."

"Not agreed," Bren said. "Thinking about it."

"Tomato, tomahto," Ty said with a wave of his hand. He disappeared into his bedroom, shutting the door as Bren shut the dishwasher and walked over to Kaida.

"Honey, what's wrong?"

"Why do you think something's wrong?"

"You have a weird look on your face."

She made a sound that could only be described as *blergh* before staring at him. Her golden eyes were glowing faintly, and her pupils were huge. She was rubbing her hands over her stomach repeatedly and he caught them and squeezed them gently. "Does your stomach hurt?"

"What?" She glanced at her stomach before shaking her head. "No, no, it doesn't hurt."

An almost hysterical laugh fell from her mouth, and Bren stared cautiously at her. "Kaida? You're freaking me out a little."

"I'm kind of freaking out a little myself," she said.

"Tell me what's going on."

She took a deep breath, her hands vibrating minutely in his. "I'm pregnant."

His hands clamped down on hers. "You're pregnant?"

"I'm pregnant," she whispered. "My period was late this month. I went to Sika, and she had a pregnancy test, and I peed on it, and it came back positive."

She pulled the pregnancy stick from her front pocket and showed it to him. Bren stared at the positive sign. "You're pregnant."

"I guess I was wrong about not getting pregnant from one round of unprotected sex," she said.

He stared silently at her, and she swallowed hard. "Bren? Say something other than 'you're pregnant'."

"You're knocked up!" he shouted and wrapped his arms around her waist. "You're having my baby!"

He lifted her in the air, whooping and hollering like he was in the packed crowd of a championship football game. "We're having a baby!"

She purred loudly before kissing him on the mouth. He set her down gently and placed his hand on her belly. "Hi, baby."

She placed her hand over his hand. "You're okay with this then? It wasn't exactly planned."

"Are you kidding? Kaida, I'm going to be a dad," he said. "You've made me the happiest guy in the world."

A tear slipped down her cheek, and he rubbed it away with his thumb. "Do you want a boy or a girl?"

"I don't care," she said. "You?"

"Doesn't matter to me. Do you think it'll be dragon or human?"

She took a deep breath. "I have no idea. But I don't care

either way. This hatchling will be a part of our clan, whether human or dragon."

He leaned down and kissed her stomach before smiling at her. "I love you, Kaida. I can't wait to meet our hatchling."

Her smile was radiant and full of sweet promise. "I love you too, Bren."

Keep reading for an excerpt of Rise of the Jaguar, Book Eight in the Shifters Series.

RISE OF THE JAGUAR EXCERPT

THE SHIFTERS SERIES BOOK EIGHT

He was big for a human. Big and – she could admit it – sexy as hell. As Paula yammered on in her ear, Emerson watched the human over her glass of wine. He was wearing jeans and a long sleeve shirt that highlighted the broadness of his shoulders and the muscles in his upper arms, and the fabric clung to his flat abdomen. She had no doubt that a very impressive set of abs were hidden beneath the black cotton fabric.

He looked dangerous, she decided. His thick dark hair and blue eyes, while attractive, weren't what set him out from the rest of the males in the crowded pub. Nor was it the fact that he was the only human in the pub. It was the caged restlessness she sensed lurking just below his skin, the way his body seemed to be both perfectly relaxed and completely on edge at the same time.

He looked like a man who would handle anything life threw at him.

He looked like a man who would run headlong into danger.

He looked like a man who would make a woman scream when she climaxed.

Emerson's jaguar trilled so loudly that Paula stopped talking, blinked, and then resumed her chattering.

Emerson nodded, only half-listening to her co-worker as she continued to study the human. His big body leaned against the bar, and when he smiled at the bartender, Emerson wasn't at all surprised to see her hurry over immediately. Emerson had only seen half of the man's smile, and *her* thighs had loosened.

The human really was on the big side. Maybe she could take him to her bed without hurting him.

Her jaguar trilled again. It was entirely on board with the idea of bedding the human. Which was odd because, generally speaking, her cat favoured other big cat shifters or wolf shifters. Emerson couldn't ever remember her jaguar being even remotely interested in a human.

She allowed herself a thirty-second fantasy of what it would be like to fuck him before averting her gaze and drinking the last of her wine. She was being ridiculous. She couldn't take a human to her bed, no matter how attracted she was to him. He might be tough, but even the toughest human was no match for her claws and teeth. And her jaguar liked to scratch and bite during sex. A lot.

"So, then I said to Joanne that I didn't care much for her tone and she said to me that I was being too sensitive. Can you believe it, Em? The woman who cries if you tell her the coffee was too strong, called *me* too sensitive. Em, are you even listening to me?"

Emerson smiled apologetically at Paula. She liked her co-worker and they had after-work drinks every Thursday night. In between 'scoping for dudes,' as Paula liked to call it, the conversation was dominated by Paula's gossipy revelations about their coworkers. Normally, Em was all for a good gossip session but wasn't feeling it tonight. Maybe it was the long day at work, maybe it was her unsettledness at her jaguar lusting after a human, but she was calling it a night.

"Hey, Paula, I'm sorry, but I -"

"May I join you, ladies?"

The low rasp sent shivers down Emerson's spine, making her jaguar sit up and purr eagerly. She lifted her gaze to see the very human she was lusting after standing next to their table.

Of course, he would have a voice that made her want to do naughty, dirty things to him.

He was balancing a glass of wine and beer in one hand and, in the other hand, whatever fruity drink Paula had ordered.

"Of course!" Paula's voice was breathless, and Emerson could smell her immediate arousal. Her jaguar hissed. It didn't like Paula's interest in the human one bit, and Emerson soothed it quickly.

She couldn't sleep with the human, not without tearing his back to shreds, but Paula was a gopher shifter. She didn't have to worry about seriously damaging the sexy human while she was banging him. It made sense that Paula would be the one who took the human home tonight.

Emerson's jaguar hissed again, real anger appearing beneath the school-girl jealousy.

Knock it off, she scolded her jaguar as the man sat beside her.

He placed the glass of wine in front of her and the fruity drink in front of Paula. "I thought you lovely ladies could use another drink."

Paula giggled and took a large swallow before Emerson could stop her. "You're right, we could."

Good God, had all Paula's brain cells flown out the damn window? In what universe did a woman accept a drink from a stranger? He could have added anything to it. Emerson gave Paula an *Oh my God, stop drinking that drink, you moron* look.

Not surprisingly, it didn't register. But in Paula's defense, it was hard to convey that kind of sentiment with only a look.

Up close, the human seemed even more dangerous. Maybe it was the dark stubble that lined his jaw, or maybe it was the hardness in his gaze even though he was smiling. Whatever it was, all the things about him that should have sent her screaming for the hills were, instead, making her fantasize about all the very naughty things she might do to him.

"I'm Paula!" Paula held out her hand, and the human shook it. Emerson's jaguar hissed again, this one more of a pout than jealousy. It wanted to touch the human, too.

Shut it. You'll get your chance.

"And you are?" The man smiled at her, an easy smile that almost made it to his eyes.

"Emerson," she said and shook his hand. Her jaguar purred loudly at the innocent contact and then purred again when the man's gaze dropped to her mouth. The smell of his arousal washed over her, and she caught her breath.

Oh shit.

Beside her, Paula made a low sound of disappointment. She'd caught the scent of the human's lust as well. Before she could look too crestfallen, a second man approached their table. Emerson could tell he was a fox shifter by his scent, and he bowed lavishly before grinning at Paula. "Care to dance, beautiful?"

"I would love to," Paula said. She jumped up, took the fox shifter's hand, and crossed the crowded pub to the minuscule dance floor at the back without a second look at Emerson.

Emerson needed to have a serious talk with her about pub safety etiquette.

"You have a beautiful name, Emerson."

She realized she was still holding the human's hand, and she pulled her hand free. "Thank you."

"A beautiful name for a beautiful woman."

She held back the eye roll with herculean effort. If she had a nickel for every time she heard that line...

The man suddenly laughed, and goosebumps shot up on Emerson's skin. Good God, how could a laugh be that sexy?

"Too cheesy, huh?" he said.

"Yes," she said.

"I'll try better with you in the future," he said.

"Cheesy and cocky," she said. "Not a great combination."

He laughed again. "I like to think of it as confidence."

"I'm sure you do," she said.

"I'm failing to impress you, aren't I?"

"Spectacularly," she said.

"To failing spectacularly," he said and held up his beer.

She clinked her wine glass against the beer bottle, watching how his Adam's Apple bobbed as he took a long swallow. He had a sexy throat.

Sexy throat? Jesus, Em, get it together.

"You're not drinking your wine." He indicated the glass she'd set back down on the table.

She just shrugged. After a few seconds, understanding crossed his face. "You think I drugged it."

When she stayed silent, he said, "You're right to be

cautious. A man like me could do all sorts of things to a woman like you."

Emerson, it is time to leave! Her inner voice was standing on the table and shouting into a bullhorn.

But her jaguar... her jaguar was purring like crazy and urging Emerson to imagine just exactly what sort of things the human might want to do to her.

He suddenly grinned at her, a boyish one that breached the barrier to his eyes and completely transformed him. She sucked in a breath, any idea of leaving buried under a tidal wave of lust so strong it made her panties wet.

She could smell her own arousal covering her like a thick blanket as the man picked up her wine glass and took a healthy swallow before setting it in front of her.

"Am I more trustworthy now?"

"Marginally," she said.

Her throat was as dry as a dusty road in Georgia, and she reached for the glass, ignoring her urge to turn it until her lips touched the same spot his lips had. She wasn't a love-struck teenager, for God's sake.

The wine washed over her tongue and down her dry and dusty throat. She toyed with the stem of the glass as she stared at him. "You haven't told me your name."

"Clay," he said.

"Tell me, Clay, what's a human doing in a pub known to be full of shifters?"

He studied the crowd. "I'm new to town. I didn't know this was a shifter's only kind of place."

"It isn't, technically," she admitted. "But not many humans come in here."

"Is that why I'm getting so many looks?"

"Partially," she said.

"Is my handsomeness the other reason they're staring?"

She laughed. "Sure, we'll go with that."

"You find me handsome. Admit it."

She cocked her head and pretended to do a slow perusal of his entire face like she hadn't already memorized every damn feature. "Handsome isn't the word I would use to describe you."

"No?" He didn't seem pissed. "What word would you use?"

"Dangerous."

He thought it over before nodding. "It's an apt description."

"You're not doing much to help your chances of me going home with you tonight."

Emerson!

That boyish grin returned, loosening her thighs and making her nipples pebble into hard points. She could smell his arousal thickening, and it intensified her own need.

He leaned forward, his gaze evaluating and appraising, "You know I'm dangerous, but you're not afraid of me. Why is that?"

She took another sip of wine. "Maybe I'm dangerous too."

His gaze shifted to her mouth again. "Maybe you are."

ABOUT THE AUTHOR

Elizabeth Kelly was born and raised in Ontario, Canada. She moved west as a teenager and now lives in Alberta with her husband and a menagerie of pets. She firmly believes that a person can survive solely on sushi and coffee, and only her husband's mad cooking skills prevents her from proving that theory.

For more information about Elizabeth, check out her website at

www.elizabethkelly.ca

facebook.com/EKellyBooks
instagram.com/elizabethkelly_author
amazon.com/Elizabeth-Kelly/e/B00EOHZ0MS
bookbub.com/authors/elizabeth-kelly

ALSO BY ELIZABETH KELLY

Tempted Series

Tempted

Twice Tempted

Forever Tempted

Breathless

Tempted Trilogy (Books 1-3)

Red Moon Series

Red Moon

Red Moon Rising

Dark Moon

Alpha Moon

Pale Moon

The Recruit Series

The Recruit (Book One)

The Recruit (Book Two)

The Recruit (Book Three)

The Recruit (Book Four)

The Recruit (Book Five)

The Recruit (Book Six)

The Shifters Series

Willow and the Wolf (Book One)

Ava and the Bear (Book Two)

Katarina and the Bird (Book Three)

Porter's Mate (Book Four)

Bria and the Tiger (Book Five)

Rosalie Undone (Book Six)

The Dragon's Mate (Book Seven)

Rise of the Jaguar (Book Eight)

The Assassin and the Bear (Book Nine)

Elora and the Crow (Book Ten)

The Draax Series

Reign (Book One)

Rule (Book Two)

Rebel (Book Three)

Surrender (Book Four)

Survive (Book Five)

Salvation (Book Six)

Harmony Falls Series

Sweet Harmony (Book One)

Perfect Harmony (Book Two)

Forbidden Harmony (Book Three)

Redeeming Harmony (Book Four)

Absolute Harmony (Novella)

Beautiful Harmony (Book Five)

Reckless Harmony (Book Six)

Seasoned Romance Series

Bet Your Heart on Me (Book One)

Take a Chance on Me (Book Two)

Place Your Trust in Me (Book Three)

Individual Books

The Necessary Engagement

Amelia's Touch

The Rancher's Daughter

Healing Gabriel

The Contract

A Home for Lily

Saving Charlotte

Shameless

The Fairy Tales Collection

Broken

An Unlikely Seduction

Holiday Romance

The Christmas Wife

The Christmas Rescue

The Christmas Nanny

The Christmas Boss

Sordid Games